RED STORM

A NOVEL

FRANK LUNA

EDITED BY:
RUTH YOUNGER

ASSOCIATE EDITOR:
SANDY BULLOCK

Gravity Bay Publishing

ISBN: 0615464653
ISBN-13: 9780615464657

FOR LILA AND MATTHEW

PROLOGUE

The giant spacecraft hurtled towards Mars at an astounding speed, marking the first time humans had traveled at such an incredible velocity. Never before had the world seen such a magnificent machine. While space travel had been a reality for decades, Mars 3 represented a radical breakthrough in spacecraft design.

At first glance, Mars 3 bore little difference to its predecessors. The cone-shaped lander and crew module were identical to Mars 2, which had made the same journey two years earlier with a crew of eight, six men and two women. Mars 3 carried a similar complement of telescopes and a communications array attached to a massive grid structure that extended a hundred yards behind the crew module. This "mother ship" would serve as an orbiting science station after the Mars 3 lander separated and touched down on the surface.

Mars 3 and Mars 2 appeared to be identical save one hidden detail buried deep within the bowels of the propulsion system at the rear of the spacecraft. Alongside the standard hydrogen engines, Mars 3 carried the first matter/anti-matter drive ever used in manned space flight, and the results were spectacular. This marked the beginning of the age of hyper-space.

Just as the jet engine made the world a smaller place, hyper-space travel would shrink the galaxy. In the amount of time it took Columbus to journey to the New World, man could now reach Mars, the New World of the modern age.

In less than three months, Mars 3 would arrive at its destination on the Grand Arroyo Plains of the red planet. That is where the Mars 2 crew was busy finishing the construction of the primary phase of Mars Base, the first permanently manned colony on another planet.

Mars 3 carried the hopes and dreams of a world already overcrowded and looking to expand. With a successful mission, the floodgates would open; and once again, adventurers and opportunists would look to the New World for freedom and riches. The nature of man's desire to conquer hadn't changed in a thousand years. The nature of Mars was about to change forever.

Mars 3's hyper-space propulsion system wasn't the only thing that set it apart from its predecessors. This spacecraft carried another secret that would also change the world. It wasn't anything as dynamic and glamorous as a hyper-drive; but it was no less ominous, and was decidedly more sinister.

CHAPTER 1

MARS BASE

Commander Matthew "Mac" MacTavish stood on the surface of Mars and considered the one certainty he faced: His space suit was running out of air. From a ridge overlooking the Grand Arroyo Plains, he gazed down upon Mars Base, the fledgling outpost consisting of three distinct structures that stood out against the rocky, rust-colored Martian terrain.

He admired Habitat 2, the most recent addition to Mars Base. This massive elongated dome dominated the site, dwarfing the smaller Habitat 1 and the conical-shaped Mars 2 crew module. Only yesterday the clear, flexible habitat roof lay deflated on the planet's surface. Overnight two massive pumps had drawn in raw Martian atmosphere and inflated the sealed dome like a giant balloon. Now the geometric shapes of the habitat panels glistened like a faceted jewel in the late morning sun.

Beep! The com-link in Mac's helmet sounded, followed by the voice of his first officer, Lieutenant Michael Traveres. "Commander, you have less than fifteen minutes of oxygen left. You are approaching redline limits."

"Copy, Lieutenant. Things look fine out here. I'm heading for Habitat 2 to check on Dr. Rechenko's progress. We should be at the airlock in under ten minutes."

"That's cutting it pretty close, sir. I'd recommend you double-check to be sure your emergency oxygen bottle is connected, just in case."

Mac patted the small bottle attached to his suit. It would automatically activate if he ran out of air, supplying about twenty minutes of oxygen. As Mac often told his crew, activation of the emergency bottle could save your life but would result in six months of paperwork and endless inquiries. "I'll be fine, Lieutenant. Rechenko and I will see you shortly."

"Copy," Traveres acknowledged from the bridge inside the crew module. "Commander, I have an incoming message from Mission Control. I'll see you at the airlock. Out."

Mac took another, satisfying look at the base. After fifteen difficult months on Mars, he and his crew of seven scientists and engineers were on the verge of finishing Habitat 2, their primary goal. He had accomplished his biggest career challenge. *Not bad for an Irish-Mexican kid from California*, he thought.

Beep! "Commander, Rechenko here." A voice with a thick Russian accent interrupted Mac's euphoric thoughts. "We have a problem with valve six. It's still not purging correctly."

Mac groaned. "I'll be right there, Victor. I'm going to drive Ratty back to the base." He climbed up the short ladder to Ratty's two-man crew cab at the front end of the large vehicle—the size of a flatbed truck. It was the workhorse of the base, used as a tractor, excavator, forklift, and heavyweight hauler. Ratty was a modified acronym for their Remote All Terrain Vehicle or RATV, which could be driven manually or by remote control from the base. Matty, the eight-passenger Manual All Terrain Vehicle, was Ratty's counterpart, used as an excursion vehicle that could take a crew to a distant drilling site and serve as a mobile home for an extended period. Mac drove Ratty down the gentle slope to the base. He entered Habitat 2 and admired the gymnasium-sized interior.

Because Mars gravity was so weak, only two columns were needed to support the clear-paneled roof, which allowed ample sunlight into every corner of the expansive structure. The floor of the habitat had been excavated down to four feet into the bare Martian surface. Six cylindrical valves, each two feet in diameter, were buried in the dirt walls along the length of the habitat, three on each side. These purge valves led to the outside and helped maintain a constant pressure inside the dome. Mac saw the rotund figure of Dr. Victor Rechenko in his space suit, bending over the troublesome valve six.

He bounded across the open floor toward the chief architect of Mars Base. Mac felt a growing anxiety in the pit of his stomach, all to aware the mission could ill afford another delay.

"Victor, we only have about ten minutes of air left. What's the problem?" His patience, along with his oxygen, was wearing thin.

"Commander, I'll need to shut down this valve to inspect internal hardware," Rechenko answered in his heavy Russian accent. "I suspect there is a bad chip in one of the controllers."

Even through Rechenko's faceplate, Mac could see the weary eyes of his chief engineer, a clear sign that he was pushing himself to the brink of exhaustion. The pride of the Russian space program, Rechenko carried the full weight of his country's honor in addition to his own high standards.

"Victor, how much time are we talking? We're already a month behind schedule. I think we need to bypass the valve and pressurize the habitat with oxygen. We have to get the hydroponics garden set up and in full production by the time the Mars 3 crew arrives."

"Commander, I prefer not to pump oxygen into H2 with one valve shut down. It is best to have all valves operational before we occupy the habitat."

"Victor, I'm sorry." Mac overruled his chief engineer and longtime friend. "Mission rules state a minimum of four valves is all that is required. Let's bypass the valve. We can purge the habitat with five valves then take a closer look at the problem after we've moved inside."

"Yes, Commander, right away," Rechenko responded as he opened the control panel for the valve.

Mac sensed his engineer's disappointment. He knew him well, having worked closely with the Russian for the past several years on the International Space Station and the Mars project. Their friendship had endured because of their strong mutual respect.

As Mac watched Rechenko shut down the valve, he suddenly found himself airborne in a cloud of red dust. In an instant, he collided with the Russian as both were sucked toward the valve.

"The valve is open!" Mac yelled as he held onto his chief engineer. The atmosphere inside the habitat rushed through the valve to the outside, pulling both of them into the two-foot opening.

"Arrrhh!!" Rechenko yelled as his left leg entered the valve.

Mac struggled to hold onto him, but was knocked off his own feet by the blast of air pressure. Just as he lost his grip, the five other valves in the habitat automatically opened, relieving the airflow through valve six.

"Victor?" Mac shouted as he pulled him away from the valve.

Rechenko didn't answer.

"Victor, are you okay?"

Rechenko started to shake and struggle, gasping for air. Mac peered into his faceplate and gasped when he saw that Rechenko's face had turned blue. Somehow the Russian's suit had been breached and the air had been sucked out of his lungs.

"Lieutenant!" Mac called out to his first officer on the bridge of the crew module. "Rechenko is down! Mayday! Mayday!"

Dr. Judy Delaney leaned back in her chair in her quarters and looked at her watch. She hadn't heard Mac and Victor enter the crew module from their Extra Vehicular Activity, or EVA, and by her estimate they should be running low on air. At age thirty-six, Judy was a veteran of several Space Station missions and considered one of the top medical officers at NASA. As always, she wore her shoulder-length light brown hair in a ponytail, which gave her a girlish appearance; but she was all business when it came to crew safety. She jumped up, slid her door open, and made her way up the ladder well to the flight deck.

She came up behind Lieutenant Michael Traveres and mission botanist Angela Lee sitting together on the bridge. They made a striking couple, Traveres with his rugged Latin good looks and Angela with her soft Asian features. They rarely missed an opportunity to spend time together as long as it didn't interfere with their daily duties.

"How's it going, Lieutenant?" Judy asked. "Aren't Mac and Victor running a little late?"

Traveres straightened up in his chair. "Yes doctor. They're wrapping things up outside. I've already given them a warning."

"Good . . . . Now if Mac would only listen." Judy rolled her eyes as she glanced at the habitat monitor showing Mac and Rechenko by valve six.

"He needs to come in right now because we've just received a message from Houston." Traveres said, staring intently at his computer. "It says stand by for a priority transmission, eyes only."

The base alarm suddenly shrieked over their conversation, causing everyone to jump.

"What's going on?" Angela shouted, covering her ears.

Traveres scanned the status panel. "Damn! H2 is decompressing!"

Mac's voice boomed over the intercom. "Lieutenant! Rechenko is down! Mayday! Mayday!"

Judy looked at the H2 camera feed, showing Mac and Rechenko struggling in a cloud of red dust beside valve six. She could hear Mac's labored breathing as he pulled Rechenko away from the wide-open valve.

Traveres keyed his com-link. "Commander, what's your status?"

"I'm fine, but Rechenko's suit is torn. He's turning blue. Get Ivory in here now!"

"How's their air supply?" Judy looked over Traveres' shoulder at the console.

"He has about two minutes before his emergency bottle activates. I can't get a reading from Dr. Rechenko. It's possible the sensors in his suit were ripped out."

She opened her com-link. "Mac, this is Judy. How are you doing?"

"I'm fine, but Victor's lost consciousness. I think we're losing him."

"What about his emergency oxygen bottle? Did that activate?"

"Yes, but he's not getting any air because his suit is ripped."

"Mac, you have to fix that tear immediately, before Victor goes into cardiac arrest."

"It'd be quicker if we brought him inside. Where the hell is Ivory?" Mac yelled. "He's supposed to be standing by in the airlock!"

"Commander," Traveres' voice stayed calm. "Ivory and La Rue are standing by, but we can't open the airlock because the atmospheric pressure in the habitat is unstable."

"Well, close the valves!" Mac yelled again.

"Sir, I can't. I have no control of valve six. You'll have to do a manual override."

Judy watched the habitat video monitor and could hear Mac's heavy breathing as he struggled with Rechenko.

"I found the tear!" Mac yelled. "I'm going to tie it off and give him my emergency oxygen bottle. That should stabilize him 'til I close the valve."

"Could we blow the airlock door to get to them quicker?" Judy asked Traveres.

Traveres shook his head. "I could blow the airlock, but it would take longer to pressurize again, meaning we might lose Dr. Rechenko."

Judy looked at Mac on the monitor as he worked on Rechenko's suit, his labored breathing resonating over the intercom. He was obviously running out of air, but Rechenko's only hope for survival hinged on Mac's being able to patch his torn suit and shut down valve six within the next few seconds.

"Okay...I've tied off Victor's suit...and...snapped in my...emergency oxygen...bottle. I'm checking his faceplate...to see if his color...has changed." Mac's words were becoming more faint and slow.

"His vitals don't look good," Judy groaned. "He's going to pass out any second now." She keyed her com-link. "Mac, please hurry and shut the valve. We need to bring you and Rechenko in as soon as possible."

Mac bent over his fallen friend, who lay motionless on the floor. He looked into his faceplate, but it was completely fogged. Letting him go, he turned his attention to valve six. His fingers felt slow and clumsy as he opened the control panel, unaware that oxygen deprivation already handicapped his movements. He struggled to remember the override procedure.

"Commander, this is Traveres. You need to prime the valve first then turn the handle to close it."

"Prime...the valve?" Mac stammered through a long exhale.

"Yes, Commander, prime the valve. Sir, you're out of oxygen. Focus on the primer pump."

Mac grabbed the primer handle and pumped it several times until the light came on.

"The light...is on." Mac inhaled deeply. The panel in front of him looked distorted and wobbly.

"Okay. Now turn the handle in front of you to the closed position."

He grabbed the handle and tried to turn it, but it wouldn't budge. He fell back to the floor, exhausted. Laboring to catch his breath, he felt like he had just run a marathon. "I think...it's st...stuck!" Mac could feel the growing panic in his own voice.

"Try again!" Traveres voice snapped over the intercom, jolting Mac into action.

Zapped of energy, and fighting off an invading tunnel vision, Mac rose up again, gripped the handle with both hands and turned it with all his might. Valve six closed completely. The remaining valves then closed automatically and stabilized the air pressure inside the habitat.

Within seconds, the airlock door leading to Habitat 2 opened. Lieutenant Christopher Ivory ran into the dome, followed closely by Damon La Rue, the mission geologist. They flew across the floor in a couple of giant leaps, and Ivory quickly snapped an oxygen bottle into Mac's suit.

"Commander, are you all right?" Ivory shouted.

Mac immediately felt the rush of fresh oxygen clearing his head. "Yes, Lieutenant, I'm fine. Let's get Rechenko inside."

At six foot two, Lieutenant Ivory, the lone African American on the crew, was the tallest and by far the strongest crew member. He and the stocky Frenchman, La Rue, picked up the large-framed Rechenko with very little effort. They carried him to the airlock with Mac following close behind. Once inside the chamber, about the size of an elevator, Ivory knelt down and unzipped Rechenko's helmet and checked for a pulse.

"Is he breathing?" Mac knelt next to his friend.

"I can't find a pulse through these gloves," Ivory answered. "Hopefully he's not in cardiac arrest."

Mac felt a dull pain in his heart as he stared at the ashen face of his Russian friend. All he could think about was the last time he saw Rechencho's wife Olga, when the three of them cruised down the Neva River in St. Petersburg, Russia. She was everything to Victor, and the last thing Mac wanted was to have to tell Olga of her beloved husband's final moments.

The pressurization chime sounded and the airlock door to the Mars 2 ready room opened. Mac moved out of the way as Judy entered the airlock and sprang into action.

"Pull back his suit," she ordered, readying her stethoscope. She checked his pulse while Ivory ripped open Rechenko's suit, exposing his chest.

"Damn! He's in cardiac arrest. Lieutenant, get the defibrillator ready." Judy started pumping Rechenko's chest. "Come on, Victor! Stay with me! Don't give up!"

Still on the floor of the airlock, Mac moved out of the way as Ivory readied the defibrillator, pulling out the paddles and handing them to Judy. He marveled at how calm and controlled the two of them were.

"Everyone back," Judy ordered as she activated the defibrillator sequence. "Clear!" she shouted. Within a few seconds the defibrillator sent a charge through Rechenko, causing him to spasm. Moments later a second charge moved his body again. Judy removed the paddles and pumped his chest again. Rechenko's right arm suddenly twitched, followed by the stiffening of his body.

"He moved!" Mac yelled.

"Oxygen mask, Lieutenant." She continued to pump his chest. "Come on, Victor, wake up!"

Rechenko let out a loud cough followed by a desperate gasp for air. Ivory held the mask as the Russian took a couple of long deep breaths, moaning and groaning and gasping for air.

"Victor, you're back!" Mac grabbed Rechenko's arm. "I thought we'd lost you."

"My lungs...," Rechenko wheezed, still out of breath, "...they're burning..... What happened?" He quickly pulled the mask over his mouth again.

"Don't try to speak. Just relax and breathe," Judy ordered as she sat back from her knees to the floor. "You had an accident, but you're okay. You took in a little freezing Martian atmosphere. That's why your lungs hurt. I want you to lay back and rest. Don't try to speak. That's an order."

Mac looked at Judy and smiled. He had worked with her on several space station missions and they had become very close. He helped her to her feet and hugged her. "You are something special," he whispered as she buried her head in his chest. The moment was short-lived as he noticed Dr. William Boyle, the mission's chief science officer, approach. The pompous British scientist had a way of conducting an inquisition after every event that took place at the base. They all knew he reported his results immediately to the European Space Consortium in Paris.

"Commander, how did this happen?" Boyle asked in his proper British accent. "Was the habitat damaged?"

It had been just a few hours earlier that Mac and Dr. Boyle had exchanged heated words about Mac's order to confine the crew to base during the habitat inspection. Dr. Boyle had insisted that he and La Rue be allowed to drive Matty out to the "Red Anvil" drilling site in a continuing effort to locate a water source. Still seething over Boyle's insubordination, Mac chose to ignore his science officer's current inquiry.

"Commander, if you are finished in the habitat, La Rue and I still have time to drive out to Red Anvil and get in a couple of hours of work."

Mac moved toward Boyle, backing him into the ready room.

"Excuse me, gentlemen," Judy interrupted. "I have a patient here who needs to be removed from the airlock. Dr. Boyle, would you please assist Lieutenant Ivory?"

"Why of course," Dr. Boyle said as he moved away from Mac, flashing him an indignant look before turning this attention to Rechenko.

As Ivory, La Rue, and Boyle carried Rechenko to a gurney in the ready room, Mac felt Judy tug his arm.

"Mac, don't start in with Boyle again. The two of you have argued enough for one day, don't you think?"

"That arrogant son of a bitch!" Mac made little effort to keep his voice down. "Did you hear that? All he cares about is his own personal quest! And while Victor is still lying injured in the airlock! I tell you, Judy, I have half a notion to send Dr. Boyle to his precious little drill site without a space suit!"

Boyle approached again. "Commander, what do you say? Can we drive Matty out to Red Anvil or not?"

"Dr. Boyle!" Mac bristled. "Do you have any semblance of decency? Your colleague almost lost his life just now!"

"Commander, while I sympathize with Dr. Rechenko's plight, he was *your* responsibility. You must understand that our time remaining here is running out and *my* responsibility is locating a usable water source. Mars 3 is on its way and we have so much to do."

Dr. Boyle's persistence irked Mac. He turned toward the Englishman, ready to verbally tear into him, when something across the ready room caught his eye. Lieutenant Traveres stood by the ladder, staring at Mac with a dark look.

"What is it, Lieutenant?" Mac asked, sparing Dr. Boyle from his wrath for a second time.

Traveres hesitated and glanced around the ready room. His odd behavior now caught the attention of the rest of the crew members, who turned to focus on him.

"Commander, I'm sorry. You received a priority message while you were busy inside the habitat." His voice was tight and stressed.

"Yes," Mac acknowledged, struck by the behavior of his usually stoic first officer. Something had rattled him.

"What did the message say?"

Traveres took a deep breath, and then pressed on. "Commander, Mission Control has lost contact…with Mars 3. They say it has disappeared without a trace."

CHAPTER 2

EARTHCONN

Traveres' stunning announcement sent Mac into an emotional tailspin. He scrambled up the ladder well leading from the ready room to the flight deck. It was a twenty-foot climb through the three-level crew module, past the mid-deck that housed the individual quarters, then onto the flight deck and bridge.

A heavy sick feeling hung over him, since he was well aware that the loss of Mars 3 could spell the end of the fragile alliance between the International Space Consortium and the Mars program. The earlier achievements of Mars 1 and now his Mars 2 mission would go down in history as the most expensive exercise in futility ever paid for by taxpayers.

Mac stepped onto the flight deck, followed by Lieutenants Traveres and Ivory, with Dr. Boyle and French geologist Damon La Rue bringing up the rear. He sat down in his pilot's seat and activated the Mission Control download, retrieving the priority message sent from Houston. Because of the distance between Mars and Earth, direct communications was not possible. Even with the high-speed laser transmission technology, it still took a signal seven to ten minutes to travel one way between the two planets.

As Mac copied the download to disk, he couldn't shake his feeling of deep anxiety—not only for the survival of the Mars Program itself, but for the eight lives on board Mars 3, including his closest friend, Commander Rusty Chandler. Twenty-five years ago, he and Rusty had become friends at the Air Force Academy and had since shared parallel careers as pilots, then astronauts, and now commanders of their own Mars missions.

Mac could only hope Rusty and his crew were not the victims of the new matter/anti-matter propulsion system they carried. If Mission Control lost contact when Mars 3 engaged the hyperdrive, he feared the spacecraft may have disintegrated into nothing more than a debris field in the blackness of space.

"Sir, the download is complete. Are you ready for playback?" Lieutenant Traveres sat down in his co-pilot's seat next to Mac, taking control of the download operations.

Mac felt the anxious stares of the captive audience crowding around him. He took a deep breath and gave the order: "Go ahead and play the disk, Lieutenant."

"Yes, sir."

It always impressed Mac that Traveres kept a stringent disciplinary posture while performing his duties, whether routine or emergency. He had worked side by side with Traveres for over a year on Mars and the two continued a strictly professional relationship with very little informality. Mac could not have asked for a better first officer, whose intelligence and dedication to duty more than made up for his stoic nature.

The screen directly in front of them went from a light blue picture to a spinning logo with the familiar corporate jingle:

"The following transmission is brought to you by EarthConn, the leading provider of global, and, now, interplanetary communications. EarthConn is the leader in VWEB access around the world. Don't forget to sign up for the new laser phone by EarthConn, so there's nowhere on Earth or Mars you can't be found."

Mac could never quite get used to the influx of corporate sponsorship in the space program. He had joined NASA shortly after the turn of the twenty-first century, just before the birth of the International Space Consortium and the advent of mass corporate sponsorship and the underwriting that came with it.

NASA had been cool to the idea of commercial sponsors, a concept readily embraced by the rest of the space community as early as the late-twentieth century. It wasn't until funding problems at NASA became unbearable that the space agency gave in. Now NASA aggressively pursued private sector funding for all its projects; and, Mac had to admit, it had helped accelerate the manned space program.

A side benefit to the growing corporate involvement was the increase in badly needed fresh blood into the agency, which included Lieutenant Traveres.

A pilot and communications expert for the Air Force, he had been working closely with EarthConn on their revolutionary Deep Space Laser Relay (DSLR). When communications problems cropped up on the first Mars mission, EarthConn played a key role in moving Traveres to the front of the line on the next Mars mission to fix the problem.

That sort of move would never have happened in the old NASA bureaucracy. Because they were paying much of the tab, corporations were not shy about calling the shots when their interests were at stake.

The onscreen EarthConn logo dissolved to a shot of a man sitting at a console surrounded by computer screens and touch pads. Mac immediately recognized Brian Montgomery, one of the British astronauts serving as the mission communicator.

"Hello, Commander MacTavish," Montgomery started. "We understand you've been busy with the habitat pressurization; however, we do have a priority situation that requires your immediate attention."

The serious tone to Montgomery's voice, absent the infamously cool "NASA–speak" of the mission communicators, caught Mac's attention. Obviously choked with emotion, Montgomery betrayed the grave mood in Houston.

"Commander, we have lost all telemetry with the Mars 3 spacecraft. Our ground-based tracking network and the deep-space radar finder have so far come up negative. To complicate the matter, we lost contact with Mars 3 as it was about to enter into hyperdrive. This obviously makes tracking difficult since the spacecraft's probable location is almost impossible to fix."

Listening to Montgomery, Mac read between the lines. The real issue here is whether Mars 3 is still in one piece. The timing of the loss of contact raised serious doubts about whether the spacecraft survived the hyperdrive burn.

"Commander, since we have not received any telemetry from the spacecraft, we are considering the possibility they may be experiencing a radiation blackout. As you know, solar storm activity is at a ten-year peak, and several solar events are expected at this time."

A solar event? That would explain a lot of things. But how long would a radiation blackout last?

"What we want you to do," Montgomery continued, "is have Lieutenant Traveres conduct a search for the spacecraft using the DSLR. He wrote the book on its operation, and we feel he would stand the best chance of locating Mars 3."

Mac's eyes locked with Traveres'. Using the Deep Space Laser Relay would mean Mars Base would lose its laser-fixed, high-speed contact with Earth, something mission planners never take lightly.

Are they already that desperate? Mac thought.

Montgomery folded his hands and leaned toward the camera. "Commander, all we ask is that Lieutenant Traveres give it his best shot. EarthConn feels that because of his expertise, he has the best chance of making contact. I know everybody here—the staff and family members of the crew—anxiously await your search results. Good luck and Godspeed. Houston out."

Flopping back in his chair, Mac shook his head. Clearly, something had gone terribly wrong with Mars 3. It was only yesterday in this very room that he and the crew watched a video feed of the Mars 3 crew's farewell transmission from Earth orbit, only hours before their hyperdrive burn. The bleak mood in Houston now tore at him.

"Lieutenant, establish a video link now. I want to send a response to Houston as soon as possible."

"Yes sir, starting uplink now. Signal acquisition in two minutes. We can send any time."

Suddenly, Dr. Boyle's voice boomed out behind them, shattering the solemn mood. "Commander, I need to send a data file to Paris. Do you mind?"

Mac snapped. "Doctor, if you haven't noticed, we seem to be dealing with a rather monumental problem—the lives of eight missing colleagues hurtling through hyperspace. A file of your latest accomplishments can wait for a later transmission."

"Commander, I beg your pardon, but this is important information that needs to be forwarded to the Consortium. Surely you can send it now."

Mac put a hand up. He had heard enough. The egotistical Brit had refocused the attention back to himself in less than a minute. Squabbling with Dr. Boyle had become a daily occurrence, and Mac was not in the mood for another fight with the pompous British scientist.

"Commander, we're ready to transmit," Traveres said, handing him the wireless microphone.

Taking the microphone, Mac dropped his head for a moment to gather his thoughts, stroking his forehead with the tip of the mic. He prepared to address not only mission control, but also the crew's families and the entire space community.

Nodding to Traveres, he looked at the bridge mini-camera pointing at the pilot and co-pilot seats. A red light below the camera illuminated, and he began to speak. "Houston, we received your priority message and, of course, share your deep concern for the safety of Mars 3. Lieutenant Traveres is confident he can locate Mars 3 using the DSLR and re-establish contact. As you know, we will be breaking our high-speed data link with you as we conduct our search, but we will maintain our low-gain signal for emergency use."

"Commander, please," Boyle interrupted, holding up a small data card. "My file to Paris. . . . I beg you."

Mac flipped the switch on the microphone and halted the transmission. "Doctor, I'm going to throw you off this bridge if you don't shut up! I don't want to hear another word about your goddamn file!"

Boyle reeled back at the reprimand. Mac could hear him flop back in the third seat on the bridge, mumbling to himself, pouting like a ten-year-old. La Rue, the French geologist and close colleague of Dr. Boyle, patted his friend on the shoulder and quietly consoled him.

Gathering his thoughts again, Mac stared directly into the camera. "Houston, we are confident we can find and re-establish contact with Mars 3, providing, of course, that their antennae array has not been damaged. Please let the families of the Mars 3 crew know we will do everything possible to locate their loved ones."

Without looking at Dr. Boyle, Mac whipped his arm toward him, snapped his fingers in his face and opened his hand. At first, Boyle recoiled then apparently realized Mac was asking for his data card.

"Houston, Dr. Boyle has a file to send and requests that you forward it to Paris. Mars Base out."

Dr. Boyle placed the card in Mac's hand, and he in turn handed it to Traveres.

"Commander, we should have EarthConn confirmation in two minutes," Traveres said. "I'll send the file then."

A silence fell over the room as Mac leaned back in his chair and let out a long sigh. "Well, Lieutenant, it looks like you have plenty of work for the next couple of days. This is a tall order."

Traveres nodded in agreement. "Yes, sir, it will take some time to re-program the DSLR. Pardon me saying so, sir, but…" He paused as if debating whether to continue.

"Yes, Lieutenant, what is it? What's on your mind? Speak freely."

"Commander, pardon the expression, but this is going to be like looking for a needle in a haystack, a very big haystack." Traveres shook his head.

Boyle leaned forward, placing a hand on the back of Mac's chair. "Commander, mission control didn't sound too optimistic."

"Yes, Doctor, I agree. It sounds like they may have exhausted all their options. But if that means we are the last hope, then we'll just have to do our very best to see if we can locate Rusty and his crew."

"If Mars 3 is lost, how will that affect us?" Boyle probed.

Mac wondered what angle the doctor was working with him. "In the short term, not at all. We have three months left here and a mountain of work to complete. I want Habitat 2 operational by the end of the week. You and La Rue have to continue your search for water and we have to get the new hydroponics garden up to full production inside Habitat 2. All this has to be done regardless of the fate of Mars 3."

"But much of this work will be useless if Mar 3 is lost." Boyle stood up. "I can't see the Mars program moving forward if eight people are lost in space."

Mac got up, standing face to face with Boyle. "Doctor, we have to go on the assumption that the crew is alive and well and experiencing technical difficulties. That's it!"

"Commander, pardon me for saying so," Boyle continued, "but we can't even get Habitat 2 operational. Rechenko almost lost his life today. God knows what else may happen as we continue to explore. I say we wait until we get confirmation that Mars 3 is okay before we move forward with any more work here."

"That's ridiculous!" Mac shot back. "We've come too far to give up on building this base. You of all people should realize that. Just ten minutes ago you were insisting on going out to drill at Red Anvil with Rechenko still flat on his back in the ready room. Now you want to cease all base operations? No, Doctor, we are going to stay on schedule."

"Even at the expense of our lives?" Boyle insisted. Before Mac could respond, a lone voice, with a heavy Russian accent, pierced the room.

"I am fine, Dr. Boyle, and so is Habitat 2."

All eyes on the bridge turned to see Rechenko, still holding onto the ladder at the entrance to the flight deck. His face was noticeably red.

"Victor, what are you doing here?" Mac asked. "You should be resting."

"I'm fine, Commander." He kept his gaze on Dr. Boyle. "And so is H2. The valve problem is a software error. I just confirmed it on the computer a few minutes ago. We are ready to pump oxygen inside the habitat immediately."

"And that is exactly what we will do, Victor," Mac said. "Gentlemen, we have our work cut out for the next two days. Lieutenant, start your search for Mars 3 immediately. Victor, I want those compressors pumping oxygen into H2 within the hour. Dr. Boyle, you have your orders. You and Mr. La Rue get together some overnight provisions and drive Matty out to Red Anvil. I want you drilling by the end of the day."

Boyle dropped his shoulders and nodded. "Yes, Commander."

As if on cue, the master alarm bell suddenly pierced the room like a sword through the heart, demanding everyone's attention.

"DSLR alarm," shouted Traveres as he turned to the computer.

"Confirmed," Ivory announced, monitoring the same telemetry. "I show acquisition failure of DSLR to the Near Earth Laser Relay at eleven thirty-seven hundred hours Houston."

Mac leaned over Traveres' shoulder. "Lieutenant, could this be a DSLR failure?"

"Negative, sir, the DSLR is operating nominally. I ran a full diagnostic this morning."

"Confirmed, sir," Ivory chimed in. "DSLR is operating at full capacity with no deviations."

"And the status of the low-gain antennae?"

Before Mac got an answer, a second alarm shrieked, sending Traveres and Ivory into a frenzy at their computers, sharing information back and forth.

The ear-piercing alarms brought Judy and Angela clamoring up the ladder to the bridge as Mac watched over his two young lieutenants desperately scanning the data at their consoles.

Suddenly aware of the bell that continued to blare in their ears, Mac reached over and turned off the master alarm and a welcome quiet permeated the room.

"Sir," Traveres started, looking first at Mac, then at the crew, then back to Mac. "Sir, it appears that we have lost complete contact with Earth, both high- and low-gain attempts have failed to acquire a signal."

"It's not a problem from our end?"

"No, sir, we are transmitting fine. It appears that Houston...uh...the entire Earth has stopped transmitting altogether."

"The entire Earth stopped transmitting? Lieutenant, how is that possible?" Mac raised his voice, incredulous that his level-headed first officer would jump to such a conclusion.

Traveres was about to speak, but Lieutenant Ivory broke in. "Sir, I'm afraid I've come to the same conclusion."

Mac turned his attention to the mission's second officer. The only person more quiet and reserved then Traveres was Lieutenant Christopher Ivory. As the chief systems officer, he maintained all operations hardware, including life support and the critical recycling system. His work ethic and deep intellect earned him everyone's respect. Reserved as he was, when he spoke, everyone knew he had something important to say.

"Commander," Ivory continued. "I show a complete loss of telemetry, as if the Earth stopped transmitting."

Mac looked long and hard at Ivory, aware he was not a man who jumped to conclusions. "What are you saying, Lieutenant?"

"I know it sounds impossible, sir, but according to the latest data, it's..." He hesitated. "It's as if the Earth has disappeared."

CHAPTER 3
IS ANYBODY OUT THERE?

Sitting in his co-pilot seat on the bridge, Lieutenant Michael Traveres stared at the data on the computer screen showing that all communications with Earth were down and not coming back soon. Three days had passed since the loss of contact; and while Mac treated it as a routine EarthConn malfunction, he knew it was much more.

Traveres thought Mac showed remarkable calm and patience early on in the crisis, agreeing with Dr. Boyle's observations that a spike in solar flare activity could be to blame for the failure. But as one day turned into three days of no communications, Mac's mood had darkened.

Today the Commander had ordered him to re-task the DSLR in an attempt to direct a transmission to the Venus Orbiter circling that planet. The complicated procedure would take time, but Traveres knew Mac had gone right to the heart of the problem. Because Mars 3 and the Near Earth Laser Relay were close to Earth, their communications arrays may also have been damaged by the same solar storm. The DSLR, however, was farther away from Earth and probably escaped damage. The re-tasking would verify whether this was the case.

After working all morning on the new program, Traveres was just about finished when he heard the familiar soft voice of Angela behind him.

"How's it going, stranger? I missed you this morning in the worst way."

The sound of her voice warmed his heart. Throughout his stay on Mars, his most precious memories were of the times he spent with Angela. No woman had ever pierced through his protective shell like she did with so little effort. Quiet and unassuming, she had waltzed her way deep into his heart and soul.

Their special connection had started out innocently enough when they first met, two years before the start of the mission. Through EarthConn's influence,

Traveres had leapfrogged over more senior astronauts to land the coveted spot as first officer on the Mars 2 crew. By the time they'd completed training, the two had become casual friends; but Traveres continued to put up barriers to anything more intimate. Eventually, Angela's playful ways and her natural beauty broke down all his resistance. They consummated their relationship during the long five-month trip to Mars.

He had never experienced anyone as soft and tender as Angela. His past relationships had been controlled and directed by him. He'd taken what he wanted and given very little of himself in return. But with Angela, he found himself in unfamiliar waters. She was so giving, so honest, so fragile that he found himself wanting to protect her.

Now, as his responsibilities on the Mars 2 mission reached its most critical phase, he began to feel anxious about their relationship. The communications blackout was a dark cloud over his head, and he didn't want Angela to think he was distancing himself from her.

Traveres turned from the computer to look at the petite figure standing behind him. He loved the way she looked in her snugly fitted bright blue jump-suit with the front zipper pulled down to the curve of her breasts. Her long, straight dark hair framed the soft features of her ageless face as she stared back with that familiar innocent, irresistible look in her eyes. She was simply the most beautiful woman he had ever seen.

"Mister, you'd better at least give me a hug in the next five seconds or I'm outta here," she said playfully, her arms extended towards him.

He quickly glanced around to see if anyone was about, then stood and held his arms out to her. She fell into his embrace and he held her close to his chest. Finally, he broke the silence. "Angela, I'm sorry I didn't see you this morning. It's just that I have a mountain of work to do and can't leave until it's done. It's very important."

"I know, sweetie. I talked to Mac earlier. He said you'd be in here all day. I just wanted to come in and stare at you for a second, maybe touch you if I could get away with it."

Traveres smiled. She always had a way of saying things that let him know she cared without putting any pressure on him to reciprocate. "I'm glad you came up. I'm just getting ready to run a critical program. If it's successful, I'll see you for lunch. Okay?"

"All right," she said, still holding him. "So how's it going? Are we talking to anyone yet?"

"No, my angel, not yet. But if you'll get your butt out of here and let me run my program, maybe I'll tell you more over lunch."

"All right." She released her hold on him and turned away. "But hurry up, Poindexter. I'm getting hungry, and I'm not just talking about food."

"It's a date." He couldn't help but laugh. Poindexter was one of a hundred nicknames she had given him. He, on the other hand, had only one nickname for her: *Angel*. Because that's what she was to him, his own angel. She had come to rescue him.

He turned back to the computer. The screen said, *Ready to run program?* He looked down at the keyboard and pressed enter. In an instant, a thousand bits of data scrolled across the screen. At the speed of light the data left Mars Base via the laser dish and beamed to the Mars 2 mother ship in geosynchronous orbit above them. The laser relay boosted the signal and sent it to the DSLR, overriding its attitude control program. The DSLR turned toward Venus, seeking the orbiting spacecraft.

Traveres estimated this would take approximately an hour, depending on how quickly and accurately the DSLR moved. In an hour they would have their answer. In an hour they would all know what he already knew.

Mac was pleased as he stood at the entrance to Habitat 2, now filled with oxygen, which allowed the crew to work inside without wearing cumbersome space suits. Angela and Judy had been busy expanding the Mars garden with Lieutenant Ivory's help. Hydroponics trays now covered nearly half the habitat floor. Rechenko worked closely with Ivory, completing all the wiring and construction required to connect the recycling system to the hydroponics garden.

Damon La Rue had buried himself, literally, in his work. The renowned French geologist surveyed, dug, and cataloged every anomaly in the virgin Martian soil that made up the habitat floor. He had taken full advantage of the opportunity to work in an environment untouched by human hands and weathered only by time and the harsh Martian conditions.

It was good to see everyone so occupied with their tasks, seemingly unconcerned with the communications glitch they were experiencing. In fact, not hearing from Mission Control for three days meant no additional work was being requested of the crew.

The only person conspicuously missing was Dr. Boyle. Mac wasn't surprised since Boyle seemed to avoid any grunt work involved in other people's projects. But curiously, he hadn't left the base for his drilling expeditions in the three days since the communication failure.

Mac noticed Dr. Boyle holed up in his lab inside HI, his face buried in a bank of computers. Whenever he spent any amount of time alone, the result was usually some sort of new project or experiment. No doubt Boyle was busy working on a theory or explanation for Earth's sudden silence. Mac decided he would give his chief scientist a little more time before asking for his observations. Besides, he hadn't had a verbal confrontation with Dr. Boyle in three days, and he rather enjoyed the peace.

Deep in thought, Mac hadn't noticed Lieutenant Traveres standing a few feet behind him at the entrance to H2. When he turned, he saw his first officer's face, showing the strain of working nearly non-stop for three days. "How is the re-tasking going, Lieutenant?"

"We should know in about an hour, sir. I just sent the program. It all depends on how long it takes the DSLR to find the Venus Orbiter. Of course, if the Orbiter has to change its position to send a response, then it could take longer."

"Can the Orbiter can change position like that?"

"That's a good question, sir. The Orbiter has one of the first field laser relays. While it is programmed to track the changing attitude of the incoming laser from the NELR, I'm not quite sure how it will respond to an incoming laser communication from the DSLR. Theoretically, it shouldn't make a difference."

"So, basically, if we get no response from the Venus Orbiter, the condition of the DSLR would still be inconclusive?"

"That's correct, sir."

Mac placed a hand on Traveres' shoulder. "Michael, why don't you lie down and take a nap? You look like you could use some rest." He rarely called Traveres by his first name, and he could tell this surprised his communications expert.

"All right, sir," Traveres said with a deep sigh. "I might lie down and close my eyes for a bit. But I want to be on the bridge in an hour to scan for a return signal."

"I'll make sure you're there." Mac patted Traveres on the shoulder as the Lieutenant turned and walked away.

Turning in the direction of the habitat, Mac was glad to see Judy walking toward him with an inquisitive smile.

"What was all that about?" she asked. "You guys having a moment there, or what? Just two hot-shot pilots smiling at each other in the doorway?"

Mac laughed. Judy observed people, their behavior, and their body language. She had a way of putting what she saw into words that made him laugh. Judy *always* made him laugh. He loved her playfulness. He felt he couldn't spend enough time with her, especially since recent events had kept them apart.

"Hey, I'm just trying to encourage the poor guy. He's been under a lot of stress lately."

"What do you mean 'lately'?" Judy frowned. "Michael's been coming apart at the seams for some time. You know, I'm worried about him, and Angela's really worried."

"Oh? Has she said so?"

"She says he seems to be getting depressed. She's afraid he's trying to distance himself from her."

Mac shook his head. "It's this problem with Mars 3 and EarthConn. He's really taking it personally. I already have Rechenko learning the communications system to share the burden. But I think emotions run pretty deep with this kid. He keeps his thoughts to himself like a well-disciplined soldier. I'm not sure there's much we can do to help."

"Well, thank you, Doctor MacTavish. That was an excellent psychoanalysis. Remind me to make an appointment with you later. I think I need some therapy, too."

Judy could be relentless when it came to ribbing him, but he knew they were in agreement.

"By the way, how serious is this EarthConn problem?" she asked.

Mac, careful not to betray his deep concern, let his gaze drop to the floor. "I wouldn't be too worried. So many factors can affect the system. That's one of the reasons my first officer is going nuts in there right now. We could conceivably be without communications for weeks. If it goes on for months in a worst-case scenario, then we may have to perform a 'blind launch' back to Earth. But I doubt that will be the case."

"Months?" Judy raised her eyebrows. "Do you really think it could take that long?"

"I just don't know," Mac shrugged.

"All right, my dear," she said in her soft, soothing voice, squeezing his biceps as she spoke. "I know you'll figure it out."

Mac looked into her eyes, momentarily losing himself in her strength and beauty. He couldn't imagine life on Mars without her.

Her grip on his arm tightened as she pressed her lips against his ear and whispered, "A blind launch? I don't like the sound of that."

Once again, Traveres found himself at the communications console, waiting for data to appear on the computer screen. This time he had company. Rechenko stood close by, familiarizing himself with the system. The Russian engineer impressed Traveres with his computer skills. He had proven himself a quick study when it came to the art of troubleshooting the complicated laser pulse communications systems. Mac continued to oversee the operation while Dr. Boyle, sitting to the rear of the room, listened and observed the procedure as it unfolded.

Traveres could see the link to the Venus Orbiter was not going as he had predicted. It had been ninety minutes since he'd sent the repositioning program and he still hadn't received the expected response from the Orbiter.

"Are you certain the DSLR responded correctly to the program, Lieutenant?" Mac asked.

"Yes, sir," Traveres answered without hesitation. "The DSLR confirmed attitude change immediately. My only concern here is our orbital information on Venus and the expected location of the spacecraft."

Dr. Boyle stepped forward and spoke for the first time. "How is a laser pulse signal going to find an orbiting spacecraft from so far away? Is it possible it's just missing the moving target?"

"No, not likely," Mac responded. "The laser pulse receiver is constantly scanning for a signal. The pulse is spread out like a radio signal, not like a narrow laser beam. The receiver will find it and focus in on the signal automatically."

Mac's familiarity with the complicated system impressed Traveres. His commander had obviously done his homework.

"The only unknown is whether or not the orbiter is hidden behind the planet," Mac continued. "But with a complete orbit every forty-five minutes, it theoretically should take no more than ninety minutes to acquire a signal if the DSLR is working properly."

Suddenly a tone sounded over the bridge speakers. The flat screen on the console between Rechenko and Traveres lit up like a Christmas tree as streams of data and signal indicators illuminated the once blank monitor. Rechenko immediately spoke up. "The mother ship has received a return signal from the DSLR! I will download it now!"

"It's data from the Orbiter!" Traveres confirmed, letting out an audible sigh of relief.

While Rechenko and Traveres celebrated, Mac could see there were no smiles at the back of the room. Mac had played his final card, hoping for a technical explanation for the communications failure. He now looked to Dr. Boyle for any possible explanation as to why Earth had suddenly fallen silent. Boyle sat with the same somber look on his face as the full implications of the transmission from Venus sank in.

Traveres and Rechenko were still celebrating when Mac decided he had to rain on their parade. "You know, this would be really good news if we were Venutians instead of Earthlings." The room fell silent as he continued. "Lieutenant, do you have the date of the last Venus/Earth transmission?"

"Uh...yes, sir!" Traveres responded with a crisp military snap. "It should be here in the downlink; it was part of the program I sent. Yes, here it is, Commander...let's see...." He paused, figuring in his head before announcing. "Yes, sir, it looks like the last Venus/Earth contact was some...eighty-four hours ago." The enthusiasm in Traveres' voice died like a deflating balloon.

Mac sat in the back of the room deep in thought, one hand covering his eyes. Never in the history of manned spaceflight had contact been lost for this long. There were simply no mission procedures that addressed this unique situation.

He looked up to see all eyes on him. As he scanned the faces, his eyes met those of Dr. Boyle. Mac chose his words carefully, hoping he would not sound lost or confused. "Dr. Boyle, I know you've been looking into this problem from a scientific perspective. Have you come to any conclusions?"

Boyle's moment had arrived, and Mac could see the Englishman was ready for it. Ever since the loss of contact, Mac knew that eventually he might have to turn to Boyle, seeking his expertise. No one at the base knew more than Dr. Boyle when it came to questions of space and orbiting bodies. The proud British Nobel Laureate appeared more than ready to save the day.

"Yes, indeed, Commander," he said. "I have been giving this a great deal of thought over the past couple of days."

Here it comes, Mac thought.

"I have come up with a couple of possible scenarios—actually, three to be exact. I am still doing some calculations, however, so I am not quite finished. Could I address the crew later this evening, Commander, say after dinner?"

Calculations? What exactly did he have in mind?

"That's fine, Dr. Boyle," Mac said. "As a matter of fact, I think it's time to brief the crew on all of this. We need to get it out on the table."

"Yes. Good show, Commander. I think that would be best for everyone."

Traveres sat by himself on the bridge, staring at the Venus data on the screen in front of him. Everything had gone as expected. He had cleared his name of any fault with the EarthConn failure, putting the crisis squarely on Mac's shoulders. He felt a twinge of pain for Angela. How would she react to this situation? Would she be strong, or feel panicked and hopeless? Her voice suddenly pierced his thoughts.

"Hi, sweetheart, I heard things went well with your test. I think that means you owe me some lunch!"

He turned to see Angela standing a few feet away. His heart pounded with a desire to shelter and protect her. "Yes, my angel," he said, hiding his foreboding thoughts. "The test went great. You'll hear all about it tonight."

"Tonight? What's happening tonight?"

"Oh, nothing much. The Commander's going to give a full briefing on what's been going on."

"Anything I should worry about?"

"No, Angel," he paused. "Nothing you can't handle."

CHAPTER 4

BRIEFING

Standing next to his bed, Mac pulled up the front zipper of his soft-pressure suit. Mission rules required anyone operating a vehicle on Mars to wear a soft suit as a precaution against unexpected cabin depressurization. He was thankful for the comfort the soft suits afforded. The bulky hard-pressure suits for outside excursions were always awkward and uncomfortable to wear.

He keyed his com-link to Habitat 1. "Dr. Boyle, are you ready?"

After some delay, Mac heard the reluctant voice of Dr. Boyle. "Commander, are sure you want to go for a drive in Matty? I would be just as comfortable briefing you here."

Mac marveled at how Dr. Boyle concerned himself with his own comfort. "No Doctor. As I told you before, I want to drive out to the Red Anvil drill site for an inspection. You can brief me on the way. Meet me inside Habitat 2 by the Matty airlock on the double. And Doctor, you'd better be wearing your soft suit."

Turning off his com-link, Mac rolled his eyes. *Patience.* Boyle had postponed his report on the communications failure for three days, requesting more time to confirm his 'findings,' whatever that meant. He sensed Boyle was milking his role as science chief. After months of squabbling with the pompous British scientist, Mac just wanted him to be a team player for once.

Sliding down the ladder well from the mid-deck to the ready room, Mac headed out the main airlock into a long white tube-shaped corridor that connected the crew module to Habitats 1 and 2. He admired what had been accomplished in their short stay on Mars. Dr. Rechenko's innovative design, the connecting tunnel, and pressurized doors to both habitats had proven to be simple, reliable, and cost-effective.

Mac stopped at the entrance to Habitat 1 to check on Boyle. He walked into the smaller dome-shaped structure that was about forty feet in diameter and crammed with spare parts, tools, and drilling equipment. At the center of the habitat was a long table with a bank of computer screens lined up next to a holographic generator, a three-foot-long, half-inch-thick platter-shaped object with several coin-sized lenses imbedded on the surface.

Boyle sat in a chair directly in front of the center flat-screen, busily typing on the keyboard, while Damon La Rue looked over his shoulder. Mac could see Boyle hadn't put on his soft-pressure suit and let out a deep sigh. "Dr. Boyle, exactly which part of 'meet me in Habitat 2 on the double' didn't you understand?"

Boyle didn't move, but Damon turned around. "Commander, is there something I can do for you?"

"Yes, Damon. Could you excuse us? I need to talk to Dr. Boyle…alone."

Angela stood perfectly still inside the cavernous confines of Habitat 2, where the red glow of the morning sun gleamed through the clear roof. She maintained a perfect Tai Chi pose, breathing rhythmically. Judy stood behind and to Angela's right, mirroring her every position, slowly moving from one pose to the next with a deliberate grace. This non-contact, martial arts discipline served as their primary source of exercise at the base. Angela had long been a proponent of alternative methods to stay in shape on extended missions.

She introduced her yoga and Tai Chi to the rest of the crew on the voyage to Mars and continued it at the base. Judy was the first to join her, followed by Mac. Traveres started showing interest in both Tai Chi and Angela about a month into the mission. Ivory, a former Navy SEAL and martial arts expert, was well versed in the discipline, but never joined in on a group sessions. The reclusive Lieutenant, always the loner in a closet full of people, preferred to practice in isolation.

Angela convinced the stuffy Dr. Boyle to try Tai Chi for a while; but, as Judy so aptly put it, "He doesn't seem to have the social desire to maintain a regimen of activity that would put him in daily contact with normal people." Boyle soon returned to his daily jog on the treadmill and left the alternative exercise to others.

The bright, open environment of Habitat 2 was a welcome change from the crowded quarters the crew had endured over the previous fifteen months. Angela looked across the habitat at Ivory, who also took advantage of the wide-open space to practice his stick fighting. She admired his strength as he leaped and thrust his body in all directions with catlike precision. Sweat rolled off his dark bare chest, revealing a finely sculpted muscular body.

Angela finished a series of poses and said, "Let's do one more set."

"I'm game," Judy answered enthusiastically. "I'm still sore from all the bending over we've done planting seedlings."

"I know what you mean," Angela laughed. "Thank God we're almost done!"

They continued their slow, predetermined movements that took time and effort to learn. The coordination between muscle movement and breathing was critical—the slower the movement, the more toning and shaping to the body. At the end of a session, most people found themselves drenched in sweat, but exhilarated by a vigorous workout of body, mind, and soul.

"How's Michael doing?" Judy asked. "I haven't seen him much the last couple of days."

"You and me both," Angela shrugged. "He's been so obsessed with the communications failure, we've hardly spoken."

"You two okay?"

"Oh, I think so. It's just...I mean...I think he's really under a lot of pressure." Angela fought the growing lump in her throat. Judy was like a sister to her, which made it easy for Angela to bare her soul. "He sometimes buries his feelings deep inside. He gets moody and doesn't want to talk about it. It's as if he thinks the communications failure was his fault or something."

"His fault? Why would he think that?"

"I'm not sure. Maybe it's because no one else has come up with an explanation for the blackout. You've got to admit, Judy, this is kind of scary not knowing what's going on. But no one is saying anything. Not Mac or Boyle. Don't you think that's kind of odd?"

Judy came out of her pose. "First off, I know for a fact that Mac doesn't blame Michael for the communications failure. He has a lot of respect for him. And as far as any odd behavior, yes, we're all on edge about this blackout; but

Mac's working closely with Dr. Boyle on the problem. They'll have it figured out in no time."

"I suppose, but what about Dr. Boyle? I thought he was supposed to brief us three days ago. What happened?"

Before Judy could respond, Angela saw the double doors of Habitat 2 open and in walked Damon La Rue, looking his disheveled self. He always managed to appear rumpled and wrinkled, as if he had just gotten out of bed. He was a far cry from the stereotypical suave and debonair Frenchman, and his appearance seemed to have gotten worse as the mission wore on.

"Pardon me, ladies, am I interrupting?" he asked as he stroked his two-day beard.

"No, Damon, we're about through," Angela responded.

"Oh, excellent. Angela, I wonder if I could ask for your assistance with preparing a special meal for tonight?"

Angela shot Judy a confused look. "A special dinner for tonight? What's the occasion?"

"It seems the Commander has ordered Dr. Boyle to brief us on his findings. It's possible he has discovered what caused the blackout."

"What makes you say that? Did Mac tell you?" Angela asked.

"No, Angelique." La Rue again rubbed the two-day stubble and revealed a slight grin. "Dr. Boyle is briefing him inside Habitat 1 right now."

Mac walked up behind Boyle, waiting for some acknowledgement from the portentous scientist, but he was ignored. Boyle slid his chair over to another keyboard and continued his work.

"Doctor...," Mac began, but Boyle interrupted.

"Commander, I am sorry, but I don't have time to go on excursions with you for tours and briefings when there is so much work to do." He continued to type, eyes focused on the screens. "While you're busy looking for a technical explanation for this communications blackout, I have been seeking a scientific one. Commander, I am a scientist, and this will take a scientific explanation."

Boyle's arrogance and his growing defiance to follow orders irked Mac, but he was determined not to fight with him this morning. He just wanted his cooperation for once.

"It's true I am an engineer and you are a scientist, and you've been in here looking at telescopic images and working your computer models; but you still can't explain what has happened to Earth, can you?"

Boyle stopped and turned toward Mac, then back to his computer to type in a few commands. Mac stepped back in amazement as two spherical objects about the size of basketballs appeared floating above the table. One was a thermal image of the Sun, the second an infrared copy of Earth. Mac had seen three-dimensional holographic images before, but none with such detail and clarity.

Boyle slowly turned around toward Mac again and fixed his eyes on him. "Commander, I know what has happened to the Earth."

CHAPTER 5
A SOLAR EVENT

Mac looked at the others sitting around the oblong table and noted the food and wine had taken effect. He had ordered fresh fish for dinner, the first from the fish farm in Habitat 2, and La Rue and Angela had outdone themselves serving up a culinary treat that would rival any fine restaurant on Earth. It wasn't often that the entire crew sat down together for a meal in the galley, and tonight promised to be memorable.

"I hope all of you enjoyed this fantastic dinner that Damon and Angela prepared for us. I'd like to propose a toast to the creators of such fine cuisine."

Everyone raised their glasses in unison and said, "Salute!"

La Rue, his cheeks nearly as red as the wine, slurred his response. "Merci, my wonderful colleagues! I'm sure you noticed how my special sauces complemented the wonderful dishes prepared by my attractive assistant. I'd like to thank my partner in this delicious adventure, the ever beautiful Angela!"

Mac and the crew cheered while Angela giggled. "Well, thank you all. I'm glad you liked it. I'm sorry it took so long to get the fish farm producing. I hope the next crew appreciates what we've left for them."

"To the Mars 3 crew!" La Rue shouted as he swayed back and forth.

"To the Mars 3 crew and my good friend Rusty!" Mac added. "May they have a safe and uneventful trip and arrive here in one piece to share this marvelous base we've built." Mac noticed about half the crew raised their glasses to toast; but Judy, Ivory, and Boyle just looked at him.

"What do you mean 'share'?" Judy asked. "We'll be long gone by the time they arrive. . .won't we?"

The table fell silent and all turned to Mac.

"Will we be gone? Well, yes, I hope so; but that is what I need to talk to you about tonight. Sit back and relax for a moment, and have another glass of

wine if you wish—or in Damon's case, if you must. I want all of you to listen
to me and later to Dr. Boyle, without asking questions until we're finished. Is
that a deal?"

"Well, mon capi'tan," La Rue bellowed, his accent more pronounced. "As
you Americans say, we're all ears!"

Mac realized La Rue was beyond tipsy. He would keep a close eye on him
throughout the briefing. The rest of the crew wore somber looks on their faces,
perhaps sensing something ominous.

"As you're all aware, we're experiencing a complete blackout of our Earth-
Conn communications. While I don't think there's immediate cause for concern, I do think it would be prudent to review our current situation since our
return launch window is only nine weeks away. Mission rules state that if a
communications blackout should occur on or before the return launch window
opens, the launch should proceed as scheduled."

The crew nodded favorably.

"However, I need to address whether or not we do face any extraordinary
circumstances. After extensive scientific investigation, Dr. Boyle has come to
some important conclusions regarding our communications failure." Everyone
at the table, with the exception of La Rue, shifted and leaned forward, ready to
hear bad news.

"This morning Dr. Boyle was kind enough to give me a thorough briefing,
not only on his findings, but including several possible scenarios we may want
to explore. Now I want to warn everybody that what you are about to hear is
based on mathematical models of possible scenarios, utilizing the latest available data. Dr. Boyle has put a considerable amount of time and thought into
what he is about to say, so please, give him your undivided attention and hold
your questions until he's finished."

Mac nodded at Boyle, who put his glasses on and opened his laptop computer. He gave a slight nod to Lieutenant Ivory who then placed the holographic generator in the center of the table.

"Very good. Thank you, Commander. Now let's get started, shall we?"
Boyle stared at his computer for a few moments then, with his head still lowered, began his briefing. "I'm afraid the Commander is absolutely right. This is
a bit of a mystery we have on our hands. I'd like to say straightaway that Lieu-

tenant Traveres has done an outstanding job, just about all anyone could ask; but this situation is perhaps beyond his control to solve." Boyle peered over his reading glasses at Traveres, giving him an awkward nod.

"Because his extensive troubleshooting has ruled out the base and the DSLR as the culprit, I focused my investigation on a *celestial* explanation. I asked myself, 'What could cause a communication blackout of this duration?' There are actually many things, the most obvious being a large solar flare interfering with our transmitters in orbit around Earth. Such an occurrence is quite a common problem; however, a solar event would only last a few hours to, at the most, a day.

"I have been forced to look at, shall we say, more unpleasant explanations, some more probable than others. I am talking about things such as a large meteor hitting the Earth or a chain of nuclear explosions causing a 'nuclear winter,' which would certainly result in a worldwide blackout. As farfetched as these sound, it was necessary to eliminate them as possibilities before I could explore further."

Mac watched as the crew listened. No looks of disbelief on any faces yet.

"With this in mind, using our telescopes on the mother ship orbiting above us, I recorded images of the Earth to confirm its nominal status." Boyle fumbled with the laptop in front of him and activated the holographic generator. In an instant a three-dimensional image of Earth appeared above the table. As it slowly rotated, everyone could see it showed a thermal relief image of the planet with varying degrees of blues, greens, and reds.

"You may notice at first glance that this image reveals nothing unusual with the Earth's surface. There are no obvious hot spots or massive ash clouds. Because this seems to rule out any nuclear or cosmotic catastrophe, I was forced to look elsewhere.

"It was at this time that I decided to revisit the solar flare question, to see if I could fit a solar event into the equation. While intense solar storms are by no means rare, what is rare is the chance of a major ejecta striking Earth."

"Ejecta?" Judy asked.

"Yes, that's correct," Boyle answered. He pressed a button on his laptop and a bright thermal image of the Sun appeared with its fiery surface erupting in a constant stream of violent explosions.

"Ejecta is a concentrated discharge of intense plasma that, through a tremendous burst of unimaginable energy, manages to escape the Sun's gravity. This concentrated radiation is thrown out into the galaxy in all different directions. A major discharge can occur about every eight to ten years."

"Eight to ten years?" Rechenko echoed. "You are talking about the Solar Maximum?"

"Oh, yes. Very good, Dr. Rechenko. Scientists have known for some time that this is a cyclical event. As a matter of fact, you may recall at the turn of the century there were mass predictions that the Sun would explode and fry everyone on the planet. It just so happens that the Solar Maximum, as it is called, coincided with the new millennium. It made for good fodder; the increase in solar activity seemed to confirm all those doomsday predictions. Of course, the activity eventually subsided and the Earth made it through the end of the millennium unscathed."

"Well, Dr. Boyle," Judy asked. "Are you telling us that the Earth may not have made it through this cycle?"

The room fell silent. Mac could see that all eyes were on Boyle, who pressed a few keys on his computer. The holographic Sun reduced to the size of a soccer ball and a softball-sized Earth appeared about six feet away. The two images hovered over the table for all to see. Then a bright flare shot from the Sun and a simulated solar storm moved slowly toward the Earth.

"I have uncovered evidence that the Earth may have experienced a recent solar event. In fact, we may know the exact time the event took place. Lieutenant Traveres informs me that the DSLR lost contact with Earth at exactly eight-oh-six a.m. Houston time on the morning of the fourth of June, exactly ten days ago."

Above their heads the solar storm impacted the hologram of the Earth and the thermal image turned almost completely red. Mac wondered whether the simulated storm wasn't a bit too dramatic. Judging from the stunned faces in the room, he could see that Boyle had made his point clear.

Finally Judy spoke again. "So, Doctor, what exactly do you think happened to the Earth? Is there evidence of mass destruction? How can you come to such a conclusion so quickly?"

Mac admired Judy asking all the right questions. Skeptical by nature, she insisted on drawing her own conclusions.

Boyle typed in a few commands and two holograms of the western hemisphere appeared. The crew leaned forward to study them.

"The picture on my left is a thermal image of the western hemisphere captured eleven months ago. The picture on my right is a thermal image taken four days ago—the same hemisphere, eleven months apart. Although you cannot see it with your naked eye, the thermal readings indicate an increase in surface temperature of between five and ten percent across the board. Remember, we're talking percent, not degrees. I'm afraid this indicates a near-catastrophic temperature escalation on the surface of the planet that could only be explained by a handful of events."

"What sort of temperatures are we talking about?" Judy asked.

"I estimate a temperature range of one hundred and ten to one hundred twenty degrees Fahrenheit across the mid-western United States. At the poles, the data shows a temperature of ninety to a hundred degrees."

"Dr. Boyle," La Rue interrupted, "...is this just the western hemisphere or is it Europe and Asia also?"

Boyle stroked the keyboard and the hologram changed, revealing two more Earth images. "I'm afraid much of the eastern hemisphere shows the same thing. Curiously, it appears that the highest temperatures are in Europe and Africa, which has led me to believe that the east took the brunt of whatever it was that struck the Earth."

"What do you mean struck the Earth? Like a meteor?" Judy asked.

"Not a meteor. I believe the Earth was struck by an enormous solar flare, ejecta, from the Sun. I think it initially hit the eastern hemisphere and, through the Earth's rotation, continued to impact the planet until it died out about halfway through the western hemisphere. I show a dramatic drop-off in temperature through Alaska, Canada, and the extreme western United States."

Mac studied the reaction of his crew. The ones with close family ties appeared the most disturbed, particularly Angela. Her face was ashen as she glanced fitfully at Judy and Traveres.

Ivory and Traveres appeared to be taking things in stride, the ultimate military professionals, stoic and rigid. La Rue, perhaps due to his inebriated condition, maintained his cocky, devil-may-care attitude even though his beloved France might have taken the brunt of this cosmic fireball.

Rechenko remained quiet during the briefing, looking down, most likely thinking about his wife, Olga. Mac knew this had been the longest time they had been separated and, if Boyle's scenario proved accurate, his homeland had been hit the hardest.

Mac wasn't surprised by Judy's reaction. Her rugged background, growing up on a cattle ranch in Colorado, helped her maintain composure.

"What about San Francisco and the Pacific Ocean? Were they affected?" Angela asked, obviously concerned about her hometown and family.

"This is another curiosity," Boyle continued. "It seems that ninety percent of the land mass was affected, but not the largest ocean, even though it accounts for a fourth of the surface area."

"Why is that a curiosity, Doctor?" Judy asked.

"Well, I am getting off the subject a bit, but let me tell you a brief story. When I studied at Cambridge, I was an aide to a very well-respected professor of Humanities. I will not say his name, but he had the curious hobby of studying the accuracy of psychic predictions. It is really quite amazing, but he found an undeniable link between historical predictions and actual events. There was one such event I will always remember because it made the hair on the back of my neck stand up when I heard it."

Mac bit his lip, wondering where Boyle was going with this, as once again everyone at the table hung on every word.

"This professor claimed a psychic had told him that an intense solar flare from the Sun would hit the Earth around the turn of the century. The unusual point about this case is that the psychic claimed the flare was not a random occurrence but a planned celestial event."

"Planned?" Judy broke in immediately. "Planned by whom?"

"The professor told me the psychic would only say it was planned by a higher power and, to prove it was no accident, only the major land masses would be affected, leaving the Pacific Ocean untouched."

Boyle paused long enough to let his words sink in. Mac looked around the table and could see everyone deep in thought.

La Rue finally broke the silence. "Dr. Boyle, correct me if I am wrong, but in essence you are saying God sent a giant fireball to destroy the Earth? Because if that is what you are saying, then I am afraid I cannot accept it. You see, I do not believe in God. I do not think God exists; and if he does not exist then he certainly would not destroy the Earth! God may have destroyed *your* Earth, but not mine!"

"Okay, Damon, that's enough!" Mac had heard all he wanted from his drunken geologist. "Dr. Boyle, I think it would be best if we stick to the scientific facts tonight. This is traumatic enough without adding religion to the mix."

"Of course, Commander," Boyle said, clearing his throat. "Let us continue, shall we?"

"Continue? Continue where?" Judy demanded. "I'm afraid Damon is right. You're claiming through your scientific study that God, or a higher power, caused the Sun to shoot a solar flare at the landmasses of Earth? I'm sorry, but I find that difficult to accept!"

"Dr. Delaney, I did not say I thought a higher power caused this solar incident. In fact, I am not even sure it was a solar incident. All I am saying is that it is curious that the mean temperature of the landmasses of Earth has risen substantially, leaving the largest area, the Pacific Ocean, untouched. This phenomenon simply reminded me of the story by my college professor. I assure everyone here that it was not an attempt on my part to explain this curiosity, and I apologize for even mentioning it."

"Okay, Doctor, I accept that," Judy said. "So, scientifically speaking, what will this rise in temperature mean for the population? I mean…do we have a home to return to?"

"Well I'm afraid that is going to take a little more time to determine; however, I do have a list of scenarios as to how this temperature shift may have affected the population. I took the liberty of breaking down solar events into five levels. Level one is the daily solar radiation colliding with the Earth's magnetic field and causing the occasional crackle of a mobile phone. Orbiting satellites are thermally protected and unaffected by this exposure. There is virtually no residual radiation for the population to worry about.

"A level-two event, while infrequent, causes a little more concern. Satellite transmissions are affected, leading to navigational problems for sea and air travel; mobile phone service can be disrupted for short periods of time. Some orbiting satellites have to shut down to protect their electronics. Residual radiation is of little concern.

"A level-three event is a bit more serious, I'm afraid, although very rare indeed. Entire satellites can be destroyed; most will be put out of commission for weeks. Communications of all kinds can be lost for days. In rare cases, there is measurable radiation present afterward and ozone levels can be affected. Thankfully, the Earth has experienced just two level-three events in the past fifty years.

"A level-four solar event, while never known to have occurred, would result in catastrophic damage to the environment and population of Earth. Any satellite in its path would stand little chance of survival. Communications worldwide would be lost for an indefinite period. Energy production, public utilities, international and local banking, air travel, even car travel, would be affected. The operation of government business would be near impossible, resulting in a social breakdown. Hospitals, police, and fire protection would probably fail for an extended period. The radiation blast from the Sun at its apex would kill hundreds of thousands of people instantly, and perhaps millions more of radiation sickness in the months and years to follow. Environmentally, the Earth would experience a change that would affect the entire population. The heat generated in the atmosphere would stir up weather systems that would spawn killer tornadoes and massive hurricanes of a magnitude never before seen on Earth. The polar ice caps would start to break up and possibly melt altogether, causing catastrophic flooding."

Mac observed the grim mood around the table. The look on their faces betrayed thoughts of all they had left behind. Their earlier disbelief now turned to an acceptance of what they faced.

Boyle continued to speak as if lecturing at Cambridge. "Possibly the most dangerous environmental problem would be the depletion of the ozone layer due to the changing temperatures. For the people who survived the initial radiation blast, and there would be billions, the residual radiation from the Sun would likely reach unsafe levels for an extended period. Yes, it is possible that the remaining population would be forced to live inside or underground until the ozone layer could repair itself."

"Dr. Boyle," Judy interrupted again. "Would the Earth have a chance to recover from such a catastrophe?"

"Let me put it this way, Dr. Delaney. It would all depend on the extent of the environmental damage. How many species were lost? How was plant life affected? Was the food chain still intact? Remember, I told you there would be tremendous storms. Well, perhaps that would be the Earth's way of cleansing itself, ridding the planet of the weak, flooding the continents to bathe the scorched land. Keep in mind, people would have very little to do with the environmental recovery. Interestingly, humankind has always battered the environment it so depends on. This is a shining example of the absurdity of that action. Everyone's future would depend solely on whether or not the environment could reestablish a balance. Ironically, the annihilation of much of the Earth's human population would actually hasten the recovery."

Mac knew nobody liked the sound of that, but he understood the necessity for Dr. Boyle to speak with such candor. What an odd feeling to hear of the possible destruction of your planet while being so far removed from it.

It again fell to Judy to ask the question seeping into everyone's mind. "What does this mean to us, Dr. Boyle? Does it mean we cannot or should not return to Earth?"

Mac stood up and spoke. "That is what we are here to decide. Dr. Boyle and I have discussed at great length what our options are. I suggest we take a break right now, think about what we've heard, and come back to the table in an hour to discuss our options."

Everyone nodded in agreement and started to rise. Rechenko, though, had one more question. "Pardon me, Dr. Boyle, but just out of curiosity, what would a level-five solar event do the Earth?"

The entire crew paused, some standing, some still sitting. All attention focused on Boyle, who leaned back in his chair and took off his glasses to rub the bridge of his nose. He then leaned forward and pressed a button on his computer, and the two Earth images floating above the table disappeared. Looking at Rechenko, he simply shook his head.

"With a level-five solar event, this briefing would be over. There would be no Earth to return to."

CHAPTER 6
SCENARIOS

Dr. Judy Delaney stood in her quarters and stared at her image in the mirror. Her eyes were red from crying, but also from rage. She couldn't believe the Earth had met the fate Dr. Boyle had suggested. She also couldn't understand why her good friend—no, her *best* friend, Mac—hadn't at least briefed her on what was to come at dinner. She felt betrayed.

Thoughts of her family and friends in Colorado weighed on her mind. If a solar catastrophe did indeed hit the Earth, she was helpless to do anything to ease their pain and suffering. Even deeper inside her grew a fear of her own fate. Could this really be the end of the world?

Get a hold of yourself! You are not alone. You are part of a crew of hand-picked professionals trained to survive in the most forbidding environments. What better company could you ask for? Where the hell is Mac?

Just then, someone knocked. Judy wiped her face clean. She opened the door and saw Mac standing there. He had the same somber look on his face he'd worn during Dr. Boyle's presentation.

"Yes, can I help you, Commander?" she said in an icy tone.

"Judy, don't be like that. I'm sorry I couldn't say anything to you earlier, but there was a lot to sort out, and it wouldn't have been fair to the crew."

Judy felt her eyes widen and her nostrils flare.

"Fair to the crew? What do you mean fair to the crew? You're about to tell us the world is ending and you want to stick to protocol? I love you military men! Did you see the reactions of Traveres and Ivory? Those idiots didn't even flinch! You might as well have told them the blender in the kitchen was broken!"

"Now, Judy, don't say that. The crew was deeply affected by the briefing. Traveres is staying strong to support Angela. Rechenko went to his quarters to be by himself. La Rue is so drunk it probably hasn't hit him yet. I will agree with you about Ivory though. He seems very stoic about the whole thing, but I'll bet he's falling apart inside." Mac stepped closer to her.

"And what about you?" she asked, pointing her finger at his sternum to halt his advance. "How are you holding up? Do you really believe this is happening?"

"I have to tell you that I honestly don't know what to believe. But with the lack of any other evidence or explanation, I have no choice but to go along with Boyle. I'd like to give it more time, but this seems to be the best explanation so far."

"That's just great!" Judy shouted. "Years of training for this mission and nobody ever told us what to do if the world should happen to end while we were away!"

"Well," Mac continued, "that's exactly what we're going to talk about right now. Everyone is absorbing what they've heard. In a few minutes I'll call everyone together and we'll try to decide where to go from here."

Judy studied the man standing in front of her and tried to read his face. Was he as afraid as she was? Could she trust him to be completely honest with her after the bombshell Boyle dropped at the briefing?

"What exactly are our options?" she asked, dropping her shoulders in resignation.

"To put it simply, we can stay here and try to make a go of it, or we can try to return to Earth. I'm just not sure what we'll find there. We could also decide to split up the crew, leaving some here and letting others take a chance on returning to Earth."

Judy slid her hands up Mac's chest and gripped both sides of his collar and pulled him toward her until they were inches apart. "Well, whatever anyone else does, I'm sticking with you. But only if you promise you'll keep no more secrets!"

She fell into his embrace as he whispered into her ear, "I promise no more secrets."

Mac saw that the mood in the galley had changed considerably in the hour since the briefing ended. The crew had gathered around the table talking heatedly.

"Commander," Rechenko said. "Dr. Boyle says there could be a chance the Mars 3 crew may still be alive! He says they could have been hit by the solar flare before Earth was and it knocked out their communications. Could they have survived the solar flare and still be on course? Is that possible, Commander?"

"Of course it is," Mac said, loud enough for all to hear. "Let's quiet down for a moment, and then Dr Boyle and I will address the Mars 3 situation."

Adjourning the meeting for an hour had taken the gloom and doom out of their faces. This highly trained crew thrived at surviving in a hostile environment, always ready to face any challenge put before them.

"Dr. Boyle and I both think there is an excellent chance the Mars 3 crew survived this solar event. I'm sure a warning from the external sensors gave them plenty of time to retreat to the double-lead–lined radiation chamber. Even with the long duration of the solar storm, there are plenty of provisions in the chamber to sustain the crew. What we don't know is the condition of the craft.

"We know all the navigation and computer equipment is shielded; however, their high- and low-gain arrays are vulnerable so they may not be able to communicate. That would explain why Houston lost contact with them, probably moments before they went into hyperdrive.

"Even with their communications down, as long as the guidance computer is operating, the Mars 3 craft will land here inside of twelve weeks regardless of the condition of the crew. This is why we need to start looking at our options. Dr. Boyle has come up with a list of scenarios. Let's listen to them and see if we can agree on how to proceed with what may, for some or all of us, be our final weeks on Mars."

The crew stirred noticeably at the last statement. Mac suspected they were asking themselves who would remain here and who would leave.

Boyle put his glasses on again. His well-weathered face and bald head revealed age spots, making him appear older than his fifty years.

"Let us get started, shall we?" he said, clearing his throat. "As the Commander stated, there is an excellent chance the Mars 3 crew has survived and will arrive at Mars Base in less than twelve weeks. As most of you are aware, the Mars 3 craft is using the new matter-antimatter accelerator, which means their trip will last only three months as opposed to our six-month journey. This will be an important factor in our future decision making.

"Now, as you know," Boyle continued, "this base cannot support the combined crews of two Mars missions, even for a short time. That is why the missions have never overlapped. This means we would need to hit our launch window in nine weeks. However, before we leave, we must have confirmation that the space station in Earth orbit has survived intact with a working shuttle, or at the very least, an emergency escape vehicle for the reentry through the atmosphere."

Mac looked at each of the eight members of the crew and wondered if any of them had thought about that point. Surely Traveres and Ivory had.

"So," Boyle went on, "what are our options? After meeting with Commander MacTavish for several hours, we came up with a list of scenarios we all need to consider.

"In the first scenario, we plan to launch as scheduled, regardless of whether we reestablish contact with Earth or the Mars 3 craft. Within nine weeks, we may not be able to tell if there is an Earth to return to, but we would still prepare for launch. We would execute a 'blind launch' and take our chances that there will be a return vehicle waiting for us in Earth orbit.

"Scenario two, we prepare for launch on schedule, but miss our window and wait for the Mars 3 crew to arrive. Remember, even though they can't communicate, they still might be able to receive transmissions from us and Houston. They may have a better understanding of what is happening on Earth. Once we debrief the arriving crew, we should have a clearer picture. If it looks like there has been just a moderate solar event and it is possible for us to return, then we'd launch at our next available window. That would get us back to Earth in eight months instead of six.

"If it looks like the Earth has sustained substantial damage, we will still need to have four volunteers leave the base and return to Earth, taking their chances."

"This would leave the total number of people remaining at Mars Base at twelve, assuming there were no fatalities on Mars 3. It would be difficult, but there should be adequate life support to sustain that number for a couple of years. However—and this is critical—if we find ourselves in this scenario, we must locate a reliable water source here."

"Dr. Boyle," Judy asked, "Am I to understand that our only two options are to return to Earth as a full crew of eight and possibly all die, or to split up the crew…"

"Dr. Delaney," Boyle interrupted, obviously annoyed by the directness of her question, "If you will let me finish, you will see where all the risks lie in each of these scenarios. Now, if I may continue? In the third scenario, the Mars 3 craft lands and some or all of the crew has perished. In this case, we will be able to use the Mars 3 mother ship and its matter-antimatter accelerator to leave Mars at our leisure.

"As I see it, and the Commander agrees with me, we must be ready to follow any of these scenarios should the situation dictate. But beyond that, not only should we prepare for departure as planned, but we must prepare this base to accommodate more than eight people. In order to do that, Dr. Rechenko needs to start immediate construction of Habitat 3. Lieutenant Ivory must expand the recycling capabilities as best he can. Ms. Lee should expand the Mars garden to its full potential, and Mr. La Rue and I will step up our search for a permanent, reliable water source.

"While we are doing this, the Commander and Lieutenant Traveres will be readying the lander for launch while continuing to monitor the Earth and Mars 3 for any communication."

Mac could see the crew thinking. This had been quite an evening for all of them. To be told that the Earth may be experiencing a cataclysmic solar event…that their friends and loved ones may be suffering…that some of them may have to stay on Mars and try to survive while others may have to leave to an uncertain fate on Earth…was clearly overwhelming.

Mac stood up and addressed his crew.

"While you are digesting what you've just heard, I'd like to remind everyone that this situation could change at a moment's notice. Contact with Earth or Mars 3 could be reestablished. We may determine that it is safe for all of us to return together to Earth on time. But whatever we do, we must take immediate steps to assure the safety of not only ourselves, but also of the crew on its way here.

"In the coming days, I want everyone to think about how you would like to see us proceed. Think about whether you prefer to remain here at the base or try to return to Earth. We have a lot of work to do in the next few weeks, work that our very survival depends on. I ask you all to remain focused on the tasks ahead and, if you should be so inclined, to pray. Pray for the successful conclusion of this mission and for the lives and safety of our friends and families. Now, Dr. Boyle and I will try to answer any questions you have."

There were many questions that night. Some were to Dr. Boyle about the Earth's condition. Some were to Mac about timetables and work schedules. Judy sat silently at the table staring at Mac, thinking to herself of one thing: her relationship with this Commander of an isolated base on a faraway planet. How did she end up here with him, this man she cared about so much? No matter what they faced, Judy knew she loved him; and whatever happened, she wasn't going to leave his side. That is where she felt most comfortable, most natural, and most secure.

Besides Judy, one other person stared at Mac from across the table—not out of admiration, but out of curiosity, much like a poker player trying to read an opponent's intentions. Did the Commander really think the Earth was destroyed? This was important to know and, like in the game of poker, things were not always as they appeared.

CHAPTER 7
PIANO IN THE NIGHT

Angela walked into Habitat 2 and stood in the middle of the open floor. The glow of the Martian sunset pierced the clear roof and gave an orange tint to the spacious interior. Only the slight hum of the water pumps from the hydroponics trays broke the quiet. She raised her flute to her lips, closed her eyes, and began to play. With the help of the intercom, her evening recital echoed throughout the base to all who wished to hear.

In an odd way, the stress of the past six weeks of lost contact with Earth inspired her. Throughout her life music served as a safe sanctuary from all her concerns and fears. She never felt alone when she played. And tonight, she was not alone. A silent figure stood just inside the habitat, hidden from her view, watching her closely, listening intently to every note.

Mac and Judy sat inside Matty, parked on Sunset Ridge above the base, and admired the colorful streaks of light that painted the glowing sky. As darkness fell over the Grand Arroyo plains and Mars Base, Mac savored a rare moment alone with Judy, away from the pressures and distractions of the normal workday.

"Can you believe it's been six weeks since we've lost contact with Earth?" Judy asked. "Did you ever think this would go on for so long?"

"Honestly? No. I was surprised when we didn't re-establish contact after a day, and I certainly didn't imagine six weeks without so much as a radio call from Earth."

"So you think Dr. Boyle's assessment is accurate? Could the Earth have been hit by a giant fireball from the Sun?"

"I certainly don't want to believe it, but considering Boyle's evidence, I see no other viable explanation."

Mac leaned back and tried not to continually process in his mind whether everything that could be done was being done. He had pushed the crew hard, ordering Angela and Judy to double the size of the Mars garden in H2. He worked with Ivory to improve the efficiency of the recycling equipment, squeezing every last drop of water from the system.

Mac had ordered Rechenko to use Ratty and begin the excavation of the foundation for Habitat 3, which progressed rapidly. Rechenko would be ready to pile drive the footings for the roof supports in one week, a remarkable feat even for the industrious Russian.

Mac worked daily with Traveres on the virtual reality program, practicing launch procedures while maintaining a close vigil on the communications console. Earth continued to remain silent.

But Mac knew the busiest crewmembers were Boyle and La Rue, who didn't spend any time at the base. He had them step up their water drilling activity, and they sometimes spent three or four days at a time at the drill site, returning only for provisions and equipment.

One issue that concerned Mac was Boyle's decision to go for broke and continue the deep drilling at the Red Anvil site. La Rue strongly disagreed, preferring to drill at two or three promising sites up the canyon towards Angel Rock. Mac finally helped the two come to a compromise and sent Ratty to the other sites for some remote drilling as soon as Rechenko finished his H3 excavations and pile driving.

"Mac, do you think there is any chance the crew of Mars 3 survived?"

He glanced at Judy sitting next to him with her feet up on the console, the fading red glow of the sunset washing across her face. He wanted to give her hope but knew she would see right through any glossy explanations. "I have no idea. I'm troubled that Rusty hasn't found a way to at least signal us that they are still on the way. He's a brilliant engineer and I'd expect that he and his crew would figure out some way to communicate with us—if they survived."

Mac reached his hand around the back of Judy's neck and massaged her gently. She closed her eyes and let out a soft moan and uttered a few fading words. "I feel in my heart that they're okay."

Mac smiled. Judy always knew the right thing to say to make him feel better. "It looks like our sunset is gone," he said, looking at the now pitch-black Martian sky. "How about a little music?"

"You read my mind. Turn on the monitor for H2. I'll bet Angela is playing her flute in there right now."

Angela stood in the middle of Habitat 2 and played with all her heart and soul. She pretended she was back in the middle of Golden Gate Park in San Francisco on a summer afternoon performing for the birds, the trees, and anyone who should happen by. She had spent many summer days in the park joining other neighborhood musicians for an improvised concert.

She played a long final note on her flute and slowly opened her eyes, chasing the San Francisco summer away. She saw Lieutenant Ivory standing a few feet away, quietly listening to her play. Angela jumped back and gasped.

"I'm sorry, Angela," Ivory apologized. "I didn't mean to startle you."

"No, no, that's okay, Lieutenant. I just thought I was alone," she said, placing her hand on her chest.

"I love listening to you. Is it your own music?"

Ivory's attitude and demeanor caught her attention. In the fifteen months on Mars, he had barely spoken a friendly word to her, keeping to himself on his free time, never partaking in the weekly poker games or exercising with the crew. Michael had told her Ivory was obsessed with professional protocol, but she suspected he was mostly shy.

"Yes, it's my own music. It's melodies I made up and like to improvise with." Angela blushed, uncomfortable talking about her music. "Do you play?"

"No, not the flute, but I do have this." Ivory held up a flat keyboard, about three feet long, eight inches across, and only an inch thick.

"Is that a keyboard?" she asked in surprise. "I didn't know we had one on board."

"It's my personal piano. I play it in my room wearing headsets, but I rigged it so the habitat speakers will pick up the sound. Listen."

He sat down on the floor in front of her and flipped a few switches on the keyboard. He then pressed middle "C" and Angela gasped at the clarity of the piano. She watched and listened in amazement as Ivory played a simple, yet beautiful, melody.

When he finished, she could barely contain herself. "Christopher, I had no idea you were so talented. Did you compose that yourself?"

"Yes, it's a little something I made up," he answered shyly. "You see, I've never taken music lessons so I don't really know if this sounds good to anyone else. I play by ear for my own enjoyment."

"It's so beautiful. Play some more and I'll join in."

Angela listened closely to his music then raised her flute to her lips. She could barely contain her smile as she enjoyed the human side of Lieutenant Ivory.

"Is someone playing a piano?" Judy said as she and Mac listened to the music coming from Habitat 2.

"I don't know. I'll call up the H2 camera and see." Mac leaned over and pressed a few keys on the computer. A picture of Habitat 2's interior came up and clearly showed two people in the middle of the floor.

"I think that's Ivory," Judy said, straining to see the figure sitting on the floor.

Mac zoomed in the habitat camera. "I'll be damned. That *is* Ivory. I didn't know he could play, or that he had a keyboard here."

"It sounds beautiful," Judy sighed as she sank back into her seat. "It just goes to show that even though you spend two years with someone, you may not know the person all that well."

Mac had to wonder how well he knew Ivory, or even Lieutenant Traveres for that matter. Ivory went out of his way to remain isolated and mysterious; and aside from his relationship with Angela, Traveres was pretty good at keeping to himself. *Maybe that's the way the Space Agency is training the new blood,* he thought.

Mac leaned back, letting the music from Habitat 2 fill his senses. "You know what this reminds me of, the music playing at night as I lay back and close my eyes?"

"Tell me," Judy whispered. Mac noticed she was dozing off.

"It reminds me of when I was a kid back in camp in Southern California. My Irish father and Mexican mother were good Catholics and sent me to our church's boys' camp up at Big Bear in the San Bernardino Mountains. One of the Brothers who supervised the thirty or so kids in my cabin used to turn out all the lights at bedtime and play the guitar until we all fell asleep. There was something about the sound of that guitar in the darkness that made me, and most of the other boys, I guess, feel secure and unafraid of being without Mom and Dad."

"Do you miss your parents?" Judy asked, with one eye open.

Mac listened to the music, and pondered her question. How were his parents doing? Were they suffering? Didn't Boyle tell him the temperature west of the Sierra Nevada was nearly normal?

"Sure I miss them, but I know my mom and dad can take care of themselves. They retired to the foothills of Northern California ten years ago. Dad built a log cabin on top of a hill outside the little town of Lotus. They have ten acres with a couple of horses, some goats, chickens, and three dogs to keep the deer and varmints away from the garden. They love to hike down to the American River, a mile or so away, and fish for fresh trout. I think they'll survive okay. In fact, I'm looking forward to taking you to Lotus to meet them some day in the not-too-distant future."

"I would like that very much. I only hope we *have* a future," Judy said, her eyes still closed

"I'd like to think we have a long life ahead of us," Mac paused. "I bought some land next to a private reservoir about an hour's drive from my parents' home. I've already designed the cabin and plan to start construction when we return. I love the serenity of a high mountain lake, especially when I'm quietly gliding across the surface in a canoe. It reminds me of Big Bear and my childhood."

"It sounds wonderful, Mac. I'd sure like to be there with you, but only if I can bring my horses."

"You got yourself a deal, young lady."

Mac let Judy doze off as he sat quietly for the next several minutes, listening to the soothing music from the habitat. He closed his eyes and reminded himself how lucky he was to have Judy at his side. There was only one woman that Mac had previously let into his life, and that failed relationship still haunted him three decades later. It was thirty years ago, the summer of his high school graduation. He'd been accepted to the Air Force Academy for the fall, and his mother had arranged for him to stay with his Uncle Guillermo's family in the resort town of Cuernavaca, Mexico.

It had always been her dream for him to learn Spanish and better understand his Mexican heritage. Being an only child, Mac's closest cultural experience had been spending time with his cousins in San Diego, playing on the beach. But they were mostly "Americanized" as he was, so his mother's hopes had remained unfulfilled.

Mac remembered he had been reluctant to spend the remaining months of his civilian life away from his friends in Santa Monica. But when he arrived in Cuernavaca, something convinced him he was in for an unforgettable summer.

His Uncle Guillermo and his cousin Magdalena met him at the bus station. To say she was beautiful fell woefully short of describing this striking young woman with her long dark hair, deep blue eyes, and flawless golden brown complexion. She carried herself with an air of warmth and confidence. Mac quickly found himself smitten with his lovely cousin.

Together, they made frequent trips to Mexico City and the surrounding area. Magdalena explained the sometimes-painful history of Mexico, from the great Indian empires of the Aztecs and Mayans to the brutal Spanish conquest led by Hernando Cortez.

He learned a great deal about his heritage from Magdalena, and at the same time his love for her deepened—a love she eagerly returned. What had started off as a friendly relationship between distant cousins grew into something more intimate. It wasn't long before they found themselves in each other's arms, exploring the depths of their passion.

They were both all too aware that their relationship would come to a quick end if Magdalena's father discovered their secret. So they agreed it would be necessary to wait for the right moment to reveal the true nature of their friendship. Their self-imposed abstinence resulted in an almost unbearable sexual tension between them.

With only a few weeks to go before Mac was to return to the United States and begin his career at the Air Force Academy, he decided to take Magdalena for his own. They returned to their favorite spot, the Pyramid of the Sun at Teotihuacán outside Mexico City.

These ruins of the ancient city were among the most impressive and mysterious in the world. The complex included two large pyramids, a grand avenue, and several smaller structures. The entire site was a technological marvel for its alignment to astrological points in the sky. As best as anyone could determine, its inhabitants had abandoned Teotihuacán a thousand years before the Aztecs arrived.

The beauty and mystery of Teotihuacán lured Mac and Magdalena to its highest point. As they stood atop of the great Pyramid of the Sun at sunset, he took her in his arms and asked her to marry him. He could tell his proposal shocked and surprised her, but he was confident she could never leave him, no matter what the consequences might be. She finally said yes, and he felt on top of the world. But it was a world that would soon crash around him, leaving a trail of pain and betrayal.

Mac shuddered at the dark memories, a reflex that brought him back to the present. It always amazed him the even now, thirty years later, the thought of Magdalena still shook him to his core. Buried in a successful career and countless failed relationships for three decades, Mac found himself finally at peace with Judy.

He noticed Angela had long since gone to bed, allowing Ivory to continue his recital alone. The piano in the night gave Mac that secure feeling he knew as a boy. He hoped the rest of the crew felt much the same way.

Lieutenant Traveres sat in the darkness of the bridge, illuminated by the dim lights of the flight console and his computer screen. He too listened to the music emanating from Habitat 2, but his focus was on the data before him. The DSLR had located an object traveling though space on a rendezvous course with Mars. And while he wouldn't reveal his findings to Mac for several weeks, he was gratified to know that he had found the needle in the haystack.

CHAPTER 8
INCIDENT AT RED ANVIL

Michael Traveres sat at the communications console and listened to the static on the Mars receiver. Nothing had changed in the ten weeks since the loss of contact. Earth remained silent. Mac also had him constantly searching for Mars 3, but Traveres continued to report that all he had found was empty space.

He turned his attention to the matters at hand. Three different crews were on outside excursions today, keeping him busy monitoring their status throughout the afternoon. Boyle and La Rue had driven Matty to the Red Anvil site thirty miles away and continued to drill for water. Mac and Ivory drove Ratty to the fuel processor to ready the transfer of propellant for Mars 2. At the base, Rechenko and Angela conducted an inspection of the H3 panels.

Traveres wondered if anyone noticed the significance of today's date. Had they not lost contact with Earth, today was the day that Ratty was to carry the crew module back to the launch site to be mated with its ascent stage and fuel tower. This should have been their last day at Mars Base.

Missing their primary launch window meant one thing. Every week they stayed on Mars extended the length of their journey to Earth. If they waited too long, a return to Earth would be impossible for nearly two years. With the Mars 3 arrival still an estimated two weeks away, a launch decision would have to be made with little delay.

Traveres pressed a few buttons on the keyboard, calling up the positions of the three crews outside. With the help of the mother ship in stationary orbit over Mars Base, he could pinpoint the exact position of any crew member wearing a locator badge. Ratty and Matty also had internal beacons that transmitted their locations. In the event of crew disorientation or remote malfunction, it would be nearly impossible to find them without a locator beacon.

He noticed Mac and Ivory had left the pressurized cab of Ratty and were walking around the fuel processor a few miles from the base. He could listen in on Mac and Ivory's conversation if he wanted to, but it wasn't his normal practice.

Traveres switched to a shot of the Red Anvil site. Glancing at the screen, he did a double-take. *What the hell?* Zooming in tighter, he noticed the image showed only the locator beacon of Dr. Boyle, nothing else.

Mac gave Ivory a nod as they wrapped up their inspection of the fuel tank connected to the giant processor. Everything looked good.

"We'll have little margin for error when it comes time to fuel the lander," Mac said. "As soon as Mars 3 lands, we'll need to debrief the crew immediately then make a decision on who will leave and who will stay."

"Commander, that will leave us only five days to move the crew module to the launch site and load the fuel," Ivory said. "That's not much time."

"I know, Lieutenant, but it's too risky to have a fully fueled vehicle so close to the Mars 3 landing site. All it would take is one pebble striking the fuel tank and we'd really be in a fix."

Mac's redline alarm suddenly sounded, grabbing his attention.

"Base to Commander, do you copy?"

"Go ahead, Lieutenant, what's up?"

"Commander, sorry to bother you, but we may have a problem."

Mac winced. "Problem, what kind of problem?"

"Huh…well, sir," Traveres hesitated. "I just finished talking to Dr. Boyle and it seems that Damon and he had an argument. Mr. La Rue left Boyle at the Red Anvil site and drove off in Matty by himself."

"What?" Mac blurted in disbelief, fogging the faceplate on his helmet for a second. "Goddamn it, Lieutenant, what the hell are those two idiots doing out there? I don't have time for this!"

"Sir, it seems Mr. La Rue has turned off his locator badge, but I've tracked Matty near the Angel Rock formation."

"Okay, Lieutenant," Mac said, through clenched teeth. "What is Dr. Boyle's situation? Is he in any immediate danger? How's his oxygen supply?"

"Sir, he said he would be okay for about four to six hours, a little more with the emergency oxygen at the site."

"All right, Lieutenant. That shouldn't be a problem. We can get to him in an hour if need be. Are Rechenko and Angela still outside?"

"That's affirmative, sir," Traveres answered.

"Okay, Lieutenant. This is what I want you to do. Have Judy prepare a tranquilizer syringe and emergency medical supplies. Got it?"

"Copy, Commander. Can I assume the syringe is for Mr. La Rue? Dr. Delaney will want to know."

"Yes, Lieutenant, that's a safe assumption—unless, of course, we don't find Matty. Then the tranquilizer is for me!"

Driving Ratty at top speed toward Red Anvil, Mac tried to calm himself, but his geologist's reckless behavior concerned him. *What had gotten into that crazy Frenchman?* He had noticed Dr. Boyle and La Rue arguing more and more about where to drill for water. Mac suspected that argument had finally come to a head.

"Commander to Dr. Boyle. Do you copy, Dr. Boyle?" Mac said, cueing his intercom. "Commander to Dr. Boyle, please acknowledge."

"Yes, Commander, Dr. Boyle here. I am dreadfully sorry you have to be involved in this. My apologies for taking you away from your work."

"That's not a problem, Doctor. How are you doing? Are you all right?"

"Yes, yes, Commander, I am fine. I wish you didn't have to come out here, but I am not sure when Mr. La Rue is planning to return. You see, Commander, I am afraid we got in a bit of a row and he just beggared off. I am not quite sure what has gotten into him."

"Dr. Boyle, we'll have plenty of time to discuss that later. I just wanted to make sure you weren't in any immediate danger."

"Oh, yes, I am fine, Commander. Thank you."

"One more thing, Doctor. Lieutenant Traveres has located La Rue. He is currently near Angel Rock. I'm trying to get hold of him and have him return to Red Anvil. Should he return before we arrive, I do not want you to board Matty. Is that clear? I want you to wait for us."

"Oh, yes, Commander. That is perfectly clear. I think that would be the prudent thing to do."

"Thank you, Doctor. We'll see you in about an hour. Out."

Mac's redline suddenly beeped. "Base to Commander, do you copy?" Traveres said.

"Go ahead, Lieutenant," Mac said, thinking to himself, *what now?*

"Sir, I contacted Mr. La Rue and told him to return immediately to Red Anvil."

"What did he say, Lieutenant?"

"Sir, he sounded rather reluctant and wanted to speak with you first."

"Goddamn it! You're the safety officer! He's not supposed to question your orders! He's supposed to comply, no questions asked!"

"Yes, sir," Traveres spoke with added caution in his voice. "I have him online. Would you like me to patch him through?"

"Yes, Lieutenant, go ahead."

Mac waited, purposely making La Rue speak first. "Hello? Commander MacTavish? Do you read me?"

"This is Commander MacTavish," Mac said in an icy tone. "I want you to turn that vehicle around and immediately return to Red Anvil. Is that clear, Mr. La Rue?"

"Oh, yes, sir. Very clear! I am already on my way back, Commander," La Rue said, turning submissive. "I am sorry you had to be involved. I was just trying to get some additional drilling done. I meant no harm."

"Mr. La Rue, I will not discuss this until we meet face to face. Return to Red Anvil immediately. Should you arrive before we do, stay in your vehicle. Do not attempt to pick up or contact Dr. Boyle. Is that clear?"

"Commander, please. I assure you, I meant no harm. But that Dr. Boyle is a fool! He is not a geologist. All he is doing is wasting valuable time and putting us in danger. He is not listening to reason. You will see."

"Mr. La Rue! I told you I will not discuss it now! Your only concern is to get Matty to Red Anvil immediately. Out!"

Mac glanced at Ivory sitting next to him. "Lieutenant, we have a couple of scientists who are not only fighting with each other, but are apparently a long way from reaching their main objective, finding water on this goddamn planet! That's bad news for everyone!"

La Rue's blatant criticism of Boyle surprised Mac. He had his doubts about being able to break up a fight between his two bullheaded scientists. That's why he had brought along Ivory as the enforcer. His martial arts expertise meant there would be no messing with him. Ivory was literally the strongest man on the planet.

As they approached the Red Anvil site, Mac decided he would deal with La Rue, and that Ivory should return to base with Dr. Boyle. "Lieutenant," Mac said to Ivory, breaking a long silence. "Let's pressurize our suits. We're getting close to the site."

Since Ratty didn't have an airlock, they had to zip up their helmets then pressurize their soft suits. Once oxygen flowed in their suits, they could depressurize the crew cab to open the door and pick up Boyle.

The Red Anvil drill site came into view as Ratty crested a high ridge. The ancient riverbed had been aptly named for a large rock formation shaped like a giant anvil. Millions of years ago, water had flowed through the area, carving all kinds of unusual formations. The slight depression at the site led Boyle to speculate that the water had drained deep into the soil there.

Mac stopped Ratty at the top of the ridge looking down into the basin. He could see Dr. Boyle leaning against the drilling equipment. Across the depression and out of Boyle's line of sight, Matty obediently waited. Dr. Boyle looked up, spotted Ratty, and waved.

"Dr. Boyle, do you copy?" Mac said.

"Yes, Commander, I read you loud and clear. It's good to see you. I have not seen a sign of that damn fool La Rue yet."

"Take it easy, Doctor, he's right above you," Mac said, shaking his head. Diplomacy wasn't one of Boyle's strong points.

"Commander, it is good to see you!" La Rue broke in. "I have been here for some time!" he said, chiding Boyle.

"All right, you two, I don't want to hear any chatter," Mac warned. "Dr. Boyle, you will ride back to the base with Lieutenant Ivory. Mr. La Rue, I will ride back with you."

Mac took over manual control of Ratty and drove toward Dr. Boyle. La Rue drove down the ridge and met them as Ratty reached the stranded Doctor. Mac opened the door and Dr. Boyle quickly approached, already pleading his case.

"I cannot say enough how sorry I am for all this, Commander," Boyle said. "I am really quite embarrassed by Damon's behavior. I just do not know what got into him."

"Lies!" La Rue shouted from inside Matty, where he was listening in on the com-link. He drove Matty forward toward them while he pleaded his side. "Don't you believe a word this man says! They're all lies!"

Before Mac could answer, Dr. Boyle cut in. "I can assure you, I will tell the Commander nothing but the truth! In fact, I will apologize for your reckless behavior!"

"Apologize for me?" La Rue's com-link crackled. His French accent turned heavy. "You ignorant nothing! You should apologize for yourself and your pompous, stubborn ways! We are all going to die of thirst because of you!"

"All right, that's enough!" Mac shouted as he jumped off Ratty's high crew cab. "Dr. Boyle, Damon, I don't want to hear another word. Let's get going!"

Mac entered the rear airlock of Matty to depressurize his suit then stepped into the spacious cabin. Matty was designed to carry a crew of eight but also doubled as a mobile habitat affording comfortable living and sleeping quarters for two people for an extended period. Boyle and La Rue had spent many nights together on their drilling excursions. *Perhaps too many nights,* Mac thought.

Instead of an agitated La Rue, Mac found him calm and in control, ready to speak rationally about his actions. Mac sat down in the front passenger seat, ready to listen.

"Commander," La Rue began, "I am sorry to have troubled you when there is so much work to be done. Forgive me for this incident, but I felt compelled to stop this madness going on with Dr. Boyle. He is the most stubborn man I have ever known; and if we are not careful, he will lead us to disaster."

"Damon, it's hard to find any justification for leaving your colleague stranded in such a dangerous environment. What possessed you?"

"Commander, there is something I must show you, but it means taking a thirty-minute drive up Highway One. Then you will see why I left Dr. Boyle on his own."

Highway One was the main road forged by Dr. Boyle and Damon La Rue on their many excursions up the Grand Arroyo Plains. The highway passed numerous drill sites, the supply drop area where unmanned cargo was delivered from Earth, and Angel Rock, a solid granite formation on the far northern border of their exploration.

Mac had been so busy constructing the base he hadn't had time to inspect the entire length of the highway. Now was as good a time as any to see the far reaches of the science team's excursions. Another point of interest was a small crater that Dr. Boyle and La Rue created with the help of Lieutenant Ivory's chemist skills. La Rue needed some seismic readings in the area and had enlisted Ivory's Navy Seals demolition experience to build a homemade explosive charge. With Mac's reluctant approval they drilled a deep hole and set off the device while La Rue took seismic readings. The powerful explosion created a crater the size of a backyard swimming pool and rained rocks and small boulders down on the crew, which had taken refuge behind Angel Rock.

La Rue got his readings, but Mac was less than thrilled that they had put themselves in harm's way.

"Commander, this business with Dr. Boyle has got to end. I am the geologist on this crew, am I not? We have wasted ten weeks doing ninety percent of our drilling at Red Anvil. I have identified five other promising sites, but that pompous sonofabitch won't listen. Just because we've found high moisture content in the permafrost, he insists on continuing there. We are not looking for permafrost! We are looking for an aquifer and underground lake deep enough so that it is not frozen solid.

"Commander, please. You must intervene for the sake of the crew and the success of this mission."

Mac felt that La Rue was probably right. Boyle wasn't used to being overruled. He was larger than life, a world-renowned scientist, Nobel Laureate and Rhodes Scholar, who carried his credentials on his sleeve—along with his ego. Mac had no choice but to treat him with kid gloves.

"All right, Damon, how about if I give you Ratty to drill at the other sites? You can take Lieutenant Ivory with you. Is that satisfactory?"

La Rue smiled. "Oh yes, Captain, that would be most helpful."

"All right, Damon, I..." Mac stopped mid-sentence and gazed out the front window in amazement. Only a few hundred yards away a large granite rock formation loomed out against the surrounding rust-colored landscape. A slender oblong slab of granite shot a hundred feet in the air like a pair of folded wings. A shorter slab leaned against the taller one and appeared to have a rounded boulder on top representing the angel's head. Like a sentry overlooking the Grand Arroyo Plains, this natural sculpture took Mac's breath away.

La Rue smiled at him. "Mon Capitan, welcome to Angel Rock."

Traveres shifted in his seat at the communications console. He monitored the day's events on the computer, tracking Ratty's return to base and Matty's progress toward Angel Rock, but a new alert from the orbiting telescope captured his attention. It was a contact alarm. The sensors had detected a celestial anomaly. Could it be a comet, or perhaps an errant asteroid? Traveres knew better.

With great patience and deliberate precision, Traveres focused the telescope's infrared camera to a new set of coordinates. His eyes froze on the small dot on the screen as the data scrolled by confirming velocity, course, and probable ETA.

Traveres nodded with satisfaction. With visual confirmation, he knew it was time to tell Mac. It was time to tell everyone.

Mac watched as La Rue maneuvered Matty around the deep manmade hole in the ground while giving ongoing commentary.

"As you can see, this explosion gave me excellent readings on the surrounding bedrock profile. There are three or four promising sites for drilling I would like to get started on."

Mac looked out the window and noticed tire tracks heading farther north into the mountains above the Grand Arroyo.

"How far north have you explored into these mountains, Damon?"

"Oh, not far. There is no reason to go into the mountains looking for water, but the view from up there is spectacular. Would you like to see?"

Beep! Mac's redline sounded. Traveres was calling.

"Yes, Lieutenant, what is it? Did Ivory and Dr. Boyle make it back to base okay?"

"No, Commander, they are on their way but still about ten minutes out."

"Good, we will be returning shortly. Is there anything else?"

"Yes, Commander, I just received a contact alert from the orbiting telescope a few minutes ago."

Mac and La Rue shot each other an anxious glance. "A contact alert? Any idea what it might be, Lieutenant?"

"Sir, I have confirmation. It's Mars 3."

CHAPTER 9
THE ARRIVAL

The Mars 3 lander separated from the mothership and fired the retro-rockets to bring the craft out of orbit above the Grand Arroyo plains. With flawless precision, the central computer used the control thrusters to position the heat shield toward the surface. In the next few moments the g-forces would steadily increase as Mars 3 entered the upper atmosphere.

Mac had the crew gather on the bridge so they could watch Mars 3 streak through the sky like a meteor. Traveres had assured him that the long-range camera at the base would bring in a beautiful picture of this once-in-a-lifetime event.

The base buzzed with activity all morning. Mac had La Rue and Ivory prepare Matty for the retrieval mission while Judy readied her first-aid supplies and reviewed the crew manifest from Mars 3 to familiarize herself with her new patients.

Mac had assigned Angela and Boyle to prepare the evening's welcome dinner. They spent most of the morning gathering fresh fruits, vegetables, and fish for the social event of the year on Mars.

Mac noted the growing excitement among the crew ever since Traveres announced he had found Mars 3 right on course two weeks ago. With the spacecraft's flawless performance, there was a growing optimism that the crew had survived. Considering the Mars 3 communications array was damaged by the solar storm, it was likely there would be no radio contact with the arriving crew—no communication until Mac opened the hatch to welcome the weary travelers.

"How much time, Lieutenant?" Mac asked, his eyes focused on the screen. The crew had split up four and four, crowded around the two large flat screens on the flight deck.

"Any moment now, Commander, the computer program has hit every event right on cue."

"I think I see something!" Angela jumped. "Is that it?"

Everyone squinted at the screens, but Mac wasn't so sure. Then a bright yellow streak appeared, and everyone erupted into a collective cheer. Hugs and kisses abounded, and Mac felt a lump in his throat as he fought to hold back tears.

He could only imagine the excitement and exhilaration Rusty's crew must be feeling right now with the g-forces building up against their bodies after three months of weightlessness. He didn't envy them, though. In fact, he looked forward to strapping himself inside Mars 2 and taking off from this planet in one week. There was a lot of work to be done before then.

"Okay, everybody," Mac put his hands up to quiet his excited crew. "Mars 3 will be landing shortly, and it's been over two years since we've seen any new faces. Keep in mind that some of the arriving crew may need assistance so let's be prepared."

"Commander, are you going to bring the entire crew to the station right away?" Angela asked. "I need to know what I should have ready to go as far as appetizers." That put a smile on everyone's face. No doubt there was going to be a party tonight.

"I'm not sure how soon we'll bring them over, Angela. We'll have plenty to do in the first few hours, so I wouldn't anticipate anyone coming over right away. That reminds me, Dr. Rechenko, did you put additional scrubbers on line yet?" He was referring to the carbon monoxide filters needed to purify the air at the base.

"I planned to do that while you retrieved the crew."

Mac looked around at the smiles in the room. "Then I think we're ready. Judy, Lieutenant Ivory, Mr. La Rue, let's get to Matty. We'll watch the landing from there."

A hundred thousand feet above the planet, a drogue chute deployed, helping to stabilize Mars 3. The main chute then opened, jolting the craft and at the same time jettisoning the heat shield.

For the next fifty thousand feet, the lander swung at the bottom of the giant parachute until it reached a predetermined altitude and the descent engines fired. The landing radar continued to send the location information to the computer to allow for the necessary adjustments in rate of descent and forward velocity.

The automated landing cycle needed no human intervention unless there was a total computer failure. Pilots practiced for months, training for a manual landing, but had yet to be called on to execute this contingency.

Mars 3's engines throttled forward to maintain its current altitude safely above the surrounding terrain. The radar array started a sweeping search for the landing beacon as the spacecraft increased its forward velocity. The computer contained a detailed profile of the landscape and knew exactly how far it needed to go.

At twenty thousand feet, Mars 3's forward velocity decreased as it approached the base. Finally, with thirty-three percent of its fuel remaining, the radar array locked onto the beacon that Mac and Ivory had positioned a few weeks earlier. The computer zeroed in on its target and activated the final landing cycle. Eight miles from Mars Base, the spacecraft passed through fifteen thousand feet. It would be on the surface in five minutes.

"Bingo! Mars 3 radar has acquired the landing beacon," Traveres announced over the com-link. "We should have a visual any time now. The lander will appear about fifty degrees above the horizon."

Mac listened to Traveres' play-by-play from inside Matty. Ivory and Judy sat behind him, and La Rue was strapped into the driver seat next to him. Mac wanted to be ready to go as soon as Mars 3 touched down. The base camera had lost a visual after the spacecraft entered the atmosphere, but as Mars 3 got closer to the base, it would reappear on the screen. Ivory and Judy sat forward to get a better view of the large screen between Mac and La Rue.

"Shouldn't we be seeing it by now?" Judy asked as she squeezed Mac's shoulder from behind.

"Soon enough, with the landing beacon activated. I'm sure Traveres has the base camera zooming in on the exact coordinates."

"There it is!" Rechenko shouted over the com-link from the bridge.

Mac saw it immediately as the remote camera locked onto the lander and zoomed in for a spectacular look.

"That's fantastic!" Judy said. "I don't see any flame coming out of the engines. Is that normal?"

"Yes it is," Mac answered. "It should be practically invisible, but you can see what looks like a slight vapor trail. That's the hydrogen reacting with the atmosphere."

Three and a half miles from base, the Mars 3 lander passed through an altitude of seven thousand feet. The computer adjusted the thrust to slow its rate of descent. It had used up nearly eighty percent of its fuel and would need to land inside of three minutes.

"There it is! I see it!" Angela yelled over the com-link. "I can see it through the window! Oh, it's beautiful!"

Mac scanned the skies through Matty's window as Traveres continued his dialogue.

"They're looking good. They're coming right down the middle of the arc. Looks like Commander Chandler is doing one for the books."

Mac smiled. Rusty wasn't actually at the controls, but as he had done before him, Mac knew his friend was closely monitoring the terrain, making sure they weren't going to land on a boulder or clip a mountain peak as they approached.

After hundreds of hours in a simulator flying this very approach, Mac knew one thing for sure. Rusty wasn't actually flying the lander.

The computer increased the engine thrust again as the lander passed through one thousand feet. With sixteen percent of fuel remaining, it was right on target for touchdown with plenty to spare. Approaching three hundred feet altitude, the thrust increased again, and the lander slowed its descent. A gentle landing was imperative since a broken strut would spell disaster for the crew.

"They're starting to kick up some dust," Mac said, watching the final few feet through binoculars out of Matty's front window. He felt Judy's hands tighten their grip on his shoulders as Mars 3 inched downward. Traveres made the call over the com-link.

"Fifty feet! They're kicking up a dust storm. Forty feet! We've lost visual!"

Mac watched as the spacecraft disappeared in a red cloud of dust and vapor.

At thirty feet, the radar showed no large boulders or obstructions below. The computer reduced the thrust and the lander dropped softly to the surface. Mars 3 now stood on the Grand Arroyo Plains.

CHAPTER 10

INSIDE MARS 3

"Touchdown! Main engine cut off! They're down!" Traveres shouted over the radio. Sitting inside Matty with La Rue, Judy, and Ivory, Mac stared at the monitor showing a cloud of red dust clear to reveal Mars 3 on the surface.

Overwhelmed by the sight of the lost spacecraft's textbook landing on the Grand Arroyo Plains, he couldn't speak. But his excitement was tempered by the unknown. What would they find inside Mars 3? He finally regained his composure and found his voice.

"Matty to base, we're on our way." Mac nodded to La Rue, and Matty lurched forward.

"Commander, that was incredible!" La Rue said as he steered Matty down the well-traveled road to the landing site. "I have never seen anything so fantastic!"

"I have to agree, Damon. It was beautiful," Mac said, happy to see the troublesome Frenchman in a good mood.

"Mars base to Mars 3, do you copy?" Traveres' voice echoed over the radio. Mac had asked Traveres to radio Mars 3 at regular intervals as soon as they started for the landing site. No one spoke inside Matty as the radio remained silent. The first call to Rusty and his crew went unanswered.

Mac felt Judy's reassuring pat on his shoulders. He knew she was trying to be optimistic, but he sensed her growing concern, which mirrored his own.

"The lander is going to take a few minutes to power down and vent any residual fuel. Damon, let's bring Matty to within two hundred yards and make a visual assessment," Mac ordered.

"Okay, Commander, we are about a half-mile away," La Rue said. "I have a good visual from the external camera."

"Mars 3, this is Mars base. Do you copy?" Traveres called for the second time. Again there was no response, just slight static from the radio.

"Commander, it is likely the radio array on Mars 3 was damaged," Ivory said from the back seat.

"I agree, Lieutenant. And judging from how well the spacecraft performed, I'd say there's an excellent chance the crew survived as long as they made it to the radiation chamber."

Mac tried to believe his own words, but something told him escaping to the lead-lined chamber in the center of the crew module may not have been enough protection against the massive solar flare. If they were alive, Rusty surely would have found a way to communicate by now.

"There she is, straight ahead," La Rue said, steering Matty directly toward Mars 3

"Mars 3, this is Mars base, please respond," Traveres radioed again.

"Commander, we are at two hundred yards." La Rue brought Matty to a stop.

Mac looked out the front window at Mars 3, still venting excess thruster propellant. The spacecraft dominated the barren horizon, standing nearly fifty feet tall. A thick vapor swirled around Mars 3 as fire and steam shot out of various portholes, giving the lander the strange appearance of being alive.

"Mars 3, this is Mars base. Do you copy?" Traveres voice echoed over the radio.

Silence.

"Mars 3 lander, this is Mars Base. Do you copy?"

Mac turned and looked at Judy. He could see her eyes searching for any sign of hope in his face. He gave her a tight-lipped smile and nothing more.

"Lieutenant, let's get to the airlock and prepare for egress. Mr. La Rue, bring us to a one hundred yards directly in front of the bridge window," Mac ordered.

"Why aren't they answering?" Angela blurted out, right into Traveres' ear.

"Calm down, Angela. You have to give them time. They're very busy right now running through their checklists and shutting down systems."

Traveres glanced at Rechenko and Boyle sitting next to him on the bridge and knew by their expressions that they weren't buying it. After several unanswered radio calls, the mood on the flight deck had shifted from excitement to dread.

"Look, we already know their radio doesn't work; otherwise we would have heard from them weeks ago, right?" Traveres said as he turned to Angela and gently squeezed her arm. "Mac is sure to get visual confirmation as soon as they get close to the lander."

"Look, they're coming out!" Rechenko shouted, pointing to the screen.

Traveres turned around and looked at Mars 3 but saw no movement. Then he realized Rechenko was referring to Matty. Two figures emerged from the airlock and moved toward the silent spacecraft. Mac and Ivory were about to enter Mars 3.

Mac was certain someone would have spotted them by now—unless they were too busy to look out the window. But after traveling in space for three months and landing on an alien planet, Mac was pretty sure their eyes would be plastered to every available window.

In one-third gravity, he and Ivory covered the hundred yards to the base of Mars 3 in a short time. Standing next to the lander, the windows were even less visible because they were so high, but just twelve rungs on the exterior ladder separated them from the airlock door.

Mac marveled at the great spaceship as it towered over him. It was a technological marvel, with three separate and independent sections that fit together to form an interplanetary vehicle.

The lower section held the versatile descent/ascent engine with a variable thrust that had the ability to fire several times throughout the mission.

A series of large oblong-shaped fuel tanks comprised the second section of the lander. The tanks were strapped to a grid structure called the tower, which wrapped around both the lower engine section and the upper crew module.

"Let's get up the ladder to the airlock. You can tap into the computer outlet by the door and see what's going on with the ship," Mac said, as he grabbed onto the rails of the landing strut and started to climb up.

"*Commander, this is Dr. Boyle. Have you seen any signs of life?*"

"Negative, Doctor. Nothing so far."

Mac could sense everyone had the same sinking feeling. The euphoric mood among the crew a few minutes ago now turned to one of anxious antici-pation. Listening in, they now hung on his every word.

"We've reached the airlock door. Lieutenant Ivory's going to tap into the external terminal and get a reading from the central computer."

There was barely enough room at the top of the ladder for two people to stand on the 'front porch'. Ivory bent down and opened the cover to the exter-nal junction and plugged in his computer tablet.

"Commander, I'm not receiving any data. It's possible the connectors have been damaged."

"Well, that sounds like status quo for the past three months. Can you bypass the connectors and hard-wire to your hand-held?"

"Yes, sir, I've already started."

Mac leaned against the porch railing to give Ivory room to work. He looked over the landscape in front of him where Matty stood, and in the distance he could see the glint of the afternoon sun reflecting off Habitat 2. *This is a sight Rusty and his crew should be looking at. . .if they are alive.*

"Commander, I have data from inside," Ivory said. "The computer just completed the shutdown procedure for the engines and the auxiliary power units are cycling down as well. The environmental systems are functioning normally and the internal temperature is sixty-nine degrees."

"And no signs of life?"

Ivory hesitated a second and looked at his tablet. "I can only confirm auto-mated commands to the computer. Sorry sir, there's no evidence of any other activity."

Ivory's words hung in the air as the reality started to set in. Mac felt a dull pain in his heart as it became clear that Rusty and his crew hadn't survived the radiation from the massive solar event. He and Ivory were about to see the grizzly results.

He took a deep breath and said, "Let's go inside, Lieutenant."

Traveres felt Angela nudge up next to him and wrap her arms around his waist. Everyone had heard Ivory's words, and Traveres could see their mood had changed from one of optimism to one of total despair.

"Michael, what does it mean if they're all dead inside? Are we going to have to stay here?" Angela spoke in a mere whisper.

Traveres turned and looked at Boyle and Rechenko staring back at him. "I don't know, Angela. I wouldn't have thought everyone on board would be dead. It's hard to imagine the scope of what must have hit them, but don't give up hope yet. They're about to open up the lander. Maybe they'll find someone alive inside the radiation chamber."

Mac and Ivory waited for the pressure inside Mars 3's airlock to stabilize. After some discussion with Judy, Mac decided he and Ivory would stay in their pressurized suits when they entered Mars 3, which would spare them any unpleasant odors they might encounter.

It took about thirty seconds to equalize the airlock pressure. When the large green "ready" light came on, Mac spoke to the crew listening in at the base and inside Matty. "We are ready to enter the lander."

Mac pressed the "proceed" button and the door automatically started to move. As it opened, it revealed a dark room lit only by the light coming through the galley window. Mac and Ivory held up their flashlights as they strained to see through the filtered light into the dark corners of the ready room.

Neither of them attempted to walk out of the open airlock for fear of stumbling on something or somebody. Shining their flashlights at the floor, they could see various bits of debris: clothing, wrappers, tools, and a variety of objects that had been floating through the craft.

"Commander, it looks like several breakers are off," Ivory said. "The radiation alert shut them down to protect the equipment that's not shielded."

"We'll have to go up to the flight deck to turn them on," Mac answered. "Let's do a quick scan of the lander first."

Mac and Ivory carefully moved out of the airlock and into the darkened ready room. The beams from their flashlights and the breathing sounds in their suits made for an eerie feeling as they searched through the debris and clutter strewn about the floor. Mac moved through the hydroponics garden, overgrown from neglect, as Ivory pushed aside containers of food in the galley searching for the unthinkable.

"The hydroponics garden and the galley are deserted," Mac announced to the listening crew. "The lower level is clear as far as we can tell. We're heading up the ladder to the crew quarters."

Stepping off the ladder to the second level, Mac moved slowly down the dark corridor amid unopened containers, personal belongings, and equipment. It appeared the crew had barely started unpacking supplies and personal items before their routine was interrupted. He dreaded looking into each room, expecting to find a grotesque body lying on the floor, only to find nothing.

"Ivory and I are in the corridor. All the doors to the individual quarters were open, but there's no sign of anyone inside." Mac started to think about the radiation chamber the crew had obviously retreated to. He wasn't looking forward to opening that hatch.

"Second level is clear. The crew quarters are empty. We're now climbing up to the flight deck." Mac motioned to Ivory to head up the ladder.

With the first two levels of the lander empty, Mac started to piece together the painful reality of what had happened. The crew had made it to the radiation chamber, only to die together, huddled like helpless victims of an unavoidable disaster.

Mac made his way onto the bridge, Rusty's bridge. In a way, he had secretly hoped he would find Rusty's body at the controls, fighting his last battle, doing everything in his power to save his crew and die with dignity. That was surely better than dying huddled together in a death chamber.

The lights suddenly came on as Ivory flipped the main breaker, revealing the deserted flight deck. Rusty's chair was empty, as was the entire bridge. The time had come to confirm the inevitable. Mac walked up to the radiation chamber hatch and put his hand on the lever. The actual chamber was in the center of the crew module with its top hatch on the flight deck floor, and its bottom hatch on the ceiling of the ready room two levels below.

"We have found no one on the bridge. I am now going to open the hatch to the radiation chamber." Mac could feel his stomach tied up in knots. He took a deep breath, steadied himself, and opened the hatch.

He and Ivory leaned forward with their flashlights and looked inside.

"Oh my God!" he said, at first in a whisper, then louder. "Oh my God, this can't be!"

"Commander, what is it?" Traveres shouted over the radio.

"Mac, what do you see?" Judy radioed from inside Matty.

As Ivory continued to peer inside the chamber, Mac fell back to the floor. His heart raced and his hands shook as he unzipped his helmet and breathed the stale air of Mars 3 for the first time. Nothing could have prepared him for what he saw in the chamber. Or more accurately, what he didn't see. Slowly, he started to speak.

"Th…there's no one inside the radiation chamber! The cr…crew's not here. Mars 3 is empty!"

CHAPTER 11
A VOICE IN THE NIGHT

Mac sat on his bed with his eyes wide open, the day's awful events still fresh in his mind. Judy lay next to him, fast asleep with the help of a strong sedative.

It had been an ugly scene earlier when he and the retrieval team returned to base after discovering no one on board Mars 3. *How could that be?* He saw the panic in everyone's eyes as they tried to make sense of it all.

Even Boyle was speechless. "Commander, this is most puzzling. I cannot imagine how...I mean, where...I just don't know...."

And La Rue responded, adding fuel to the fire. "You don't know? I thought you knew everything. Maybe aliens abducted them on the way here."

Mac had put an immediate stop to the reckless exchange. He called for a vote to see how many of them wanted to leave Mars immediately, which prompted another wild tirade from La Rue. "We've been abandoned here!" he'd shouted. "I don't want to spend another day on this damn planet. I vote we leave immediately."

All but one crew member had voted to leave Mars as soon as possible. Only Boyle tried to convince everyone to stay, speaking with an eloquent resolve. "Commander, with all due respect, I don't see how we could ever consider leaving now, before we know exactly what happened to Mars 3. There is still so much we need to learn here; and remember, we don't know the true condition of Earth."

Rechenko stepped forward. "I'm afraid I have to disagree with you, Doctor. If I am going to fight for my life, I want to do it on my own planet."

"We will leave by the end of the week," Mac had told his crew. But he secretly wondered if they should leave without solving the mystery of Mars 3.

Replaying the day's events in his head didn't make him any sleepier. Mac closed his eyes as he gently stroked Judy's hair while she slept peacefully beside him. He considered joining her in sleep by taking a sedative himself.

Finding himself at his washbasin, he splashed cold water on his face and rubbed his weary eyes with his hands. As he slowly opened his eyes and looked in the mirror, his body froze and he could feel the hair on the back of his neck stand straight up. Staring back at him was not his reflection, but the image of his friend Rusty Chandler. Gripped with fear, he couldn't move away from the mirror. He tried to speak, but Rusty spoke first, in a voice he didn't recognize.

"WHY DID YOU LEAVE ME? COME BACK, HELP ME!"

Paralyzed, Mac tried to break free from where he stood, finally letting out a loud grunt. "Ahhh!!" He found himself still sitting on his bed, drenched in sweat and breathing heavily. He'd been dreaming! Mac covered his face with his hands. *Get a grip on yourself!*

He jumped out of bed and stumbled into the dark corridor of the mid-deck, still sweating and trembling. Climbing up the ladder well to the flight deck, he sat in his Commander's chair, a place that helped him think.

A few panel lights and monitors softly illuminated the otherwise dark bridge. He tried to collect his thoughts. For the first time in his life, he felt overwhelmed. *Would this nightmare ever end?* Nothing in his years of training prepared him for this. *Why was Mars 3 empty?*

Then the voice again pierced the quiet night.

"WHY DID YOU LEAVE ME? COME BACK, HELP ME!"

Mac stiffened in his chair. *Could I be dreaming again? No! This is real!*

"WHY DID YOU LEAVE ME? COME BACK, HELP ME!"

He glanced at the communications console. The voice came from the radio! That meant it came from Mars 3! Someone was still alive there! He grabbed the mic and spoke. "Hello! Who is this? This is Mars Base. Who is this? Identify yourself!"

"COME BACK, HELP ME!"

"Who is this?" Mac shouted. "Hello, this is Mars Base, Rusty! Do you copy?" His heart was racing. As fast as he could, he reached down and sounded the bell.

The blaring alarm shook everyone out of bed. Ivory bounded up the ladder to the flight deck, followed closely by Traveres. "Commander, what is it?" Ivory shouted over the alarm.

Mac reached over and flipped the bell off. "Lieutenant, get Matty ready. We're going over to Mars 3 ASAP!"

Ivory and Traveres gave each other a puzzled look. "Right now, sir?"

"Yes, Lieutenant, right now! There's a survivor on Mars 3. I just heard a voice over the radio from the lander."

Traveres moved to the communications console as Dr. Boyle came on to the flight deck. "What's going on, Commander? Did you ring the bell?"

"Yes, Doctor, I heard a voice coming from the Mars 3 radio link."

"A voice from the radio?" Boyle jerked his head back and lowered his gaze. "How is that possible? What did it say, Commander?"

Mac brushed off Boyle and turned to Ivory, voice booming. "Lieutenant, I told you to get Matty ready, on the double." He glared at his second officer. ". . . and make sure La Rue is up. I want him to drive!"

With a glance at Boyle, Ivory scampered down the ladder. Mac turned his attention to Traveres, who was talking on the Mars 3 radio link.

"Mars 3, this is Mars Base, do you copy?" Static. "Mars 3, this is Mars Base, acknowledge." Static again.

"Lieutenant, have you picked up anything?"

"Negative, Commander. May I ask what you heard, sir?"

"Yes, of course," Mac said as Rechenko entered the room. "I was sitting in that chair when I heard a voice on the radio say, 'Why did you leave me? Come back, help me!' I heard it twice."

Traveres and Boyle glanced at each other, and Rechenko furrowed his eyebrows. "You heard a voice on the radio say that?"

Mac nodded as Boyle pressed him. "Did you recognize the voice? Was it male or female?"

"I couldn't tell," Mac admitted, surprised at himself. "It was such a strained voice that it could really have been either. It didn't sound like Rusty. It sounded exactly like the voice...." Mac stopped himself, fearing he had gone too far.

"Exactly like what voice?" Boyle probed. "I thought you said you didn't recognize it."

"Well, I didn't, I, uh....." Mac knew he was going to regret it, but he had to continue. "You see, I had a dream earlier that I heard this voice."

"A dream? What sort of dream?"

"It was just a dream," Mac said, determined to press on. "But in it I swear I heard this voice saying, 'Why did you leave me? Come back, help me!' It was the same voice I heard here on the bridge coming out of the radio."

"You had a premonition," Rechenko said, willing to take Mac at his word. "You had a psychic vision of someone in trouble."

Angela walked into the room, squinting from the lights. "What's all the fuss about? Damon's running around complaining about having to drive Matty somewhere?"

"Is Judy up?" Mac asked.

"I don't think so. I didn't see her in the corridor," she said, yawning.

"Angela, get her up and tell her to meet me at the Matty airlock immediately, and make sure she brings her emergency gear."

Angela disappeared down the ladder, not questioning Mac's orders, but Boyle remained obstinate. "Commander, forgive me for saying so, but are you sure you didn't just fall asleep in the chair and your earlier dream reoccurred?"

Mac knew it was a fair question, one he might very well have asked of someone else; but he had no doubt about what he was going to do.

"Doctor, I appreciate what you're saying, but I know what I heard. I would not put any member of this crew in harm's way if I weren't absolutely sure. We've got to get to Mars 3 as soon as possible. Lieutenant, continue to monitor the radio. I want to know immediately if you hear anything."

La Rue drove Matty across the moonless pitch-black surface of Mars with much more care than usual. Driving on the Martian surface at night, even on a familiar path, was difficult and dangerous. What would have been a ten-minute drive during the day turned into a half-hour journey at night.

Mac sat next to Judy, who fought to shake off the effects of the sleeping pill she had taken earlier. He sensed the crew had doubts about his story. The fact that Traveres had heard no further transmissions didn't help, and he risked his credibility and authority by insisting on this rescue mission if they found nothing.

It gave him chills when he thought about the image of Rusty he had seen in his dream. Was Rechenko right? Had it been a premonition or an actual call for help? Maybe it was just the survivor's guilt he felt over the Mars 3 crew.

"Okay, Commander, there's the lander," La Rue said in a patronizing tone. "Do you want to hook up to the portable airlock tunnel?"

Mac ignored his rudeness. "Hook up to the airlock. Lieutenant, let's go."

With the portable airlock tunnel in place, Mac and Ivory didn't have to wear space suits. Once again they stood on the threshold of Mars 3. Mac's heart raced as he opened the door. This time the interior lights were on, but it was quiet inside.

"Let's get to the flight deck," Mac said, moving to the ladder well. Within moments he stood at the entrance to the bridge. It was empty and silent. His heart sank.

Ivory followed behind him and looked around. He stepped over to the radio and picked it up.

"Mars 3 to base, copy?"

"This is base to Mars 3," Traveres responded. "What did you find?"

"Nothing yet," Ivory answered. "We're starting our search now."

Mac slumped into the commander's chair and shook his head. Had he taken half of his crew on a dangerous midnight trek across the surface of Mars in search of a phantom voice? This looked bad. He watched Judy as she made her way up the ladder and looked around the empty flight deck.

"Maybe we should do a thorough search now and check every nook and cranny," she said as she walked up to Mac and placed a hand on his shoulder. "Look, I know you heard something and that you wouldn't jeopardize the crew if you weren't positive, so let's at least take a good look around, all right? I'll check the crew quarters."

Judy disappeared down the ladder as Mac leaned back into Rusty's chair. He was lucky to have her, and he always listened to her counsel.

"DON'T LEAVE ME. PLEASE DON'T LEAVE ME!"

Mac gripped the arm rests. *That voice!* He could barely muster the courage to look at the radio as he started to shake, convinced he was on the verge of a nervous breakdown. Then he heard Traveres' voice over the radio.

"...base to Mars 3. We heard the voice! Mars 3, do you copy? We heard the voice!"

Mac could hardly believe his ears. He wasn't cracking up. Traveres had confirmed the voice transmission, but from where? He stood up, looking around.

"Commander!" Ivory yelled. "I've found something. I need some light."

Mac leaped out of the chair. Miscalculating the one-third gravity, he nearly flew across the bridge into the bulkhead. Ivory was on his knees, peering down through the open hatch of the radiation chamber.

"Commander, there's someone down there! I can see movement. I don't have my flashlight; you'll have to flip the breaker."

Mac jumped across the room to the breaker panel as Judy came up the ladder. "What's going on?"

Traveres' voice continued to boom across the room from the radio. *"Do any of you copy? We heard the voice! We heard the voice over the radio! Commander, are you there?"*

"Judy, get the radio," Mac ordered. "Tell them we think we located someone in the radiation chamber."

"Commander, there *is* someone down here!" Ivory said, lowering himself into the chamber. "I may need your help pulling her out."

Her?

"It's a female crewmember. We'll have to check the manifest," he yelled at Judy, who was already talking on the radio. "It looks like we found a female survivor. Have them standing by with the crew's bios."

Mac looked down into the chamber and saw that Ivory already had her in his arms. She looked like a sack of bones, pale and thin, with her arms wrapped tightly around his neck. Mac could hear him talking softly to her in a nurturing voice.

"You're all right, you're safe now. We're here to help you. Let me lift you up to the Commander. See, he's right above us. He'll help you out of here."

As soon as he said that, Mac saw her grab him even tighter.

"Okay, okay, I won't let go of you. I'll take you out of here myself."

With her wrapped tightly in his arms, Ivory made his way up the footholds and out of the chamber. He laid her on the floor of the flight deck, but she refused to let him go. Judy came up and looked at her. "Oh my, she's dehydrated. I left my bag on the mid-deck. Be right back."

Ivory managed to peel her off enough for Mac to see the name 'Gibson' on her jumpsuit. She buried her face in Ivory's chest again.

"I vaguely remember a Jeannie or a Jenny or a Joan Gibson when I reviewed the crew manifest recently," Mac said.

He backed out of the way as Judy hurried back up the ladder and knelt beside her patient. She reached out to check her pulse.

"Careful," Mac said. "She isn't taking much of a shine to strangers."

"Well, I'm her doctor so she'd better like me."

No sooner had those words left her mouth than the woman reacted with lightning speed, landing a powerful punch on the bridge of Judy's nose. Judy tumbled back and crumpled to the floor. Stunned by the speed of the woman's attack, Mac moved to restrain her, but she was tightly clutching Ivory again, her head buried in his chest.

Mac turned to Judy, who slowly sat up, dazed, holding her nose and rubbing her watery eyes.

"What the hell happened?"

"She hit you," Mac said. "Are you all right?"

"Wow, she's quick! I didn't see that coming. You'd better hold her arms while I sedate her. We'll have to carry her to Matty."

Mac got up and walked over to the radio. "Damon, this is Mac, do you copy?"

"Go ahead, Commander."

"Damon, we need you on the flight deck on the double."

"What?" La Rue protested. "I'm not going inside that ship. It's haunted."

"Mr. La Rue, I said on the double! Out!"

Mac continued on the radio. "Mars 3 to base, do you copy?"

"We copy, sir. Go ahead," Traveres answered back.

"Lieutenant, look up Gibson in the crew manifest. I believe it's Jeannie or Jenny Gibson. I need the medical file on her."

"Yes, sir, I have it right here. Her name is Regina Gibson, AKA Gina Gibson. She's the chief botanist for the crew. Thirty-three years old. No significant allergies."

When Mac returned, he found Ivory sitting on the floor with the girl asleep in his arms.

"Did you give her the sedative?"

"Nope, didn't have to," Judy said standing over Ivory. "She fell limp in his arms. We're going to have to get her to the base so I can get some fluids in her and stabilize her."

Mac leaned over Ivory and gently pulled the woman's dirty hair from her face. "How did we miss her on our first search?"

"I think she was hiding in one of the storage lockers," Ivory speculated. "I saw a pillow and some blankets and food wrappers in an open bin. With the sudden increase in gravity, it probably took her a while to get to the radio in the chamber."

"Are you sure she's going to be all right, Judy?"

"Physically, yes, but emotionally she may have a long road to travel before she can talk about what happened here."

Mac looked at the now-peaceful face of the mystery girl and leaned forward to speak directly to her.

"I can't wait to hear your story," he whispered. "Welcome to Mars, Gina Gibson."

CHAPTER 12
ORBITAL MECHANICS

Gazing out the Mars 2 bridge window, Mac admired the mid-morning Martian sky. The deep red streaks of the jet stream foretold the coming of the red storms to the hemisphere. They had already endured one season of gargantuan dust storms. With the discovery of Gina Gibson, it looked inevitable that some of his crew would endure another dusty season.

Although he had slept only a few hours, Mac felt invigorated by last night's rescue. After the confounding mystery of an empty Mars 3, he was thrilled to find a survivor who would be able to explain what happened to Rusty and the crew—that is, if she ever became coherent.

"Mind if I join you?" Judy plopped into the co-pilot's chair next to him.

Mac could see by her disheveled appearance that she had had a rough night. "How's your favorite patient?"

Judy cocked her head and shot him a fake smile with an exaggerated grin. "Oh great, my favorite subject. Well, she woke up with a fever and the 'shakes' this morning, but she wouldn't let me near her, so Ivory gave her something for her fever. A few hours later I tried to draw some blood; but again, I couldn't get near her. She's forced me to try a different approach."

"Oh? I hope it didn't involve violence."

"No, not from me anyway. I've been that road with her before." Judy rubbed her tender nose. "Actually, I sent Angela in there to see if she could gain Gina's trust."

"Angela? Hey, that's not a bad idea. They're both about the same age and share the same background. Did it work?"

"Like a charm. Ivory is particularly happy. Gina finally let him leave the room without throwing a fit."

"So how soon before I can talk to her?"

"Talk to her? No, no, I don't think that's going to happen any time soon. Physically she's getting better by the hour, but emotionally she's a wreck. I haven't heard a coherent sentence out of her yet, just a lot of crying and grunting with an occasional left hook thrown in if I get too close."

Mac could see Judy was taking Gina's behavior personally. "Come on Judy, you're the one probing and sticking her with instruments. Give her time, and you'll gain her trust."

Judy shrugged and sank deeper into the chair.

Mac stood up and leaned against the console with his arms crossed, facing her. "We have to launch Mars 2 by the end of the week, before our window closes. But before we leave, I need to know what happened to Rusty and his crew. I have to know what Gina knows."

"Mars 3 to base, Commander, do you copy?" Traveres' voice came over the radio.

"I copy, Lieutenant. How are things looking over there?" Mac responded. "Commander, I think I have some good news."

"Good, Lieutenant, I could use some."

"We completed our systems diagnostic check about an hour ago and found all software applications have been damaged or compromised in some way."

This is good news? Mac thought.

"Fortunately, the central core computer memory was not affected, most likely due to the added protection of the radiation chamber. That's why Mars 3 landed safely with no pilot or crew."

"What about the communications array? I expect it's fried."

"Sir, we have more good news there. Dr. Rechenko checked out the array first thing. While it appears the receiver and controller chips have been damaged, these are all replaceable; and he has begun the repairs on the full array and its systems. We also ran a check on the Mars 3 mother ship, and the laser link is fully operational."

"That's excellent, Lieutenant! What would be your best guess for bringing Mars 3 to full launch status?"

"For full operation, that's hard to say since we haven't checked every system yet." "Well, give me your best guess."

"With Ivory and Dr. Rechenko's help, it shouldn't take more than a week."

"Okay, finish what you can today. I need you back here this evening for a complete briefing. Base out."

Mac noticed Judy giving him a quizzical look. "What's the hurry with Mars 3, Mac? They have eighteen months to get it ready, don't they?"

"Yes, they would if they were going to stay. But it may be possible for all of us to return home in both spacecrafts a few weeks apart."

"What?" Judy gasped. "That would be wonderful! Do you really think we can do it?"

"It's only a possibility right now," Mac said, holding up his hand to quell Judy's enthusiasm. "Boyle is working on some launch scenarios, but it's very complicated. It's all a matter of orbital mechanics, weight to fuel ratios, and the positions of Mars and Earth. If we have enough fuel, we may be able to pull this off."

Someone cleared his throat behind Mac and Judy, startling both of them. Mac turned to see Boyle standing at the entrance to the bridge holding his computer tablet. "Yes Doctor, how are your computations going?"

"Sorry to disturb you, Commander, but I need to speak to you...." He paused for a moment and glanced at Judy before adding, "...alone."

The entire crew gathered in the galley for a late dinner. The previous twenty-four hours had been by far the most stressful of the mission. Mac knew the time had come for him to announce a final course of action.

"May I assume Ms. Gibson is sound asleep?" Mac asked, ready to start the briefing.

Angela answered first. "Yes, she's sleeping like a baby."

"And how *is* your patient today?" Mac asked, looking at Judy.

"Her day was better than mine, I can assure you. I spent most of it trying to convince her to give me a blood sample, with no success. However, Angela managed to clean her up and even calmed her. Ivory was kind enough to spoon-feed her lunch and dinner. She should make a full recovery as long as she starts to eat regularly. That's the best analysis I can give you from three feet away."

"Has she said anything yet?"

"Besides growling, no, she hasn't uttered a peep to me."

"She's spoken a few basic words to me," Angela said. "Mostly baby talk. She still looks scared."

"And Mr. Ivory?"

"I've gotten her to say her name and my name. That's about it," Ivory smiled. "She seems pretty withdrawn. Although when I returned from the processor and walked in the room, she did give me a big smile."

Mac marveled at the amazing change in Ivory's demeanor since he rescued Gina last night. Her dependence on him certainly lightened his stoic personality. He actually smiled as he spoke of her.

"It would be nice if she could tell us what happened to her and the Mars 3 crew sometime in the not-too-distant future," Mac said. "And speaking of the future, I have arrived at some final decisions regarding *ours*."

The room fell silent. All eyes focused on Mac.

"It had been my hope that we could launch Mars 2 in five days and Mars 3 before the twenty-eight-day launch window closes. But I'm afraid that's not the case. Even though Lieutenant Traveres can have Mars 3 ready in plenty of time, our problem is fuel. Earlier today Dr. Boyle informed me that we only have enough fuel to launch one vehicle. Because I ordered a delay in fueling Mars 2, the processor was not able to manufacture at its full capacity for this past month. I take responsibility for this error, and I am afraid it leaves us with only one option."

Mac watched the crew closely as they absorbed his words.

"First off, I have decided to postpone the launch of Mars 2 for sixteen to eighteen months."

Everyone in the room gasped. La Rue banged on the table then buried his face in his hands.

Mac ignored La Rue's theatrics and continued. "Second, Lieutenant Traveres has assured me Mars 3 will be ready for launch prep in one week, meaning we will be able to launch within two weeks, easily making Mars 3's launch window."

This time the gasp from the crew was one of excitement.

Mac continued. "Lieutenant Traveres has agreed to accept a promotion to Lieutenant Commander and assume my duties as Commander of Mars Base and the Mars 2 mission upon my departure. Lieutenant Ivory will serve as his

First Officer and co-pilot. Dr. Boyle has enthusiastically volunteered to remain at the base and continue his exciting Mars research. Angela will remain and continue to maintain the Mars Garden. She will also undertake the role of medical officer. Gina Gibson will remain at the base, assisting Angela while, we all hope, making a full recovery."

Mac could see smiling faces all around him. After all the speculation and second-guessing, the crew finally had a plan. "For those of you returning to Earth on Mars 3—Judy, Damon, Victor—I thank you for your willingness to face the unknown. Believe me, I would not ask for volunteers to return to Earth if it were not for the fact that we have a limited water supply here. This base cannot sustain nine people without a permanent source of water.

"We have a busy two weeks ahead of us," Mac continued. "First thing tomorrow, Angela, I want you to ride over to Mars 3 with Traveres and Rechenko. You need to get the hydroponics garden back in operation as soon as possible for our return trip. Judy should accompany you since it will be her responsibility to maintain it. Mr. Ivory, you and Dr. Boyle will handle the Mars 3 fueling. Let me know if you need my help. Mr. La Rue, you will be in charge of provisions for our return trip. You'll need to divide up the rations as best you can. We will be in transit for five months."

The excitement and eagerness the crew displayed put a smile on Mac's face, but he had one more item to cover. "Before I say good-night to you, I would like us all to pause for a moment out of respect for the memory of the Mars 3 crew members who lost their lives. As you know, I lost my best friend, whom I will never forget. Some of you may have known other crew members as well."

With all heads bowed in reverent prayer, the unmistakable sound of footsteps echoed nearby. All heads at the table turned around, looking into the darkness of the galley entrance. A thin, gaunt figure emerged from the shadows like a ghost. It was Gina Gibson.

Ivory reached out to help guide her to a chair, but she refused to sit down. Managing to shuffle her frail body to the edge of the galley table, she pulled back her dirty blonde hair, revealing deep, empty eyes. Looking toward Mac, she softly whispered, "Thank...you...."

CHAPTER 13
GINA GIBSON

Mac sat in the privacy of his quarters and called up the file of Gina Gibson, chief botanist for the Mars 3 mission. Traveres had downloaded her personal file from the Mars 3 mainframe computer in an effort to shed some light on her. After a week on Mars, she still refused to discuss her traumatic solo journey, forcing him to seek other sources of information that might be useful in getting her to talk.

Gina's file came up on the screen. He barely recognized the photo with the fuller face of a woman in her mid-thirties with deep blue eyes and straight blond hair—a far cry from the ghostly figure Ivory had pulled out of the radiation chamber.

He heard a knock on his door, then Judy's voice. "Busy?"

"Come in," Mac leaned over to open the door. "I want you to take a look at this."

Judy stepped in and glanced at the screen. "Is that her? Hmm, she's lost a lot of weight, and the lack of sun has really changed her complexion. She's beginning to look a little more like her picture after a week of eating, though."

"How's she doing? Is she gaining strength?"

"Oh, she's made remarkable progress. Even though she's thin, she has good muscle tone in her arms and legs. I just left her and Ivory in Habitat 2. They're sparring with those sticks again."

"They're stick fighting?"

"Yes, they've been doing it all week after Tai Chi. She's really quite good at it. Ivory's working hard to get her into shape. I think that will help with her mental health, too, working out the frustration she may feel as a sole survivor."

Mac started to scan Gina's file. "I don't see anything here about formal Martial Arts training. Ivory must be a good teacher."

"What about those two?" Judy asked, raising her eyebrows. "They make quite a cute couple, I think. Could the plan be any more perfect—leaving Angela and Michael, Gina and Ivory together on Mars? I know this planet isn't exactly the Garden of Eden, but it's nice to think of those four as the Adams and Eves of a New World."

"That would make Dr. Boyle the evil serpent, wouldn't it?"

"No. I think he would prefer the role of the Almighty," Judy laughed.

Something caught Mac's eye as he scanned the file. "Well I'll be. Listen to this. Gina received her advance degree in Agricultural Engineering from the University of California at Davis, just outside Sacramento. Isn't that where Angela went?"

"You know, I think you're right. I remember hearing somewhere that NASA recruited whole classes from U.C. Davis Bio-tech program when the Mars project was approved. What a coincidence."

"So Angela doesn't recognize her?"

"She hasn't said anything to me."

Reading further, Mac stopped and raised an eyebrow. "Talking about coincidences, listen to this. Gina's parents live near the town of Coloma in the Sierra Nevada foothills, due east of Sacramento. That's only a few miles from Lotus, where my parents built their retirement home. Could they be neighbors?"

"Why don't you ask her yourself? You've been looking for an excuse to talk to her."

Before Mac could respond, the intercom tone sounded, followed by Dr. Boyle's voice. "Dr. Delaney to Habitat 2 on the double...Dr. Delaney, you're need in H2 immediately!"

"Oh-oh, what's this?" Mac moaned. He followed Judy, who had grabbed her medical bag and shot out the door and down the ladder to the airlock tunnel. Entering Habitat 2, Mac saw Ivory, Gina, and Boyle standing over Angela, who was lying on the floor flat on her back, covering the side of her head with her hand and moaning in pain.

"What's going on?" Judy demanded, like a mother scolding her mischievous children.

Ivory, Gina, and Boyle scurried out of Judy's way as she knelt next to Angela. "Angela, how do you feel? Where are you hurt?"

Mac strained to hear her soft voice as she tried to respond. "I...I don't know. Where am I? What...happened?"

"What do you remember?"

Angela closed her eyes and shook her head. "Why am I on the floor?"

Judy gave Mac a disgusted look then pulled a small flashlight out of her bag and shined it in Angela's eyes. "Tell me what you *do* remember."

Angela took her hand away from her forehead to reveal a sizable bruise. Mac and Judy gasped at the sight of the large red welt.

Mac turned to Ivory, Boyle, and Gina. "How did this happen?"

Boyle spoke first, as Gina held onto Ivory. "Apparently Gina and Lieutenant Ivory were stick fighting—you know, sparring, nothing serious. I guess Angela came along and asked if she could join in. She's quite good at it, you know. She had a go at it with the lieutenant first, then she and Gina squared off. Well, I guess, the two were going at it pretty good, and it got a little out of hand."

"A little out of hand?" Judy interrupted. "Angela might have a concussion! What the hell were you guys thinking? You can kill someone with this!" Judy held up a hard plastic dowel about five feet long. Mac recognized it as one of the cross support struts for the hydroponics trays.

"Lieutenant, why were you stick fighting, and how could you let this happen?" Mac asked.

"I'm sorry, Commander, it's my fault. Gina and I were doing it to get her strength back. It's an excellent exercise, and she is qualified in this discipline. However, when fighting Angela, she let the stick get away from her."

"Mr. Ivory, I would think you'd use better judgment, particularly so close to the launch. I trust I won't see you doing this again?"

"No, of course not, sir."

"Excuse me, sir, it was really my fault. I shouldn't have been so reckless." Everyone looked in the direction of the unfamiliar voice. Gina was talking, saying more than she ever had before in the presence of the other crew members. Her voice was mysterious to everyone but Mac. He had heard it in his nightmare and over the radio the night they rescued her. To his surprise, she sounded just as haunting as she had on the first night he had heard her.

"No, sir, it was my fault," Ivory insisted. "I should have known better than to expose them to injury."

"All right, I don't care whose fault it is; just don't let it happen again. Judy, how's Angela doing?"

"She's had a pretty good knock on the head," Judy said, still kneeling over a dazed Angela. "It could be a mild concussion. I'll have to keep a close eye on her."

Angela sat up with Judy's help. The large welt on her forehead looked so bad that Ivory and Gina looked away.

"Let's get her to her quarters," Judy said.

Boyle and Ivory reached under Angela's shoulders and helped her up. They started to walk to the airlock tunnel with Gina close behind.

"Gina, could you wait a moment?" Mac asked. "I'd like to speak to you."

Gina froze, staring at Ivory, who continued to walk Angela to the airlock tunnel. Only after Ivory looked back and nodded to her did she turn to face Mac.

As Judy walked by Mac, she whispered to him, "Be careful. She's already clobbered two of us."

Mac wasn't sure whether Judy was joking or not because his eyes were on the woman in front of him. It amazed him the way Gina had transformed herself from the frail, near-catatonic specimen to the slender, attractive woman who stood before him. But for all her physical improvements, Mac sensed her fragile, emotional state.

"How are you doing, Gina? You look well."

Gina dropped her gaze to the floor and fidgeted from side to side.

"Are you feeling better?"

"I'd like to go now, please," she whimpered, still looking straight down.

"Did you know your parents and mine live in the same area in Northern California?"

Gina continued to stare at the floor.

"Gina, I'd really like to talk to you about your experiences on Mars 3. Any information would be helpful."

This time she shook her head and looked up. "Commander, I'd like to go now, please. I'm sorry." She turned and hurried to the exit.

Mac dropped his head and let her go.

Standing at the entrance to Angela's quarters, Mac watched as Judy removed the freeze bag from Angela's head wound and said, "Sit still, Angela. I'll be right back. Okay?"

"Thanks, Judy, I'll be all right. You don't have to fuss." Angela leaned on a pillow propped against the wall.

Mac motioned for Judy to follow him to his quarters where she closed the door behind her.

"How's she doing? Is she going to be okay?"

"She still doesn't know what hit her." Judy shook her head. "She doesn't even remember sparring with Gina. I'm sure she has at least a mild concussion."

"I've had a mild concussion before," Mac said, almost proud. "I was riding a motorcycle in a friend's driveway and accidentally gunned it into a telephone pole. I lost my memory for hours."

"Lost your memory?"

"I'll say. I still don't remember the accident to this day. I only know what happened because the people I was with told me. For all I know, I could have made a pass at someone's wife and gotten clobbered for it."

Judy slapped Mac on the arm. "I'm willing to believe that story rather than the motorcycle accident version."

"Well, regardless of what happened, I was diagnosed with a concussion. I didn't remember anything for ten hours after the accident. And to this day, the last thing I recall was having lunch with my friends. The next thing I remembered was looking at my buddy standing by my hospital bed praying over me. The point is, Angela will be all right. She'll just need some time to get her marbles lined up again."

"Well, I hope so," Judy said as she turned to him. "So was the 'friend' you saw praying over you Rusty?"

"Yes, as a matter of fact it was."

"I'm sorry, I know you miss him. I gather you didn't get any information out of Gina?"

"No, I'm afraid it was a dead-end today. She looked very uncomfortable. I'm beginning to wonder if she'll remember anything from Mars 3. She's probably just as traumatized emotionally as someone with a concussion would be affected physically."

"Well, maybe so…and call me crazy if you like, but I can't shake the feeling that she's hiding something. I'm not sure I fully trust her."

"What are you saying? Do you think today's incident wasn't an accident?"

"Mac, I'm sorry if I sound too negative about Gina, but you have to remember that the first time I saw her she popped me in the nose. Then she's continually refused to have anything to do with me. No examination, no blood test, nothing! But she'll gladly talk to Ivory and Angela. What's that all about? I don't know. So I asked Angela to try to persuade Gina to let me examine her and draw some blood. Next thing you know we're picking Angela up off the floor. It's as if Gina thinks we're getting too nosey."

A knock at the door caused them both to jump. "Come in," Mac said.

The door creaked open, and Mac and Judy stared in shock at Gina Gibson, who stood in front of them.

How thin are these walls? Mac wondered.

"Can I come in?" Gina asked.

"Yes, of course," Mac said without hesitation. "There's not much room, but you can fit."

Judy quickly stood up. "Look, I need to check on Angela. Why don't the two of you talk? I'll leave."

"How is she doing?" Gina asked Judy in her soft voice. "Will she be all right?"

Judy stopped, surprised by Gina's willingness to talk to her. "She'll be fine. It's just a mild concussion. She'll be up and around in no time." Judy glared at Mac for a moment then left the room.

"Sit down," Mac motioned Gina toward the only other chair in his small quarters. He couldn't help but notice what an attractive woman she was. Her straight long blond hair framed an oval face featuring pearl-white skin that accented deep blue eyes. "What can I do for you?"

"First of all, I want to thank you for being so patient with me. I understand you were the one who heard me calling on the radio. Thank you for coming back for me."

The sound of Gina's voice gave Mac chills, reminding him of the dream he had had in this very room. "Forget it, I was thrilled we found someone who survived. It must have been very difficult for you."

Gina looked down at her lap, then up again into his eyes. "I'm ready to tell you what happened on Mars 3."

Mac took a deep breath, careful not to say anything that might change her mind. "I appreciate that Gina. I know this isn't easy for you."

She sat up straight and nodded at him.

Mac turned on his voice recorder and smiled at her. "How much do you remember?"

She leaned back and placed her hand over her mouth. Mac could hear her take several short breaths as her eyes started to water. After a long pause, she spoke in a broken voice.

"I remember everything."

CHAPTER 14
A LIVING NIGHTMARE

Mac watched Gina wipe tears from her face as she tried to maintain composure. Sitting face to face with Mac in his quarters, Gina was finally exposed, unable to bury her head in Ivory's chest to avoid eye contact and scrutiny. She had volunteered to bare her soul.

She had in an incredibly short time transformed herself from an emaciated near-catatonic specimen to a lean, healthy woman. But Mac still feared her mental state might not match her remarkable physical recovery.

She gave him a weak smile. "All right, Commander, I'm ready to begin."

"Okay, Gina. Let's take it slowly. If you feel a need to stop and collect your thoughts or take a break, feel free to do so."

She nodded and took a deep breath. "Where would you like me to begin?"

"Why don't you start with what was going on before the radiation alert. Make sure you mention anything unusual you may have overheard, particularly about radiation warnings."

Gina closed her eyes for a moment. The slightest smile crossed her face. "I remember Commander Chandler was very pleased after the hyper-drive was engaged. He thanked the crew, and I think everyone was excited to finally be underway. Shortly after that, the Commander asked me to start clearing the radiation chamber of some storage bags because he wanted to run a drill as soon as possible."

Mac remembered that at the beginning of his own mission, supplies for the Mars Garden and the galley had been stored inside the radiation chamber. It took the crew several weeks to clear out all the items so he'd run the radiation alert drills when bags of supplies were still in the chamber. The fact that Rusty wanted to run drills early in the mission indicated that he might have been concerned about frequent radiation alerts.

"Please go on, Gina."

"I took a complete inventory of what could be moved first and what should stay. I even started to move some supplies out of the chamber. Katie Thompson, our chief geologist, helped me."

She paused for a moment and put her hand to her mouth and took several short breaths. "Oh, poor Katie! I'm sorry, but I haven't thought about her for awhile. She and I were very close, Commander. If she had stayed in the chamber with me, she would probably be alive today. Instead, she kept moving back and forth between the lower chamber hatch and the garden, storing supplies for me."

"Gina, it's not your fault. You were just following orders. There's no way you could have known what was about to happen."

Gina nodded. "I'm sorry, Commander, I'll try to stick to the facts."

Mac wondered if she had the strength to continue.

"I had just given Katie the last storage bag for the galley. She floated through the bottom hatch of the chamber, and that was the last time I saw her...alive."

"Was the upper hatch to the bridge open at that time?"

"No, it was closed. Because I was moving things around, I didn't want anything to float out onto the flight deck. As a matter of fact, I was about to open the top hatch when I realized I'd forgotten to log off the computer at the chamber control station. Just as I pushed away from the hatch and started to float to the computer, the radiation alert sounded. It scared the hell out of me...but that was nothing compared to what happened next. Without any warning, the lights went out. I was in complete darkness, but I could tell it was more than just a blackout. There was complete silence, no hum of equipment, air pumps, or fans. For a moment, as I was floating weightless in the pitch-black silence, I thought I was dead. Then I slammed into the computer station and bounced off into some storage bags."

"So you're saying you couldn't see or hear anything? What about the emergency lights and the control console in the chamber? They didn't come on as they were supposed to?"

"No. Not right away. About every five minutes they would try to power up for a few seconds and then they would go dead. That went on for maybe about an hour until they finally stayed on, along with all the warning lights."

She hesitated for a second before adding, "...there's something else..."

"What is it?" Mac watched her fidget in her seat.

"I didn't think about it right away, but I realized I *could* hear something." Her bottom lip started to quiver.

"What, Gina? What did you hear?"

She let out an eerie wail that faded to a whimper. "Oooooooh..." She covered her ears, reached out and grabbed Mac's shirt, and burrowed her head into his chest.

He patted her back. "Don't worry. You're all right. It's all over. You're safe here with us."

She pulled away from him, still sobbing. "I could hear people screaming!" She cried as if just realizing it for the first time. Again, she collapsed into Mac's arms, and he held onto her so she wouldn't fall to the floor. He wished Judy were here to help. This was more a therapy session than a briefing.

"Gina, do you mind if I call in Dr. Delaney to help?"

"No! Don't call the doctor! I want Christopher. Please get me Christopher."

Mac wasn't surprised she wanted Ivory. Perhaps they could get through this with his help. He started to get up to summon him when Gina grabbed his arm.

"Wait, Commander," she said, still sobbing. "Let me try to continue. I think this is helping...I need to do this on my own."

Even though she appeared weak and fragile, her formidable grip, along with her iron determination to work through her trauma, surprised Mac.

"I guess I never realized it before," she continued, "but just after the power failure, in the darkness, I could hear screams. I was so disoriented and confused that I wasn't sure what I was hearing at the time. I could have saved them. I feel so ashamed," she cried, covering her face with her hands.

"Gina, you aren't responsible for their deaths. Had you opened the chamber to try to help, you would have died also. And that wouldn't have done anyone any good. It wasn't like they were banging on the hatch, right?"

Gina looked down and shook her head. "That isn't exactly true, sir."

"What do you mean?"

"Well, after an hour of the power going off and on, the computer console in the chamber finally activated. I was pretty scared, and I wondered why I

hadn't heard from anyone. I checked to make sure life support was still functioning throughout the spacecraft. Then I tried to contact Houston, but there
was only static on the radio. That's when I heard a tapping sound at the bridge
hatch."

"Tapping?" Mac repeated. "Did you open the hatch?"

Gina covered her eyes again, sobbing softly as she spoke. "Commander, I
wanted to open the hatch in the worst way. I was scared and all alone. The radiation warning light was still on, so I had to decide if I should go against procedures and override the safeties to open the hatch. I had to consider whether
any equipment might be damaged."

Mac pondered her answer for a moment. There were strict rules against
opening the hatch to the radiation chamber once it was sealed. The computer
and life-support functions were all located in the protective chamber. To open
the hatch during a warning could doom the craft and everyone inside.

The spacecraft and all its functions could be controlled from the remote
console in the chamber. In theory, the crew should be able to survive several
weeks, if necessary, inside a space the size of a large bathroom. Mac was
sure Gina wasn't looking forward to spending that time inside the chamber
alone. She faced the unenviable decision of whether to chance her own life
to save others. No amount of training could fully prepare someone for such
a situation.

"Gina, you had to make a very difficult choice. No one could blame you for
not opening the hatch. Given the situation, you did the right thing."

Gina looked up at Mac. "I opened the hatch, sir. I didn't want to be alone."
She paused and closed her eyes for a moment. "But in retrospect, it was the
wrong thing to do."

"Wrong? Why was it wrong? What happened to the survivors?"

"There was only one survivor, sir. Just one person made it to the hatch
alive. You see, I overrode the safety on the hatch and opened it. The first thing
I saw was the bright light of a flashlight, which blinded me. Next I heard mumbling, first in Russian, then in broken English. 'Stop the burn, we must stop the
burn! Everyone is dead!' While I couldn't see his face, I knew it was Alexander
Holshevnikoff, the first officer and co-pilot. He tried to push me out of the way
and get to the control console. He was frantic, but very weak. He could barely

move. I assumed he was trying to stop the hyper-drive burn. I didn't know if I should try to stop him or not, but he was talking crazy."

"So did you try to help him?" Mac asked.

"I wasn't altogether sure what I could do for him, but I didn't let him near that console. I told him to tell me what to do and I would put it into the computer. But he was too weak. All he could talk about was how I shouldn't allow the burn to continue. His directions were rambling and confusing; and in the end, he finally lost consciousness. I was alone again, only this time I knew I was the only one alive on the entire ship."

"So you let the hyper-drive burn continue as scheduled?"

"I didn't see any other alternative. I couldn't revive Alexander, I couldn't contact Houston, and I knew I couldn't turn the ship around by myself. At the time, I thought my best bet was to stay with the ship and wait on Mars for the next crew to come. Had I known how difficult it was going to be, I would have committed suicide that very day."

Her casual mention of suicide surprised Mac. "So the nightmare was just beginning?"

Gina nodded thoughtfully. "Commander, I already had one dead body with me in the chamber. I knew six other bodies waited for me throughout the spacecraft. Six of my crewmates, my friends, the companions I had worked with so closely for two years.

"The real nightmare started after the ship finished the hyper-drive burn. The radiation alarm stopped and I got the all-clear to exit the chamber, knowing I was the only one alive on board. The spacecraft's lights didn't work so I floated through the dark ship with only a flashlight. First I went to the bridge where I found Commander Chandler still strapped to his seat. His eyes and mouth were wide open and his skin was burned and discolored."

Fitting he should die at the controls of his ship, Mac thought, swallowing hard and wondering if Rusty ever knew what hit him.

Gina continued. "I also found our science officer, Dr. Thomas Peterhaus, floating above the Commander. He had a gash on his face, and I could see globules of blood floating about. On the mid-deck, I found our surgeon, Dr. Daniel Sherwood, and our chief engineer, Luis De La Torre, floating dead above their beds. I'm still haunted by those memories."

Gina's behavior shifted subtly. The more gruesome the tale, the more matter-of-fact her attitude became. Mac wondered if she wasn't in some sort of denial. He looked forward to hearing Judy's impressions of the recorded interview.

"But the most difficult find of them all…" she continued, "…was when I finally located Katie Thompson in the hydroponics garden, with the last bags I'd given her floating around her."

Gina paused for a moment and bit her lip before she continued. "I located the last body, the chemical engineer, John Beletti, in the galley kitchen. He had been preparing the day's meals.

"Death was everywhere. I began to wonder if I weren't dead myself." She laughed to herself for a moment, then her smile faded before she added, "That was wishful thinking."

Mac tried to imagine floating his way through the entire ship in total darkness and finding the bodies of his crewmates. It must have been surreal for Gina.

"So what did you do with the bodies?" he asked, trying to sound matter-of-fact.

Gina took a deep breath, as if preparing to unload another burden from her thoughts. "At first, I tied them all together so they wouldn't float off throughout the ship. I considered putting them in the storage bins, but I knew they would start to decompose. I finally decided I had no choice but to get them off the ship."

"How did you accomplish that?"

"Well, it wasn't as easy as I thought. First off, it was still dark, and the controls for the airlock weren't working. I knew I had to figure out how to turn everything back on. I went into the computer and called up the restart procedure for the spacecraft. It took me about half a day to get the power and lights back on. I was so happy to have gotten the ship back up and working, I immediately tried to call Houston again, but I couldn't reach anyone. When I finally went down to the ready room to deal with the bodies, I just wasn't prepared for what I saw."

She started to shake again. "What did you see, Gina?"

Her eyes welled up with tears and her voice strained as she spoke. "I wasn't prepared to see the entire crew bundled up together, floating around the ready room in the full light. In the dark...it didn't seem so real...I could deny it was really happening. But in the fully lit ready room, the terror of it all really hit me. I panicked. All I could think of was getting the bodies out of the ship and out of my sight.

"I fumbled with the airlock, pushing the group of bodies inside and closing the door. It was difficult because I was shaking so badly. I decompressed the chamber and opened the outer door. But they didn't float away like I thought they would. They just stayed in the airlock!"

Gina panted and her face became flushed. Mac was about to stop her when she held up her hand and slowed her breathing. After a moment, she started speaking again in a detached tone. "Then I realized I shouldn't have depressurized the chamber before I opened the outer door. I closed the door and pressurized the airlock about ten percent. I hit the emergency door release and wow! You should have seen those bodies fly out into space. It shocked me for a second. Then it sunk in like a heavy weight on my shoulders; I would be alone for three months on the ship and, I thought at the time, eighteen months on Mars."

Gina looked Mac straight in the eyes. "Can you blame me for contemplating suicide?"

"No, I don't think most people would have survived what you went through. I'm not sure I could have. How did you manage to keep your sanity?"

Gina shook her head. "Of course, you know, I didn't keep my sanity. At first I tried to maintain my normal duties, being the chief botanist on a ghost ship. But that didn't last. The first radiation alert I had, I stayed in the chamber for a week, even though the alert only lasted an hour. I found myself spending more time inside the chamber and away from the empty corridors of the ship. It was too painful to move around rooms that were once filled with my friends and crewmates. Since I could monitor the entire ship from the remote console in the chamber, I found it easier to just stay there. I let the garden go and survived on the food storage. Not that I had much of an appetite. In the end, I mostly slept. I turned the lights out and hid in one of the storage compartments in the chamber."

"What about when you arrived here? Were you aware that you had landed?"

"Yes, I could actually feel the vibration, the shudder of the lander as it entered the atmosphere, but I ignored it all. I figured I was about to die. The surge in g-forces caused me to black out. When I regained consciousness, I knew I had landed because the vibration had stopped and gravity pinned me to the floor."

"But you heard us when we looked through the lander, didn't you?"

"Yes, of course I heard you. But you have to remember you were supposed to be long gone. I wasn't expecting anyone to visit for another two years. I thought I was dreaming when I heard someone walking around the ship. By the time it dawned on me that I wasn't dreaming, I realized I couldn't move. I hadn't been exercising for two months. I couldn't even lift my head, and I found speaking to be way too challenging. I heard Christopher open the chamber hatch and look inside. But he couldn't see me in the storage bin, and there was nothing I could do. You gave up too quickly. It literally took me hours to get to the radio and figure out how to contact you."

It all made sense to Mac. He remembered the first search of the lander. They were so stunned not to find anyone there that they left without doing a thorough search.

"I'm sorry about that," Mac apologized. "We were in a state of shock ourselves. Do you know that I had a dream about you asking for us to return to the ship?"

"You had a dream? About me?" Gina asked, surprised.

Mac stopped the recording. No sense in documenting his disturbing dream. "Yes, the night we found you, the evening after our first search. I was lying on my bed and fell asleep. I had a dream that I was standing in front of the mirror, only the reflection I saw was Commander Chandler's."

Gina rubbed her arms as if she had a chill. "Whoa...that's strange!"

"Well, that's not the strangest part...," Mac said just as the intercom tone sounded, making them both jump.

"Commander? Sorry to bother you." La Rue was calling from the bridge. "Lieutenant Traveres wanted to give you an update from Mars 3."

"Okay, Damon, I'll be right there."

"Commander, are we through?" Gina asked. "I wanted to look in on Angela to see how she's doing."

"Yes, by all means. We're done. Thank you for sharing your experiences. I know it must have been difficult."

"Thank you for asking, Commander," she said with a smile. "I think it did me a lot of good."

"Gina, do you mind if I play our interview for the crew tonight? I think it would really shed some light on our situation."

Gina hesitated for a second. "No…I don't mind, as long as I don't have to be there to hear it."

"Of course not, Gina. I wouldn't think of putting you through that again."

She reached out and squeezed his arm. "I'm also looking forward to hearing about the dream you had about me, Commander."

Mac blushed. He wished he hadn't mentioned it, and now he was going to have to talk about it again. "Sure, some other time," he said, dismissing the thought. "I'll play the interview tonight then."

Mac shut off the recording of his conversation with Gina and looked around the galley table at the six people sitting in grim silence. Angela and Gina were the only ones not present. The crew showed mostly watery eyes and blank stares. Finally, Boyle broke the tension. "I can't believe how fast the ship was disabled. Did you notice there were only seconds between the initial alarm and the blackout? It's amazing anyone survived."

"It's possible no one survived," Judy said.

"What do you mean?" Mac asked.

"While I haven't been able to examine Gina, I suspect she won't survive the high levels of radiation she's been exposed to, even inside the protective chamber. I'm afraid the solar storm was too strong."

Mac noted a conciliatory tone from Judy, not just from a concerned doctor, but a genuine sympathy for Gina's welfare.

"I think you may be right, Doctor," Rechenko said. "During our inspection we found some damage to the central core, but enough nano-processors survived to rewrite the automated program. That's why the computer kept turning off and on after the blackout."

"Commander, I think this shows the severity of the solar storm," Boyle said. "It's no wonder we haven't been able to re-establish communications. Still as conditions improve on Earth, I'm optimistic you will hear from Houston on your return voyage."

"And I'm ready to leave," La Rue spoke up. "Solar flare or not, if Mars 3 can survive the brunt of a radiation storm, things couldn't be that bad on Earth."

Mac leaned forward and looked at each member of his crew. "One week. We have one week to launch. Will we be ready?"

"I'll have the Mars 3 computer ready to go in another day or so," Traveres responded. "We should be able to run a launch dress rehearsal in three days."

"La Rue and I will fuel Mars 3 tomorrow, Commander," Ivory said. "The recycle system is running and the water tanks are full."

"The garden is in good shape and ready for launch," Judy added.

"And I've already moved about half the supplies to Mars 3," La Rue announced proudly. "I should easily be finished in the next few days."

"Okay, let's keep to our schedule and we should be ready in time," Mac said. "Is there anything else?"

Rechenko spoke up first. "Sir, I'd like to say something about Gina..."

"Excuse me," Traveres interrupted. "I need to check on Angela." He got up and walked out of the galley.

Mac watched his first officer leave, realizing that just as Judy's attitude was softening toward the newcomer, Gina had made a new enemy. Traveres was clearly upset by Gina's violent action against Angela earlier in the day. He'd seemed uncomfortable listening to Gina's recording and obviously didn't want to sit around and listen to everyone talk about what a brave person she was.

Traveres sat on the edge of Angela's bed and watched her sleep. She looked so peaceful, unaware of the danger she faced—a sharp contrast to the anger and rage he was feeling . He reached into his breast pocket and pulled out a silver video disk and clutched it tightly. The time had come for him to take control of the mission.

CHAPTER 15
DRESS REHEARSAL

Lying flat on her back, Angela finished her final yoga stretch and got up to turn off the music inside Habitat 2. It had been four days since her concussion, and she felt a hundred percent better. She walked between the rows of hearty fruits and vegetables growing well over her head, transforming more than half the gymnasium-sized habitat into a luscious green garden. She always looked forward to her morning yoga and daily garden inspection, but today was different. Today she was alone.

Mac, Rechenko, and La Rue were busy at Mars 3, conducting their first launch simulations. Judy, her usual morning companion, was with them, working on the in-flight hydroponics garden. The base felt empty with them away, and Angela worried that it would be difficult to say goodbye to them when the time came.

It had occurred to her that the people leaving Mars Base for Earth tended to be more warm and friendly than those staying behind. The serious Dr. Boyle always buried himself in his scientific projects, Christopher Ivory continued his introverted ways, and Gina was cold and distant. Angela noticed Gina would get somewhat moody when the conversation turned to something personal, such as her acquaintances or interests. Ever since the stick-fighting accident, Gina was aloof, never apologizing to Angela and referring to the incident as a careless lapse of control by both of them.

If it weren't for Michael, she couldn't endure eighteen more months on Mars. He was her refuge, and lately she had noticed a delightful change in his attitude. It started when she emerged from the fog of her concussion. His constant foreboding had been replaced with a surge of optimism and excitement. In the midst of all the problems they faced, Michael was acting as if a huge weight had been lifted off his shoulders. Every day since the accident, he would tell her everything was under control and she would be all right. While she wasn't quite sure what he meant, she enjoyed his renewed energy. Finished with her routine, Angela hurried to the bridge to be by Michael's side.

When she reached the flight deck, she was surprised to find him conducting the premier launch dress rehearsal on his own. "Where is everyone?" She squeezed his shoulder and gave him a peck on the cheek.

"Everyone's busy. Boyle's in his lab, and Gina and Ivory are preparing the big dinner for tonight."

"So how's the rehearsal going? Is the program working okay?"

"We're about to find out," he said with a grin. He guided her to the co-pilot's chair and motioned her to sit. "I want you to watch this. I threw Mac a little curve ball on the first launch simulation. Let's see how he handles it."

Mac sat down in the Mars 3 Commander's chair. He never expected to be sitting in Rusty's seat, preparing to go home.

"Commander, the computer is ready for the virtual simulation program," Rechenko reported from the co-pilot's seat.

"Thank you, Victor. How does it feel to be a pilot on an interplanetary spacecraft?"

"I'm ready."

Mac keyed his mic. "Mars Base, this is Mars 3. The computer is loading the launch program."

"We copy that," Traveres answered. "We are receiving telemetry from your high-gain antennae, over."

"Roger, base, we're putting our glasses on now." Mac nodded to Rechenko. "Be sure to call out any anomalies as the gauges start registering. You know the drill. We're probably going to go through this a couple of dozen times today."

"Got it, Commander."

Mac adjusted his glasses, settled in and started thinking about being a pilot again. His view of the cockpit wouldn't change until the gauges started to register during the simulated launch. Even the view out the window would mirror the spacecraft's virtual altitude all the way through the ascent and docking with the orbiting mother ship. The only difference in a virtual launch was the lack of vibration, which could be substantial in the early stages of an actual liftoff.

He looked around, his gaze stopping on the overhead camera mounted above the two seats. Rusty had addressed that camera while sending his greetings to the Mars Base crew just before Mars3 had entered hyperspace three months ago. Mac had meant to look at the recording of that last transmission, but he hadn't gotten around to it. It would be nice to see Rusty one more time. Then it occurred to him that Rusty would have made a copy of the transmission and left it in his disk tray, as was standard procedure for pilots. Mac reached down to the tray release, below the console.

"Commander, the computer has loaded the launch program."

"Thank you, Victor." Mac keyed his mic again. "Base, this is Mars 3. The program is loaded. Waiting for the accept prompt, over."

"Copy, Commander, waiting for accept," Traveres responded.

Mac released the disk tray and looked inside. Sure enough, Rusty's transmission record disk sat right where it should be. He grabbed the small silver disk and slipped it into the playback tray and hit the button. Instantly on the screen in front of him appeared a picture of Rusty and his co-pilot looking into the camera. Mac, looking at his old friend, smiled sadly. Knowing that Rusty had died less than forty-eight hours after this video was recorded gave Mac an eerie feeling.

"Commander, the computer accepted the program."

"Okay, Victor. Base, we have a go; we are ready to initiate launch sequence."

"Copy, Commander, we have good telemetry. You are go to initiate at your discretion."

"Roger, base. T-minus sixty seconds and counting." It was all automatic now. As long as Traveres and Rechenko had written the program correctly, things would run smoothly.

Mac scanned across the control panel, checking his gauges. His fuel tanks were at capacity and hydraulic pressure was nominal. He glanced up and noticed that Rusty's transmission disk continued to play. It was at the point where Rusty was introducing the entire crew as they crammed onto the bridge.

"Thirty seconds," Rechenko called out. "Auto launch sequence engaged."

Mac paused the disk, freezing the Mars 3 crew floating in front of the camera. He would look at it later.

"Fifteen seconds, ignition sequence start. Ten…nine…"

Mac scanned the gauges. Everything looked good.

"We have ignition!" Rechenko announced. "All engines are firing."

"Mars 3, this is base. We show four good engines."

"Copy that." Mac said, responding to Traveres' launch dialogue. He looked at Rechenko, whose head moved back and forth scanning the gauges.

"Thirty seconds, five thousand feet, Commander."

"Copy, Victor. Continue your read-outs." Mac smiled at Rechenko, who was a quick study and seemed to be enjoying himself.

"Approaching fifteen thousand feet at fifty seconds, Commander."

Mac looked up. With the virtual glasses on, the view outside the window changed quickly. The sky darkened as the landscape fell away.

"Ninety seconds, forty thousand feet. Attitude is good, fuel consumption nominal."

"Okay, Victor, we're at maximum velocity, approaching roll program."

"Fifty thousand feet, starting roll program," Rechenko announced.

A computer alarm shrieked as warning lights flashed across the console.

"We have main engine cutoff! Power is off across the board!" Rechenko shouted.

"Mars 3, this is base. I show main engine cutoff, copy?"

Mac slammed his hand on the console. "Dammit, Lieutenant! We have no power and no engine! What's going on with your program?"

"Commander, initiate restart on your computer and fire engines at full throttle. You can still complete the roll manually," Traveres said, still conducting the simulation as if it were really happening.

"Lieutenant, I'm not interested in wasting time saving the ship. I need Victor to complete a full launch to docking before we throw any problems his way."

"Of course, sir, it will take Dr. Rechenko and me about ten minutes to reload the program. Stand by."

Mac took his glasses off and sat back in his chair. The frozen image of the Mars 3 crew drew his attention. As he studied their faces, a sudden chill rushed through his veins and down to his core. He couldn't believe what he was seeing, or not seeing. He leaned forward and counted the crew. "Six, seven, eight...."

All eight crew members were accounted for, but there was a catch. The Gina Gibson he knew wasn't one of them.

Sitting in the front passenger seat of Matty as La Rue drove back to base from Mars 3, Mac felt increasing nausea stalking him. He had little doubt that Gina was not a member of the Mars 3 crew. The very thought tightened the already multiple knots in his stomach.

Who was this woman, and what was she doing on Mars 3? How did she get there? Was she a stowaway? Impossible without a lot of outside help, but from whom? Someone in Houston—or worse, someone here at the base? What about the Mars 3 crew? Did she murder all eight of them? If so, why?

Get a grip on yourself! Mac looked out the front window at Mars base glowing in the golden sunset on the Grand Arroyo Plains. If Gina was a stowaway and had outside help, then he faced a conspiracy situation. But to what end? He had to talk to someone, but who could he trust? He looked to the back seat where Judy and Rechenko sat. He had known Victor most of his career, but how well? He turned to Judy, who was lying back with her eyes closed. If he couldn't trust her, he couldn't trust anyone.

Lt. Michael Traveres paced nervously inside Habitat 2 by Matty's airlock door, thinking of the best way to broach a sensitive subject with Mac. His commander hadn't been in the best of moods today. It had started with the aborted simulation on the first launch test. Mac reacted angrily to the engine failure Traveres had written into the program. While the subsequent simulations ran smoothly, Mac had been uncharacteristically short with the crew in general and Traveres in particular. This would make their conversation all the more difficult.

A chime sounded as the indicator light above the airlock changed from red to green. The hatch swung opened and La Rue slipped out of the tunnel.

"So, is dinner ready yet? I'm starving!"

"Almost, Damon. They've been cooking all day. We eat in half an hour."

Rechenko climbed out next. The airlock tunnel connected to Matty was six feet long and only three feet in diameter, making it a tight maneuver for the large Russian.

"Let the celebration begin!" he said, obviously in a mood to party.

Traveres helped him out and waited for the next person to come out, but the chime sounded again, indicating that Matty was ready to undock from the airlock.

"What's going on?" Traveres said. "What are they doing?"

Rechenko closed the airlock hatch, allowing Matty to release from the other side.

"Mac and Judy wanted to go for a final drive on Mars together," Rechenko said. "I think they want a little private time before the big party tonight. Kind of romantic, yes?"

Traveres bowed his head in frustration. His conversation with Mac would have to wait.

After releasing Matty from the airlock, Mac drove down Highway One a short distance and turned up a side road that led to an overlook called "Sunset Ridge." This spot was a favorite for the crew because it looked out on the base and the landing area on the Grand Arroyo plains. Mac brought Matty to a stop, and he and Judy looked across the rust-colored terrain. With the setting sun, Mars 3, and the fuel processor were clearly visible. The metal and composite structures were a stark contrast to the surrounding barren red horizon.

Since they were launching in two days, this was probably their last sunset on this ridge together. They took a moment to savor the bright reds and oranges of the Mars landscape before Judy spoke. "You know, as much as I miss the colors and sweet smell of Earth, I know I'm going to miss this place. I will always have fond memories of our time here because of you." She turned her gaze from the sunset to him. "I only hope our love will survive whatever we have to face back on Earth."

Mac took a deep breath. "Judy, I have to show you something...that is...I want your opinion on something."

Judy sat up, giving him a quizzical look. "I noticed something was on your mind. You've been acting funny all day. What's the big secret? You going to ask me to marry you?"

Mac let out a nervous chuckle. "I only wish it was something that simple, but it's not."

"Wow, this is serious," Judy recoiled in her seat. "What's the matter Mac? Just tell me."

"No, I'll show you." Mac opened up the computer and inserted the silver disk. "Look very closely at the crew. This is the last transmission we received from Mars 3, three months ago. You remember it?"

She looked closely at the screen as Rusty introduced his crew. *"This is Dr. Katie Thompson, and next to her is Gina Gibson, our chief botanist..."*

"Yeah, I remember this. That was the day before we lost contact with them, and with Earth."

"Look carefully...at the crew."

Judy stared at the screen for a moment, then squinted and leaned forward for a closer look. Mac could tell she was counting the crew. "Oh my God! That's not Gina!" She stiffened in the chair and her mouth hung open. "How can she not be there, Mac? That's impossible..., isn't it?"

"Yes, you'd think so, but how do you explain that woman back at the base? Rusty introduced a Gina Gibson, but it's not the Gina we know."

"How did she get on Mars 3? Is she a stowaway? How is that possible?"

"With a lot of help, that's how. She would have had help getting to the space station where Mars 3 was docked. Then someone would have had to help her on board Mars 3. I think she might have been part of the launch prep crew that had access to every part of Mars 3. After their work was done, she stayed behind, probably hiding in the radiation chamber for several days before the crew launched."

"You mean to say she just lucked out when the solar alert hit, making her the only survivor?" Judy asked.

"No, I think it's worse than that."

"How can it be worse?"

Mac called up Gina's biography and photo on screen. "Remember this picture? I showed it to you the other day."

"Yes, I remember. That barely looks like her, but she'd lost a lot of weight and body mass. But in this picture of the crew, I don't think that's her, no matter how much weight she'd lost."

"I agree, so who put this picture in our computer file?" Watching Judy trying to process this turn of events actually relieved some of the burden Mac felt while dealing with this on his own.

"You think someone here at the base is helping her?"

"Possibly."

Judy stared right into his eyes. "Someone on our crew?"

"I don't want to believe it, but that's what it looks like," Mac said. "There's a chance Gina, or whatever her name is, isn't working alone. Somebody here altered the files, somebody with computer skills and the time to do it."

"Couldn't Gina have done it after she arrived?"

"I thought about that, but I called her file up the day after we found her. How would she have accessed a computer and changed her photo so quickly? The only explanation I can think of is that she had help here. And who knows more about altering files than any of us?"

Judy closed her eyes and shook her head as if she didn't want to hear what she was about to say. "Traveres?"

"He's my first choice. But it could go deeper than just Gina and him. We have to look at reasons behind this ruse. Why would she murder the Mars 3 crew? What is her purpose here? I think it goes without saying that we are all in grave danger."

"Wait a minute. If Gina killed everyone on board Mars 3, then you're saying there was no solar event, that...that Earth is okay?"

"I think that's a good possibility."

Tears welled up in Judy's eyes as she clasped her hands together. "Oh Mac, you mean my family is okay? I can't believe it. After all these months of worrying, this could all be just a charade?"

"Let's not get ahead of ourselves, Judy. Right now that scenario is impossible to verify. I tried to use the Mars 3 radio to contact Earth today, but it wasn't working. I couldn't even uplink to the mother ship or the DSLR. If Traveres is involved, he could be jamming any radio signal so we can't send or receive."

Judy shook her head as if she didn't want to believe. "Traveres...he's the communications expert. Oh my God, Angela will be devastated."

Mac raised an eyebrow. "Who's to say Angela isn't part of the conspiracy?"

"Beep!" The intercom tone made them both jump as Angela's voice boomed over the speaker. "Hey, you guys. Wha'cha doing up there? Making out?" Her voice was barely audible over the sounds of laughter and celebrating in the background. "You guys hurry up and finish whatever it is you're doing. Dinner's almost ready and you're missing cocktails." The intercom cut out with a thud.

"She can't hear us, can she?"

Mac looked around. "Nothing's on, unless they're bugging us."

Judy leaned forward, almost to the point of putting her head between her knees. She took a couple of deep breaths and rocked back and forth. "I can't believe Angela would be involved in a conspiracy against the mission. I just refuse to believe it."

"Judy, hear me out on this. I've had all day to think about this. Look at the people who are staying here and the ones who are leaving. That is the most likely split on who is and who isn't a conspirator. Who volunteered to stay? Boyle was adamant about remaining here. No surprise there, especially since he's the one who's producing all those intricate holograms on how bad Earth's been damaged by the solar event. I wouldn't trust him for anything. And the two military men, Traveres and Ivory, have handled all the communications. Maybe they're just following orders."

"And Angela?" Tears started to roll down Judy's face.

Mac reached out and squeezed her hand. "She was the most insistent of all about staying. I'm afraid she can't be trusted either. Not now."

"She just wants to be with Michael," Judy's voice trailed off, and then she buried her face in her hands.

Mac looked out the window at Mars base, already in the shadow of darkness. "One thing I don't understand is why? Why would you eliminate an entire crew and put on a ruse like this. The loss of Mars 3 will effectively end the Mars program. Is someone hell-bent on halting exploration here?"

"What are we going to do, Mac? What can we do?"

"The first thing we do is return to base and act like nothing's wrong. We have to observe everyone's behavior and see if we can figure out whether anyone is working with Gina. It could be that she's working alone. I just don't know. I have to have more evidence. I'm going to do something tonight after dinner."

"What?" Judy sat up and grabbed his arm. "Don't do anything foolish. I don't want to lose you."

"Don't worry. After everyone's asleep I'll go to the bridge and access the communications console to see whether I can figure out if our radio signals are being jammed. Maybe I can contact Earth."

"Beep!" The intercom tone sounded and they could hear more laughter, glasses clinking, loud conversation, and then, the haunting voice of Gina Gibson.

"Hi, you two, just wanted to let you know, your dinner's ready."

CHAPTER 16
THE LAST SUPPER

Mac and Judy walked into an unexpected scene in the galley. Rechenko had traditional Russian folk music blaring as he tried to demonstrate dance steps to Angela and Traveres, who giggled uncontrollably as they faced each other. Boyle and La Rue were also quite a sight as they danced about the room in an awkward embrace, attempting to keep pace with the rhythm. Meanwhile, Gina and Ivory moved in perfect choreography, spinning and twirling as they placed platters of food on the neatly set table.

Mac felt a twinge of guilt that he could suspect any of his hardworking crew, his family for the past two years, of any treasonous behavior. He felt Judy squeeze his hand, and the weak smile on her face mirrored his thoughts.

"Let's enjoy this final night together with everyone," she said under her breath.

Mac leaned to her ear and whispered, "I'll keep an open mind."

"Sit! Let's all sit down!" Rechenko shouted from across the galley. "Our guest of honor is here! We can eat!" Everyone gave a collective cheer as Boyle, Angela, Traveres, and Rechenko took their places at the dinner table. Mac poured himself a glass of wine and sat down next to Judy. She laid her head on his shoulder.

Ivory and Gina came to the table, he carrying a large bowl of fresh salad, she a tray of piping hot bread.

Dr. Boyle stood proudly before everyone and toasted. "To those departing on Mars 3, this is your farewell dinner! Enjoy!"

"Before we eat, I'd like to ask you all to bow your heads for a brief blessing." Mac said.

Everyone joined hands and lowered their heads respectfully.

"Dear Almighty God," he started. "Bless this food you have so graciously provided for us. And bless those who toiled so hard to prepare this final feast we are about to share as one crew." Mac stopped for a moment. He felt a lump in his throat as thoughts of saying goodbye hit him hard. Judy squeezed his hand.

"Thank you for guiding us and keeping us safe from harm and danger this past year. Please protect us as we embark on a most difficult and dangerous chapter in this noble mission. We humbly ask for your wisdom and guidance as we are faced with important and difficult decisions in the coming weeks. We beseech Thee to watch over us as we walk hand in hand amidst the dangers that surround us. As I relinquish my responsibility for the crew remaining here...," he paused again as his voice cracked, "...I ask you to shield them from any harm that may come their way. In all your power and glory, Amen."

"Amen," everyone responded. Mac could see tears in Judy's and Angela's eyes as they looked at each other. Rechenko had his hands over his face, hiding his red, swollen eyes.

"My, my, Commander, those are some touching words for a career military man," Boyle said. "If I may so humbly salute the first crew of Mars Base!" he began. "It has been an honor to be associated with each of you. We have faced incredible dangers; indeed there may be many more trials and tribulations to go before we're done. I would especially like to thank our brave Commander MacTavish, to whom we all owe our lives. It is through his leadership that we have succeeded in building this wonderful base. Cheers!"

"Cheers! Salute! Strovia!" they responded.

There were several more toasts throughout the night, each crew member taking a turn to express his or her feelings. Mac was heartened as Boyle and La Rue put their differences aside and joked with each other, and even Gina and Ivory laughed the evening away with their crewmates.

The magical evening left Mac wishing he were mistaken about Gina. After all his crew had been through together, saying goodbye tonight was overwhelming. By the end of the evening, he had purged any thoughts of betrayal from all but Gina. She still remained a mystery.

As the party broke up, Mac walked with Judy, anxious to hear her impressions of the evening. Before they could leave the galley, Traveres intercepted them. "Commander, I haven't had an opportunity to apologize for the initial launch program I wrote. I should have warned you about the abort test."

Poor Traveres, Mac thought. He had been short and demanding and outright rude to his right-hand man all afternoon.

"Forget it, Lieutenant," Mac said as he gave Traveres a slap on the shoulder. "I've been distracted for the past couple of days. You were right to put the abort test in the launch program. I should have reacted better."

"If you want, we could run the 'RLS' program tomorrow for our final rehearsal."

Mac knew Traveres had probably worked hard on his Return to Launch Site (RLS) and he didn't want to seem ungrateful. "If we have time, but my main priority tomorrow will be the rendezvous simulation. I think I need more work on that."

"Of course, sir. Good night."

Mac waited until they got to his quarters before asking Judy, "So what are your thoughts about tonight?"

"I saw a lot of love and sincerity around the dinner table," she said. "Even Gina seemed normal and approachable."

"I feel the same way. I sat there tonight and felt ashamed I could suspect the crew of some kind of conspiracy. But that still doesn't answer why Gina is not on the image of the Mars 3 crew transmission. I can't leave here until I'm convinced she not a stowaway, an imposter, or a murderer."

"I know what she is!" Judy grabbed Mac's upper arms as she knelt on the bed. "She's an alien!" She made her eyes bulge and hissed at him before she rolled back on the bed laughing.

Mac watched her and sighed. "I think you've had too much wine. You'd better get some sleep."

"Aren't you coming to bed?"

"No, I'm going to check on some things. I'll be up late. Get some sleep. We have a big day tomorrow."

After two hours of searching through computer files in the middle of the night, Mac was ready to give up. He placed both elbows on the bridge console, leaned over, and ran his fingers through his scalp. After reviewing pages of data, he saw no evidence of any tampering with the communications network to Earth. Auto log entries clearly showed Traveres' ongoing efforts to re-establish contact with anyone who may be listening.

But what about Gina? He called up the frozen image of the Mars 3 crew again with Gina's picture and bio next to it. Was she lying to him? Was she ready to betray them all?

Betrayal, particularly from a woman, stirred up deep, painful emotions from Mac. He leaned back, closed his eyes and let his mind wander to the one woman in his life who epitomized the ultimate betrayal: Magdalena, his beautiful cousin in Mexico. The last time he had seen her was thirty years ago, atop the great Pyramid of the Sun in Teotihuacan. He had asked her to marry him, and she had said yes.

The euphoria they shared on top of the Pyramid of the Sun quickly disappeared when they revealed their plans to Uncle Guillermo. He reacted with anger and accusations. He screamed of Mac's disloyalty. "Shame on you!" he yelled. "You bring dishonor to your family and to mine! You cannot marry your cousin! I forbid it!"

In the face of his uncle's anger and hate, Mac had stood his ground. "We are not asking for your permission, sir," Mac had said. "We are adults. We've made our decision and we are going through with it no matter what you think."

Consumed by rage, his uncle ordered Mac to leave and never return. Not to be derailed, Mac continued his defiant tone. "I will leave as you ask, but I will return for her. Make no mistake about that."

Uncle Guillermo got in the last word as Mac walked out the door. "It is you who are mistaken, my foolish nephew!"

Mac returned to the United States, but not before arranging to rendezvous with Magdalena on top of the great pyramid in two weeks. That would give her father time to calm down, and she would have a chance to slip away.

When he returned to Santa Monica, his mother greeted him with mixed feelings. She told him she knew they were very much in love and she was happy for them, but she worried about how their marriage would affect her relationship with her brother. In the end, she supported Mac's decision to return to Mexico to bring back his bride. As usual, his father said little, only advising him to be absolutely sure that is what he wanted.

When Mac returned to Teotihuacán, full of excitement and anticipation, the red glow of the setting Sun added to the warmth in his heart. Eager to see what Magdalena had carefully chosen to wear to their fateful rendez-vous, he quickly climbed to the summit of the great pyramid. His excitement subsided when he reached the top only to discover Magdalena had not yet arrived.

Mac searched for his love among the scores of tourists making the trek up the pyramid to see the sunset. His heart pounded with anticipation, confident she would be in the next crowd of people. But as the sun continued to drop, Mac's disappointment grew. Then, through the crowd, he saw a familiar face. Uncle Guillermo, not Magdalena, was walking toward him.

"Where is she?" Mac demanded. "Where is Magdalena?"

His uncle shook his head, reached in his pocket, and pulled out an envelope. "You are a fool!" he said, handing Mac the envelope. "You do not understand what is going on here. This is bigger than you."

Mac opened the envelope and found a note inside. He instantly recognized Magdalena's handwriting, but he wondered if the words were hers.

My Beloved Cousin,

I am so ashamed. I fear I have misled you to this awkward and unfortunate situation. I let you fall in love with me and allowed you to believe I had done the same. I am sorry to say this is not true. I have a way of life here I could never leave. I know you have a life in California and will some day become a famous pilot.

You must believe I am speaking of my own free will. I am so sorry if I have caused you any unnecessary pain. You must know I will always cherish the time we spent together.

Magdalena

Mac stood frozen in front of his uncle. He knew in his heart that Magdalena had written the note. Overcome with despair, his shock turned to sorrow—for himself and for what he had put his family through.

His uncle spoke again, this time in a lecturing tone. "Now go home, my foolish nephew. And let this be a lesson to you. In life things are not always what they appear to be." He turned and walked away, leaving Mac at the top of the great pyramid just as the sun disappeared behind the mountains.

Mac opened his eyes and caught himself. He had fallen asleep on the bridge thinking about that fateful summer, many years ago. In a way, Magdalena's betrayal had been a blessing to him. After the events in Mexico, he started the Air Force Academy and immersed himself in his studies to ease his pain. He buried himself in work, avoiding long-term romantic relationships for years.

This dedication helped accelerate his career in the Air Force. And most important of all, if he had married Magdalena he would never have met Judy. He sat up and stared at Gina's picture on the computer screen. "Who are you?" he said out loud.

"Come back, don't leave me…" Mac stiffened in fright as he felt a hand slide from the end of his shoulder to the nape of his neck. He whirled around and saw Gina staring at him.

"I'm sorry. Did I frighten you, Commander?"

Mac's heart pounded as he caught his breath. "Gina, what are you doing here?"

"I couldn't sleep. In fact, I haven't slept very much since I've been here. I mostly wander like a ghost in the night, haunting the corridors of the base."

Mac raised an eyebrow at her and thought about Judy's comment about Gina being an alien.

"I'm joking, Commander," she squeezed his arm and left her hand there. "You can see I'm not a ghost. You can feel my grip, can't you?" She squeezed again, harder this time.

"Gina," Mac said, pulling away. "Yes, I know you're not a ghost, but why did you say those words right now?"

"You mean, 'Come back, don't leave me'?"

Her voice sent a chill through him. "Yes, why did you repeat that again?"

"Oh, I just remembered what I said over the radio the night you rescued me. You see, I had no memory of that night until recently, when it all started flooding back to me. I'm sorry if it has haunted you. Maybe I really am a ghost," she smiled.

"No, I think you're real enough."

"My God, is that really me?" Looking at the computer screen, Gina plopped on to the arm of the chair, practically sitting on his lap. "I look completely different than my picture, don't I?"

"Yes, as a matter a fact, I have noticed that."

"I've lost so much weight, and my hair is longer and straighter. Not all bunched up like it does when I'm weightless."

Mac watched as she put her hand out to the image of the Mars 3 crew. She ran her fingers over each one of their faces and sighed. "I miss them so much. Why was I the only survivor?" She dropped her hand to Mac's thigh and leaned back against his chest.

The warmth of her body against his stirred a forbidden fire deep inside that he couldn't ignore. Was she coming on to him, or did she just need to be held as she worked through her pain? He reached around and gave her a reassuring hug. "Things happen for a reason, Gina."

An alarm broke the quiet on the bridge. Mac jumped, pushing Gina away before he realized this wasn't a base-wide alarm but a detection warning from the meteorological science station. He heard someone coming up the ladder. The lights came on as Ivory stepped onto the flight deck.

His second lieutenant flinched with surprise when he saw Mac and Gina on the bridge. "Good evening, Commander," he said, walking to the console. "I'll just be a second. I want to check this alarm."

Before Mac could respond, Traveres bounded up the ladder and entered the bridge. He reacted with the same surprise as Ivory when he saw Mac and Gina. "Good evening, Commander," he said. "Is everything all right?"

"Yes, I'm just catching up on a little work."

"What do we have?" Traveres asked, looking over Ivory's shoulder.

"It looks like the mother-ship radar has detected an increase in high wind activity to the northeast of us about five hundred miles," he answered.

"A red storm? What direction is it moving?" Traveres asked.

"It's moving due south. If it stays on that course, it should just skirt our perimeter in about a week."

"Well, let's hope it doesn't shift. That looks like one hell of a blow," Traveres said.

The team work between his two lieutenants impressed Mac. Watching them made him feel confident about leaving them in charge of the base.

"We're all through here, sir," Ivory said respectfully. "It was just a red storm warning—nothing to be concerned about."

"I'm also done, gentlemen." Mac said before he turned and looked at Gina. "Let's all have a good night's sleep. We have a big day tomorrow."

Mac slipped into bed beside Judy and closed his eyes. It had been a long, stressful day. As he dozed off to sleep, he tried to put his mind at rest about Gina. He decided he would reveal his concerns about her to Dr. Boyle after he and the returning crew were settled inside Mars 3 for their flight back home. It was the least he could do.

As he fell deeper into sleep, he started to dream. He found himself at the base of the great Pyramid of the Sun in Teotihuacán. The past evening's thoughts had entered into his dream. He looked up to the top of the pyramid, knowing she waited for him. He'd had this dream before. As usual, he floated effortlessly up the steps of the pyramid to the summit where he found his beautiful Magdalena waiting for him. Her long dark hair and flowing dress blew in the breeze.

The glow of the sunset included an unmistakable tinge of Martian red. Magdalena turned toward him and put her arms out to hold him. He grabbed her and held her tight to his chest. It had been nearly thirty years since her betrayal, but he still had deep feelings for her.

As always, she spoke to him in his dream without moving her lips. This time she grabbed his hand and said, "Come with me. I have something to show you." She led him to the edge of the great pyramid.

Looking over the side, he saw a sheer cliff that dropped off to a rust-colored landscape. The familiar Martian terrain stretched to the far horizon as the sun set, not over Mexico but over the Grand Arroyo plains. Standing on the edge of the pyramid, he gazed down upon Mars Base from the perspective of Sunset Ridge where he and Judy had parked last night.

Still holding her hand, he turned to Magdalena, but she was no longer with him. Instead, he was holding the hand of his Uncle Guillermo! His uncle looked at him with that familiar evil grin while clutching Mac's hand tightly. "I told you you're a fool," he said. "Things are not what they appear!" Pulling Mac with a strong tug, they both fell off the edge of the pyramid. Mac suddenly found himself several thousand feet above ground, falling toward Mars Base.

He tried to brace himself. That reaction woke him up, and he lay twitching in his bed. He exhaled loudly, waking up Judy.

"Are you okay?" she said in a deep throaty voice. "Did you have a bad dream?"

"I'm sorry," he said, out of breath. "It was a bit of a nightmare. It...it's nothing. Go back to sleep."

"Are you're sure you're all right?"

Mac lay back on his pillow, emitting a deep exhale. "No, I'm not at all sure."

CHAPTER 17
FAREWELL

7:30 A.M.

Strolling arm in arm with Angela through the thick rows of vegetation in Habitat 2, Judy savored the moment. This was their final morning walk together, and she felt the lump building in her throat. She had so much she wanted to say—words of friendship, encouragement, and caution. "You're like a sister to me, Angela. If Doctor Boyle is right and the Earth is returning to normal, then I'm looking forward to going on a shopping spree in San Francisco with you when this is all over."

"That would be great!" Angela said with a wide grin. "And I can't wait to go horse-back riding with you on your ranch in Colorado."

"That's a date." Judy could feel the tears welling up in her eyes. "Only a few more hours before I go."

Angela tightened her hold. "I wish we didn't have to say goodbye. I hate goodbyes. We have to stop talking like this. I'm already a mess and we haven't even had breakfast!" Tears rolled down her face. "I've learned so much from you, Judy. I hope you realize what an important person you've become in my life."

"You've learned from me? Not half as much as I've learned from you! You're an incredible person, Angela—very unique, very special. And you seem to have found a wonderful man to share your love. What could be better?"

"What could be better?" Angela wiped the tears from her face. "We could all be going home together with no catastrophic solar event destroying half the world. Michael and I could be getting married in a church in San Francisco with you as my maid of honor."

"That will happen soon enough. You'll be home before you know it."

"That's if there is a home to return to," Angela said, rolling her watery eyes.

Judy lowered her voice to a whisper. "I've wanted to talk to you about Gina."

"Gina? What about her?"

"Look, I know you guys get along pretty well, and I think that's great, but I just want to caution you."

"Why? She didn't hit someone else, did she?"

"No, nothing like that. I just wanted to warn you to keep an eye on her behavior. You'll be the chief medical officer for the Mars Base crew after I leave. It's your responsibility to monitor not only the physical but the mental well-being of the crew. If you think anyone is becoming a danger to the rest, you need to take appropriate action."

"Don't worry, I'll do my best. I'm ready for this, really."

Judy sighed and nodded in agreement. "I know you are. Forgive me for trying to 'mother' you one more time before I leave."

They embraced again but were startled by a figure near the entrance to the habitat. Gina Gibson stood at the doorway, staring at them. She walked toward them with a somber look on her face, and said, "It must be very difficult for the two of you to leave each other after being through so much together."

Judy fidgeted nervously, wondering whether Gina had heard her warning to Angela. "Yes, it...it is difficult," she stammered. "We've become very close."

Gina looked straight into Judy's eyes. "Don't worry about Angela. I'll keep an eye on her."

7:50 A.M.

Michael Traveres sat in front of the bridge flight computer, inputting the day's final simulation programs. Excitement and anticipation had replaced the pressure and stress he had felt earlier in the week. This would be a pivotal day in his career. As the new commander of Mars Base, he and he alone would shoulder the responsibility for the safety and well-being of the crew.

He ran a check on all Mars 3 systems. The spacecraft was ready for its simulation runs as Mac expected. He looked around to make sure no one was nearby. Then he typed in his code. Once the security program let him in, he worked swiftly, verifying he had control of all Mars 2 systems. Then he limited the main-frame access terminals and wireless connections. Next, he encrypted all base systems and microwave uplink programs, giving him complete remote control of Ratty and Matty.

Finally, he checked the uplink to the orbiting mother ship and completed the link to Mars 3's main computer. He looked at the text on the computer.

Ready to run encrypted program?

He pressed 'yes'.

Encryption program running, the computer verified.

Traveres looked up at the clock and smiled. It was a few minutes before eight in the morning. He was ahead of schedule. With a simple keystroke, he set into motion his secret plan. With all systems at Mars Base under his control, he had reached the point of no return. He had one more item to check before he was through. He slid open the drawer directly under the console to make sure his emergency oxygen mask was still there. It was.

8:15 A.M.

Mac looked around the table at his crew finishing their final breakfast together, and searched for some appropriate words. "Since we all said our goodbyes last night, I won't bore you with any speeches. I would like to remind you that Dr. Rechenko has prepared a small plaster slab for the departing crew to sign before we leave. Perhaps that will be the start of a tradition that will last for generations.

"As far as this morning's crew assignments go, Lieutenant Ivory will drive Matty for us and conduct a final exterior inspection of Mars 3. Judy and Damon will continue to secure the galley and ready room for tomorrow's launch while Victor and I work on flight preparations. At approximately one o'clock this afternoon, we will commence a final launch and docking simulation. I don't want to go more than two and a half to three hours on simulation. It's more important that we don't burn ourselves out for tomorrow's launch."

"Yes sir," Traveres answered smartly.

"Our launch window opens tomorrow at ten-seventeen. I expect to launch at exactly ten-thirty-five. Now, let's enjoy this last breakfast together, and we'll meet at the airlock at nine-fifteen for a short departure ceremony."

"Commander, if I may," Boyle spoke up. "I'd like to report some good news."

"Of course, Doctor. I can always use some good news."

"Thank you, Commander. I just wanted everyone to know I took some thermal readings of Earth, and I am happy to report that the planet surface temperature has, with a few exceptions, returned to normal. The only anomaly is an unusually high concentration of storm activity out in the Pacific."

"That is good news, Doctor!" Mac's face erupted into a rare grin. "Perhaps there will be someone to greet us upon our return."

9:10 A.M.

Mac stared at the two sealed envelopes on his desk in his quarters, one addressed to Traveres, the other to Dr. Boyle. He still wasn't sure about Gina Gibson, so he decided to warn Traveres and Boyle to keep a close eye on her.

Picking up his duffel bag, he gave his Commander quarters one more glance and left on his final base-wide inspection. This had become a tradition for him when commanding space station missions. He always went through the entire station just before he left, giving him a sense of accomplishment and closure for the mission.

Walking through the mid-deck, he dropped the envelopes inside the appropriate desks. Next, he climbed the ladder to the bridge and gave the flight deck the once-over. He had spent a lot of time in that pilot's chair; and regardless of the circumstances, giving up command of Mars 2 wasn't easy.

Climbing down the ladder to the lower level, he realized that he felt guilty over leaving half his crew behind. In a way, he should be the last one to leave, but his years of experience and his piloting skills would be needed to successfully bring Mars 3 back to Earth safely.

After inspecting the galley and ready room, he walked down the airlock tunnel to Habitat I. Inside, he found a mountain of tools and equipment. This was the staging area, machine shop, office, and headquarters for the exploration and settling of Mars.

It was a typical working environment with cables and torches and half-opened components strewn about the room. It made him think about what he had missed by not being able to spend more time with Boyle and Ivory and La Rue as they went out on their various excursions. These men were the real Mars explorers, the ones who mapped the Grand Arroyo, created Highway One, and wrote the book on Martian survival.

He felt a twinge of regret over the missed opportunities. He could only take solace in the fact that his willingness to administer the day-to-day operations allowed the rest of the crew the time and freedom to do what they did best.

As he left Habitat I, he realized that he had not seen a single person throughout his inspection. He hurried down the airlock tunnel through the double doors to Habitat 2 and stopped in his tracks. Lined up by Matty's airlock stood the entire crew staring back at him. They all shared the same serious look. He started to say something, but they spoke first.

"Atten...hut!" Traveres ordered as they all snapped to attention.

"Commence singing!"

"For he's a jolly good fellow, for he's a jolly good fellow!" The crew started to sing to him as smiles broke out on all their faces.

Mac bit his lower lip to prevent himself from breaking down. Tears welled up as he looked for an escape from the emotional tidal wave.

As they finished singing, they let out a tremendous cheer, and Mac started to laugh. "That was terrible! One more verse and I'm sure you would have cracked some panels on the habitat!"

They converged on him with congratulations, hugs, and slaps on the back. As they quieted down, Gina stepped forward and held up something in her hands. "Commander, please accept this as a token of my appreciation for all you've done for me," she said, handing him a small medallion. "This is a St. Christopher's medal. He is the patron saint of safe travel. He will help protect you and ensure you a safe flight home. I wore this around my neck throughout my journey here. I prayed to St. Christopher every day and he helped see me through."

Choked with emotion, Mac avoided looking up at Gina as he uttered a barely audible "Thank you."

Next, Ivory held up what appeared to be a red Martian rock with some white marks on it. "Commander, this is a little something to remind you of your stay here—in particular, to remind you of *my* stay here. As you can see, this rock is scored with the white paint from Matty's high-gain dish. This is the rock that took out that antenna during our ill-advised explosion experiment."

Mac chuckled as he took the rock from Ivory's hand. "Thank you, Lieutenant. I'll be sure to leave that entire incident out of my mission report."

"Thank you, sir," Ivory said, as he shook Mac's hand. "Good luck on your journey home."

Dr. Boyle spoke up next, holding up a computer disk. "Commander, I would like to present you with this personal journal of our mission. I think it appropriate that you take this with you, and please read it. It contains much about the quality of your leadership and skills as commander of this mission. And may I add on a personal note, that it has been an honor to serve under you. Best of luck on your flight home."

"Thank you, Doctor. I deeply appreciated your help and wise counsel."

Angela stepped forward and handed him an audio disk. In a trembling voice, she spoke softly: "Commander, I know how you always enjoyed the mini-concerts Christopher and I gave at night here in the habitat. I made a recording and it came out great. Please think of me and your pleasant memories here when you listen to this." She reached out and hugged him tightly.

He held on to her and whispered in her ear. "Thank you, Angela. Take care of yourself."

Finally, Traveres stepped forward. "Commander, I would like to present you with your favorite deck of cards—the one you used to beat us all at poker. The cards have the Mars 2 mission emblem on the back. Their return to Earth with you will serve as a symbolic completion of the Mars 2 mission."

Mac reached out and gave Traveres a hug and a slap on the back. Turning to his crew, he spoke in as strong a voice as he could muster. "As of this moment, I officially relinquish my responsibilities as Commander of Mars Base to Lieutenant Commander Michael Traveres." Everyone broke into spontaneous applause as Mac shook Traveres' hand.

"Commander, you must come and sign your name before the plaster dries," Rechenko said. Mac noticed another plaster patch with the names of the Mars 3 crew that had perished in space. He reached out and fingered Rusty's name to say goodbye before he turned to the Mars 2 patch and signed his own name under the title.

Ivory opened the airlock tunnel to Matty, and Judy climbed in first, followed by Rechenko, La Rue, and Ivory. Mac turned to Traveres, snapped to attention, and saluted. "Permission to disembark, Lieutenant Commander."

"Permission granted," he answered.

With that, Mac climbed into the airlock, taking what he considered his first steps toward Earth.

12:50 P.M.

Mac sat on the flight deck of Mars 3 and looked out the window at Ivory, who had just completed his final inspection of the external fuel lines. While he appreciated his deliberate approach, Mac's concern about falling behind schedule grew. He and Rechenko still had several hours of simulator practice to complete, and he was getting anxious.

"Commander, everything looks nominal from here. I recommend you keep the valves primed. That should prevent them from freezing up tonight."

"I copy, Lieutenant. Is there anything else? We really need to start the sim-program."

"No, Commander, I'm finished here. I will return to base. Have a good flight, and good luck."

Mac called Traveres immediately. The complicated rendezvous program ran forty minutes, and once it was started, completing it in real time was necessary. "Base to Mars 3," Traveres called. "Commander, are you ready to get started?"

"Affirmed, Base," Mac answered. "Hold on to your hat; we have a lot of work to do."

3:00 P.M.

Angela had kept busy all day working in the Habitat 2 garden, but she already missed Judy and Mac. She knew she would never be that close to Gina so she now focused her attention on her work and on Michael. The next two years, she told herself, would be wonderful with him. She smiled as she thought back to his amorous behavior this morning. Drifting off into a daydream, Angela flinched in surprise when she discovered Gina standing a few feet away. She jumped back, thinking she must have been deep in thought not to have heard her approach. "Gina, you scared me!" She noticed that Gina looked different somehow, as if her shyness had melted away.

"So, how about a little exercise?" Gina asked, holding up the sticks they had sparred with before.

"Oh, no thank you, Gina," she answered, bewildered by the odd request. "Besides, I don't think we're supposed to do that anymore. Commander's orders."

Gina pressed on. "Well, in case you haven't noticed, your boyfriend's the commander now. I don't think he'll mind us doing a little sparring." Gina tried to hand her the stick.

Angela quickly stood up, trying to put some distance between the two of them, but Gina continued to move closer. Angela thought back to Judy's words of caution about Gina's behavior. "Gina, I do not want to spar, so please don't ask me again!" she shouted, her face turning red. "I'm going to my quarters!"

Angela managed to maneuver around Gina and head for the exit. To her relief, she saw Ivory standing by the habitat entrance. He would be able to talk some sense into Gina, she thought.

"Christopher! Am I ever glad to see you!" she said, walking briskly toward him.

"What's the matter? Don't you want to spar with Gina?"

Angela stopped in her tracks. A chill came over her as she listened to him. He, too, sounded and acted different—cockier, not his usual reserved self.

Ivory held up another fighting stick and threw it at her so she had no choice but to catch it. "Your weapon," he said.

From behind, Gina threw the second stick she was holding to Ivory, and they both assumed a classic attack position.

Angela clumsily turned back and forth between Gina and Ivory, not sure whom to face. Fear began to grip her body. *What's wrong with these two? Are they just playing a joke on me?*

"I am not going to fight!" she said, lowering her stick. "Leave me alone!"

"Raise your weapon and defend yourself!" Ivory's voice was deep and cold. In an instant he sprang at her with an overhead jab. Angela instinctively raised her stick and easily blocked his swing. From her right, Gina cried out, unleashing a series of strikes. As Angela blocked these, the sharp crack of their sticks echoed through the habitat.

"Why aren't you countering?" Ivory demanded, taunting Angela as he circled around her. "You should counter at the very least!"

Angela breathed heavily in and out. Adrenaline coursed through her veins and her mind raced. She felt like a child alone in a schoolyard confronted by two bullies when no one was around to help her. *I must get to the exit!* she thought.

Ivory and Gina continued to circle her, trapping her in the middle of the habitat, no matter how she tried to maneuver. Then she noticed another figure standing by the door. It was Dr. Boyle! *Maybe he can help me!* she thought. But he just stood there, reading a piece of paper he held in one hand. He held an open envelope in the other.

Gina screamed again and charged, forcing Angela to block several strikes. Ivory then picked up the assault with several close body jabs. Angela blocked most of them, but Ivory managed to strike her in the kidneys. She looked at Boyle, who now watched passively, as if nothing unusual was happening. Her heart sank.

Exhausted, she tried her best not to cry, but the blatant betrayal weighed heavily on her. She felt utterly alone. Her tears flowed, nearly blinding her as Gina and Ivory started their next assault. Ivory came at her first and managed to hit her shoulder with a forceful blow that almost knocked her off her feet. Gina followed up with rapid-fire jabs and a roundhouse swing that caught Angela on the knee, sending her to the ground grimacing in pain. Already breathless and paralyzed by fear, she succumbed to her tormentors.

Ivory and Gina continued to circle her, maintaining their attack position. She felt like a wounded animal surrounded by hungry predators. Boyle stepped forward and yelled, "Don't hit her in the face! I don't want any unnecessary suspicion!"

After hearing those words, Angela knew she was about to die.

CHAPTER 18
THINGS ARE NOT AS THEY APPEAR

3:55 P.M.

Lieutenant Ivory drove Matty over the uncharted terrain, careful not to raise any dust and betray his presence. Weaving around rocks and boulders of all sizes, he approached Mars 3 from its blind side, opposite the flight deck windows where he knew Mac and Rechenko were sitting. He came to a full stop one hundred yards from his destination.

Turning on his receiver, he eavesdropped on the conversation between Mac and Rechenko as they conducted their virtual reality docking simulation. With a clear path before him, he estimated thirty seconds of drive time to the Mars 3 airlock; another minute to hook up and pressurize the connecting tunnel; then the hard part—dragging Angela's limp body from Matty to Mars 3.

4:00 P.M.

"Victor, there it is, right on time!" Looking through his virtual glasses, Mac pointed out the bridge window at the simulated image of the mother ship orbiting in front of them. It appeared as a bright star on the horizon.

"Beautiful," Rechenko answered. "What do we do now?"

"Just stay on course. The computer will do most of the work. I'll take over manually when we're inside fifty meters. That's when it gets intense. I'll need you to call out the data to me as we're closing in for capture."

Mac felt his heart rate jump as he prepared to take over control from the computer. He couldn't afford any distractions. If he failed to complete the docking in the allotted time, he would have to start the forty-minute program from the beginning. It added to the realism of the simulation, and he was anxious to get it done.

As he concentrated on his next series of calculations, the redline alarm went off in his headset. Someone was trying to get hold of him. "What is it?" he snapped, careful to keep focused on the program.

"Commander, I'm sorry to bother you." It was Dr. Boyle.

"Doctor, can this wait? I'm very busy right now," Mac shot back.

"I think not, Commander. I'm afraid we have a bit of an emergency."

"Emergency? What is it?" Mac rolled his eyes. *The timing couldn't be worse*, he thought.

"Well, apparently, about twenty minutes ago Angela went into convulsions. Gina and Lieutenant Ivory tried to stabilize her, but it appears she may have slipped into unconsciousness."

Mac groaned. "Dr. Boyle, I want you to drive over here immediately and pick up Dr. Delaney. Did you hear me? Immediately! I'm going to switch you over to her right now. Do you copy?"

"Commander, Lieutenant Ivory is already on his way, and he's bringing Angela with him."

"What?" Angela was in danger, but he was reluctant to abandon the simulation at its most critical phase. "All right, Doctor. I wouldn't have moved her, but since she's already on her way, I'll alert Judy and have her standing by. What is their ETA?"

"They should arrive within five minutes," Boyle answered.

Christ sakes! Why did they wait so long before they told us? Mac thought, then gritted his teeth as he responded to Boyle. "I copy, Doctor. Mars 3 out."

"Commander, we are at a thousand meters," Rechecko said, referring to the distance to the mother ship. "We are right on course."

"Okay, Victor. Keep an eye. Remember, I want to go manual at fifty meters." Mac keyed the redline to Judy.

"Yes, Mac, go ahead."

"Judy, I just finished talking to Dr. Boyle. We have a problem. Apparently Angela went into convulsions about twenty minutes ago."

"Oh my God!" she interrupted. "I have to go over there right now!"

"It's too late. They're already bringing her here."

"What? That's ridiculous! They shouldn't be moving her. She could have a blood clot or an aneurysm. They could kill her!"

"I know, I know, but she's going to be at the airlock in less than five minutes."

"Five minutes? Those idiots! I swear, Mac, if they've done irreversible damage by moving her...."

As upset as Judy was, Mac knew she was going to explode over what he was about to say next. "Judy, you're going to have to get La Rue to help you with Angela until I'm finished here, okay?"

She did not respond.

"Five hundred meters to target," Rechenko said.

"Judy, I'll be done here in fifteen minutes. I'll be down to help as soon as I can. It's critical that I complete the simulation."

"Goddammit, Mac! This is Angela we're talking about! What the hell's the matter with you?" She shouted so loud he could hear her voice rising up the ladder well.

Mac clenched his teeth, "Dr. Delaney, I'll be down there as soon as I can. Out!"

"You bastard!" she yelled.

He winced. As usual, timing was everything, and right now the doctor had to be with the patient and the pilot had to be with the ship. He focused on the mother ship image looming in front of him.

"A hundred meters, Commander, braking thrusters are firing," Rechenko said. "Slowing to five meters per second."

Did she really call me a bastard? Mac wondered as he was speculating what had happened to Angela. Could it be a result of the concussion? Most likely yes, but considering the mystery with Gina, something more sinister was possible.

"Seventy-five meters. Slowing to three meters per second," Rechenko called out.

The airlock chime on the console in front of Mac sounded, indicating Matty had arrived and was docking with Mars 3. Angela would be on board in a few minutes. He placed his hands on the controls and prepared to disengage the autopilot.

"Sixty meters, two meters forward. Standing by for manual control."

The airlock door chimed and Mac could hear voices emanating from below. He heard Judy giving orders to La Rue as they hurried about the ready room. There were more loud voices and hurried footsteps.

Concentrate.

"Fifty meters, Commander, ready for manual transfer."

"Okay, Victor." Mac gave his full attention to the simulation. "I've got manual control, holding at two meters per second."

Docking two objects traveling thousands of miles an hour through space required a choreography involving a delicate mathematical dance between orbiting bodies. The higher the orbit, the slower the craft moved. The trick was to intercept the mother ship at exactly the right time. When it went right, it was a thing of beauty. But one wrong move could cost time, valuable fuel, and lives. "Forty meters, two meters forward," Rechenko said.

Mac squeezed the thrusters again. "Slowing to one meter forward," he said as he scanned the data stream in front of him.

"Thirty meters."

As he tapped the thruster handle again, he thought he heard the faint voice of Judy yelling his name. Before he could react, the intercom blasted with her voice. "Mac! Come down here! Something's going on."

"What is it? Is Angela all right?"

"No, it's not Angela! It's Ivory. He just left and La Rue went with him!"

"What?" Mac shouted, too stunned to move. "Are you sure?"

"Goddammit, Mac! They both went into the airlock and sealed the door before I knew what happened!"

Mac ripped off his glasses and stared at the control panel. The airlock light suddenly went off right in front of him, accompanied by a chime. Matty had disengaged from Mars 3.

He jumped from his seat, yelling at Rechenko as he bounded for the ladder. "Abort the program!" He slid down the ladder past the mid-deck, barely touching the rungs. He landed on the floor of the ready room where Judy was bent over Angela on the roll-out gurney.

Leaping over to the airlock control panel, he confirmed that Matty was indeed gone. Grabbing the communicator, he called Ivory. "Lieutenant Ivory, this is Mac, do you copy?" There was no response. "Lieutenant! Return to the airlock immediately! Do you copy?" No response.

"Lieutenant! Damon! I want you two to return to the Mars 3 airlock immediately! Is that clear!" Silence.

Judy continued to work on Angela.

"How is she?" Mac asked.

"She's not in a coma, thank God, but she appears to be sedated."

This time Mac used the 'all call' button on the panel, alerting anyone near a communicator. "Mars Base, this is Mars 3. Lieutenant Traveres, anyone, I've lost contact with Lieutenant Ivory inside Matty. Please contact him and tell him he is to return to the Mars 3 airlock immediately."

Again, there was no response to Mac's order.

"Mars Base, this is Mars 3. Lieutenant Traveres, do you copy?"

No one answered.

"Mac?" Judy said.

He ignored her. "Mars Base! Matty! Anyone who can hear me! Please respond!"

"Mac, come look at this."

He turned around and saw Judy holding a piece of paper in her hand.

"What is it?"

She held the paper out to him.

He took it from her hand. It was a note scribbled on a piece of Angela's stationery.

Beware!
things not as they appear.
no launch! no fuel 4 orbit
ky angelatraveres

Mac stared at the note for a moment until a familiar sound caught his attention and sent an instant chill through his body. The engine primer pumps were turning at high speed.

"Do you know what it means?" Judy asked, oblivious to the sounds that Mac had focused on.

Before he could answer, Rechenko's frantic voice blared over the intercom. "Commander! Commander! The launch sequence is starting! We're launching! We're launching!"

"Shit!" Mac grabbed Judy by the collar and screamed in her face. "Strap yourself and Angela down! We're going to launch!"

In one leap, Mac grabbed the ladder and pulled himself up. Every second counted. With the engine already primed, they could launch in as few as fifteen seconds.

The ladder well above Mac shuddered as the main engine fired, causing him to lose his footing and dangle from a ladder rung. In a matter of seconds, the engine would blast full throttle, kicking the large craft into the air.

As he reached the mid-deck, Mac yelled to Rechenko. "Abort! Abort!"

The vibrations increased along with the deafening roar of the engines. Things appeared to move in slow motion as he lunged, hand over hand, toward the bridge. He knew he had to be off the ladder before Mars 3 lurched into the air.

He managed to grab the bottom rung on the flight deck when the engines hit full throttle. Thousands of pounds of thrust poured out of the bottom of Mars 3, blasting the craft upward with a violent kick. Mac's knuckles turned white as his grip slipped finger by finger. The powerful thrust upward proved too much, and he slammed to the floor of the mid-deck.

He lay flat on his back, stunned. A million thoughts raced through his head. He had been played beautifully. Ivory had primed the engine, and Traveres kept him tied to the bridge with the virtual simulation. Boyle skillfully laid down the tale, which he swallowed. With precision timing, as Mac switched to manual control in the docking simulation, Ivory struck with lightning speed. Dropping off Angela, he knew Judy would be distracted. Damon and Ivory probably hit the airlock door the first time she looked away. They were inside Matty and released from the airlock within seconds, signaling Traveres to start the auto-launch sequence.

Mac righted himself against the vibrating wall. He cleared his mind of all thoughts but survival. Fighting against the increasing g-forces pressing against his body, he picked himself up from the floor and made the first move to regain control of his ship.

The launch shook and vibrated Mars 3, sending anything not strapped down flying about the cabin. Judy found herself hanging on under the galley table while the evening's dinner and accompanying cookware turned into lethal projectiles, crashing into walls and splattering about the room.

As best she could, Judy kept a close eye on the gurney, secured to the wall but still bouncing up and down in the ready room.

Mac crawled back to the ladder and managed to grab the closest rung. The constant shaking combined with the increasing g-forces against his body meant it would take all the strength he could muster to make it the final fifteen feet to the flight deck. He could barely hear Rechenko's panicked voice as he called out for help. Out of breath from his climb, Mac tried to shout instructions to him. "Abort to launch site! Abort to launch site!" Mac yelled. "Key in ALS! Key ALS!" He reached the flight deck and crawled across the floor to the bridge.

"We're at twenty-five thousand feet!" Rechenko yelled back, as he typed feverishly on the keyboard. "Nothing is happening. The computer is not responding!"

"Try to reset." Mac grabbed the back of his seat and pulled himself off the floor.

"The computer is not resetting!" Rechenko shouted.

"Try to reboot!" Mac hollered, working his way around his chair.

"I already did! Nothing's working! It's out of our control!"

Mars 3 continued to climb with its main engine at full throttle. Pulling nearly four times the force of gravity, Mac finally climbed into his pilot's seat, trying desperately to think of a way to shut down the engine and restart it for a return to the launch site. He remembered the note Judy had found: "Beware!... things are not as they appear...no launch!...no fuel 4 orbit..." Someone was trying to warn him that they would never make it to the mother ship for rendezvous, but who?

"Forty thousand feet!" Rechenko shouted. "Commander, maybe we should go to orbit and try to rendezvous with the mother ship."

"No, we can't go into orbit. We don't have enough fuel."

"Can we orbit until we gain control of the computer, then land at the launch site again?"

"No, we don't have a heat shield; we'd burn up in the atmosphere. Victor, I think our only hope is to cut the power and shut down the main computer and break the link controlling the ship. If that works, I'll restart the computer and input an encrypted access code to lock out any external signal. Victor, you're going to have to hit the main breaker. Shut it off for ten seconds, and then turn it back on."

Rechenko nodded, unbuckled his seat belt, and struggled out of his chair toward the breaker, only ten feet away. Mac checked his altitude. They were at forty-two thousand feet; the auto-roll program would start at fifty-five thousand feet, only seconds away.

Rechenko pulled the breaker. All of the lights and the console went dead, but to Mac's surprise, the engine continued at full throttle. How could the power be cut without affecting the engine? Rechenko counted ten seconds, and threw the breaker again. The lights and the console flickered to life at the same time the engine shut down. The sudden halt of the engine at full power knocked Rechenko off his feet. Mac almost flew out of his chair, barely grabbing the handles and cursing himself for not remembering to fasten his seat belt. He checked the altitude. Mars 3 had just passed through fifty thousand feet when its engine shut down. Its upward inertia would carry it up another few thousand feet before it would literally stop in mid-air. Everything inside would be weightless, but only for a few moments. Without power, even in the light Martian gravity, Mars 3 would fall back toward the surface like a rock.

While pinned to the floor under the galley table, Judy found herself in total blackness as the lights and power went out. Then the lights came back on but the engine shut down, throwing her into the underside of the table. Now she felt a new sensation, one she hadn't felt in months: weightlessness. Had they gone into space? She pushed herself over to Angela, who was still unconscious on the gurney. While reaching for Angela's arm, Judy felt herself floating upward. She tried to grab the gurney rail but missed. Suddenly another feeling came over her. She realized in a matter of seconds that everything in her stomach would force its way out of her mouth, and there wasn't a thing she could do about it.

Mac helped Rechenko back into his seat as he waited for the monitors to reset. Shutting down the main power meant everything had to be rebooted. He had no time to waste. Mars 3 would be falling any second.

"Damn these monitors!" Mac yelled. "I can't very well encrypt the computer if I can't see it. Damn it!"

Mars 3 started to fall, slowly at first, but then with incredible speed. Mac tightened his seat belt. He had experienced a similar situation many times as a test pilot, coaxing a fighter jet out of a flat spin before blacking out. He could feel the inevitable nausea coming, but he had to remain conscious; blacking out now would be fatal. The screen in front of him came on and he quickly keyed in a code, but to his surprise the computer indicated that there was already an encryption program running. That made no sense. How could a program be running if the main computer had been shut down? Unless…the computer never did shut down!

Then why did the engine cut off at fifty thousand feet?

The scenario seemed familiar to him, almost like deja vous? *Engine cut off at fifty thousand feet* echoed in his head.

Then it hit him. He had seen this very situation in Traveres' abort program, the one he had refused to run a few days ago! Could they be in that very program now? Mac quickly keyed in ALS (Abort to Launch Site). The screen lit up and the computer asked if he was ready for main engine start.

"I'm in! I'm in!" He turned to Rechenko, who leaned over the side of his chair groaning. Mac knew he could also black out at any moment so he took the only option left to him. Chancing that he could potentially throw the spacecraft into a violent spin and rip it apart, he initiated an emergency engine start. He thought about warning Rechenko of the impending jolt and spin, but what did it matter at this point? He only hoped the encrypted program would accept the request. If it was Traveres' abort program running, the engine should re-ignite. He keyed in the command and held on.

Approaching thirty thousand feet, he felt the main engine fire at full throttle. Mars 3 immediately began to tumble, causing his and Rechenko's arms and legs to flail around as though they were rag dolls. Mac worried that Mars 3's downward velocity would push the threshold of the maximum allowable stress to the spacecraft's structure.

He gritted his teeth and tried to focus on the read-outs in front of him. Twenty thousand feet, still tumbling, descent rate not increasing as before— good news. At least the engine had slowed their fall.

Through the window he could see alternate views of red sky and red terrain as Mars 3 spun toward the surface. It suddenly occurred to him that he had seen this before, in a nightmare. He recalled that in his dream of Magdalena, she had led him to the edge of the great pyramid at Teotihuacán; but when he looked over the edge, he saw the Martian surface from a great altitude. Then, Uncle Guillermo pulled him over the edge and he fell helplessly, just as he was falling now.

As the encroaching tunnel vision signaled he was about to pass out, Mac caught one more glance at his readings: twelve thousand feet. *It won't be long now,* he thought. Mac closed his eyes, resigning himself to fate. *Magdalena, why did you betray me?*

Mac felt as though he had just blinked his eyes when he began to feel a heavy weight on his chest, as if someone were standing on him. He realized he was pulling g's, in only one direction!

He opened his eyes and glanced at the altitude and rate of descent. Fifteen hundred feet and still falling like a rock. Twelve hundred feet and the spacecraft shuddered and shook. A thousand feet and the mighty engine throttled to one hundred and ten percent of normal. Eight hundred feet! It felt like Mars 3 would tear itself apart.

Mac braced for impact. He didn't want to die like this, betrayed by his crew. He felt shame in his heart. Four hundred feet...three hundred feet. The main engine roared. Barely conscious, Mac noticed the g-forces lighten slightly. The engine throttled back, a hundred and fifty feet. Mac could see the surface outside. Altitude one hundred feet and holding! The engine hummed at idle power. Mars 3 was hovering!

The engine throttled up again as the computer started to bring the craft to a higher altitude. Nausea crept back into Mac's body when he sat up too quickly to monitor the flight data. The ship rose to one thousand feet and started to move laterally, seeking the landing beacon. But where were they? Mac hardly felt he was in any condition to take manual control of the ship, but he knew where he wanted to go.

As Judy regained consciousness, she felt sick to her stomach. Her spinning head made it impossible to stand up, so she crawled, hand over hand, to the top of the gurney. Angela moaned. A good sign, Judy thought. At least her friend was still alive.

"Angela! Angela! Wake up!"

Angela continued to moan. Judy pulled down part of Angela's jumpsuit and gasped at the sight of several deep bruises up and down her arms.

"What did those bastards do to you?" she cried.

Mars 3 locked on to the landing beacon and adjusted its flight path. Their violent tumble from the skies had left them about five miles to the south of the base. Because of his condition, Mac decided to let the computer take the approach to within a quarter-mile of the landing zone before he would switch to manual control.

Rechenko came to and began apologizing for what had happened. To Mac's surprise, Rechenko thought he had somehow started the launch sequence himself.

"Victor, this was not your fault," Mac said. "They launched us automatically."

"They?" Rechenko said. "Who are 'they'? You mean Lieutenant Traveres and Dr. Boyle?"

"I'm not sure. Stand by. I'm ready to switch to manual control. Victor, keep an eye on my heading. I'm going to be awfully busy here."

"I will do what I can, Commander; but to be honest, I do not feel so good."

Mac input the manual command override. The computer promptly accepted. He now controlled Mars 3, a gangly beast that wasn't designed to travel laterally across the surface of Mars.

Mac could see the fuel processor about three miles to his left. That meant the base should be dead ahead. "Keep an eye out, Victor. The base should be right in front of us."

Suddenly a warning alarm sounded on the bridge. "It's a fuel warning, Commander," Rechenko said. "Two minutes of fuel left, sir, according to the computer. But I'm not sure that is correct. If you look at the fuel indicator, it says we have plenty."

"Don't pay any attention to the indicators; they're not correct. Start a countdown from right now," Mac ordered. "We have two minutes of fuel, maybe a little more."

"Commander, we should land as soon as possible, yes?"

"We will, but not before we get to the base. I want those sons-of-bitches to see us land at their doorstep!"

"Can we get there in two minutes?"

"I don't know, but we're going to try." Mac throttled the power back. "Descending to six hundred feet. The base should be right in front of us. Keep watching, Victor."

"About ninety seconds of fuel, Commander."

"There it is!" Mac shouted. "Dead ahead! Increasing forward velocity."

The difficult task of flying Mars 3 manually required all of Mac's skills as he battled with the flight controls. Fuel consumption rates and forward velocity estimates ran through his head as he tried to figure how close to the base he could land.

"Sixty seconds of fuel, Commander."

"Descending to three hundred feet." Mac felt beads of sweat roll down his face. With the base still a half-mile away, he decreased his forward velocity to avoid overshooting the target. Mars 3 wouldn't exactly stop on a dime.

Lights inside Habitat 2 were now visible. Mac thought how he would love to be a fly on the wall and see the reaction of his betrayers as Mars 3 came over the horizon directly at them. What a sight it must be!

"Forty-five seconds, Commander." Rechenko's voice tightened.

As the base came into full view, Mac felt the anger inside him swell, but he knew he had to get down on the ground in one piece first.

"One hundred-fifty feet, thirty seconds of fuel!"

An alarm sounded and a digital voice blared out at them. *"Warning! Thirty-seconds of fuel remaining. There is no reserve."*

Rechenko twitched nervously as he read out the altitude. "One forty...one thirty...one twenty..."

Mac had picked out a glide slope and adjusted his rate of descent to intersect at his preferred target.

"Eighty feet! Fifteen seconds fuel!" Rechenko yelled.

The engine thrust started to kick up some dust, and the base disappeared behind a dark red Martian cloud. Mac flew completely blind, praying he wouldn't drop a landing strut on a large boulder.

"Ten seconds! Sixty feet, Mac!"

Mac throttled back fifteen percent to increase his descent rate slightly.

"Five seconds! Forty feet!"

"Come on, baby, just a little more!" Mac coaxed his engine to keep going.

"Twenty-five feet, Commander, no fuel!"

The engine continued to fire for a few seconds. Mac kept the throttle up until the engine shut down.

"Brace for impact!" The lander hit the surface with a jolt. Mac and Rechenko bounced in their chairs.

The dust around the windows of Mars 3 gradually cleared. Mac lay his head on the console, and sweat rolled down his face as he let out a deep exhale. He was spent, mentally and physically. Slowly, he raised his head and gazed out the window at a sight he never thought he would see again.

Looming directly in front of him, a mere hundred yards away, stood Mars Base, bathed in the fading orange of the setting sun. Too exhausted to say anything, he stared out the window with only one thing on his mind.

CHAPTER 19
EVIL FORCES

"Damn! What the hell happened?" Boyle slammed his fist on the console next to Traveres, who pretended to troubleshoot the situation on the computer. Ivory, La Rue, and Gina all stared out the bridge window as the red dust settled around Mars 3.

"I thought you said they wouldn't be able to override the launch, Lieutenant!" Boyle screamed a few inches from Traveres' ear.

"I don't know what happened, Doctor. I seem to have lost all contact with their computer. It's possible Mac discovered the laser link and managed to shut us out."

Traveres watched Boyle's face turn red, his eyes bulging. "Goddammit, Lieutenant, you'd better reestablish control of their bloody computer and this entire operation, or it will be your neck! Is that clear?"

Traveres said nothing; he knew he didn't have to. He had control of the operation, and it was progressing nicely. In his mind, the only glitch was the amount of time it had taken Mac to gain control of Mars 3 and save the ship. His main concern now was how to get everyone off the bridge so he could be alone.

"That was one hell of a maneuver to abort the launch and land right next to the base," Ivory said, still looking out the window. "You gotta hand it to Mac; he showed some incredible skills."

"What skills? He's just a lucky bastard!" Boyle yelled. "And a lot of good it did him. They're stuck out there now, and that's where they're going to die."

Traveres noticed Boyle hated to see Mac get credit for anything—a fact he might be able to exploit in the future against the ego-driven scientist.

"We should be wary of what Mac plans to do next," Traveres spoke up. "They have pressure suits, and they're certainly close enough to walk to the base. They just have to find a way in."

"I agree," Ivory said. "We need to think about setting up a perimeter and defending the base."

Traveres watched Boyle closely. The doctor was frustrated by Mac's heroics and certainly wouldn't stand for being bested by him.

"Maybe you're right," Boyle conceded. "Mac may not be the brightest commander in the space program, but even he knows his only option is to retake this base, and that's not going to happen. Mr. Ivory, I want you and La Rue to secure H2 and the airlock entrance. Keep an eye on that lander and report anything suspicious immediately. Gina, get down to the galley and start fashioning some weapons. As for you, Lieutenant, get control of their computer! As soon as you do, I want you to kill their life support. I don't want to see these bastards take another step toward this base."

"Yes, sir," Traveres nodded. He was happy to hear that Ivory and La Rue were headed to the habitat where he could easily isolate them. Boyle's watchful eye prevented him from making any obvious moves; but very gradually, he began to change the environment inside Mars 2. The moment Boyle left the bridge, he would secure Mars Base. He only hoped Mac and the crew would sit tight for a few hours and let him handle the situation.

Mac was sitting on the Mars 3 bridge, staring out the window when Judy made her way onto the flight deck.

"What happened? Did we do that?" She wobbled onto the bridge. "Mac, tell me it was an accident. Those guys didn't launch us, did they?"

"I'm afraid they did." Mac leaned back in his pilot's chair and wiped the beads of sweat off his brow. "It's pretty obvious they were trying to get us into orbit, short of the mother ship, so we'd be marooned in space until we burned up in the Martian atmosphere."

Rechenko perked up. "Who launched us? Why would anyone try to kill us like that? I don't understand."

"I'm sorry, Victor. I guess I owe you an explanation. We have reason to believe that Boyle, Traveres, Ivory, La Rue, and Gina have conspired to take over Mars Base and eliminate us, preferably without a trace."

Rechenko wrinkled his nose and opened his mouth but said nothing.

"I also suspect Gina Gibson stowed away on Mars 3 and somehow managed to gain control of the ship and eliminate Rusty and his crew."

"Why?" Rechenko shook his head. "Why would anyone want to kill all those people on Mars 3 and control the base? There's nothing here but rock."

"I wish I had an answer for you, Victor; but right now, all I can tell you is that they are trying to kill us too. We have been set up throughout this whole mission. Think about it. Who's in control of communications? Who gave us detailed explanations of a major solar event and Earth's condition. Who stays and who goes? Who's controlling the main computer? Every detail, down to making sure we were busy and distracted when they brought Angela here tonight and La Rue skipped out with Ivory. It was all timed so they could launch us into orbit without enough fuel to reach the mother ship."

Rechenko shook his head. "I don't believe it."

"Look, don't you think it's a little peculiar we've just launched to fifty thousand feet, tumbled and rolled back to a landing in front of the base, and no one has tried to contact us?"

"Da," Rechenko answered.

"Okay, listen to this." Mac activated his communicator. "Mars Base, this is Mars 3, copy?" No response. "Mars Base, this is Mars 3, please respond."

The Russian stroked his beard. "So Earth wasn't hit by a solar storm?"

"It's doubtful."

"And they are responsible for launching us?"

"That's what I'm saying, Victor."

Rechenko let out a long sigh. "What do we do now, Commander?"

Mac stood up and looked out the window at Mars Base. "We do everything we can, use every resource available to us to get back in control of that base. We take back the base, or we die trying."

Traveres looked up at Boyle, who stood frozen in position, waiting for Mac to finish speaking on the communicator. After a few moments, Boyle looked at Traveres. "He seems rather calm, considering what he's just been through. Could it be he doesn't suspect that we blasted him into the sky?" He laughed. "Could it be the great Commander has no idea he and his crew are the victims of 'Evil Forces'?"

As Boyle proudly referred to his team as the 'Evil Forces,' the thought crossed Traveres' mind that the egotistical doctor would be the perfect antagonist in a James Bond film. To him, power was the ultimate elixir, fueling his increasingly flamboyant personality.

Traveres had first met Dr. Boyle over ten years earlier, during his days at the Academy. The doctor had come to give a presentation on scientific coalitions between the private sector and the military. Boyle recruited him to work with EarthConn, arranging a joint research project with the large communications contractor. It amazed him that he had been recruited so long ago to play such a key role in this sinister plan.

He noted the change in Boyle's demeanor since he had taken charge. It must have been difficult for the British doctor to play a subordinate role to Mac for so long. He appeared eager to make up for the years of frustration he'd endured waiting for this moment.

Traveres ignored Boyle's increasing arrogance, knowing he would foil the doctor's plans the minute Boyle left the bridge. He had to be patient and pick the right time to take action.

"Nyet!" Rechenko slammed his hand on the console. "This encryption program will not let me in to any of the base systems. I am sorry, Commander, there is nothing I can do."

"Victor, we have to find a way into the computer. Our lives depend on it," Mac pleaded. "The sooner we assault the base, the better our chances of survival. We need to get into their main computer."

"Assault the base?" Judy asked, returning to the flight deck after checking on Angela. "Who's going to do that?"

"We are," Mac answered, reaching out to reassure her.

Judy turned away, keeping her distance. "Right now? Couldn't we wait? Maybe we can negotiate with them in the morning."

"Negotiate?" Mac shook head. "You've got to be kidding! Those traitors over there just tried to kill us! You can bet they're thinking of how to finish us off right now. Our best chance is to attack the base as soon as possible, before they have time to shore up their defenses."

Judy kept her back to Mac, not allowing him to see the tears rolling down her face. "Mac, I don't know anything about fighting! And what about Angela? Do you expect her to join in your attack on the base?"

"How's she doing?" he asked.

"Oh, she's awake now," Judy's voice cracked. "But she's sore from that beating they gave her."

"Did she tell you anything?"

Judy took a deep breath and turned around. "Mac, she told me the last thing she remembers is working inside Habitat 2 when Gina came along, pushing her to stick fight again. When she refused and tried to leave, she says Ivory came in and cornered her. Then the two of them beat her."

The story confirmed everything Mac had feared. The conspiracy included everyone inside the base; and Gina and Ivory, the two experts at martial arts, were the enforcers.

"The last thing she remembered," Judy continued, "is hearing Dr. Boyle warn them not to hit her in the face to avoid raising any suspicion."

"Really? I guess it makes sense. If Ivory had brought a bloodied Angela to Mars 3, we would have been alerted much sooner to what was going on. Well, we know one thing for sure. It looks like Dr. Boyle's in charge. What about Traveres? Did Angela see Michael at all?"

"She says he's not involved in the plot."

"Not involved?" Mac raised his voice. "How can she say that? He's the only one who could have launched us like that! It's his encryption code that is preventing us from gaining control of any computers! How can she say he's not involved?"

Suddenly, a familiar voice pierced the room. "Because he gave us the password for the encryption program," Angela said, surprising everyone as she staggered into the room.

"Angela, what are you doing?" Judy moved quickly to steady her friend. "You should be lying down, getting some rest."

"I don't need any rest," Angela said more forcefully. "Commander, you're right, we have to take control of the base as soon as possible. Michael is alone with those ruthless people. We need to help him now."

"What did you mean that he gave us his password to the encryption program?" Mac asked, skeptical about Traveres.

"That note that you found on my chest. Michael put it there this morning. He told me not to read it until tonight. Judy showed it to me. Look at the last line, it says, '...ky angelatraveres.'"

Mac looked at the note again. Of course! Key in angelatraveres! The answer had been in front of him all along. Before he could turn to Rechenko, the Russian had already keyed in the password.

"It worked!" Rechenko shouted. "We have control of our computer."

"What about the base computer?" Mac asked. "Can we tap into that?"

Rechenko keyed in a few more strokes on the computer. "Da! We are in! I can monitor the base habitats, and most of the Mars 2 systems."

"That's perfect. All we need is a way to get into the base undetected." Mac peered over Rechenko's shoulder. "Victor, start looking for a way to get us in there."

"I have a couple of good ideas; after all, it is my design."

Mac turned to Judy, sensing her mood. "What's troubling you?"

"What's troubling me?" she asked with a tone of sarcasm. "Even if we sneak back into the base, what good would it do? Ivory and Gina are combat experts. Look at what they did to Angela. How are we going to get control of anything with those two thugs around?"

"We don't have a choice. If we don't move on the base as soon as we can, we'll die here. Those thugs will have no mercy on us. Our only hope is to do what they probably don't expect: Attack immediately and aggressively."

"So you have some kind of plan for me to 'attack'? I'm not the greatest fighter in the world, you know."

"Look, we've surprised Boyle and his crew to this point. I'm sure they didn't anticipate us surviving that launch and landing right on their front porch. They don't have any weapons we can't make. We just have to draw on our unique knowledge and expertise to get an edge. I don't see that we have any choice."

"I've got it!" Rechenko said, still working on the computer. "I know a way to get you in!"

Everyone gathered around the Russian. "Commander, I think I can get at least two of you inside Habitat 2 without being detected."

"That's great, Victor!" Mac said, already planning his assault. "Angela and I will go."

"Nyet, Commander. You cannot go. It will have to be Judy and Angela."

Mac studied Rechenko as the Russian leaned back in his chair, stroking his beard, looking back at Mac as if he was sizing him up from head to toe. "Victor, what's going on in that Cossack head of yours?"

"You cannot go, Commander, because you're going to be the decoy."

CHAPTER 20
THE QUIET BEFORE...

Lieutenant Michael Traveres watched for any sign of activity coming from Mars 3 as Dr. Boyle paced nervously back and forth behind him. The bridge windows were completely dark as the disappearing sun brought a deep blackness to the moonless Martian landscape.

"Damn! I can't see a bloody thing out there! It'll be impossible to tell if anyone's coming out of Mars 3," Boyle complained.

Traveres noted the doctor's cockiness had disappeared. The deep worry lines on his flushed face betrayed his growing frustration with this unexpected standoff. Boyle was a scientist, not a commando. Unaccustomed to thinking on his feet, he required time for meticulous planning and preparation when something went wrong.

Boyle keyed his communicator to Ivory, on guard in Habitat 2. "Lieutenant, can you see anything out there?"

"Negative, Doctor. We're completely blind here."

"Any suggestions?"

"Yes, Doctor. We could tap into the infrared camera on Ratty and aim it at the lander. We should be able to detect anybody leaving the airlock."

"Excellent idea, Mr. Ivory. We'll take care of that straightaway."

Traveres knew what was coming next as the doctor turned off the intercom. "I'm surprised you didn't think of that," Boyle glared at him. "Bring Ratty into position. I want to see that infrared camera shot as soon as possible."

"It's going to take some time," Traveres stalled. "I'm running a de-bugging program on the mainframe. I need to comple..."

"Lieutenant!" Boyle interrupted. "I don't give a shit about your bloody computer program! I want to see that infrared picture now! It's your incompetence that has us in this bloody mess! Now, do as you're told!"

"Yes, sir." Traveres added the proper humility to his response. The truth was, he had thought of using Ratty's infrared camera long before Ivory suggested it. He had run through every possible scenario long before this day had come. It surprised him that Ivory took this long to come up with the idea.

"Sir, would you like me to activate the infrared camera on Matty also?" Traveres offered, trying to endear himself again.

Boyle looked at him with a blank stare. "Of course, Lieutenant. I'm sure that's what Ivory had in mind," he said, not willing to give any ground.

"Yes, Doctor, right away," Traveres obediently answered.

Just then Gina walked onto the bridge carrying a long rod with a kitchen knife taped to the end, making it look like a spear. She also had numerous kitchen knives sheathed in her belt. She would have looked funny if it hadn't been such a serious situation, Traveres thought.

"What's all this then?" Boyle asked, peering over his reading glasses, looking her up and down.

"What do you mean? My weapons?" Gina slowly turned around, revealing more knives hidden on her belt.

"Yes. Is this all you could come up with? A couple of knives on your belt and a homemade spear? Look at this! How long have you been at it?"

Traveres could see Gina took offense to Boyle's insinuation that she hadn't accomplished much. "Hey, I've been working on these knives for almost two hours!" She pulled one out of her belt and held it up. "They're razor sharp! You could shave with them. These are for Ivory and me. Don't you worry; we'll make quick work of them when they come."

Looking at Gina and her homemade knives and spears, Traveres laughed at the irony. Here in this hi-tech environment amid sophisticated equipment, something as basic as defending the base came down to relying on rudimentary weapons.

In this regard, he still had to concede Boyle's team had the superior edge. With two trained martial arts experts and La Rue, who willingly took on the attitude of a renegade mercenary, any attack on the base would be a useless gesture. But Traveres knew that, given enough time, he could eliminate them all in one swift stroke.

"Dr. Boyle, the infrared cameras are on line." Traveres pointed to two video screens showing the ghostly image of the Mars 3 lander in white set against a dark background.

"Excellent," Boyle smiled. "Nobody's coming out of Mars 3 without us knowing about it."

Down in the galley, Mac helped Judy tape together a couple of crude spears when Angela walked in holding a copper tube.

"Judy, do you think you could spare a needle or two? I think I can make a pretty good dart blower from this. We could put some type of sedative on the needle tip and knock everyone out from a distance."

"Could you make your own darts for that thing?" Mac asked.

"Oh sure. That's not a problem. When I was a kid I used to do this all the time. If you do it right, you can shoot a dart fifty, sixty feet with amazing accuracy."

"Angela, I don't think you could deliver enough sedative to knock someone out," Judy said. "And even if you did hit your target, there's no guarantee you'd get enough injected to put someone down."

"How much sedative do you need?"

"It depends on who your target is. But it wouldn't be an instantaneous effect. It would take time."

"What about cyanide?" Mac asked, looking at Judy.

"Cyanide? We have cyanide?" Angela raised her eyebrows.

Judy shook her head. "Do you really want to use cyanide?"

"I don't see how we have any other choice," Mac answered.

"You know it will kill them," she shot back. "One shot and they're dead."

Mac didn't hesitate. "Better them than us. We're not playing around here. They tried to kill us all today, and we have to respond the same way. It's very likely they were responsible for the murder of the entire Mars 3 crew. You can bet they have the same plans for us!"

"I'm a doctor! I don't kill people!"

"Judy, we have a choice. It's us or them. It's that simple."

"I'm sorry," Judy's voice tightened, "But there's nothing simple about kill-ing. I'll help you because it's our only hope for survival, but there's nothing simple about it."

Boyle's spirits were lifted now that he had eyes pointed towards Mars 3. "Lieutenant, go down to the galley and get yourself something to eat."

"No thank you, Doctor," Traveres answered, surprised by Boyle's change in mood. "I want to finish on the computer first."

"Suit yourself. Gina, why don't you take some food to Ivory and La Rue. I don't want them to leave the habitat."

Traveres hid his excitement. With Gina, Ivory, and La Rue inside Habitat 2, they could all be eliminated at once! That would only leave Dr. Boyle to deal with.

Gina left the flight deck, disgruntled that she had to play waitress to the crew. She didn't appear in any hurry, which made Traveres all the more anxious. He'd have to wait until she entered H2 before he activated the rapid depres-surization.

Traveres preferred to be alone on the bridge when he depressurized H2, but Boyle seemed reluctant to leave the flight deck for any extended period of time. Traveres kept a close eye on the airlock indicator, which would signal Gina's entrance into the habitat. All he could do was wait and hope she didn't take too long.

"They have both infrared scanners on us, Commander," Rechenko said, monitoring the computer. "They'll know as soon as we open the outer air-lock door. The good news is, it looks like they are content to leave Ratty in place."

That news relieved Mac, since Ratty's remotely controlled arms could eas-ily tear apart and destroy Mars 3 if Boyle chose to do so. Mac figured either they didn't want to chance damaging Ratty or the possibility hadn't crossed their minds.

"Is there any way we could get control of either vehicle?"

"Negative, Commander," Rechenko answered. "All higher functions, such as life support for the crew module and remote communications, are controlled through the Mars 2 computer, which I have not been able to access. I only have control of the H2, HI, and airlock systems outside the lander; but I'm still looking to break into the Mars 2 data bank."

"All right, Victor. Just keep an eye on Ratty for any sudden moves. I'll be with Judy and Angela, getting ready. I want to be inside H2 within the hour."

Traveres worked on the computer, while Boyle stared at the infrared Mars 3 images and rambled on about the mission. The doctor's cocky mood had returned, and he let Traveres know about it. "I wish I could have seen the look on Mac's face as he realized Mars 3 was about to launch. Yes, I would have paid good money to see the terror in his eyes!" Boyle made no attempt to hide his disdain for Mac. Traveres preferred the burdened and stressed Boyle to this cocky version.

"I hope you don't miss your girlfriend too much. Angela's a fine-looking lass, and you did an excellent job with her. I will be sure to include that in my report."

Traveres tried not to react. His blood started to boil every time he thought about how they had beaten her until she passed out.

"I know you took quite a fancy to her these past few months," Boyle continued. "Indeed, I found her quite attractive myself. She turned out to be a remarkable woman—stronger than I thought. I must admit I had some concerns about you becoming too attached to her. I'm glad to see that wasn't the case."

Boyle was testing him, Traveres thought. Could it be the doctor suspected his allegiance had waned? Traveres acted indifferent, doing his best to hide any anger from the probing doctor. "She was okay," he answered without looking up, "but she really wasn't my type. Too tiny and whiny. I can't wait to get my hands on a real woman when we get home."

Boyle laughed out loud, slapping him on the back. "That's the spirit, my boy! And you will have the pick of the litter when we return! We'll all be able to write our own tickets. Set for life!"

Traveres felt ashamed. He thought of Angela, inside Mars 3, being nursed back to health. He would get his revenge soon enough. Patience, he thought, patience! It would all be over soon, and Angela would be back in his arms.

He called up the locator screen. Gina was still in the galley! What's she doing there? Cooking a turkey dinner?

Suddenly the communicator chimed. Boyle jumped up. "Talk to me, Ivory. What do you see?"

"Nothing, Doctor, I just wanted to run an idea by you."

"Go ahead, Lieutenant. What is it?"

"Yes, sir, I just wanted to say, we don't have to sit here and wait for these guys to come out and attack us. We can get to them right now."

"How do you mean?"

Traveres knew what was coming next.

"We can use Ratty to pick apart the lander with its claws. It could easily rupture a bulkhead without doing damage to the vehicle."

"I like the sound of that," Boyle said. "I'd prefer to get these guys out of my hair now rather than wait for them to attack us."

"I agree," Ivory said. "I'll come in and run the virtual remote right now."

Boyle looked at Traveres with an evil grin. "No, Lieutenant, you stay put in case they make a break for the habitat. Gina and I will be standing by to lend a hand. Lieutenant Traveres will handle Ratty. He's the best virtual operator," he said, nodding to Traveres.

Traveres couldn't decide whether this development was a good thing or not.

In the ready room, Mac helped Judy and Angela with some final adjustments on their soft suits. "Remember, these suits are designed for daytime use only so it's going to get cold. The important thing is, don't panic. If you keep moving, you should make it to the far side of the habitat in five minutes."

"No problem," Angela said, her strong voice showing confidence.

Mac felt a deepening foreboding as he looked at Angela and Judy. He could very well be sending them to their deaths, a risk that weighed heavily on his mind. They would all put their lives on the line tonight, and this could be the last time they would see each other alive.

He zipped up the front of his soft suit and placed the communicator in his ear. "Test, test," he called to Rechenko on the bridge.

"I copy, Commander."

Mac looked at the variety of makeshift weapons and equipment on the table in front of him. "So what do we have here?"

"This is the hollow dart Angela made," Judy responded. "We have three of them, all laced with cyanide. As long as they penetrate the skin into muscle, the effect should be immobilization then death within thirty seconds. A hit around the neck area would be ideal. However, a strike anywhere deep enough in the body would do the trick."

"Obviously, Ivory is the primary target," Mac said. "With his strength and quickness, he's the one I'm most worried about—along with Gina, who's obviously a trained fighter." Angela nodded. "I'll be ready. I just need a clear shot and I'll put 'em down."

"I also made up some syringes with a strong narcotic sedative," Judy continued. She held up a paper tube with a plunger on the end. "All you have to do is jam this into a leg or an arm and push the end down. Depending on how much sedative you inject, the drug could take several minutes to start working. If you find a vein, it could take as little as thirty seconds."

Mac wasn't surprised to see Judy had come up with an effective way to immobilize someone without killing them.

"Nice job, you two," Mac said. "We can't put this off any longer. They have Ratty poised and ready to attack. We should be prepared to go at a moment's notice."

Just then, Rechenko called over the communicator. "Commander, you'd better come up here."

"What is it, Victor?"

"Ratty's on the move, Commander, and it's headed straight for us."

Looking through his goggles, Traveres eased Ratty ever closer to Mars 3. He and Dr. Boyle argued back and forth about what part of the spacecraft to attack. All the while, Traveres really had only one thing on his mind: When was Gina going to enter H2? Finally, Ivory chimed in with his opinion. "Doctor, I agree with Traveres. I think we should just punch out one of the galley windows. That would be the safest. Rupturing a fuel line would put Ratty at risk, which is something we can't afford to do."

Slamming his hand on the console, Boyle relented. "Okay! Okay! I've been overruled by the military! Let's just do it and get it over with!" Traveres could see he had been looking forward to seeing Mars 3 explode into a fireball even though the ship didn't have enough fuel on board to light a cigarette.

"How close, Victor?" Mac asked, as he opened the airlock door for Judy and Angela.

"Approximately one hundred meters and closing. And Commander, its claws are extended."

"Don't do anything until I get there." Mac looked at Judy and Angela standing in the airlock. "All right, you two," he said, his voice starting to quiver. "Be careful out there. Use your heads and don't do anything foolish. Your primary advantage is in stealth and surprise, so remain hidden as long as possible. Listen for my cues. I'll know when it's best to run, walk, or crawl."

Looking at Angela, he extended his hand and lightly brushed her cheek. "This is the second time I've said farewell to you on this mission. I expect to be saying hello again in about twenty minutes."

She smiled and gave him a hug. "I'll see you in twenty," she said.

Mac turned to Judy. Without saying a word, they gave each other a long, tight hug.

"Okay, my love," Judy whispered. "Take your own advice and don't do anything stupid. I love you."

Rechenko called out again, "Commander, Ratty is about fifty meters out!"

"I'll be right there!" Mac yelled.

"Okay, don't step out until I say to. Is that clear?" They both nodded as the airlock door closed.

Mac glanced at Judy through the window, making eye contact with her. He mouthed the words "I love you" to her, and turned and walked away. As he made his way up the ladder to the flight deck, he yelled at Rechenko, "Hit 'em with the lights! Hit 'em now!"

"All right, I'm closing in," Traveres said, staring at the infrared image in his goggles. Without warning, he saw a bright white flash, temporarily blinding him. "Ahhh...shit!" he shouted, as he ripped the goggles off his head. "I can't see a thing!"

Boyle, who had been watching Ratty's progress out the window, covered his eyes. He'd been staring at the dark night for so long that the powerful lights outside Mars 3 impaired his vision. "What's going on?" Boyle yelled. "Where did that come from?"

Traveres smiled as he rubbed his eyes, appreciating the simple solution Mac had come up with to stop Ratty in its tracks and render the machine useless. "Those are the docking lights on the lander. I'm afraid we won't be able to operate Ratty with them on."

"Ram them!" he ordered, launching into a tirade. "I don't care if you can't see. Ram them and knock that bloody lander off its feet!"

Boyle's orders stunned Traveres. He had to refuse and hope Ivory would back him up. "Doctor, I can't ram them! If I do, we'll lose Ratty! Do you know what that means? We'll be marooned!"

"Goddammit, Lieutenant! Ram them, I say! I want them eliminated! Now!"

Consumed by rage, Boyle had lost control. Traveres put his finger on the keyboard. With a single keystroke he could depressurize H2, killing Ivory and La Rue. He looked over at the panel instinctively and to his horror, noticed the airlock light was on! With all of the distractions he had failed to notice Gina had already entered the airlock. But where was she now?

Ivory started to plead with Boyle not to ram Mars 3, but Traveres heard nothing. Before he depressurized H2, he decided to make one last check of Gina's position. He called up the locator program and searched for Gina's badge. Boyle continued to argue with Ivory, giving Traveres a couple of seconds to check.

The computer showed that she was still in the airlock. Traveres backed off for a moment. He decided to wait until she entered the tunnel leading to H2. If he depressurized too soon, she could get back to the airlock and save herself.

"The lights are out!" Ivory yelled. "Check the infrared!"

Traveres looked at his Ratty monitor. The screen was blank. It would take the thermal sensors ten to fifteen seconds to recalibrate the available heat. He looked back at the airlock light and his heart sank. The light was off, meaning Gina had made her way back inside Mars 2, a golden opportunity missed. Gina had probably entered H2 when he had the goggles on. He wasn't sure he'd have another chance like that.

He thought about his next best alternative, waiting for Boyle to leave the bridge so he could barricade himself on the flight deck and suck the oxygen out of the rest of Mars 2. It was more risky, but done correctly, quite effective.

The monitor of Mars 3 showed the landing struts slowly reappearing on screen. Without warning, the image was suddenly obliterated again.

"Bloody hell! The lights are on again!" Boyle yelled in frustration. "What the hell are they doing?"

"They're trying to stop us from advancing Ratty toward the lander," Ivory answered, "and it's damn effective too."

"I don't care what they're trying to do," Boyle shot back. "Eliminate them now!"

"Doctor, time is on our side," Ivory countered. "Let's wait until daylight, then we'll have a better chance of taking out the lander and not damaging Ratty."

"All right!" Boyle barked. "We'll wait until morning, but nobody sleeps! We're going to watch that ship all night!"

Traveres breathed a sigh of relief; he now had until morning to carry out his plan. The next time Boyle left the bridge, Traveres would blow the valves on H2, eliminating Ivory and La Rue. Then he would start to depressurize Mars 2, which would take about eight to ten minutes. He had already sealed the radiation chamber so the ladder was the only way to gain entrance to the flight deck.

That would be the "choke point" Traveres would have to defend as Boyle, and presumably Gina, would be fighting to gain entrance and regain control of the ship. He had his oxygen mask secretly stowed away and had already disabled the remaining masks inside Mars 2.

Boyle stared out the window, cursing again while the lights from Mars 3 continued to turn off and on, making it impossible to focus on anything with the naked eye or the infrared sensors.

"Why do they keep flashing those lights?" Boyle complained. "We stopped moving Ratty!"

Why indeed? Traveres wondered. *Be patient, Mac,* he thought. *I'll take care of everything.*

Mac stood over Rechenko as they both monitored the two blips on the screen showing Judy's and Angela's positions.

"How much farther to the berm?" an out-of-breath Angela asked over her com-link.

Mac could hear the shiver in her voice. "The berm is about a hundred feet in front of you. You can make it in two more sprints. Get ready to move."

He nodded to Rechenko, who switched the lights on. "Run!" Mac said, counting ten seconds. "Down!" he ordered, nodding at Rechenko to turn the lights back off.

Rechenko looked up at Mac. "Isn't it about time you get to the airlock?"

Mac nodded. "You're right, my friend. It's time to go. Thank you for everything, Victor. Be sure to keep me posted on everyone's position."

"Dobreya chisca, Commander," Rechenko said, wishing him good luck in Russian. "Be cautious, my friend."

"Thanks, Victor. I will see you shortly."

Boyle rubbed his eyes as he tried to stare out the window. "Oh bloody hell! I refuse to take any more of this!" He got up and turned to Traveres. "I am going to lie down for awhile. Call me if those fools out there do anything besides flash their lights."

"Yes, sir," Traveres said anxiously. The time to act had arrived. As soon as Boyle hit the ladder, he would depressurize Habitat 2. With his finger on the button, his heart beat like a scared rabbit's.

Suddenly, Ivory's voice came over the communicator, yelling excitedly about something. Boyle stepped back onto the bridge. "Come again, Lieutenant. Please repeat your transmission."

"I said, someone has come out of the lander! Don't you see? Someone is standing right in front, out in the open!"

Traveres looked out the window. There appeared to be a figure standing in front of Mars 3. The light from the lander was directly behind the person, making it difficult to see, although Traveres had a pretty good idea who it was.

Squinting out the window, Boyle asked, "Is that a man standing there?"

Traveres simply nodded and replied, "It sure is."

CHAPTER 21

...THE STORM

Judy collapsed next to Angela at the bottom of the three-foot-high Habitat 3 berm and shivered. They had only traveled three hundred yards, but she was exhausted and cold. The soft suits they wore were great for mobility, but poor protection against the bitter Martian nights that could be a hundred degrees colder than daytime.

They had exited Mars 3 and run in the opposite direction from the base. After about fifty yards, they started a loop toward the berm. With the bright lights shining directly at the base, Judy was sure they had gone completely undetected.

She was surprised that her body could feel so weak after traveling such a short distance. Shivering from the cold, Judy started to doubt whether she could perform her assigned tasks, much less make it to the habitat. Suppressing her panic, she fought the urge to bolt back to the safety and warmth of the Mars 3 airlock. "I...I don't know if I can make it Angela. I'm f..freezing."

"Yeah, I'm cold too, but we have to keep moving," Angela urged. "We can make it a straight sprint to the back of the habitat. No one will see us behind this berm." She got up and grabbed Judy's arm to pull her to her feet.

Judy looked over the berm at the surreal scene before her. Mars 3's bright lights pierced the black night, casting long shadows on the surrounding rocks and boulders. At the base of Mars 3 stood a lone figure, like a statue, out in the open.

"Judy," Angela tugged at her again. "Let's go. Run!"

The Mars 3 airlock door slid open and the cold night hit Mac like a thousand miniature knives. As he stepped out onto the surface, he worried about how Judy and Angela were faring in the bitter temperatures. At least they could keep warm by moving. He, on the other hand, had to stay in one place and stall. The bright lights from the lander cast a long shadow in front of him as he faced the base, a mere fifty meters away.

"Commander, I'll keep the lights on. They're almost there," Rechenko said over the direct com-link. "It's time."

A multitude of thoughts ran through Mac's mind as he started to walk toward the base, and very possibly, to his death. Here he was staring down his betrayers, coming back for more after their initial attempts to kill him had failed. For as long as he could remember, he never backed down from a fight— always too proud, or too stubborn, to surrender.

When he reached the halfway point between the base and the lander, Rechenko gave him his first intelligence report. "Commander, the locator badges show Ivory and La Rue inside the tunnel, waiting by the airlock entrance. Gina is in the ready room and Boyle and Traveres are on the flight deck."

Mac stopped about twenty meters from the base. Without going through the usual formalities, he keyed the base-wide channel on his com-link and began to speak. "Dr. Boyle, I am going to enter the airlock tunnel to Habitat 2. There you will surrender control of Mars Base immediately. You and your crew of mutineers are to be incarcerated and returned to Earth to stand trial for treason and the murder of the Mars 3 crew."

He continued his slow walk toward the base.

"Can you see anything?" Judy asked, shivering as she followed behind Angela.

"Not yet, but we should be getting close. Hang in there."

Judy could feel her soft suit stiffen in the extreme cold. Her hands could barely hold her flashlight and she couldn't feel her toes. "Angela, I don't know how much more I can take," she said, trying to keep pace. "You may have to go on without me."

"Judy! Stop talking like that. I'm freezing too, but we have to keep moving. We're almost there. Besides, Mac is counting on both of us."

"I'll try, Angela. I'm sorry," she said through her chattering teeth.

"Look! We made it!" Angela stopped abruptly in front of her. "There it is!"

Judy shined the flashlight on the circular plate on the side of the habitat. They had reached their destination. They were standing in front of valve six.

Mac stopped short of the airlock entrance, waiting for Rechenko's signal that Judy and Angela were in position. He stalled by again announcing his intentions, making sure he was as obnoxious as possible. "Dr. William Boyle, Lieutenant Michael Traveres, Lieutenant Christopher Ivory, Damon La Rue, Gina Gibson. You are considered mutineers and co-conspirators in the murders of Commander Russell Chandler, Lieutenant Alexander Holshevnikoff, Dr. Thomas Peterhaus..."

"Mutineers!" Boyle bristled, his face beet red. "Criminals? Incarceration? This man is delusional!" He yelled, pacing back and forth on the Mars 2 bridge.

Traveres noticed that Boyle seemed to be particularly incensed by the way Mac spoke as if he were still in command. Mac's aggressiveness had taken Traveres by surprise. At this point he needed Mac to stay away from the base and let him handle eliminating Boyle and the rest. If Mac entered the base, Traveres wouldn't be able to carry out his plan. His only option now was to immediately blow all the valves in Habitat 2, killing Ivory and La Rue instantly. Then he would take his chances fighting off Boyle and Gina.

He put his finger on the emergency valve purge switch, but a status light on the panel made him stop. He couldn't believe his eyes! The external door on valve six was opening!

"Victor, I'm ready," Angela called over her com-link to Rechenko on the Mars 3 bridge.

"Opening the outer valve," he responded.

The six valves on the habitat, designed and built with Rechenko's close supervision, were two feet in diameter by six feet long. Each valve unit had an internal and external aperture door that worked independently of each other, letting atmosphere escape from the habitat into the valve chamber through the internal door, then purged into the Martian air through the external door.

It was a crude airlock of sorts, with just enough space for a smaller person to climb through.

The outer valve opened and Angela bent over and slid into the cold chamber. At this point Rechenko closed the outer door and slowly opened the internal valve, letting the habitat air seep inside and equalize the atmosphere. Angela felt the warmer habitat air start to rush over her, but she still shivered. It would be two minutes before she could enter the habitat.

"Commander, Angela is in the valve," Rechenko said over the com-link.

Mac walked up to the base airlock, opened the door and stepped inside, relieved that no one was there to challenge him. Enveloped in the warmth of the pressurized airlock, he moved his arms and twisted his body in an effort to loosen up. He had no idea how he would be greeted on the other side of the door. His main mission was to stall and occupy the attention of Ivory and La Rue in order to give Angela and Judy a chance to get in position. He had to be ready for anything.

The airlock chimed and the door started to open. Mac unzipped his helmet and made sure his com-link was on and his earpiece secure. With his first step, Mac and Angela entered Mars Base at exactly the same time.

"Doctor, what do you want me to do?" Ivory called out to Boyle, as Traveres watched the monitor showing the drama unfolding in the airlock tunnel.

Boyle slammed his hand on the console. "That bastard called me a traitor! Let him in," he yelled. "Let him in, and kill him before he can say a word!"

Angela crawled out of the valve onto the habitat floor, giving Rechenko the all-clear signal. She stood up and hid behind some corn stalks and unzipped her soft helmet, taking in a deep breath of warm air. The sixty-six-degree air felt good on her face, though the rest of her body still shivered. As she stretched and turned and flapped her arms trying to warm up, Angela thought about the beating she took in here from Ivory and Gina. It helped wash away any nervousness she might feel about the task ahead. With an iron resolve, she loaded the copper tube with a cyanide dart; and in a slight crouch, she moved through the numerous hydroponics trays stalking her first victim.

Mac stepped into the tunnel leading to the two habitats and the lander. Ivory and La Rue stood before him, fifteen feet away, holding their crude weapons but saying nothing. La Rue had a cocky stare on his face, which Mac knew spelled trouble. Ivory had his familiar blank stare, absent of emotion.

Mac decided to take a passive posture with these two in an attempt to buy Angela and Judy more time. He allowed La Rue to walk a circle around him, showing them he trusted his former crewmates. Mac turned to Ivory and started to speak, "Let's all take it easy..."

Whack! A sharp pain on the back of his legs brought Mac to his knees. Realizing La Rue had just hit him, he tried to calm the situation. "Wait! Listen to me..." La Rue walked around him and rammed the end of his stick into Mac's gut, forcing every last bit of air from his lungs. Mac fell flat on his stomach, gasping for air, but before he could catch his breath, La Rue jumped on his back and pulled on Mac's head, nearly snapping his neck. Mac let out a desperate gasp, still trying to get some air inside his lungs as he felt the Frenchman put his full weight on him.

Mac felt La Rue's razor-sharp knife against his neck. He fully expected to feel the cold steel slice through his throat when a tone sounded inside H2. Mac recognized the decompression chime on Matty's airlock.

"Hold it!" Ivory snapped, stopping La Rue. "I'll handle Mac. Go check out Matty's airlock. Someone may be trying to gain access to the habitat."

La Rue reluctantly released Mac's head, but not before slicing a shallow three-inch slash in his neck. "Let that be a preview of things to come, mon capita'n," La Rue whispered in his ear. Mac gasped for breath, as blood flowed down his neck.

"You shouldn't have come back," Ivory said, walking toward him.

Mac lifted himself up to a kneeling position, amazed that he could still breathe. "I don't see that I had much of a choice. You see, someone forgot to fill the fuel tank before we launched."

"You're lucky to be alive. If that crazy Frenchman had had his way, your head would be rolling around in front of me right now. You wouldn't have much to say about anything then, would you?"

Mac sensed Ivory had only a little more patience than La Rue. He could see how the brutality of this group had caught Angela off guard. Even though Mac had urged a merciless attack on his former crewmates, he hadn't been able to muster the cold-hearted ruthlessness they had displayed. If Angela was already inside the habitat, he hoped she would bring the same ruthless attitude to bear on whomever she encountered first. If she didn't, they wouldn't stand a chance of retaking the base.

Angela had been slowly making her way to the front of H2 when she heard the chime from the Matty airlock. It wasn't in the plans for that to happen, but she knew she must investigate. Chances were Ivory or La Rue would be there, too, presenting a perfect opportunity for ambush.

Mac had barely caught his breath when Ivory dragged him into Habitat 2 and threw him on the floor. He saw La Rue approach Matty's airlock door and look through the porthole to the entrance tunnel leading to Matty.

"What did you find?" Ivory called out to him, still standing over Mac.

"I see nothing here. Perhaps we missed them and they're hiding inside the habitat. We should do a full sweep of the area," La Rue said.

Ivory grabbed Mac and shoved him against a support pole in an open area of the habitat. Using a hard plastic tie wrap, he put Mac's arms around the pole and tied his wrists together. "You start your search from there," Ivory yelled to La Rue. "I'll check the far side of the habitat."

Mac watched Ivory and La Rue disappear into the foliage while he remained lashed to the pole, wondering if he was standing on the spot where he would die.

From her vantage point, Angela could see Ivory on one side of the habitat, and La Rue searching the other. She made a split-second decision. She would take La Rue out first without using a dart. It would be quick and painless and leave her time to set up a good blow dart shot at Ivory from a distance.

With catlike precision, she moved to intercept La Rue as he made his way along the wall of the habitat. She reminded herself to be quick, efficient, and brutal. *Light on your feet, Angela. Stay centered, strike without mercy.* She paused when she saw La Rue moving toward her, still unaware of her presence. If she did it right, he would never know what hit him.

Angela coiled like a snake, ready to strike. *Just a couple more steps.*

Despite the sixty-six-degree air coming into the chamber, Judy continued to shake from the cold. It had been two minutes since she entered the chamber, yet the internal valve remained closed, preventing her from entering the habitat. She kept her helmet on and tried not to panic, unaware that Ivory stood only a few steps away from the valve, completing his sweep of the far side of the habitat. Because Rechenko had been closely monitoring the positions of Boyle and his crew, he had delayed opening the internal valve.

Standing in the center of the habitat, with his hands wrapped around a support pole, Mac had a commanding view of the drama before him. To his left, he saw Ivory disappear behind the thick foliage of corn and wheat stalks. To his right, he had just lost sight of La Rue, who searched behind some equipment along the near wall. While he hadn't seen her yet, Mac knew Angela was somewhere in the middle, hopefully with her blow darts, ready to strike.

Mac's hands were free enough that he could reach into his collar and reattach his communicator earpiece, which had fallen out. As he struggled to set the piece in his ear, he thought he saw movement to his right.

La Rue continued his deliberate search along the perimeter when he suddenly felt himself unable to breathe. Before he could gasp for air, he felt his testicles being smashed between his legs. He collapsed to the ground, and someone jumped on his back, pinning his head to the floor, rendering him completely immobile.

La Rue struggled to see his attacker, but a sharp pain, like a needle plunging deep into his neck, overwhelmed him. As he slipped into unconsciousness, he thought he saw Angela standing above him. *Where did she come from?*

Ivory sprang into action when La Rue didn't respond to his calls. He moved swiftly to the far side of the habitat where the Frenchman had been. Hurdling hydroponics trays and equipment, he kept a wary eye, always on the lookout for anything out of place. In just a few moments, he came across La Rue lying on the ground in a fetal position. He was unconscious with no visible wounds—just a large hypodermic needle sticking out of his neck.

Boyle's impatience grew as he paced the floor, anxious to hear from La Rue or Ivory. Traveres quietly continued his work on the computer, all the time monitoring the changing situation on the habitat cameras. He did whatever he could to help Mac, already having depressurized Matty's airlock just as La Rue prepared to slash the Commander's neck. He wasn't sure how much of a reprieve Mac would get.

"Ivory, report!" Boyle barked. "Did you find anyone in the habitat?"

"Yes, sir, I found La Rue, lying unconscious on the floor with a needle stuck in his neck."

"What?" Boyle shouted. "Are you telling me there's an intruder?"

"That's exactly what I'm saying."

"Well how in bloody hell did someone get in there without being detected?"

"Doctor, my guess is Rechenko found a way to enter the habitat without using the airlock. After all, he designed this thing."

"Who do you think got to La Rue?"

"I have a pretty good idea whose handiwork this is. I think Angela is here, and she's watching me right now."

Traveres perked up. He found it difficult enough, dealing with Mac spoiling his secret plan. Now his love, Angela, could be in harm's way, upsetting everything he had arranged to gain control of the base.

"Doctor, let me go in and help Ivory search for Angela," Gina yelled over the com-link from the ready room. "We'll take care of her."

"No! Absolutely not! Don't open the airlock. That may be what they're waiting for. Ivory, I'm afraid you're going to have to find Angela on your own; and when you do, eliminate her immediately! And while you're at it, eliminate our former Commander. I don't know why he's still alive."

"Actually, Doctor, I need him alive," Ivory said. "You've given me an idea."

Angela crouched down behind some vegetation and waited for Ivory to walk out onto the open floor. She knew he would eventually return to Mac's side, which would afford her an open shot with the blow dart. If the first shot didn't kill him, she would have plenty of time to reload for a second shot before he could find cover. She reached for her blow-dart shooter and her heart sank. To her horror, the copper tube she had carried at her side had bent in three places, rendering it useless.

How could this have happened? Then she realized La Rue must have landed on it when they fell to the floor together. Now she would have to battle Ivory hand to hand, something she did not look forward to. She made sure the two knives on her belt were secure, and she reached around her back to make sure her third smaller knife was still hidden. Looking around for anything else she could use to defend herself, she found two hard plastic dowels, each about two and a half feet long.

Finally, as she expected, Ivory emerged from the far side of the habitat and walked across the open floor toward Mac. If only she had her dart shooter, Ivory would be a dead man. She decided to remain hidden as long as she could.

Her heart pounded as she watched Ivory grab Mac by the back of his suit and push him to the ground. He unsheathed a long knife and pulled Mac's head back, exposing his already bloody neck.

Judy desperately tried to raise Rechenko on her communicator. Still sealed inside the cold dark chamber, she tried to relax and chase away the panic. *Have they forgotten about me? What if everybody's dead and I'm trapped in here?* Suddenly, a beam of light hit her face as the internal valve started to open. *Finally!*

She unzipped her helmet and crawled out of the chamber. The warm air inside felt good on her frozen face. It would take time to warm up her stiff, numb body before she could start looking for Angela. She was attempting to contact Rechenko when she heard someone shouting from across the habitat.

Mac winced in pain when Ivory grabbed his hair and pulled his head back, reopening the knife wound La Rue had given him. He felt the blood flow down his neck as Ivory slipped his knife against the three-inch slit below his chin.

"Are you ready to die, Commander?" Ivory whispered in his ear.

Kneeling on the floor with his hands strapped to a pole and blood running down his neck, Mac could think of only one response to Ivory's question. "Why am I dying? Why do any of us have to die?"

Ivory whispered in his ear again. "The real tragedy for you is that you will never know why you had to be eliminated. Let's just say you're in the way of something much bigger that yourself. But I'll promise you one thing. You won't die alone. I'll make sure Angela goes with you."

Ivory looked up and shouted across the habitat. "Angela! I know you're in here. I'm not going to waste time looking for you. Show yourself."

Mac looked at the thick foliage inside the habitat, knowing there were a hundred places to hide and take up a strong defensive position. Ivory was using him to flush her out for one final battle.

"Angela! I promise you a fair fight—just you and me and a couple of sticks. What do you say to that?"

With no response from Angela, Mac felt Ivory's grip tighten.

"Look here, Angela! If you don't show yourself by the count of five, your commander will die a slow and painful death!"

Mac felt the knife slide into his wound. With his strength, Ivory could easily decapitate him.

"One!" Ivory yelled, looking at the foliage in front of him. "Two...three... four! Angela, I'm not bluffing!"

Mac heard some rustling noises then saw Angela emerge across the floor in front of them, holding two sticks, each nearly three feet long. To Mac, seeing her safe and uninjured was a beautiful sight. He had to assume she had already eliminated La Rue, which would account for Ivory's brutality. She walked to the middle of the open floor and posed in a ready position, a challenge to her adversary that left no doubt she was ready to fight.

Traveres sighed under his breath as he looked at the monitor. Angela looked great considering what she had endured. She moved gracefully across the floor, stretching and limbering up in preparation for Ivory's onslaught.

"Doctor! I'm going inside the habitat!" Gina yelled from the ready room. "I want a piece of that bitch!"

"No, Gina!" Boyle said. "Stay where you are. This should be interesting."

Traveres felt a large lump in his throat as he tried to hide his emotional turmoil. The love of his life was about to engage in a fight to the death, and all he could do was watch! As a thousand scenarios ran through his head, he let his fingers slip to the emergency valve purge. The tactile feel of the switch gave him the clarity he was seeking. With Boyle focused on watching Ivory and Angela square off, he knew what he had to do.

Traveres and Boyle watched the monitor as Ivory picked up his six-foot stick and twirled it around his body and up in the air. He stepped deliberately across the floor in a sort of passive counter-dance to Angela. They both stretched and warmed up, Ivory with his long fighting stick, Angela with her two short "swords," mimicking the age-old art of the samurai.

It was well known that Ivory excelled at his single stick sparring, but Traveres had never seen Angela display her obvious command of the ancient discipline. He hoped the unknown would level the playing field somewhat. He felt any surprises she might have up her sleeve afforded her an outside chance for survival, maybe even victory.

"This should be good," Boyle said, as if watching a title fight on TV.

Ivory came to the center of the floor and bowed smartly. Angela responded in kind. Immediately, Ivory went on the offensive—prodding, testing, probing weaknesses and defensive strategy. Angela met each stroke of his stick with efficiency and grace, never counter-striking, never moving backward, constantly gliding laterally, allowing the energy of his blows to pass by her, not through her.

Traveres knew Ivory hadn't yet begun his power onslaught. He was testing her, seeking her weaknesses. She refused to counter, giving him nothing to go on. Then it came. He feinted one way, spun, and struck repeated blows at her body from alternate ends of the stick. The awesome display of quickness and power seem to impress everyone but Angela. He managed to graze her forehead, prompting her first counter-strike to his rib cage as she spun to avoid his blows. Neither hit was threatening; however, from Traveres' vantage point, he thought Ivory reacted with surprise at Angela's jab to his ribs.

"Excellent!" Boyle said, obviously enjoying the battle. "She's pretty good!" he added, looking at Traveres, who just stared at the monitor, careful not to reveal his readiness to step in and help. *Timing is everything,* he reminded himself.

Angela tried to control her breathing, at the same time being careful to remain in an attack position. It had felt good to experience her first contact, which built her confidence.

"An excellent exchange," Ivory laughed. "You've been holding out on me!"

Angela, trying to stay focused, didn't want to respond; but she couldn't avoid answering such an idiotic comment with a little psychological warfare. "I am still holding out!" she responded with a wry grin.

Ivory lost his smile. Angela knew his ego had been bruised by her ability to counter-strike him. No one here had ever come close to laying a stick on him. Setting himself up for another offensive, Ivory ran at her, swinging his stick with alternate ends striking at Angela with blazing speed and power. The loud crack of their colliding weapons echoed throughout the habitat.

Angela did not back up or even move laterally to avoid him. She stood her ground and managed to block his strikes by turning her body sideways, letting him brush by her. As he passed her, she landed a strike at one of his ankles, causing him to lose his balance; but she wasn't through with him yet. As he wobbled, still trying to maintain his center, Angela spun away from him, landing a blow squarely on the back of his head.

Ivory tumbled forward, rolling head over heels on the ground but immediately popped up to a ready position. He came at her again, this time with rage in his eyes, jabbing and poking with lightning speed. Angela continued to sidestep and block, saving her counter-strikes for the right moment.

Even though Ivory expended much more energy, Angela felt a growing fatigue. Her arms and legs ached all over. She knew Ivory could wear her down to the point at which he would go for the kill. Aware that she had to deliver a decisive blow while she still had the strength, she decided to draw him in and counter with a crippling onslaught of her own.

Ivory bolted toward her again; and on his next jab, Angela stepped into it, blocking it, then dropped to the floor as he swung the other end of his stick around, just missing her head. She immediately struck his left knee with all her might, and, using her inertia, she swung her leg around and kicked the opposite leg from under him. Ivory crashed to the ground beside her, letting out the groan of someone who had had the breath knocked out of him. As she swung her stick again, rolling away from him, Angela paid the price for her aggressive move. Using the inertia of his fall, Ivory's stick came crashing down on her back, striking her left shoulder blade, causing her to drop a stick. In an attempt to get away, Angela rolled and struck with her remaining stick, first pushing away his stick, then connecting with the center of his forehead. The blow drew blood as Ivory reeled away in the opposite direction.

Angela struggled to her feet and moved to the far end of the floor. There she collapsed in pain, her shoulder aching from the full force of his hit.

Gina screamed over the com-link to Boyle. "I'm going in there, goddammit!"

Boyle jumped from his chair next to Traveres and flew down the ladder, yelling at him not to let her open the airlock. Traveres sat in his chair, stunned. This was the moment he had been waiting for all night. He was alone on the flight deck with Gina and Boyle distracted in the ready room. Traveres leaped from his chair and pulled the hard plastic grate over the ladder well. He secured it with some rope and rolled a couple of chairs on top. He could hear Boyle and Gina in the ready room, yelling at each other. His heart raced as he thought about Mac, Judy, and Angela. They had to be warned about what was coming.

Out of breath, Angela lay on her side and looked across the open floor at Ivory, kneeling on all fours, his head down. She had hit him not once, not twice, but four times, knocking him down and drawing blood! She had given him her best shot, but she knew it wouldn't be enough. Overcome with exhaustion, she needed to regain her strength to continue. If he recovered before her, the match was his. She looked over at Mac who had been watching the battle, still tied to the pole. She noticed him struggling with something on his collar, using his hands as best he could. She heard a faint voice yelling over her communicator, which had fallen out of her ear during the fighting. She put it back and quickly realized what Mac was doing.

"Okay, Angela, let's stop messing around with these play things!" Ivory yelled at her as he stood up and threw his stick to the ground. Limping toward her, he pulled two long knives from his belt and threw one on the floor in front of her. "It's time to play for real."

Angela looked at the knife, lying about ten feet in front of her. Ivory continued to approach her, his knife at the ready. She started to get up, slowly slipping her hand to the back of her belt. There she gripped her own knife and waited for Ivory to move in a little closer.

"Go ahead, Angela, pick it up. Pick up the knife and prepare to die."

In one swift motion, Angela rolled over and flung her knife end over end with deadly accuracy. The blade buried deep into Ivory's thigh, and he let out a loud wail as he fell back to the floor. Instead of coming in for the kill, Angela sprang up and bolted for the deep foliage of the habitat. As she ran she zipped her helmet closed and the airflow automatically started. She continued to move through the thick foliage, aware Ivory was in pursuit with a razor-sharp knife in his hands.

"You're dead, Angela!" Ivory yelled across the habitat.

Angela could hear him through the external microphone on her helmet. She knew she had to disappear.

"You can't hide forever!" he yelled.

Angela collapsed beneath a row of corn. This would have to be good enough. She pulled out her last knife and waited.

In seconds, Ivory appeared before her, hobbling from his wounds but determined as ever with his long knife at the ready. She could see the rage in his eyes as he moved toward her. Then he stopped and turned away for a second. When he turned back, she saw a look of sheer terror on his face as the base alarm echoed through the habitat.

In an instant, the surrounding foliage became airborne as all six purge valves opened, forcing the oxygen in Habitat 2 outside. Angela grabbed onto a leg from one of the trays as she was pelted by vegetation flying toward one of the open valves. Then she felt the tight grip of Ivory's hand on her ankle as he struggled to hold on to her.

She tried to push him away, afraid he might try to slice at her suit in an attempt to get at her oxygen flow and somehow save himself. She kicked him in the head but his grip only tightened. It seemed an eternity, but she finally felt his grip loosen as the cold Martian atmosphere seeped into his lungs.

Angela pushed Ivory's hand away and caught a glimpse of his discolored face. There was no doubt. Lieutenant Ivory was dead.

CHAPTER 22

PURSUIT

"What the hell's going on?" Boyle yelled, standing inside the ready room with Gina, watching the camera feed from Habitat 2. Dust and foliage flew around the habitat in a violent windstorm as the roof sagged to the floor. "Shit! Someone blew the purge valves!" Boyle slammed the com-link button to the bridge. "Traveres! Who blew the valves?" With no response, Boyle jumped over to the ladder well to yell to the bridge; but when he looked up, he saw the flight deck entrance was blocked. "Goddammit! That bastard did it!" he yelled at Gina. "That bloody sod betrayed us! We've got to get to the bridge!"

He started to climb up the ladder when the base alarm sounded, stopping him on the first rung. "What the hell is that?" He motioned to Gina to check the computer.

She glanced at the screen. "Oh my God, the module's decompressing!"

"What?" Boyle ran over and pushed her aside. "Crew module decompressing?" he read out loud. "That son of a bitch is trying to kill us! Gina, get the soft suits out of the locker. We're going to be out of air in about ten minutes. I'll see if I can stop him on the computer."

Boyle desperately worked the keyboard, trying to access the environmental controls. "Damn that bastard! He's encrypted everything! We're locked out!"

"Doctor Boyle!" Gina screamed as she sank to the floor next to an empty locker. "All of the soft suits are gone!"

Breathing deeper with the thinning oxygen, Boyle turned around and looked at the H2 monitor. The dust had settled and debris was everywhere. In the middle of the picture, he noticed a figure slowly standing up, arms still wrapped around a support pole. "He managed to get his soft suit sealed," Boyle whispered to himself, shaking his head. "Mac lives."

"Commander, are you okay?" Rechenko's voice blared over Mac's com-link as he shimmed his way against the pole to stand up. The force of the valve purge had knocked him off his feet.

"Yes, Victor, I'm okay. I barely got my helmet on when you blew the valves."

"I didn't do it, Commander. Lieutenant Traveres did."

Mac sighed, relieved that Traveres really was helping them. Up to that moment, he wasn't completely convinced he could trust Michael. "How are Judy and Angela? They get your warning?"

"I'm okay," Angela's voice cut in over the com-link as Mac watched her emerge from the pile of foliage and debris strewn about the floor of the habitat. She ran up to him and cut the ties holding him to the pole.

"Angela, thank God you're all right. Where's Judy?" he said, rubbing his wrist then pressing his neck with his hand to put pressure on his bleeding wound.

"I never saw her come into the habitat. We'd better look for her."

"Her locator badge indicates she's by valve six," Rechenko interrupted.

"Judy, can you hear me? Judy, are you all right?" Mac shouted as he ran, following Angela into the tangled maze of pipes, trays, and foliage piled chest high along the walls of the habitat. He stopped for a moment when he saw Ivory's body lying face down. Hoping Judy hadn't met a similar fate, his heartbeat quickened. She was everything to him. *Did he send her to her death?*

"Judy! Answer me!" Mac's voice cracked.

"mmmuhh...Mac...I'm here...," Judy moaned over the com-link.

"Where are you?" Mac leaped at the sound of her voice.

"I...I don't know. It's dark and cold, and I'm covered in plants."

"I think she's inside the valve," Angela shouted as she cleared away a pile of wheat and corn stalks around valve six.

"There's her arm," Mac said, reaching out and grabbing her. "Victor, we found her. She's stuck halfway into the valve." They pulled her out onto the floor and helped her stand up.

"You okay?" Angela asked, brushing Judy off.

"I don't know," she said, flexing her arms and legs. "No broken bones. How is everyone else? Where are Ivory and La Rue?"

"They're dead. Michael blew the valves when he knew we had our helmets on. He saved our lives," Angela said.

"And now we gotta save his." Mac keyed his com-link. "Victor, can you pinpoint Traveres, Gina, and Boyle's locations inside Mars 2?"

"Yes, Commander, a moment please. It appears that they are in close proximity to each other at the top of the ladder well."

Mac looked and Judy and Angela. "Let's go get him."

Traveres stood above the flight deck ladder well and took deep breaths with the help of the emergency oxygen mask. He had already fought off two separate assaults from Gina and Boyle in the last four minutes. The hard plastic grate blocking the entrance to the flight deck had held up surprisingly well, but he expected more desperate attacks.

Five more minutes, he told himself. Five more minutes and he'd rid himself of the remaining evil in his life. It didn't bother him in the least that he had just killed Ivory and La Rue inside H2. In a few short minutes, Gina and Boyle would start to feel the effects of the oxygen deprivation, weaken, and finally succumb without a struggle. Five more minutes would buy him a lifetime with Angela without dark and evil secrets.

He heard Gina and Boyle making their way up the ladder whispering to each other, then Boyle addressed him in a calm, almost fatherly tone.

"Michael, we have to stop this game we're playing. I don't know why you're doing this; but as you know, there is important work to be done here—work which you were a part of. Work you can still be a part of. You can't let your feelings for Angela cloud your judgment. As a matter of fact, Angela could join us and help complete our mission. You can make all that happen, but you have to decide right now. Are you going to be a part of the most important discovery in history, or responsible for one of mankind's most dismal failures? It's up to you to decide right now because we are running out of time."

Traveres' only concern was for time to move faster. Whatever Boyle wished to talk about suited him fine, particularly if it took five minutes. With no compelling reason to answer, he just waited.

"Be silent if you wish, Michael, but there is something even you are not aware of. Something you have no power to control but which is catastrophic, not only to you and me, but also to your friends outside. We are all in grave danger unless you act soon. Do you understand me, Michael? Do you understand what I'm saying?"

What was he talking about? How could Boyle speak of threats with his air running out? Traveres thought of Angela and Mac outside, only a few feet away, probably trying to open the airlock. Could Boyle really possess something that would kill everyone? Or was he just bluffing?

"Damn, this door is heavy!" Mac said, as Angela and Judy helped him push the airlock open. It had taken them five minutes to manually purge the Mars 2 airlock.

"Any change in their positions, Victor?" Mac keyed his com-link.

"Negative," Rechenko answered. "They're all on the flight deck right now."

As they stepped into the Mars 2 airlock, Mac thought about how Boyle probably reacted when the habitat decompressed. It shouldn't have taken him long to realize who did it. Traveres had put his life on the line for them; now he needed their help. Mac could see that Angela couldn't wait to get inside the lander to save Michael. The fight inside her amazed him. She had held her own in a toe-to-toe battle with Ivory. For all his previous displays of prowess and skill, Angela dismantled the mighty beast with grace and efficiency.

Mac put a hand on her shoulder. "Thank you for coming to my rescue," he said. "Is there anything you can't do?"

"Yes, I can't make this airlock pressurize any faster," she cried. "All I care about is finding Michael alive."

"Let's move carefully," Mac urged. "We could be walking into an ambush, so keep your helmets on until we verify there is breathable atmosphere inside."

"The pressure is almost equalized," Judy said, gripping a long stick she had picked up in the habitat.

As Mac started to open the door, he heard Rechenko talking excitedly in his ear. "Commander! According to the locator badges, Traveres has moved to the radiation chamber, separating himself from Boyle and Gina."

"Great news. Keep us posted."

"Let's go," Angela urged, holding a knife in each hand.

"Remember to watch your back," Mac warned.

They slid the airlock door open and entered the Mars 2 ready room. Mac checked the environmental control panel before he unzipped his helmet. He never thought he'd see the inside of this lander again. Mac made his way to the ladder well and looked up to the flight deck. *No one in sight.* He motioned Judy to check the galley and Angela made her way to the bottom hatch of the radiation chamber on the ceiling of the ready room. She jumped up on a chair and tapped three times on the hatch.

The quiet inside the lander unnerved Mac. Boyle and Gina could easily be lying in wait for the right time to strike. He nodded at Angela, and she reached up and opened the chamber hatch. Mac stood guard by the ladder as Angela pointed a flashlight up into the chamber. Judy came over from the galley and suddenly gasped, looking at Angela's outstretched hand. "Are you bleeding?"

Angela flinched at the sight of her blood-soaked arm. She rotated her hand around and saw red droplets of blood landing on her from above. Before she could react, Traveres rolled out of the chamber, crashing on top of her as they both fell to the floor.

"Oh my God!" Judy screamed. "He's covered with blood!"

Angela tried to push him off her, but when she saw his chest was soaked in blood, she cried, "No! What have they done to you?"

Suddenly, Gina swung down from the open hatch, landing directly on Traveres and pinning Angela to the floor. Gina pulled out a knife, ready to strike; but Judy swung her stick with all her might, hitting Gina's wrist.

The knife flew out of her hands and across the floor. Gina jumped toward Judy, kicking her in the chest and knocking her back into the galley entrance. Before she could hit her again, Mac came from behind and slashed her across her back with his makeshift spear. Screaming in pain, Gina whirled and kicked the spear out of his hands. While Angela struggled to get Traveres' dead weight off her, Mac pulled a knife from his belt and faced Gina. He saw her eyes were empty, void of any emotion—the eyes of a cold-blooded killer. Just as Gina began her attack, Judy came up behind swinging her stick. Gina blocked her blows, and in one swift move, threw her into Mac and bolted for the ladder. As she vaulted up the rungs, Mac dove across the floor and grabbed her ankle to prevent her escape. Hanging from the ladder, Gina delivered several kicks to Mac's head and shoulders, trying desperately to free herself. Mac resolved not to let go of her, and using all his might, buried his knife deep into her calf.

"Aughh!" she screamed in pain, weakening her grip.

Just then, Mac heard a booming voice from behind. "Let Gina go or she dies!" Boyle yelled from across the room. He turned around, and saw Boyle standing at the galley entrance with his arms wrapped around Judy, holding a knife to her throat. *The bastard must have been hiding somewhere in the galley and surprised her from behind*, Mac thought as he pulled his knife from Gina's calf and watched her dart up the ladder and out of sight.

"You know I won't hesitate to slash her throat, Mac! Now drop your weapon or say goodbye to your girlfriend."

Mac instinctively took a step forward, but stopped when Boyle tightened his grip on Judy. Angela crouched on the floor between them, slowly pulling Traveres to the side of the room. Mac could see that Michael was still conscious but breathing in sporadic gasps.

"Don't take another step, Mac!" Boyle screamed. "Drop your knife! I'm not bluffing!"

Finally face to face with Boyle, Mac refused to back down. "Why are you doing this? Why do people have to die?"

"Don't question me!" Boyle shot back.

Mac noticed Judy fumbling with something on her pant leg, and finally realized she held a small paring knife in her free hand. He tried to stall for time, giving Judy her best shot at stabbing Boyle without being slashed herself.

"Doctor, I've tried my best to help guide this mission through some extraordinary challenges, some of which I suspect were of your own fabrication. Now ten people are dead. More may die tonight. I don't think it's too much to ask you to explain your reasons for..."

"Shut up!" Boyle interrupted. "I don't answer questions coming from a dead man! That is what you are, didn't you know? You're a dead man."

Mac noticed Angela had also caught sight of the knife in Judy's free hand and readied herself.

"Dead man?" Mac stalled. "Why am I a 'dead man'?"

Boyle grinned at him. "Never mind. You wouldn't understand. This is bigger than you are. Just know that you've served your purpose, and that's all that matters. You're a dead man now."

In one swift motion, Judy sliced across Boyle's right wrist, causing him to drop his knife. He jerked to one side, screaming in pain but still holding Judy's left arm. That split second of hesitation provided the opening Angela needed. She sprang from the floor and kicked Boyle in the chest, allowing Judy to break free.

Mac plowed into the doctor before could regain his balance, which sent them both flying into the galley. They rolled under the table in a tangled ball.

Angela moved to help Mac when Judy screamed at her. "Angela! Look!"

Gina came sliding down the ladder well. As she hit the floor of the ready room, she turned to face Angela, who now saw that Gina was holding a knife in each hand.

Mac managed to stay on top of Boyle long enough to land a crushing punch to the doctor's left ear, followed by a backhand to his nose. Blinded by his watering eyes, Boyle released his grip. Mac pulled him to his feet by his collar and said, "No mercy." With all his might, Mac drove his tight fist into Boyle's face, sending him crashing to the floor.

"Mac, sit on him and keep him still," Judy said, holding a large syringe. "This will knock him out for hours." She stuck the needle into Boyle's arm and the doctor moaned as he slipped into unconsciousness.

Mac turned to the ready room as Gina and Angela, both with knives in each hand, collided in their first exchange, blocking swipes and jabs. Gina paused only for a moment then charged again, but Angela emerged unscathed and managed to slash Gina across the cheek as they parted. Mac considered helping, but as he saw blood flowing from Gina's face and calf, he realized Angela was playing a cat-and-mouse game with her.

He even considered taking pity on Gina, but knew Angela had no such thoughts. With Michael bleeding to death in the corner of the room, he was sure Angela would show no mercy to her tormentor.

Gina favored her good leg as she readied herself for another attack. Even though she had taken the brunt of the punishment, she continued to stay aggressive, looking to land a fatal stab to Angela.

They came at each other again, arms flailing, holding nothing back. They were so close to each other, they might have been hugging. As the two separated, Angela no longer had her knives. Mac looked at Gina, who stood in a defensive pose, only her eyes revealing the shock of the last exchange. One of Angela's knives protruded from Gina's chest. She dropped her own knives as a look of horror came over her face. She fell to her knees, and finally collapsed to the floor, revealing another knife protruding from her back. Gina was dead.

Angela ran over to Traveres, who lay on the floor moaning. Judy had ripped open his shirt, revealing a deep red pool of blood. "My God, what did they do to you?" Angela cried. "Judy, please! We've got to help him! Don't tell me it's too late."

"Angela, honey, I'll try."

Through his labored breathing, Traveres tried to speak. "Angela." He softly brushed her cheek. "I...I love you. I did this for you. Angel, please get Mac."

"I'm here, Michael." Mac knelt down next to him.

"Commander, I'm sorry...for the trouble...," he started.

"Michael, you saved us."

"You...you're not safe yet."

"Why?"

"A bomb...on board," he coughed, blood flowing from his mouth.

"Where is it?"

"I...I think...Gina's room. They said they had a bomb...would blow up the ship unless I let them on the bridge."

"Then you never saw the bomb?"

"No, I heard them talking. He told Gina to deactivate it. I think she rearmed the bomb, just in case you retook the base. This is a suicide mission... we are expendable."

More than anything, Mac wanted to ask Traveres the reason for the mutiny; but now he had a bomb to worry about. "I'll look for the explosive. I want you two to put your helmets back on. If this thing blows the side off the crew module, I want us to be able to survive, if the blast doesn't kill us."

Mac zipped up his helmet and ran to Gina's room, searching every corner of the sparse quarters. He found nothing but her clothes and a laptop computer, not quite closed. He opened it up and saw number forty-nine displayed on the screen, then forty-eight, then forty-seven. He realized in horror that he was seeing a countdown display on the screen with only forty-seven seconds left!

He keyed his com-link. "Victor! Unlock the outer doors on the habitat tunnel now! I have to get outside."

"I copy, Commander."

Mac closed the laptop and put it under his arm. *Thirty-five seconds.* He started counting mentally in his head as he made his way down the ladder to the ready room.

Judy and Angela turned as Mac hit the airlock entrance.

"Did you find it?" Judy asked.

Ignoring them, Mac closed the door behind him and activated the airlock as his count reached twenty-seven seconds. He knew the decompression took about fifteen seconds, leaving him about ten seconds to get outside. He double-checked the oxygen in his suit. The decompression cycle seemed to take forever. "Victor, make sure those outer airlock doors are unlocked!" he yelled.

"They're unlocked, Commander." Rechenko radioed back.

Twenty seconds, Mac counted to himself. The cycle reached the halfway point—too close for comfort. Then he remembered that he could blow the outside door anytime. He just had to be careful the pressure didn't throw him out of the airlock or knock him to the ground.

He hit the emergency release and found himself being pushed out the door. *Fifteen seconds, run!* His legs dug into the ground. Mac felt as if he were moving in slow motion. He hit the inside habitat airlock door at eight seconds. He pushed through the outer door counting five, four...

He stopped and flung the laptop out toward the H3 berm in one motion. Two...one.... He dove to the ground and waited. Zero...he saw a bright light in the direction he had thrown the laptop. Mac curled into a fetal position and buried his head in his arms.

"My god! That was close!" he heard Rechenko say, witnessing the drama from the Mars 3 bridge. "Are you all right?"

Curled up in a ball, Mac was physically exhausted and mentally spent. They had retaken the base at a terrible cost. Three more people were dead, another was dying, and he still didn't know why.

"Mac! Are you okay?" Judy called frantically. "Are you there? Answer me!"

"I'm here, Judy. I'm fine," Mac said, barely mustering enough energy to speak.

"Please come back inside," she pleaded.

Mac sensed something amiss in her voice. "Judy, how is Traveres?"

After a long silence, Judy answered, her voice cracking. "Michael's dead."

CHAPTER 23
AFTERMATH

Mac sat alone at the galley table and stared into a cup of cold black coffee. The horror of the day's events only now started to sink in. Four crewmates died at Mars Base that evening and no one except Boyle seemed to know why, and he wasn't talking.

Rechenko and Mac had strapped Boyle to a chair inside the radiation chamber. Judy placed an IV in his arm with a continuous flow of sedative to keep him under. Taking no chances, Mac locked and secured the chamber, leaving only a camera trained on Boyle so he could be interrogated. But grilling him with questions would have to wait.

Mac and Rechenko had to complete the gruesome task of recovering the bodies of Ivory and La Rue and putting them in plastic bags as they had with Gina's and Michael's. The four of them were laid side by side on the cold floor of Habitat 2 as it was being pressurized overnight. Judy suggested they bury their comrades on Sunset Ridge, overlooking the base. Mac agreed, as long as it didn't interfere with their launch preparations.

Mars 3 would need to be refueled and the master computer re-calibrated and loaded with a new launch program. They had five days to complete all these tasks, or they would be sentenced to two more years on Mars.

Mac pushed back his chair and started to get up from the galley table when Angela appeared at the door. "May I come in, Commander?" she said, in a soft, gentle voice.

"Of course, Angela." Mac sat back down. "What can I do for you?"

Angela sat next to Mac and rested her hand on his arm. "First of all, Commander, Michael repeatedly told me how ashamed and sorry he was for being a part of this."

"I know, Angela. He gave his life to save ours. I hope he knew we were grateful."

"He admired you so much. Michael was honored to be your right hand."

"Thanks. That's nice to hear."

"It's so unfair he had to die," she said, tears welling up in her eyes. "But he didn't want to die in vain. He had several things he wanted you to know—information that would help you deal with Dr. Boyle."

"Hey, I need all the help I can get."

"The first thing he said was that under no circumstances should you try to contact Mission Control through EarthConn or any other method."

For the first time in over three months, Angela finally confirmed what Mac only recently suspected; Earth had not been hit by a solar catastrophe.

"Why shouldn't I?"

"Michael said you would understand when you looked at the media files in his computer. Besides, he said only Boyle has the encryption code for Earth-Conn."

"That figures. Did he say what was in the files?"

"No, he didn't have time; but he said you should read them first thing."

Mac guessed the files of the world's newspapers and electronic media would reveal the cover story explaining the disappearance of Mars 3 and the fate of Mac and the other innocent crew members. That would be helpful in interrogating Boyle.

"Did he say anything else? Such as why half my crew turned on me?"

"Yes, he said you should check the VOTS file on his computer."

"VOTS? What does that mean?"

"I don't know for sure. Michael said he was mostly kept in the dark, but he knew Ivory, La Rue, and Boyle were planning a week-long EVA to the Valley of the Sun."

"Where the hell is that? I don't remember that on any of the maps."

"I don't know either, but I'm pretty sure VOTS is the Valley of the Sun."

Mac flinched. "That would make sense."

Angela leaned over and kissed him on the cheek, then hugged him tightly. "Commander, he admired you so much. I didn't realize it until it was too late, but he carried a huge burden inside him. I feel terrible that I didn't recognize it for what it was. Maybe I could have helped him sooner and he'd be alive today."

"Don't think for a second you could have done anything more than you did. You saved our lives. Michael was a victim of a ruthless group of people. If he hadn't kept silent, we might all be dead."

Angela stood up and nodded. "Thank you, Commander. Your words mean a lot. Good night."

"Good night. Sleep well." As Angela went off to bed, Mac thought of the turmoil she must be feeling. She saved everyone's life but the one that mattered most to her.

Even though it had been an exhausting day, Mac rushed to search through Michael's computer. The sheer curiosity about it all would have prevented him from sleeping anyway.

Traveres' media file revealed a series of headlines from the world's newspapers and periodicals. He was shocked by the extent of the lies and deceptions perpetrated on the public. **Mars Commander Murders Crew. Betrayal and Murder on Mars! MacTavish Goes Mad! Mass Murder on Mars!** His horror only grew as he read some of the articles about himself and the Mars Mission. He was accused of going mad and taking control of the base, including all communications with Earth. He supposedly murdered Rechenko and Judy and was threatening the rest of the crew.

Worse yet, Dr. Boyle was portrayed as the hero, responsible for saving the mission by convincing Mac to give up his murder spree and surrender to Boyle's authority! Boyle was now considered the mission leader and an international hero!

Mac thought about his family at home, his mother and father and the obvious hurt and shame they must feel for their only child. Were they being held up to ridicule, having raised one of the most notorious traitors in history? He needed to contact them as soon as possible to set the record straight and ease their pain.

Curiously, he saw little about Mars 3 until he came across a reference to the impending doom of the Mars program due to Mac's treachery and the catastrophic failure of the Mars 3 mission. As he searched further, he found the fabricated story of how Mars 3 disappeared shortly after the attempt to go into hyper-drive with the new plasma-injected matter/anti-matter booster. NASA had concluded that the engine had exploded and killed the crew instantly.

In the wake of the tragedy, the International Space Consortium postponed the Mars 4 mission until the new hyperdrive could be thoroughly reexamined. This resulted in the fractionalization of the Space Consortium and the withdrawal of several participating nations. The entire Mars program had come to an end—all orchestrated by Dr. Boyle and whomever he was working with inside the program.

It was clear to Mac that the purpose of Boyle's mission was to end all further exploration of Mars. But why would a prominent scientist, with a career built on exploration and discovery, be an agent for forces wishing to discourage interest in the red planet?

He searched for Traveres' VOTS file, which revealed a series of maps starting with Highway One leading out of the base and passing by Red Anvil, Angel Rock, and beyond. Boyle and La Rue had explored much more territory than Mac had been led to believe.

Highway One followed up the Grand Arroyo for several miles then cut off into mountainous terrain. There were several switchbacks in the road indicating a steep vertical climb to a high mountain pass. The road then wound down into a depression. Traveres had labeled the depression the Valley of the Sun. From Mac's estimate, it was about a hundred miles from Mars Base.

So this is why Boyle, Ivory, and La Rue found it necessary to spend so much time away from the base. The distance they had to travel made overnight stays a necessity. It appeared Traveres had not been briefed on the valley since his map showed no details of any kind. Mac figured Boyle's computer contained all the pertinent information, protected by his encryption code. Traveres had warned Mac not to use EarthConn to contact Houston. Boyle probably had an operative back inside Mission Control who could remotely sabotage the mission in the event that Mac managed to regain control of the base. After all, Traveres did say this was a "suicide" mission.

There were so many more questions than answers. How big was this conspiracy? How high up the chain of command did it go? Could it be an international conspiracy or solely a European operation? The people responsible obviously wielded an enormous amount of power—enough to manipulate mission crews, the world press, even independent corporate contractors and space agencies. They were even willing to send an entire crew to their deaths.

His thoughts drifted back to his parents, holed up inside their cabin. The only man who could vindicate Mac was heavily sedated and sitting strapped to a chair in the radiation chamber.

The sun broke over the Grand Arroyo, its rays piercing the windows of the crew module and Habitat 2. Walking through the base, Mac saw the signs of the previous night's battle everywhere. Bloodstains marked the walls and floor of the ready room. Habitat 2, now pressurized, was strewn with debris piled around the six purge valves.

Angela and Judy were preparing the bodies of Michael, Gina, Ivory, and La Rue. They were placed on the floor of the habitat, each covered with the flag of the International Space Consortium, with the exception of Traveres. Angela insisted on placing an American flag over his body.

Mac stood over the bodies and felt the anger building up inside. Angela and Judy walked up and stood by him, saying nothing.

"This is all such a waste." He shook his head. "I want to pledge to you both right now that no more lives will be lost." Mac felt Judy squeeze his hand tightly. "An hour before sunset we will meet here for a burial ceremony. Now, let's get to work."

At midday, while Mac and Rechenko worked inside Mars 3, Angela was on the Mars 2 bridge, mastering the remote controls for Ratty. Traveres had been the expert operator for the ungainly beast, as he called it, so Angela had benefited from watching him manipulate the virtual reality system.

With Mac's permission, Angela remotely guided Ratty up to Sunset Ridge and commenced digging the four graves. Once she got the hang of it, she became quite good at using the virtual goggles and hand controls to dig into the Martian surface.

As Ratty's arms scratched the surface, responding to Angela's hand and arm movements, tears rolled down her face. Digging into the soil, the reality of the moment penetrated deep into her core. Instead of planning their wedding, she planned a funeral and dug Traveres' grave.

"If you want, Commander, I could fuel the tower tonight," Rechenko said as he and Mac walked back to the base from Mars 3.

"No, Victor. That won't be necessary. We should have plenty of time to re-fuel Mars 3 tomorrow. Besides, Angela is using Ratty to dig graves up at Sunset Ridge."

Rechenko nodded. "Angela is taking this very well, I think."

"She's a rock, Victor. I don't know how she does it. It will be difficult to bury them tonight."

"Commander, you should have had Dr. Boyle dig the graves. After all, he is responsible their deaths, is he not?"

"Yes, he is; but I'm not planning to let Boyle out of the radiation chamber until we move him to Mars 3 just before we launch."

"That's more than he deserves. We should just leave him here."

"Don't think I haven't considered that, but he has to answer for his crimes before a world court. That reminds me…" Mac keyed his com-link. "Judy? Do you copy?"

After a short pause, Judy answered. "Yes, Mac, go ahead."

"I'd like you to wake up Boyle for me, please. It's time for a conversation."

"Okay. He'll be ready when you are. I can remotely deliver the stimulant through his IV. It won't take him long to become fully conscious."

"Thanks, Victor and I are walking back to the base right now. We'll be there in a few minutes," Mac said as he stopped and looked along the horizon.

"The sky is changing," Rechenko said, as if reading Mac's mind. "There is a Red Storm coming, I think."

"Yes, the season's beginning. Ivory recorded a Red Storm warning two nights ago. I'm glad we're launching in a few days."

As he walked back to the base, Mac considered the two unpleasant tasks remaining today: burying four crewmates and resurrecting a hated adversary.

Dr. Boyle felt a deep hunger pang as he slowly woke up from his drug-induced slumber. He shifted his position and felt the soreness in his body, the result of sitting in the same spot for over eighteen hours. In an instant, he remembered the disaster in Habitat 2. The deaths of part of his crew didn't bother him as much as realizing the lowly Commander Mac MacTavish had gotten the better of him.

He turned his head from side to side, wincing at the throbbing pain in his jaw where Mac had punched him. His arms were strapped to the chair, rubbing against a slash on his wrist; and his face was swollen from the punches he had absorbed. The pain pulsing through his body reminded him he was alive when he should be dead.

He had given Gina enough time to set the explosive that would kill them all. So why was he still alive? Something had obviously gone wrong. He deduced he was a prisoner, but whose? Did Mac manage to retake the base?

He knew Ivory and La Rue had been killed in the habitat, and he presumed Angela had taken out Gina in a final knife fight. He shook his head in disgust. Angela had been the one person he had underestimated.

How could things have gone more wrong? At least he had eliminated Traveres, preventing him from divulging any sensitive information about their true purpose here. Since he was the sole survivor, he knew his ultimate responsibility would be to ensure that no one else would leave Mars Base alive.

Mac sat in his chair on the flight deck and looked at the monitor showing Dr. Boyle strapped in the chamber. He appeared haggard and disoriented, but obviously awake. Mac realized he had to be sly and cautious, bluffing his way into making Boyle believe Mac knew more than he really did.

Mac activated a monitor in front of Boyle, allowing the groggy doctor to see him. To Mac's disappointment, the doctor glanced at him for a moment then averted his eyes. *Was this shame?* Mac wondered. *Possibly embarrassment? Definitely not guilt or remorse!*

"So, Dr. Boyle," Mac paused for a long moment to see if Boyle would acknowledge him. "I have one thing to say to you. I'm not dead." Boyle continued to look away.

"I'd like to thank you for that premature send-off you gave us yesterday. I can't say we were in the best of moods when we landed, as you and your crew found out."

Frustrated with Boyle's failure to react, Mac stepped up the rhetoric. "You know, we are burying three of your colleagues in about an hour on Sunset Ridge. I am holding you responsible for their deaths."

Boyle quit twitching and glanced at the monitor.

"When we return to Earth, you will be charged in the murders of Lieutenant Ivory, Gina Gibson, and Damon La Rue." Boyle cocked his head slowly, as if he was about to ask a question, but remained silent. Mac knew Boyle had to be wondering about Traveres' fate.

"You are also responsible for the life of Lieutenant Traveres, who is recovering from the wounds you inflicted upon him last night."

Boyle looked away again.

"Dr. Boyle, Lieutenant Traveres has briefed me on the purpose of your mission here. With his help, I have obtained information on your secret activities. He told me about the Valley of the Sun." Mac stopped and waited for a reaction. Boyle finally turned to the monitor and spoke to Mac for the first time since their fight in the ready room the night before.

"Tell me, Commander, have you contacted Mission Control yet?"

Mac hadn't anticipated that question and stumbled as he answered.

"No...no, I haven't, not yet. I'm still waiting until I have all the facts before I uh...call them."

"Waiting for all the facts?" Boyle continued. "Then the Lieutenant hasn't divulged the true nature of the Valley of the Sun. Of course, he couldn't have since he didn't have any knowledge of what we were doing there. You see, he was just our chauffeur. This mission that you are interfering with was strictly on a need-to-know basis. Only Ivory, La Rue, and I knew the true purpose of this expedition, and now I am the sole guardian of the secrets of the Valley of the Sun."

Much to Mac's dismay, the cockiness in Boyle's voice had returned. He obviously knew he had something Mac wanted.

"So, Commander, since you've probably tried and failed to get any information out of my computer, and you have to launch soon, you will have precious little time to waste driving a hundred miles across Mars to find out what is so interesting about the Valley of the Sun. My guess is you probably want me to give you my encryption code and save you the time. Am I right?"

Mac knew he had to be careful. Boyle obviously thought he could make some sort of deal. He decided to hit the doctor in his most vulnerable spot, his ego.

"Doctor, it would save me some time having access to the information in your computer; but, believe me, I am prepared to drive out to the Valley of the Sun myself and take whatever I find back to Earth as my discovery. I will be the one to shock the world, not you."

Boyle seemed ready to react to Mac's threat, but then a slow grin came over his face. "Commander, if you've seen any of the headlines from Earth over the past few months, then you are aware that you are certainly one of the most hated figures in world history. Because of your heinous crimes against your own crew, you are vilified across the planet. Now you want to steal my discovery and return to Earth expecting the population to believe you? I would venture to say that you and your returning conspirators wouldn't get two feet inside the International Space Station before you were arrested and charged with the murders you are so anxious to pin on me."

Mac could see Boyle intended to play all the cards available to him. Could he be right? Would the world believe him if he were to return with very little evidence of what had transpired on Mars? One fact remained. Mac needed the information inside Boyle's computer, but what would he have to give up in order to access it?

"All right, Commander, I have a proposal for you. If you really have the time to drive all the way to the Valley of the Sun," Boyle started, "then let me go with you. I can assure you that once you get to the Valley, you will have no idea what you are looking at. You will waste valuable time trying to decide what to do—all the while, missing the most significant and fascinating secrets hidden there."

Mac felt tempted, but he didn't want travel a hundred miles across Mars with Boyle at his side.

Boyle continued. "Commander, I could be your guide through an unbelievable discovery that will change the world. You would be among the first to see what the origins of Mars, Earth, maybe even our entire solar system. Together, we'll return to Earth, triumphant explorers, celebrated as equals with Columbus, Magellan, and Drake."

It amazed Mac how Boyle could make such an evil scheme seem so inviting. Mac let Boyle see his interest.

"How would we explain the deaths of Ivory, Gina, and La Rue?" Mac said, careful to exclude Michael. "The headlines already said I was the betrayer."

"Easy," Boyle answered. "We just say the others had controlled all communications until you and I subdued them."

Boyle's willingness to casually brush aside his colleagues outraged Mac. He pressed the sedative button causing Boyle to lose consciousness almost immediately. Mac had heard enough from this cold-hearted killer. He turned to Judy and Rechenko, who sat with him during the interrogation. They too appeared stunned by Boyle's callous behavior.

"I can't believe that sonofabitch actually thought you would take him up on his offer," Judy said. "I'm surprised you let him talk that long."

"Well, I'm no closer to finding out what's in the Valley of the Sun, other than its being some sort of remarkable discovery that could rock the world. If we can't figure out how to access the information on his computer, I'm going to have to drive a hundred miles to see what's worth the lives of twelve people."

"Commander, it is only speculation on my part...," Rechenko said, "...but I may have a way to get at the information on Boyle's computer."

"Really, Victor? How?"

"I discovered a program that Lieutenant Traveres used to control the Mars 3 computer. It gave him access to all our computers with the use of optical laser technology, the same technology we use to track our locations with the badges we wear."

"I don't understand," Mac said. "You mean he could eavesdrop on our computers by using a laser from the mother ship? How is that possible?"

"I am not quite sure how it works, but I ran some tests on my own computer, and I was able to upload files using his program."

"Upload files? That's fantastic! We can get at all of Boyle's files. That means I don't have to deal with him anymore. Great!"

"Commander, there is a problem with just uploading the files off his computer. They are still encrypted. Without the code, the files would still be useless."

Mac's mood sank as his hopes for an easy solution disappeared. "So if we upload his files, we wouldn't be able to find his code on there somewhere?"

"I am afraid not. In fact, I already ran a test on his laptop and came away with nothing but encrypted code. He would have to input his code for this to work. Then we would be able to upload his unprotected files."

"But how are you going to do that?" Judy interrupted. "You can't just give him his computer. He'll be suspicious, particularly because he probably knows of the existence and capabilities of Michael's program."

"Judy's right," Mac said. "The last thing I want to do is tip off Boyle that we're trying to steal his files. So how do we get him and his computer together without raising any suspicion?"

"Dr. Boyle would probably like nothing more than to get to his computer and destroy all his files," Rechenko said.

Mac nodded. "I agree. I'm sure his biggest fear is that we would return to Earth with his findings to vindicate us. We have to find a way to get him to input the encryption code without trying to destroy anything. Victor, how long would it take to upload his hard drive after he put in the code?"

"I do not know for sure," answered Rechenko. "It works pretty fast though. I uploaded the launch program from Mars 3 in about ten seconds. It would obviously take a lot longer for an entire hard drive."

"What are you thinking?" Judy asked, crossing her arms and shooting Mac a stern look.

"I'm not sure yet," Mac said, knowing Judy would probably object immediately to what was on his mind. "So what you're saying, Victor, is that if I can get Boyle to open up his files, you may be able to upload them within, say, a couple of minutes?"

"It is possible. Of course, it would depend on how much information he has stored."

Judy glared at Mac with an intensity he had never seen before. "Mac, you're not thinking of taking that crazy doctor to the Valley of the Sun with you, are you?"

"Maybe," Mac said, looking at the monitor, which showed an unconscious Boyle still sitting in the chamber, tightly strapped into a chair.

"Well then you're as crazy as he is!" she shouted. "Except there's a big difference between you and him. He's a cold-blooded killer and apparently you want to be his next victim—all because you want to clear your good name and return a hero!"

"Judy, stop it! I can't believe you'd say that. I *have* to get the information from his computer or I can't guarantee we'll be able to return to Earth safely. Not just me, but none of us. There is some sort of network of conspirators within the space agency, or maybe the government, that is prepared to discredit any evidence we bring back, particularly if it's encrypted and we don't know what it is. In order for us to be cleared of all blame for this tragedy, we must know what Boyle is hiding."

"So you have to take that murdering son of a bitch to the valley with you? Isn't there a better way?" she cried in exasperation.

"Look, I don't have to take him all the way to the valley. All I have to do is have him turn on his computer and access his files. Victor will upload his hard drive and give me the all clear. Then I'll return to the base immediately. I don't have to see what's in the valley. It should all be cataloged in his files."

Judy shook her head and turned her back to him.

"We're running out of time," Mac pleaded. "If you can think of a better way, I'm all ears; but right now I think we ought to plan for doing this in three days. That way we'll have Mars 3 fueled and ready to go."

"I just want this nightmare to end." Judy turned to him again. "I don't know how much more of this I can take. Go ahead if you must, but if you get into trouble out there, I'm not going to rescue you, understand? You're on your own. It's bad enough that Angela lost her hero…"

As if on cue, Angela came up the ladder and walked into the room. She wore her soft pressure suit and she'd applied makeup to her face in an attempt to camouflage her deeply swollen eyes.

"Commander," she said. "It's an hour until sunset."

Mac gave her a reassuring nod. The time had come to bury their comrades.

CHAPTER 24
VALLEY OF THE SUN

Mac woke up early and slipped out of bed, careful not to wake Judy. It had been two days since they had buried their colleagues at Sunset Ridge, and he hadn't had a decent night's sleep yet. He stepped out into the dark corridor and climbed up the ladder to the flight deck. The morning's early light filtered through the bridge windows, just enough for Mac to make out Rechenko's rotund figure slumped over the console.

"Victor, wake up." Mac shook him.

"W…what?" Rechenko sat up. He had fallen asleep next to Boyle's computer.

"What are you doing? You sleep here all night?"

"No, I've been up for about an hour, trying to break this damn encryption code so you won't have to go to the Valley of the Sun today."

Mac plopped down into his pilot's chair and gazed out at the deep red sky to the east. The Valley of the Sun had beckoned him from the moment he learned of its existence. "I've been in command of this mission for more than two years. I've traveled over two hundred and sixty million miles and managed to lose half my crew through mutiny. I'm a failure, Victor, the most hated person in the galaxy. I don't really give a damn about Boyle's encryption code. I'm tired of relying on someone else to save my ass. I'm going to the Valley today to see first-hand what in God's name is worth twelve lives."

"Are you going to take Boyle with you?"

Mac reached over and turned on the camera pointed at Boyle, strapped in the chamber. He pressed the remote button that would bring the doctor out of his drug-induced sleep. "I'm going to ask him. If he says yes, then we go. I still want you to try to upload his files when he logs on to his computer. We'll need the code to access EarthConn and talk to mission control."

"Da, as you wish," Rechenko nodded.

Mac watched Boyle stir as the stimulant took effect. He appeared thin and drawn and in need of a shower and shave. In contrast to his surly behavior a few days earlier, he immediately started to talk to the camera with a deep wail. "What are you doing to me? I'm starving to death in here! My mouth is dry, and I need solid food. Why are you torturing me?"

"Doctor, we've just been very busy readying Mars 3 for launch. We'll try to get you some solid food in a couple of days."

"A couple of days? Are you bloody crazy? Get me out of this chair! I have sores and cramps. This is inhumane!"

"At least you're alive," Mac said coolly. "That's more than I can say for your cohorts who were buried a few days ago."

Boyle lowered his voice and stared at the camera. "What do you want from me? I had a mission to accomplish and I failed. You can return me to Earth to stand trial, but you don't really have any conclusive evidence against me, do you?"

"Not yet, but I will by tonight. You see, Lieutenant Traveres provided some very detailed maps of the Valley. I should be able to make my way around and catalog plenty of what I see."

Boyle raised an eyebrow. "You're going to the Valley today?"

"Gonna leave in an hour. Of course, if you went with me, I could complete my investigation more quickly."

Boyle chuckled. "Do you mean that I might help you with your investigation? Why in the hell would I do that?"

"Because with you or without you, I'm going to get to the bottom of this. I'm offering you a chance to show me your discovery personally and claim credit for your work. You'll still face criminal charges, but at least you'll have the credit you are so concerned about. That's more than you deserve, Doctor; that's more than you offered the people buried on Sunset Ridge."

He could see Boyle seriously considering his offer, but Mac decided not to let him think it through too long.

"I'm not going to try to convince you to help me. I have the whole day to explore the Valley on my own. Plus I have your computer. Encryption code or not, a way will be found to get to your files. Then I will be the one to show the world what I've discovered."

Mac watched as Boyle fidgeted in his seat. "What's the matter? Have you gotten used to intravenous feeding and being strapped to that chair?"

"All right! I'll do it!" Boyle's face turned red. "I can't believe I'm going to help you, but I see I have no other alternative! Not that anyone would believe you could come up with such an extraordinary discovery."

"Fine, I'll send in some food. I want you to have your strength for the trip." Mac switched off the camera and turned to see Judy standing behind him.

"So that's it," she said, arms folded. "Just the two of you will be traveling a hundred miles across Mars? Why don't you take one of us? I'll be glad to go and watch over that sneaky bastard."

"No, I'm doing this on my own. He's my responsibility."

"But Boyle is a maniac with nothing to lose."

"Look, he'll be strapped to his seat. I'll be in constant contact with you on my redline. As soon as he accesses his files, Victor will upload them. When you give me confirmation that you have his files, I'll simply stop and turn around."

Judy rolled her eyes. "Don't talk to me like I'm a fool, Mac. Here, take this." She handed him a large syringe.

"This won't do me any good. We're going to wear hard-pressure suits."

"Stab him in the neck. The needle will puncture the soft collar. It won't take much; this is cyanide."

Mac raised his eyebrows. "You mean business."

"All right, that should hold you," Mac said, as he and Rechenko secured the restraining belt behind Boyle's seat inside Matty.

"Is this absolutely necessary?" Boyle asked. "It's not as though I can run away."

"Just a precaution. You'll have to earn my trust."

Mac walked Rechenko to the back of Matty and entered the small airlock where Boyle couldn't hear them. "Victor, are you prepared to fly Mars 3 on autopilot if you have to?"

"You mean, by myself?"

"Yes. With Judy and Angela's help, could you launch from here, rendez-vous with the mother ship, and perform a hyperspace burn to return to Earth?"

"I suppose I could, but I don't want to."

"I don't want you to either, but in forty-eight hours Mars 3 has to launch, with or without me."

Mac drove Matty along Highway One at a good clip, sometimes reaching fifty miles an hour on the well-traveled road.

"Is the Valley of Sun on the guidance system?" Mac asked, speaking his first words to Boyle since leaving the base.

"Type in 'site 13'. That will take us where we want to go," Boyle said, not bothering to look at him.

At first Mac wondered if he should trust Boyle, but it was clear the doctor was just as eager to see the Valley. He entered site 13 into the computer and the auto guidance system took control of Matty, allowing Mac to take his hands off the wheel. A combination of road sensors and a laser relay from the orbiting mother ship would lead the vehicle to its destination.

Mac reached between the seats and pulled out Boyle's computer. "Here you go, Doctor, I thought you might need this if you're going to explain everything to me."

Boyle seemed to chuckle under his breath as he took the computer and set it on his lap, but didn't open it. He quietly stared out the window.

Judy paced the flight-deck floor like a caged tiger. Rechenko and Angela sat next to each other and listened to every sound coming from Matty.

"I think Mac just handed Boyle his computer," Rechenko said.

Judy stopped. "Did he turn it on?"

"Not yet. I'll let you know."

Judy went back to pacing while Rechenko and Angela listened for any sub-tleties in the ambient sound coming from Matty.

"Are you feeling okay?" Mac asked, breaking the long silence.

Boyle turned his head to look at Mac. "I'm okay," he said, pausing as he turned to look out the window again, "considering what I have had to endure the past few days."

Mac bristled at the thought that Boyle would complain about his treatment, but suppressed his disdain. "So you feel good enough to do some exploring outside?"

"What makes you think we need to go outside?"

"I don't know, Doctor. Why don't you tell me what I should expect? Don't you think it's time to let me in on your little secret?"

"All in good time, Commander. Everything you need to know is right in here," Boyle, patted his computer. "I'll let you know as we approach the Valley."

"So you're saying we won't have to leave Matty to explore the Valley?"

"No, I didn't say that. If you're any kind of a scientist, you'll want to get out and experience the magnificence."

"Damn! I thought we had him!" Rechenko yelled. "I think he had his computer in his hands. It sounded like he was ready to power it up, but I show no signature from the laser scan."

Judy turned away from the communications console and resumed her endless walk. After enduring the last week of violence and mind games, manipulations and deceptions, she just wanted Mac safe by her side.

Matty bounced across the surface at top speed. They had cruised past Red Anvil in less than an hour, and Angel Rock loomed on the horizon. The explosion site marked the farthest point Mac had traveled away from Mars Base. The territory beyond was uncharted as far as he knew. Yet Matty sped along a well-traveled highway that stretched as far as the eye could see. According to the navigational display, Mac could see they would travel for another thirty miles of open landscape, gradually climbing up into a towering mountain range that formed the far boundary of the Grand Arroyo.

"How long will it take from here, Doctor?"

"About another hour until we reach the summit above the Valley." Boyle looked at his watch. "One more hour and you'll have your answer, Commander."

"I'm not even sure what the question is. You seem to think this is bigger than I can comprehend. Suppose you give me a little preparation so I don't die of shock?"

Boyle opened his computer and turned it on. He typed feverishly on the keyboard, pulling up files and looking at data. *This was it!* But Mac hadn't heard anything on his redline from Rechenko.

"A signal!" Rechenko barked. "He's turned on his computer!"

Judy moved to the console. "Has he logged on yet?"

"I don't know. I'm switching to an active scan." Rechenko watched the read-out from the laser relay. "It's a strong signal."

"I hear typing!" Angela said.

"Rechenko activated the program, commanding the laser relay to scan the output of Boyle's computer. Almost instantly, the screen filled with a data stream of information.

"What is that?" Angela asked. "Are we looking at Boyle's computer?"

Rechenko studied the screen. Something looked familiar, and he felt a pang of anxiety in his stomach. "No!!!" he shouted, causing Judy and Angela to jump. He quickly severed the links to the laser relay, cutting off all communication with Matty. Every locator indicator, camera, and microphone instantly went dead.

"I've lost audio contact with Matty!" Angela shouted. "I've also lost the road camera and all location emitters!"

"What?" Judy yelled in alarm.

Rechenko sat, shaking his head and covering his face with his hands. "I'm afraid we just blew our cover."

Mac watched Boyle as he studied the data on his computer.

"Interesting," Boyle finally said, "very interesting."

"What is it?"

"I would have thought your friends back at the base would have been monitoring us pretty closely, yet I see no indication the laser relay is even being used."

Mac tried not to show his panic. The first thing Boyle had done when he finally logged on to his computer was to check the status of the very instrument they were planning to use to steal his files. Rechenko must have seen what he was up to and severed the laser relay links.

"Well, they're very busy preparing for departure," Mac lied. "They have a lot to do before tomorrow's launch. I'm sure they'll take an interest as we approach the Valley."

"That is curious," Boyle said. "I would have thought you'd have microphones and hidden cameras all over the place, paranoid I might try something. I am surprised by your trust, and I think I'm ready to return a little of that trust to you."

"Victor, I can't just stand by and do nothing. We have to help Mac. He may be in grave danger. You *have* to reestablish the link!" Judy cried.

Stunned by Boyle's actions, Rechenko just shook his head. He would never have anticipated the Doctor would check on the laser link immediately after logging on. He obviously had a very powerful computer, able to monitor all the major systems on Mars. Rechenko began to wonder how wise it had been to give Boyle access to such a powerful tool, capable of controlling and manipulating much of the Mars Base hardware.

"Are you listening to me?" Judy repeated. "Mac may be in danger! We have to reestablish contact!"

"No!" Rechenko shook his head forcefully. "We cannot link up again. Not now anyway. We will have to wait until they are closer to the Valley. Boyle just checked to make sure we were not listening to them talking. We cannot get caught, or this will all be for naught."

"But how will we know Mac is all right?"

"Don't worry about Mac; he can take care of himself. I will wait about twenty minutes and activate the laser locator to see how far they've traveled. It is a passive system and Boyle shouldn't be able to detect it unless he attempts to specifically check on us."

"Will we be able to hear them?" Angela asked.

"No, not for a while. We can't risk tipping him off. Since we know his computer is activated, we will have to upload his files in one swift stroke before he realizes the laser relay is functioning."

"Well, I'm not going to just sit here and wait for bad news," Judy said. "I'm going to put on a pressure suit and prepare for a rescue operation."

Rechenko tried to stop Judy as she went down to the ready room, but Angela stopped him.

"Victor, let her go. She needs to feel like she's doing something."

"She should not worry so much," Rechenko replied. "Mac knows what he is doing. I am sure he has things under control."

Mac looked out the window and noticed the changing terrain. Matty now climbed up a gradual slope that appeared to be the beginning of a road through a mountain pass to the Valley on the other side.

"What mountain is this?" Mac asked. "The map only gives it a number."

"We named it the Mountain of the Sun, of course," Boyle said, proud to share his discoveries.

"How much longer before we get there?"

Boyle looked out the window. "We should be at the pass above the Valley in about thirty minutes."

A two and a half-hour journey? That would get them there by mid-morning, meaning they should have plenty of time to explore the Valley.

"Doctor, suppose you tell me what all the mystery is about. As I said before, since you say this is too big for me to understand, maybe you should prepare me."

Boyle pushed his computer aside, leaving it on. "I would be interested to know what you think we are going to see in the Valley."

"I don't know. I can't even begin to imagine what would be worth killing so many innocent people."

"Innocent. That's a good word," Boyle quipped. "We are all so innocent. The whole world is innocent and naive and completely oblivious to what is really going on around them. I'm interested to know what your suspicions are. You were certainly clever enough to uncover the 'conspiracy' against you. You were smart enough to save your own hide and retake the base, so what do you think you are going to see in the Valley?"

Mac disliked Boyle's condescending tone, but decided to play along—anything to get Boyle to use his computer. "I suppose it may have something to do with a mining operation? Maybe valuable minerals, diamonds, gold...something along those lines?" Even as he spoke, Mac couldn't help but think how foolish he must sound.

"Gold? Diamonds? Minerals?" Boyle said, with a devilish grin. "Oh Commander, you disappoint me so. You can't be serious! You think this is all about greed? I can't tell you how insulted I am by your—pardon me—simple-mindedness. Here I am fancying you as a worthy adversary and the best explanation you can come up with is greed?"

Mac was determined not to let Boyle humiliate or intimidate him. "Look, you didn't have to be here. I could have done this myself, without your games and insults. Now suppose you tell me what this is all about before I lock you up in the airlock."

Boyle nodded, holding up his hand. "Okay, okay, it's not necessary to threaten me. I'll cooperate. Since this will be your first time and my last time to see the Valley of the Sun, I will be glad to prepare you, as best I can, for what you are about to see." He reached for his computer and began to type again.

Mac looked at the rugged mountainous terrain outside. Matty rolled along a well-defined path that hugged one side of the mountain with a substantial drop-off on the other. Whatever happened, he would soon see the Valley of the Sun with his own eyes.

"I have contact!" Rechenko yelled. "From what I can see, they will reach the Valley in about twenty minutes. I have a lock on Dr. Boyle's computer, and I'm ready to upload."

"Do it!" Judy said. "Do it and get Mac out of there."

Rechenko hit one key, and in an instant, steams of data started to flow onto the base hard drive. He could see the massive volume of data would take some time to decipher. It was one thing to have Boyle's secret files; it would be quite another to find what they were looking for.

Matty followed the narrow path through the steep terrain. Mac gave his full attention to the slim roadway outside, rather than to Dr. Boyle's cryptic ramblings. He only wanted Boyle to explain the reasons for his treachery. Instead, Mac received a lecture on the history of the world according to Boyle.

"What you must understand, is that history as you know it, as the world knows it, has been manipulated, shaped, and written to serve the betterment of mankind. Throughout the ages, dating back to the time man lived in caves, he celebrated his mastery over his environment with simple drawings on a wall depicting his latest kill. From those humble beginnings, a pattern began that accelerated the development of man as the dominant species on the planet. By documenting his accomplishments, he could gauge how far he had progressed compared to his ancestors and his contemporaries, thus awakening the natural competitiveness innate in the human species. That awakening changed the face of the planet forever."

"That's fine, Doctor, but how does this relate to what you're doing here on Mars?" Mac asked, hoping the professor would start making sense.

"Oh, it is directly related. You see, if you study the development of man on Earth, you can see there were certain 'spikes' of intellectual advancement that could only be the result of outside influences."

"What do you mean? Extraterrestrial?" Mac chuckled as he spoke. "You're not trying to tell me you've discovered little green men on Mars, are you?" He laughed again.

Boyle glared back at him. "Nothing quite so trite, Commander."

"Oh, my God! I can't believe how much data there is!" Angela shouted as the uploading of Boyle's files reached the six-minute mark. "How are we going to make any sense of all this?"

"I don't know." Rechenko shook his head. "We will have to go about it systematically."

"What are you talking about?" Judy frowned. "Can't we just tell Mac we have the files and leave it at that? We have six months to make sense of it all, don't we?"

"I am afraid not," Rechenko answered. "We have to confirm we have solid evidence that would vindicate us before we can even contact Earth. Besides, with Mac so close to the Valley, it would be foolish to have him turn around without at least a sighting of what is hidden there."

"That was never the plan, Victor, and you know it!" Judy bristled. "Mac could be in danger right now, and we can't even listen to him. The least we can do is let him know we are downloading the files."

A chime sounded at the console. A short sentence flashed on the screen. "Upload completed."

"Great! We have his files," Rechenko said. "I will alert Mac on the redline."

Mac tried his best to understand Boyle's lecture, but there were too many loose ends.

"Commander, the evidence is right in front of you when you really look at the history of the world. For thousands of years, man had little to no impact on his environment. Then, in a relatively short span of time, he evolves from a hunter/gatherer to a farmer, then a landowner, then part of a kingdom. He builds towns, then cities. The whole story you have heard a hundred times before. But what you don't ever hear is how quickly it happens. Why does man exist on Earth for millions of years before he accelerates his intellect and impact in a mere few thousand years? That is a question no one ever asks, and why? Because they don't want to know the answer."

Mac looked out the window ahead of him. It appeared they were steadily approaching the summit pass. He estimated another five minutes.

"What if I were to tell you, evidence exists right now on Earth that would prove man was visited by beings from another planet over five thousand years ago? Would that shock you?"

"Of course not. There's been talk of extraterrestrials teaching the ancient Egyptians or the Incas or Mayans astronomy, mathematics, and so on. But if there were proof, why keep it a secret?"

"Why indeed?" Boyle answered. "Would it shock you if I told you evidence existed right here on Mars that beings had visited here thousands of years ago?"

"I could believe that, I suppose. But why would anyone want to visit this uninhabitable rock? Did you find the wreckage of an alien spaceship here?"

Boyle smiled at him and glanced out the window at the summit.

Mac noticed that the road ahead led into a narrow opening. As Matty rolled toward the summit pass, Mac anticipated an extraordinary vista. The approach reminded him of the drive he had often taken on Highway 50 from his parents' cabin, approaching Lake Tahoe from the west. After driving through narrow canyons for an hour, you reach Echo Summit and the Tahoe basin with the deep blue waters of the lake spreading out before you. It's a dramatic sight one never forgets.

As Matty rolled forward, the narrow canyon walls gave way to an open view of a deep valley surrounded by giant mountain peaks. Put in a blue lake and you'd have the Tahoe basin. But there was no lake in this valley; instead, Mac focused on some unmistakable forms he instantly knew were not rock formations. He stopped Matty so he could get a steady view. A sudden chill shot through his body.

"Commander, what if I told you the visitors to Earth came from here?"

Mac could not believe his eyes. A few miles away stood a cluster of structures arranged in a familiar grid pattern. These were structures he had climbed himself. As incredible as it seemed, Mac looked at several pyramids that had obviously been part of a great city. But most shocking of all was the fact that the structures before him appeared to be an exact replica of the great pyramids of Teotihuacán in Mexico!

"Commander, welcome to the Valley of the Sun."

Overcome with shock, tears flowed down Mac's face. "This is impossible. How long have you known about this?"

"We have known about this particular site for over fifty years."

"Fifty years!" Suddenly, the redline in Mac's ear activated. Rechenko began talking excitedly. "Commander, if you read me, we have the files. Repeat, we have the files!"

Victor's transmission broke Mac's focus on the scene in front of him. In the midst of the astounding developments, he had almost forgotten about the plan to upload the files. Boyle was surely right about one thing: This was much bigger than he could have imagined. Mac drove Matty forward as the Sun's rays bathed the great pyramids in a bright orange glow. It was now midmorning in the Valley of the Sun.

CHAPTER 25
THE FIFTH PLANET

Rechenko rubbed his tired eyes as mountains of data flashed by on the screen in front of him. Judging from the sheer volume of information, he feared it would be impossible to locate the file on the Valley of the Sun.

"This is so much information. How are we going to find anything?" Angela said, working on the computer next to him.

"What's the file name we're looking for, Valley of the Sun?" Judy asked. "Are you sure Boyle would call it that?"

"That is an excellent question," Rechenko conceded. "He may well have used a code name unfamiliar to his comrades. I will isolate and search the larger files."

Suddenly an alarm sounded at the console, causing everyone to jump in unison. Rechenko checked the computer. "It's another meteorological warning, the third this morning," he said. "That red storm is still moving toward the Valley of the Sun."

Judy looked up from her computer. "Will it affect Mac?"

"I don't think so. The storm is expected to skirt the region, but since the computer recognized Matty in the area, it sent us a warning."

Rechenko read the warning: CAUTION...HIGH WINDS AND DUST IN UPPER ATMOSPHERE COULD DISRUPT LASER TRANSMISSIONS FROM SITE 13.

"Site 13?" Rechenko slammed his hand on the console. "That must be the Valley of the Sun!" Quick, everyone, run a search for Site 13. I think we may have found the file name!"

Looking out the front window, Mac couldn't believe what he was seeing as Matty approached the pyramid city.

"This is some mining operation, don't you think, Mac?"

Straining to see every detail as they passed numerous stone structures leading to the largest pyramid, Mac tried to comprehend what it all meant. "This appears to be the same configuration as Teotihuacán, outside of Mexico City. How can that be?"

Boyle raised an eyebrow. "Teotihuacán? Why, yes, Commander, very good. In fact, this site shares the exact dimensions. I say, I'm impressed you know so much about Teotihuacán."

"I've been there many times. As a matter of fact, I once asked a gal to marry me while we were standing on top of the Pyramid of the Sun."

"You've *been* to Teotihuacán? I am shocked. I don't remember reading that in your profile. What else don't I know about you? Are you a student of archeology or is this just dumb luck?"

"Oh, I'd say it's more than a passing fancy. You see, I've been to just about all the pyramid sites in Mexico. I became fascinated by the ancient ruins and continued to visit other sites around the world when I had the chance."

"Really? May I ask where?"

"I've been to Stonehenge, the Acropolis in Athens, and of course Giza. But I must say that besides my attachment to Teotihuacán, the ancient ruins of Ephesus in Turkey is probably my favorite."

"And what did you find there that intrigued you so?"

"Well the ruins were magnificent, but I enjoyed the view from the great amphitheater overlooking the ancient city the most. You could still see the stone promenade that made up the waterfront of the city. It was easy to imagine the waters of the Aegean sea lapping up against boats tied up to the pier as the Ephesians strolled past on cool summer evenings. Of course, you had to use your imagination since the sea had receded some twenty miles away over a couple of millennia."

"Mac, I am impressed. It's not every day you run into someone who not only has seen the great ruins of the world, but also has a deep appreciation for them. Your knowledge of the ancient world will help you understand what I'm about to tell you."

"Okay! I think I have something!" Angela shouted. "It looks like a map of the Valley, except...this one seems to have several roads and buildings. This can't be right."

"That's odd," Rechenko said. "A city in the middle of the Valley?" His words hung in the air over the three of them like a huge sign.

"A city? In the Valley? On Mars?" Judy asked. "How is that possible?"

Rechenko reached over and clicked on the largest square on the grid. Instantly, a new picture appeared on screen, showing a large ziggurat-shaped, rust-colored pyramid standing tall against the Martian sky. The caption at the bottom of the page read: PYRAMID OF THE SUN

"Oh, my God. Tell me this is a joke." Judy shook her head.

"I'm afraid it's no joke." Rechenko stroked his beard. "This isn't a drawing; this is a picture taken in the Valley of the Sun."

As Matty rolled through the ruins, Mac continued to move from window to window. "How did these structures get here? Who built this city?"

Boyle gave him a wry smile. "You haven't even seen the truly shocking part. It's something so incredible, so unbelievable, that even I have trouble understanding it."

"Boyle, at this point, I think I would believe just about anything you told me; but, in spite of all I see here, I can't imagine for the life of me, why so many people had to die to keep this a secret. What is so damn important here that good people had to die?"

Boyle looked down, as if avoiding eye contact. "Of course, you know there is very little I could say that would satisfy you. I am sorry for you and your friends that were put in the middle of this situation. You are all good people. I know that. But there is a much bigger picture here that I would like to explain. And when I'm finished, if you still feel I acted criminally, then feel free to return me to Earth to face the full extent of the law. I only ask that you listen to what I have to say."

For the first time since the assault on the base five days earlier, Mac heard words of remorse and regret from Boyle's lips. While moved by his appeal, Mac knew he couldn't be trusted. Too many had died. "I will give you a chance to explain. But don't think for a moment that you can justify the blood on your hands. You will answer for your crimes."

Boyle nodded and turned to his computer. He keyed in some information then looked up at Mac. "Only a handful of people in the world know what I am about to tell you. And by a handful, I mean one hand."

"You're going to tell me how these pyramids got here?"

"No, I'm not talking about the pyramids. I'm talking about the fifth planet, and I don't mean Jupiter."

"It looks like they stopped in front of the large pyramid," Judy said. "What is Mac doing? Shouldn't we give him the all clear to return to base?"

"No, I'm sure he wants to investigate. This is a once-in-a-lifetime opportunity. We shouldn't rush him," Rechenko answered, his eyes still scanning the data before him.

Judy started to object when Angela interrupted. "What do you suppose these things are?" She pointed to the overview of the city.

Rechenko leaned over to her screen and studied the markings that appeared by each structure. "It appears to be a code of some type. I think those are laser receiver coordinates. Why would they have a laser receiver on every building?"

Another alarm sounded at the console.

"Meteorological alarm," Judy read the warning out loud. "CAUTION, DUST STORM APPROACHING SITE 13...TRANSMISSION BLACK-OUT CONDITIONS POSSIBLE WITHIN THE HOUR."

"You see, Victor!" she shouted. "We have no choice! Give Mac the all clear to return before we lose contact with him."

Rechenko looked at the warning on the screen, then back to the map he'd been studying. Something in his gut told him the laser receivers could potentially have a sinister purpose. "Okay, give him the all clear, Angela. But keep it short; I don't want to chance Boyle detecting it on his computer."

Mac and Boyle moved to the roomier part of Matty where they would have more area to maneuver in their bulky suits. Boyle called up several graphics on his laptop.

"Over the course of the past year, I have made an extensive survey of the Valley and its structures," he began. "This particular site was discovered back in the seventies, with verification and preliminary mapping completed by the Mars orbiter in the late nineties."

"What?" Mac flinched. "The Mars Orbiter? I thought that was lost before it ever reached the planet."

"No, I'm afraid the reports of its failure have been greatly exaggerated," Boyle chuckled.

"Well how did you get hold of it? Who do you work for?"

"All in good time, Mac. Please, may I continue?"

Mac leaned back and shook his head. Boyle was obviously enjoying this.

"We used the orbiter for many years before it finally succumbed after the millennium, but we acquired a great deal of intelligence, which led us directly to this site as the most promising."

"This site? You mean there are others?"

"Oh yes, many others. But this Valley had the most complete ruins in excellent condition. The Grand Arroyo landing site was chosen years before the Mars I mission arrived."

Mac shook his head. "You're saying Mars held a large population? And from the condition of the pyramids, I'd say not too long ago."

"Celestially speaking that's right. But it's difficult to predict with any accuracy how long ago this was a thriving planet."

"What happened to change it?"

"Well, that's where the fifth planet comes in."

"And we're not talking about Jupiter?"

"Right, Mac. I have found evidence here, in this valley, of a planet that once orbited the sun between Jupiter and Mars. It's an area now occupied by what is commonly known as the asteroid belt. I call the planet Atlantis. Clever, don't you think?"

"Very nice, Mr. Boyle, but you're not the first person to have made such a claim about a fifth planet. Problem is, where's your proof?"

Boyle pointed at the great pyramid. "In there, in what I call the 'Hall of Records.' It's a large chamber inside the Pyramid of the Sun." He keyed his computer and several images appeared on the screen.

"I have been able to translate these wall etchings, which are similar to those found on Earth. These are star charts that clearly reveal an orbiting body between Jupiter and Mars. By inputting the information from the star chart into a computer program, we can actually locate the position of the fifth planet."

"And this matches the position of the asteroid belt?"

"That's correct. Those etchings on the wall confirm it," Boyle said proudly.

"And, in your mind, that proves there was a fifth planet between Mars and Jupiter?"

"Beyond a shadow of a doubt. It has always been suspected, but impossible to prove until now."

Mac looked Boyle in the eye. "So tell me something, why does this have to be kept a secret? Why did you have to go around killing people and sabotaging the Mars mission?"

Boyle backed away from Mac. "You still don't get it, do you? All that matters to you is your mission, your responsibilities, and your people. How can you be so selfish? Look out that window. What do you see? A great pyramid, an exact replica of one that exists in Mexico. How do you expect that pyramid outside of Mexico City got there? Do you really think local Indian tribes built it? Even the great Aztec Empire couldn't duplicate the mastery of The Pyramid of the Sun. In the end, even they worshiped the builders of Teotihuacán as gods."

"So you're saying that beings from this planet visited the Earth thousands of years ago and built Teotihuacán?"

"Oh yes, they came to our planet all right, but they did so much more than just build one city. There is evidence on Earth right now that suggests they not only visited our planet, but also thrived there for perhaps a thousand years. They came as teachers, guiding the indigenous peoples of Earth, schooling them in astronomy, mathematics, agriculture, and higher technology—advancing civilization thousands of years in only a few centuries. That accounts for the sudden spike in the development of mankind."

"So what happened to them? Where did they go? Where is the proof they even existed and visited the Earth?"

"Well you are sitting in the midst of the most compelling evidence, Commander. But there is more. I believe we were not only visited by beings from Mars, but from Atlantis as well."

"Atlantis, as you call it, was inhabited?"

Boyle nodded. "By beings just as advanced as the population of Mars."

"How do you know that?"

"Mac, I have proof the populations of Mars and Atlantis were in regular contact with each other, shared their cultures, and both explored the Earth extensively. But perhaps most shocking is the fact that they appeared to have accomplished all this without the benefit of spaceships."

"No spaceships? Boyle, you're talking nonsense. How could they travel between their planets and Earth without spaceships?"

"I am working on a theory involving astro-kinetic travel. That's a type of sub-space transit system where travel between planets would be as simple as opening a door and stepping through. However they did it, they had a profound effect on the development of our society."

A doorway? How could that be? Mac thought. Technology like that in the wrong hands could be a powerful tool, or weapon. The redline alarm in Mac's ear suddenly sounded, follow by Angela's voice. "All clear, all clear, return to base, all clear. Out," Angela said.

Mac tried his best not to betray what he had just heard, yet he didn't know what to ask next. For the first time he began to think Dr. Boyle was right about this being too big for him. His thoughts turned to Judy and the crew back at the base. He knew they had successfully copied Boyle's files, and he assumed they were poring over them now, trying to decipher what it all meant. Since they had transmitted the all-clear signal, he was free to return; but he knew he would never have another opportunity like this.

"Boyle, I'm confused about something. You say there is a mountain of evidence on Earth that would confirm what you're telling me, but why hasn't this ever gotten out to the public?"

Boyle smiled again, obviously enjoying another proud moment. "Mac, have you ever heard of the term 'forbidden archeology'?"

"That sounds familiar. I think it's the study of all that mystical stuff you hear about—like the stone figures at Easter Island and the mystery of Stonehenge, the ruins of Machu Picchu. A lot of it sounds pretty kooky though."

"That's the idea. It's supposed to sound like a bunch of kooks making up bizarre theories. Separately, the findings are absurd, almost laughable, but collectively, the discoveries around the world are undeniably linked. But this information is always kept on the fringe of traditional archeology, only collectively no one has ever come up with satisfactory alternative explanations to debunk the crazy theories you've heard. All this wealth of information has been successfully kept from the general public simply by labeling it as the work of 'fringe' archeologists."

"Well, that will change now with this discovery, right?"

Boyle said nothing; he just turned and looked out the window at the great pyramid. Mac wondered what other secrets he had hidden away.

Without turning to look at Mac, Boyle spoke again. "Would you like to see them? Would you like to see what the Martians and the Atlantians looked like?"

Mac laughed to himself as he answered. "Sure I would. You have pictures? Maybe a group portrait of all of them?"

Boyle shook his head, continuing to stare out the window. "Not on the computer. I mean out there, inside the pyramid, in the Hall of Records."

Now Mac looked out the window. Of course he wanted to go out and walk among the ruins of the city. He longed to climb the great pyramid before him, but he knew he couldn't put his trust and his life in Boyle's hands.

He reached down and felt the syringe filled with cyanide in his leg pocket, his only protection against a surprise attack. He knew he should seal Dr. Boyle in the airlock this instant and head back to base, but the powerful draw to get outside and walk the path that few humans had ever seen proved irresistible.

"All right, Boyle, put on your helmet."

Rechenko still couldn't understand the purpose of the laser receivers on all the structures in the Valley of the Sun, but he had managed to isolate the operating frequencies of most of them. He noticed a familiar pattern emerging with each receiver linked in sequence to the next. "A chain reaction?" he mumbled out loud. "But why?"

"Hey! They're on the move!" Judy shouted, interrupting his thoughts.

"Good," Rechenko said. "It's about time Mac decided to come back."

"No, that's not what I mean! They've left Matty. They're going outside!"

"What?" he yelled. "Call Mac immediately! They've got to leave the area at once!"

"What's wrong, Victor?" Judy asked. "Is Mac in trouble?"

"I can't say for sure, but I think...I mean...I might know what those laser receivers are for."

"What is it?" Angela moved behind Rechenko to look at his screen.

"It's just a theory, but all of the receivers are linked together in a sequence. At first I thought they were simple locator beacons like the ones we all carry, but I noticed that they had a peculiar receive pattern, meaning there was a specific sequence in which they were designed to accept a laser signal."

"So why is that significant?" Judy said.

"Okay. When I started my first engineering job thirty years ago, I worked on the new highway through the Ural Mountains. I was a blast supervisor, and one of my responsibilities was programming the laser triggers on the shaped explosive charges we'd use for blasting a path through the mountains. It was imperative that the sequence be set just so for maximum effect. These laser receivers in the Valley on every significant structure remind me of a trigger sequence."

"A trigger sequence?" Judy responded. "You mean for detonation?"

Rechenko nodded. "It is a possibility."

"Why would anyone want to blow up pyramids on Mars?" Angela interrupted.

"I have no idea, but it is possible these structures are set with explosives connected to laser detonators. If that is true, they could be triggered by remote control."

"You mean like with a laptop?" Angela moved to her computer and called up the Valley of the Sun overview again.

"Yes, a laptop or even a remote control for a laptop could trigger the sequence." Rechenko ran both hands through his hair.

"We've got to warn Mac," Judy shouted.

"Oh my god!" Angela jumped to her feet in front of her computer. "They're gone!" she screamed. "Mac and Boyle have disappeared!"

CHAPTER 26
THE HALL OF RECORDS

Mac followed Boyle out of Matty's rear airlock onto the rust-colored surface at the base of the Pyramid of the Sun. He started up the center stairway, but Boyle stopped him, motioning that Mac should walk with him to the right of the steps, which revealed a small, half-hidden entrance. As they passed through the doorway, their helmet lights illuminated a dark passageway that descended gradually toward the center of the pyramid.

"Commander, you are only the second human to see the Hall of Records. Not even La Rue and Ivory were allowed in here." Boyle spoke with obvious pride. "I'm showing you this so you'll understand why this discovery should be kept secret for now."

Mac bristled at Boyle's arrogance but let him continue his condescending speech so he could cull maximum information in their limited time here.

"You must look at the overall history of man on Earth to appreciate what you are seeing today." Boyle continued down the narrow passageway. "Historians would have you believe modern man didn't make his mark on Earth until two or three thousand years before Christ. Religious leaders will ask you to believe man was nothing more than an ignorant barbarian a mere five thousand years ago. But what we've discovered here proves them all wrong. It shows conclusively that intelligent man dates back much further than most people are willing to admit."

The passageway finally opened into a small dark room. Boyle turned on a battery-powered lantern he had left there, revealing a chamber ten feet wide and thirty feet long. Mac saw familiar humanoid figures etched into the walls. Boyle stepped away, allowing him to see the entire room. The etchings looked similar to the Mayan depictions he had seen in Mexico. There were also bear-like creatures on the wall. "I've seen these before," Mac noted.

"Yes, but remember, you are in the center of a pyramid on Mars, not Earth."

"You're telling me the Mayans were not from Earth?"

"No, these are not the Mayans, but perhaps the teachers of the Mayans, the Incas, the Egyptians and other indigenous tribes around the globe. Have you ever wondered why all cultures ancient or modern have undeniable similarities? The placement of the pyramids of the world, the configuration of Stonehenge, the accuracy of ancient calendars and astronomical observations suggest that perhaps all shared the same teachers."

Mac stared at the etchings on the wall. "This is an extraordinary find. The world has to be told about this." He focused on the bear-like creatures, which seemed to be conversing with the other smaller figures. "Are these talking bears?"

Boyle nodded. "Very good. I wondered if you would notice. They're not bears. See the human-like face and the upright posture. I believe these creatures are not from Mars."

Mac glanced at the wall again. "Atlantians?"

Boyle grinned at Mac. "I am impressed by your intuitive nature. Perhaps I've underestimated you. I believe this etching depicts a meeting between the inhabitants of the two planets. It makes sense the Atlantians would come from a colder climate with their planet farther from the sun. What you may not realize is that I believe a large number of Atlantians managed to escape to Earth before their planet was destroyed, and a scattered few of their descendants survive to this day."

"Come on. Please tell me you're not talking about 'Bigfoot' or the 'Abominable Snowman'."

Boyle laughed out loud. "As crazy as you make it sound, the creatures you refer to have been sighted many times around the world. It is reported that they are highly intelligent with human-like characteristics and emotions. However, they probably did not adapt as well to our planet as the Martians did. They would have played a lesser role, or perhaps none at all in the development of man on Earth."

"What happened to them?"

"I don't know for sure, but through these etchings I have a theory as to what may have happened to the fifth planet. You see, thousands of years ago our galaxy may have included four inhabited planets: Venus, Earth, Mars, and Atlantis. I've uncovered evidence that there was a prolonged battle between Atlantis and Venus—a sort of galaxy war where both planets met their demise. Atlantis was completely destroyed, but not before they pummeled the Venutians into the nuclear winter we see that planet shrouded in today. The asteroid belt is all that's left of Atlantis.

"The destruction of Atlantis gradually changed the orbit of Mars—it probably took a thousand years—but the inhabitants of Mars saw their doom coming and, along with the survivors from Atlantis and Venus, fled to Earth to save their culture and way of life. This would account for the sudden spike in cultural advancement on Earth."

"And they did this all without the benefit of spacecraft?"

"I have a theory explaining how they traveled, and I think we're standing in it."

Mac looked around. "This chamber? This pyramid?"

"More than likely this pyramid, and its exact alignment to the stars. You see, they may well have discovered how to travel within their planet and between planets, utilizing the power of these pyramids to open a corridor to wherever they wanted to go. Imagine, Mac! Traveling between two planets simply by walking through a doorway. The power of that discovery would change our world forever. There is so much more to learn here from these beings who were our original teachers!"

As Mac listened, he began to understand Boyle's treacherous motives. He was here to harness the secrets of this fallen civilization—knowledge that could surely be put to use on Earth, either to help mankind or to enslave it. Mac had seen and heard enough. The time had come to take Boyle back to the base.

"The whole complex is set to explode!" Rechenko bellowed. "The first blast would set a sequence in motion using the laser receivers at each structure as a detonator."

Judy jumped to her feet. "We've got to warn Mac."

"There's still no sign of him or Boyle," Angela shouted from her computer. "Their locator badges are still not transmitting."

Judy turned to Rechenko. "Isn't there anything we can do?"

"I can disable the laser transmitters on the Mars 2 and 3 mother ships. That would prevent Boyle from starting the trigger sequence. But it would also cut off all communications with Mac. He'd be on his own, with no on-board guidance for Matty."

"He's already on his own!" Judy yelled. "We don't even know where he is!"

"True, but let me see if I can isolate Boyle's computer commands. I'd feel better if we didn't completely cut off Mac."

Judy let out a long sigh. "Victor, I know Mac is in trouble. I can feel it. It's driving me crazy that I can't do anything, so you do what you can here, and I'm taking Ratty to the Valley of the Sun."

"You can't do that!" Rechenko stood up, face to face with Judy. "Mac said that we were to stay at the base and launch without him if necessary. Those were his orders!"

"Well, to hell with his orders!" Judy turned and left the flight deck.

A deep red sky loomed over the horizon as Mac walked out into the open from the doorway under the pyramid steps. He followed Boyle to the base of the giant pyramid and said, "The red storm's getting closer."

"It doesn't look like it will reach us," Boyle said. "We have time for more exploring."

Mac turned and looked up the grand center staircase of the Pyramid of the Sun as memories of Mexico came flooding back to him. It wasn't hard to imagine Magdelena's flowing dress as she walked up the long stairway to the top.

"Did you have any idea this is what waited for you in the Valley of the Sun?"

Mac shook his head. "No, I must say you kept this under a tight lid."

"Well, you must have some questions as to how we did that, and right under your nose."

"All right, Doctor, tell me, who are you working for? Who sent you on this killing spree?

"I told you I am sorry about that, but you have to have a few casualties in order to protect the species."

"Protect the species? From what?"

"Look around you, Mac. What do you see? Pyramids. Not just here, but all around Mars. We've uncovered evidence of an advanced civilization here that predates our own. Can you imagine if word of that got out? We'd have a world-wide catastrophe on our hands. People would question their ancestry, their ethnicity, their religion. It would be cultural anarchy."

"What makes you so sure? Maybe it would bring people together."

"Think about it, Mac. The history of the world has already been written. The people of Egypt think their ancestors constructed the great pyramids; in Peru, they think their ancestors built Machu Picchu. Can you imagine if the Mayan pyramids turned out not to be Mayan at all? Chaos, Mac, cultural anarchy."

Mac gazed up at the pyramid summit and tried to imagine what it must have looked like here thousands of years ago. *A great, bustling city, filled with. . . Martians?*

"It's quite a view from the top, Mac. But then you already know that. Just think, you and I would be the only humans to stand on top of the Pyramid of the Sun on two planets."

Mac felt a chill shoot through his body, not sure he wanted to share such a distinction with Boyle. "You don't have to convince me to climb to the top, but I have to know. Who sent you here? Obviously someone who wields a great deal of power to be able to manipulate events, steal space probes, and appoint themselves protectors against culture anarchy. Who do you work for?"

Mac could see Boyle's smile through his faceplate. He suspected the scientist had waited for this moment.

Boyle extended his arm towards the pyramid steps. "Suppose I tell you as we climb to the top?"

Mac gave a single nod. "After you."

Judy's heart raced as she opened the base airlock and stepped out on to the surface. She ran to Ratty and climbed up to the operator's cab on the front of the large, gangly vehicle. Her plan was simple. She would drive up Highway One, relying on the satellite guidance system to lead her to the Valley of the Sun. She sealed the operator's cab and began to pressurize the small cockpit. Nervous about Mac, her hands were shaking. With a few keystrokes, Ratty lurched forward, moving slowly away from the base. Suddenly, Angela's voice boomed over the communications link.

"Judy, stop! We've reacquired their signal! Do you read me? Please acknowledge. We found Mac and Boyle. They're climbing up the large pyramid."

Judy's breathed a sigh of relief. At least he was alive. But what the hell was he doing climbing pyramids? "Have you talked to him yet?"

"Negative. The red storm's interfering with the com-link."

"Then I'm pressing on." Judy typed in more commands and Ratty picked up speed.

As Mac stood atop the Pyramid of the Sun, memories flooded his thoughts. He looked across the city to the smaller Pyramid of the Moon and marveled at the similarities in the configuration of this city and Teotihuacán. The only thing missing was the green earth, the blue sky, and of course, beautiful Magdalena standing by his side.

He couldn't help but feel her presence here—her long, dark hair, her deep blue eyes and her soft, smooth brown skin. But soon his thoughts drifted to his Uncle Guillermo and the final betrayal as he foolishly waited for Magdalena. It seemed his uncle had taken pleasure in dashing the dreams and desires of his lovesick nephew.

Thirty years and a million miles had not dimmed the pain of that betrayal as he stood atop a great pyramid. He felt sadness for the society that once thrived here. The only trace of the grandeur of this civilization was these remarkable structures. He looked at Boyle, puzzled. "Why is it necessary to keep this a secret? This is a part of our heritage, our history. We are not alone in this universe and people have the right to know!"

Boyle stared back as he walked toward him. "You are a fool. You can't understand what is going on here. This is bigger than you!"

Mac stood frozen. He had heard those very words before, spoken by another man, on top of another pyramid thirty years ago. That man was also named William, and he spoke in the same, condescending tone. Mac could no longer contain his anger.

"Don't play your mind games with me, Boyle! I'm sick of your patronizing tone. I'm taking you back to Earth to answer for your crimes."

"And how far do you think you'd get when you return? You wouldn't make it past the space station alive."

As Boyle stepped toward him, Mac could see his piercing eyes through his faceplate.

"I have powerful friends, but there is a way you could return safely to Earth in triumph. I could guarantee it."

Mac laughed. "How can you guarantee me anything?"

"Simple, Commander. Join me and the community I represent."

"Join you?" Mac wrinkled his nose, disgusted. "Why would I join a bunch of murderers?"

Boyle continued in an unwavering voice. "Join me, or die."

CHAPTER 27
THE COMMUNITY

"Nyet!" Rechenko bellowed, arguing with his computer.

"What is it?" Angela came to his side.

"This isn't possible. I'm getting a virus alert, but this is a closed system..." He paused for a moment before adding, "...unless I got the virus from Boyle's computer." He leaned forward and typed feverishly, as if chasing the virus across the screen with every keystroke.

"Can you get rid of it?"

"I'm trying but...my God, it's attached itself to the power plant systems in the mainframe. It could shut down the entire base, communications, life support."

"What's that beeping?"

"It's your laptop." Rechenko reached over and slid it near. "Virus alert." He worked the keyboard for a moment.

"What is it, Victor?"

He slammed the console with his fist. "Damn! I know how they did it!"

"Did what?"

"Remember when we retook the base and we thought Gina's laptop had a bomb in it? Mac grabbed it and threw it outside where it exploded. I saw it from the bridge of Mars 3. Only it wasn't a bomb; it was this virus. It somehow attached itself to the laptop power cells, bypassed the safeguards, and started a chemical reaction that exploded. It was small but big enough to blow a wall out of the pressurized crew module and kill us all." Rechenko pointed to the computer screen. "With this virus controlling our main power cells, the whole base could be destroyed."

"What can we do?"

"I'm not sure. The virus is in sleep mode right now, waiting to be activated." Rechenko took off his glasses and looked at Angela. "I suspect Boyle has the trigger."

Judy bounced up and down in the driver seat as Ratty whisked down the well-traveled portion of Highway One, its stiff suspension jarred by the uneven contours of the rutted road. She cursed herself for not objecting harder to Mac's crazy adventure. Surely they had enough evidence to clear their names without going to the Valley of the Sun. She didn't care if Boyle found the Statue of Liberty in the Valley; only Mac's well-being concerned her now.

"Judy, do you copy?" Angela's voice boomed over her com-link.

"Yes Angela, I copy. How's Mac?"

"As far as we can tell, he's fine. He and Boyle are standing on top of the large pyramid. The red storm's interfering with the com-link so contact is intermittent. But we have another problem."

"What is it?"

"Victor discovered a virus we downloaded from Boyle's computer. He says it could destroy the base."

"What?"

"I can't explain it, but he thinks the only way to keep it from activating is to sever the laser link with the mother ship."

"But that means you'd lose contact with Mac...and me."

"That's why we think you should turn around and return to base."

Judy bounced hard on her seat as Ratty rolled over a large boulder. "I...I can't come back." She fought her growing sense of panic, but still refused to give up on Mac. "He needs me, Angela. I know he's in trouble. I have to keep going."

After a long silence, Angela spoke, choked with emotion. "J...Judy, be careful. I don't know when I'll see you again."

Judy wiped her tears with the back of her hand. She increased the speed on the auto-drive and held on to her seat. It was still a good two hours to the Valley of the Sun.

"Join you or die?" Mac laughed. "That will never happen. What makes you think you can dictate terms to me anyway?"

"It's not me dictating terms. It's the Community."

"The Community?" Mac turned and looked around, mockingly searching for someone to appear at Boyle's side. "Is that who you work for?"

Boyle gave Mac a dry expression. "Whether you know it or not, we all work for the Community. Who do you think picked you for this Command?"

"The Community? And I suppose they chose you, too?"

"They approached me years ago, after I published a paper debunking the theories of the so-called fringe archeologists—scholars that claimed linkage between the ancient world and extraterrestrials."

Mac spread his arms, looking out over the city below them. "It looks like you've debunked your own paper, Doctor. Considering where we're standing, I'd give you an F."

Boyle shook his head. "You're missing the point. The Community has known about this site for fifty years and the extraterrestrial linkage for a thousand years."

"Then why keep it a secret? This is about our roots, our ancestry! Why keep it from us?" Mac heard a distorted beep on his redline. Then Angela's garbled voice. He could barely make out a few words.

"...danger...explosives...the Valley..."

Her warning sent a chill down his spine, but Boyle seemed an unlikely threat. Mac keyed his com-link so everyone could hear Boyle's confession.

"Power, Commander, the ultimate elixir. If you control the past, you control the future. Over a thousand years ago, it was the Roman Catholic Church that was the keeper of the past. They held the ancient scrolls from the Library of Alexandria, King Solomon's Temple, and the teachings of Socrates and Aristotle. The control of that information gave the Church enormous power to make Kings and Lords and shape the world to their liking. The inquisition squashed any challenges to their view of history. Even in the Renaissance they kept a tight rein on the likes of Da Vinci and imprisoned Galileo. Who knows how many budding scholars were executed simply for seeking the truth?"

"Are you saying the Catholic Church is the Community?"

"No, not now, although I suspect they would agree to keep this place a secret. The early Church functioned like the Community today. Controlling world events, influencing governments and manipulating the masses, but their power has been diminished. With the industrial age, a new Community was born, utilizing the foundation the Church had laid down and embracing its view of the past. An informal partnership emerged, a mutually beneficial relationship, with the Church maintaining some of its control and the Community helping to preserve world order. Through their influence, wars were fought, presidents were made."

"Presidents?"

"Prime ministers, dictators and, yes, presidents."

"The Community picked the Presidents of the United States?"

"Not exactly picked them, but to a large extent controlled their administrations and exerted influence to achieve what they wanted."

"And these presidents agreed?"

"Not all. But starting in the early twentieth century, the Community most definitely made or broke their administrations. Those who cooperated did well. Those who resisted were limited to one term, were assassinated, or were embarrassed into resigning."

"But what about the military chiefs of staff? Wouldn't they have a say in this?"

Boyle laughed. "The military industrial complex is controlled by the Community."

"How can you control every new general, admiral, or administrator?"

"You don't, as long as you can control the bureaucracy behind the power. Unbeknownst to them, the lifelong bureaucrat is the foot soldier in the Community, always careful to protect their turf, dedicated to the status quo. Policy makers come and go, but the Community knows its interests will always be served by the bureaucracy."

Mac looked out at the deep red horizon caused by the passing red storm. "This place would certainly change the status quo back home."

Boyle moved next to Mac. "A discovery like this would impact everything. The very foundations of the world's religions would crumble. Cultural anarchy, Mac, that's what we're trying to prevent here."

"Are you sure anarchy is the concern, or is it something else? It seems to me that the new world religion has been the explosion of consumerism. A discovery like this might cause people to question their values. Maybe become more spiritual, less material. Could that be why the Community fears this place?"

"The Community doesn't fear this discovery, but they do want time to understand it better. I have been sent here to unravel the mystery of the most important discovery known to mankind: the ability to transport oneself without the use of cars, or planes, or spaceships. This is the heart of my mission. Can you imagine what such a discovery would mean to our world? It would result in unlimited power and influence for our species. We could travel, not only between cities and continents, but also between planets and galaxies! Unraveling the secrets of this civilization would bring the future to us now!"

"But your Community wants to keep this discovery as its own. They don't want to share it with the rest of the world."

Boyle walked away from Mac and stopped on the edge of the pyramid. "The Community is caught between protecting the status quo and unraveling the greatest mystery of mankind."

Mac followed Boyle and stood by his side. "Imagine what Earth must have been like at the time of a thriving Teotihuacán. These teachers came to guide and nurture us. They came to us to share their spiritualism, their knowledge of how to live together and respect the good Earth. Their message, their teachings continue to influence whole segments of society to this day. Your Community represents the desecration of all that was good about this ancient civilization."

Mac heard Angela's voice again, still full of static. He could make out two words: "...Remote trigger..."

Join me or die, Boyle had threatened. Mac looked him over—helmet, suit, gloves—for any remote control he could have planted. To keep the doctor talking, he continued, "You still haven't answered my most important question: Why did so many people have to die? The Mars 3 crew, half of our crew. What was your grand plan?"

"The research here will take several years to complete. In light of this fact, two things had to happen. The Community had to find a way to keep me here for at least two to three years of uninterrupted work. That meant we had to find a way to get me here and stop the International Space Consortium from sending more crews and expanding the base.

"The best way to achieve this was to begin our work during the Mars 2 mission, then somehow delay our launch until Mars 3 arrived. We needed the

Mars 3 mother ship because of its new propulsion system that would enable us to return to Earth whenever we wanted. We then had to find a way to bring Mars 3 here without its crew, a task left to Gina, who was planted on the space-craft by the Community.

"Once Mars 3 landed, you and the remainder of your crew were expend-able. Until then, we had the option to call off the entire operation if we ran into some sort of unforeseen problem."

"It sounds like a well-written script," Mac said, eager for Boyle to continue his "confession". "But why didn't you just kill us at the base, and launch our bodies into orbit? Why all the play-acting?"

"Commander, remember, we are not hit men; we are scientists. Trying to eliminate you at the base proved too risky. We'd have had to dispose of you all at once. Launching you into orbit turned out to be the easiest course of action. But no one suspected you would uncover Gina's true identity, or perform your brilliant launch abort maneuver. I have to tell you, Mac, your performance here has impressed the Community. As a matter of fact, they have authorized me to make you a very generous offer."

"A generous offer? What the hell are you talking about?"

"Mac, I told you the Community has been watching you for some time now. They shaped your career, making sure you got a command on the Space Station. The Community positioned you in the Mars program so you would secure the command of the Mars 2 mission."

"The Community picked me? That's absurd!"

"You have the ideal profile—a skilled pilot and talented engineer, an only child, unmarried with no family to worry about. Oh yes, Mac, they had an eye on you for some time. In fact, we were about to make ourselves known to you, but it became too risky when you named Dr. Delaney and Dr. Rechenko to your crew. We knew you would never go along with a plan to eliminate them so we positioned Lieutenant Traveres, a long-time operative and pilot, as your second in command."

In his heart Mac knew Boyle spoke the truth. He recalled the battery of psychological testing he'd endured during the two years before the mission. He'd felt he was being interrogated on political, religious, and ethical questions that were intrusive and unnecessary.

"Commander, when I informed them you were able to escape from the launch attempt, they authorized me to negotiate with you, and their terms are unlimited. We can offer you a lifetime of security, riches beyond your imagination."

Mac laughed. "Dr Boyle, how can you offer me anything? You're my prisoner."

"Commander, I am afraid that isn't entirely true. You see, it is you who will be unable to return to Earth. Remember, you are a marked man. Even if you try to return and report what you've seen here, you will be soundly discredited. You have no hard evidence; no one will believe you. You've seen the headlines, Mac. You're the most hated man on Earth. But I can change that. I can make you a hero. It's really quite simple."

"You can make me a hero? How?"

"As it stands right now, the world thinks you have betrayed the mission and the crew, and I have thwarted you. Well, we can easily put the blame on Lieutenant Traveres, saying he went berserk and killed half the crew. He controlled all communications so his story is all that Earth heard. In actuality, we can say we were kept hostage until you and I managed to subdue him and retake control. You and I would return to Earth triumphantly, heroes to the world. You would be taken care of for the rest of your days."

Rechenko stopped working on the computer when Angela gasped at Boyle's last statement. He, too, was disturbed by what he heard. "Angela, don't worry about Boyle's diatribe. Mac is just trying to get him to confess and stall for time while I try to disarm this damn virus."

Mac stared back at Boyle, trying to come to grips with his twisted mind. His cold-blooded thinking came too easy. "And what of the crew at the base? What would become of them? Are they expected to go along with this charade?"

Boyle looked down at the ground and shook his head. "Mac, I'm afraid that's not possible. They would all have to be eliminated. Obviously, they can not be trusted. We would have to remain here, by ourselves. You see, before your intervention, no one was to come back alive, or so it would appear.

Traveres, La Rue, and I were to be presumed dead with the rest of the Mars 2 crew. Along with Gina, we were going to return to Earth when I completed my work here, our identities changed and our appearances altered. Remember that none of us have family to worry about. We were to live out our lives in affluent anonymity.

"But now, Mac, with your help, we can both return to Earth in less than two years as heroes, taking credit for our bravery and accomplishments." Boyle became more animated as he spoke. "Think of it, Mac! We would enjoy celebrity and wealth beyond our wildest dreams!"

Mac spoke in an unemotional, even tone, never taking his eyes off his adversary. "I thank you for the generous offer you've made on behalf of the secret Community you represent. I must admit, I'm flattered to be held in such high regard by such an influential and powerful body of people. But before I tell you my decision, I wonder if you know how I was able to uncover your little conspiracy at the base? Because without the help of one of your trusted operatives, Lieutenant Traveres, I would be floating helplessly in orbit with the rest of my crew as you made your way to 'affluent anonymity'."

"Yes, I am aware of the Lieutenant's betrayal. It was most unexpected, and I have only myself to blame, letting him carry on with Angela. But that doesn't diminish what you have accomplished, Commander. And now it's time you collect your just reward."

"Doctor, I find it interesting, almost comical, that the love of two people could be responsible for exposing the most treacherous conspiracy of all time. With all your endless planning and scenarios, the one unforeseen bump in the road for you and the great Community was the love of two young people—two people who probably share more of the spiritual philosophy of these ancient teachers than does your powerful Community."

Rechenko noticed the tears in Angela's eyes as she heard Mac's words resonate from the speakers. He returned to his debugging task with a renewed urgency. Though confident Mac had things under control, he feared Boyle might try to trigger the explosion sequence when Mac rejected his offer.

"Commander, don't be a fool. I'm offering you the world." Boyle began to pace in front of Mac. "You have no other alternative! You know I can't let you return to Earth with what you know. You have no choice but to join with me, or die."

"You're in no position to bargain or threaten me! I intend to bring you back to Earth to stand trial for the murders of twelve people. And you're mistaken if you think I don't have the evidence. I have all the evidence I need because I stole it right from under your nose!"

Boyle looked at Mac and laughed. "Perhaps you are referring to the files you uploaded from my computer using Traveres' laser program?"

Mac froze.

"You see, Mac, it is you who are mistaken about a great many things. I set a trap for you, and you have stumbled right into it, as I knew you would. You see, it is true the Community was responsible for your getting this command, but it wasn't because of your brilliance. It's because you're predictable; and true to form, you have sealed your own fate."

Once again, Mac heard Angela's voice on the redline, only this time much clearer. *"Commander, return to base, you are in danger!"*

Mac had heard enough. "It's time for us to leave, Doctor. I'm through listening to your threats and insults. I don't believe you have any trap set for me. Now either we return to base together, or I return alone. What's it going to be?"

"Commander, you are a fool! That so-called evidence you retrieved from my computer has a deadly virus in it. By allowing your crew to upload it into the base mainframe, you have given me control of all your lives."

Boyle bent his arm and pulled the protective covering off his wrist computer pad that every hard suit has stitched into the forearm. The touch pad is easy to manipulate with bulky gloves as is usually linked to a larger laptop or the base mainframe. It also displays the vitals for the suit wearer.

"Thanks to you, Mac, with one touch, I can destroy the base."

Mac folded his arms, trying to hide his own panic.

"You don't believe me, Mac?" He turned and faced Matty, parked at the base of the pyramid. "Behold your chariot, Commander!"

Mac looked down at Matty just as an explosion ripped open one entire side of the vehicle.

"What! Are you crazy?" Mac screamed.

"Did you really think you could expose the secrets of this place? Did you really think the Community would allow you to bring home evidence of its existence? I told you before, Mac, this is bigger than you. By refusing to cooperate with me, you've sentenced us both to die, along with the rest of your crew. You are going to leave this world the most hated man in history. How does that feel?"

Stunned by the sight of Matty exploding, his thoughts now turned to saving his crew. He had to rush Boyle and knock him off the edge of the pyramid.

"The only evidence anyone will ever find here is a pile of rubble. That's right, you have also sentenced this entire place to death!" Boyle motioned toward the Pyramid of the Moon.

"Behold! The end of a great civilization!"

The top of the Pyramid of the Moon disintegrated into a mass of dust and flying boulders.

"No!!!!" Mac fell to his knees. He had brought Boyle back here, in what now seemed a vain effort to protect his own name and reputation. He gave him the chance to achieve a final victory; and worse yet, the mad Doctor now held the lives of Judy, Angela, and Victor in his hands. Mac turned toward Boyle, who had his back to him, admiring his own handiwork.

"Look at this, Mac! I've started a sequence that will automatically detonate explosives from there to here." Boyle raised his arms. "What a glorious way to die!"

In one mighty leap, Mac sprang the ten feet between them, hitting Boyle in his midsection, knocking him over the edge. He expected to see him rolling down the face of the pyramid; but when Mac looked over the side, he saw that the Doctor had managed to stop his fall about twenty feet down the stairs.

To Mac's horror, Boyle regained his balance and immediately stroked the touch pad again. "Say goodbye to Mars Base, Commander; your mission has failed!"

Mac leaped through the air and came down feet first squarely on Boyle's chest, sending them both rolling down the front of the giant pyramid.

As Mac tumbled out of control, his thoughts slowed. He wondered whether he hit Boyle in time. He felt completely helpless and, prompted by a voice coming through the haze, a quiet thought entered his mind as he submitted to his fate. He repeated to himself, "Relax."

CHAPTER 28
RESCUE

"Damn it!" Judy slammed both hands on the steering wheel. Without warning, Ratty had suddenly stopped and her communications to the base had gone dead. The computer confirmed the link from the orbiting mother ship had been severed. She was stuck alone along Highway One just after Boyle had yelled something about 'destroying' the base. Now, nothing but silence. *Calm down and think.*

A growing panic gripped her as the possibilities ran through her mind. Had Boyle destroyed the pyramid city and Mac with him? Had he activated the explosive virus inside the Mars Base computer, killing Victor and Angela? Was she the last surviving person on this dreadful planet? *Settle down, Judy.*

"Mars Base, do you copy? Mars Base, can anyone hear me?" She looked out the window at the barren landscape surrounding her. Could she really be alone? She opened up all channels and called out again. "Mars Base, Mac, can anyone hear me? Come in, please! Mayday, mayday, can anyone read me?" She sat back and took a couple of deep breaths.

"Don't panic, old girl." Speaking out loud, she found that the sound of her voice echoing in the small glass-encased crew cab calmed her. "I guess I'll have to drive this thing manually." She reached down and engaged the manual drive. Ratty lurched forward. "Whoa!" Without any road signs, she'd have to be careful not to stray off the highway. Driving at half the speed she had been traveling, she tried to calm herself by repeating over and over, "Relax."

Feeling physically numb, Mac lay perfectly still. He had stopped tumbling and realized he was lying face down on his stomach with his arms at his sides. Opening his eyes, he saw the left front tire of Matty only a few feet away.

When he tried to move, a sharp pain emanating from his back cut through his entire body. A red indicator light inside his helmet told him his suit had been compromised and he had only forty percent of his air left. He had to get on his feet and make his way to Matty.

Wiggling his toes, he could tell his legs weren't broken so, ignoring the pain, he managed to crawl to Matty and pull himself up. Looking around, he saw no sign of Boyle. He glanced up the stairs of the pyramid and marveled at how far he had fallen. He wouldn't have survived without his hard-pressure suit to protect him. Had he been wearing a soft suit, he would have broken his neck.

Leaning on Matty, he made his way along the side until he reached the large hole made by the explosion. An entire side panel had been torn away, exposing severed wires and torn insulation. From the location of the hole, he assumed Boyle had planted a bomb inside his laptop, just as Gina had. Matty's interior appeared relatively undamaged. The pressurized cabin had caused the force of the explosion to blow outward, sparing the equipment inside.

The explosion had severed the cabling to the large laser communications dish on the roof, leaving contact with the base impossible. If by some miracle Matty were still operable, he would have to drive it manually out of the Valley. Mac pulled himself through the gaping hole and pushed aside the debris inside Matty. The airlock was still powered up and contained six oxygen bottles. Praying that Matty's control systems still worked, he sat down at the driver's position and flipped the manual switch. It came on instantly and Matty's transmission engaged, causing the vehicle to lurch forward a few feet.

He could hardly believe his luck! With his air running out, he would have to immediately start driving toward Mars Base. Because the six bottles in the airlock held approximately twenty minutes of air each, he figured he'd be able to make it to the emergency shed at the Red Anvil drill site and call for help. Then he could climb inside the airlock and wait for rescue.

A sudden thought cut through his excitement. What had happened to the base? He had forgotten Boyle's claim that he had set off a chain reaction explosion in the Valley. He recalled the image of the Pyramid of the Moon's top exploding, and Boyle's threat to blow up the base as well.

He stood up to look outside and was surprised to see that the city appeared undamaged. Had it been a dream? He glanced over at the Pyramid of the Moon and got his answer. The entire top had been blown off! But that was all. What had gone wrong? Better yet, what had gone right for him? Why hadn't the rest of the Valley been reduced to rubble? Perhaps his struggle with Boyle had damaged his touch pad and stopped the detonation sequence. The touch pad! What had become of it and Boyle?

Mac looked back toward the pyramid, where he could plainly see the marks his tumble had left on the steps. He could see a second set of marks, obviously Boyle's, which veered off three-quarters of the way down, ending on one of the flat tiers. Mac noticed a vapor cloud coming from that tier though the steps blocked his view of the cloud's source. That had to be oxygen escaping from Boyle's suit! He had found the madman, and now, with time running out, he had a decision to make.

Rechenko leaned over the computer and exhaled. He had been frantically working to disable the virus in the mainframe. In the end, he had severed the laser link on the mother ship as the quickest, safest alternative. He waited until the last possible second because of Judy, but once he saw that Boyle had started the detonation sequence, he killed the link.

"The virus didn't activate. You did it!" Angela came up from behind and hugged him.

"Yes, but I wonder how Mac is doing."

"I don't know, Victor. The last thing I heard, he and Boyle were screaming at each other."

"Then as far as we know, Mac and Boyle could be brawling on top of that pyramid right now."

"In a way, I'm glad Judy's driving to the Valley. She just could make the difference between Mac surviving or not."

"She's on her own now," Rechenko sighed as he returned to his computer. "It will take almost an hour to recycle the laser relay and get it back on line. We won't be able to talk to anyone until then."

As Ratty rolled along Highway One, Judy cursed herself for not being better qualified to drive this monstrous beast. Even now, in the midst of this crisis, she made a mental note that future missions should have all personnel trained to operate *all* of the vehicles. *Future missions?* she thought. *Who am I kidding? After this mission, why would anyone attempt to send someone else back here? This has been a disaster, and if what Boyle says is true? Such powerful forces would make sure a return mission wasn't possible.*

All she cared about at this point was retrieving Mac and blasting off this planet tomorrow. She prayed for his safety, knowing anything could have happened on top of the pyramid. What if Boyle had managed to overpower Mac and was returning to the base by himself? If that were the case, she would do everything in her power to stop him. She remembered the cyanide syringe she had given Mac. She knew he wouldn't hesitate to use it if he had to.

Mac reached the tier where Boyle had fallen and found him lying on his back, barely breathing. The touch pad on his arm appeared to have been shattered by the fall.

"Uhhh," Boyle groaned and lifted his head slightly.

"You failed, you miserable bastard!" Mac stood over him. "As you can see, the city is still here and so am I. And I suspect everyone at the base is okay."

"Go away," Boyle blurted through his labored breathing. A tear in the leg of his suit spewed a steady vapor cloud of oxygen.

"I'm going, but I'm taking you with me. You got the whole world believing I killed my crew and sabotaged the mission, but you're going to tell them the truth."

"Let me die here. Inject me with that cyanide you're carrying in your pocket."

Mac knelt down and opened his leg pocket and pulled out a small roll of duct tape. He patched up the tear in Boyle's pant leg then clicked a fresh bottle of oxygen into his suit.

"What are you doing? Let me die here!"

"'Fraid not. You're coming with me, you sonofabitch." Mac grabbed Boyle's collar ring and dragged him down the stairs, making sure he felt every step. By the time he reached Matty's airlock, Boyle had passed out from the pain. Mac slammed the airlock door shut, leaving his prisoner unconscious inside the pressurized chamber. He immediately started up Matty and punched the accelerator. His heart raced as he found himself hoping he hadn't made a fatal mistake. In spite of what he thought of Boyle, Mac needed him to clear his name and couldn't allow him to die. By the time he had managed to get the Doctor safely inside, he had used another bottle of oxygen, leaving himself with only four. That wouldn't be enough to make it to Red Anvil.

Even though Matty was fast, the gaping hole in its side affected the handling performance. It was a miracle it worked at all. Thankfully, Boyle wasn't a demolition expert, and his placing the laptop where he did minimized the damage.

As Mac approached the tight winding curves at the summit, he stopped and turned around to look at the Valley of the Sun one more time. Would anyone believe him? Suddenly he felt a bump on the right side of the vehicle. Slam! He had run into something. He brought Matty to an immediate stop, and realized he had been dreaming, slowly fading into unconsciousness from the lack of oxygen. He remembered looking down on the Valley. Now he found himself a couple of miles down the road, falling asleep at the wheel. His low oxygen indicator had been beeping, but he had slept right through it.

Mac plugged in another bottle of air and waited for his head to clear. He had only three bottles left. He would never make it. If the treacherous road didn't kill him, the lack of oxygen would.

As he continued down the road, his thoughts drifted back to what Boyle had told him. *What a conspiracy!* A secret Community that influences and manipulates world events? He had heard of such theories before, but to see it in action? Boyle and his co-conspirators had easily carried out this deception right under his nose. Except for a few holes in the ground, Boyle and La Rue probably never searched for water. Ivory's explosion experiment obviously served as a test for the explosives he later placed on the structures in the Valley. Traveres had total control of all communications, and the confrontation between Boyle and La Rue at Red Anvil had been a complete ruse for Mac's benefit. He had even let Ivory and Boyle fuel the Mars 3 lander for the failed launch attempt!

Through it all, Mac could see he had been the completely agreeable Commander, predictable to a fault. He wondered if it would have made a difference if he had been a little more controlling, perhaps a little more involved with each crew member's assignments. Only with Traveres' help did he have a chance to expose the conspiracy.

As soon as Mac returned to base, he would send Boyle's private files to Earth for all to see. He didn't care if he would be put in harm's way as Boyle had threatened. Mac believed that distributing the secret information for worldwide scrutiny might well protect the lives of the returning crew.

Another ten minutes and he would be clear of the narrow passes and out in the open, on a gradual descent to the Grand Arroyo. His oxygen alarm sounded again. Time to change oxygen. Two bottles left with an hour of driving to go.

Judy realized her predicament would be funny if the situation wasn't so damn desperate. After poking along at a mere ten or fifteen miles per hour, acclimating herself to handling Ratty's awkward controls, she was now pushing herself to the limits of her burgeoning driving skills. With Red Anvil now only a few minutes away, she still had over seventy miles between her and the Valley. She powered Ratty forward to make up for lost time.

Mac clicked in his last bottle of emergency oxygen then accelerated. Twenty more minutes and he'd be joining Boyle in the airlock waiting for rescue. He was confident Rechenko would see Matty's locator beacon stopped in the middle of nowhere and send help. That is, if the crew was still alive. He didn't trust Boyle's claim that he could blow up Mars Base. We wondered how the Doctor was faring inside the airlock. Was he still unconscious? Mac reached down and felt the cyanide syringe in his pocket. He had risked his own life to bring Boyle back alive, but he wasn't going to take any more chances.

Bang! Mac jumped. He had just hit something on the road, waking him up. He realized he wasn't thinking clearly, but he had to push on maybe as far as Angel Rock. He concentrated on staying in the middle of his tracks to avoid hitting another boulder.

His thoughts drifted to his mom and dad, probably still huddled in their cabin, avoiding the press. Would they ever know the true story behind this mess? Were they ashamed of their only son? He couldn't stand the fact that Boyle's lies about him would hurt either of his parents.

He called out loud to his parents. "Mom, Dad, please give me strength. I don't want to die like this!" He felt a chill enter his body. For the second time today, Mac stared death in the face.

His thoughts drifted to Judy. He had been in love with her for years and had never acted on his feelings until this mission. What was she doing now? Knowing her, she was probably on her way to meet him. That would be just like her to not sit around and wait for something to happen. He called her name out loud. "Judy, come help me! Judy, drive as fast as you can."

Matty hit something again, waking him up, although not completely. He needed to stop soon and get inside the airlock. *Just a little farther.*

Looking out the window, he thought he noticed something unusual in front of him. At first he thought it was an illusion, another dream, but it looked so real! He saw an angel, floating in front of him, beckoning him to continue on. Matty seemed to float in the air, closely following the angel as they both glided effortlessly over the terrain.

Mac felt exhilarated, almost giddy and excited that he didn't have to worry about driving anymore. He sat back and enjoyed the view, putting his complete trust in his new friend. He grabbed the giant turkey sandwich that had appeared on the console in front of him alongside a cold, frothy beer. He realized he hadn't eaten all day. Next, a small screen appeared in front of him showing a movie about an only child, the son of an aeronautical engineer and a nurse. The little boy grew up to become a great pilot. *That's nice,* Mac thought.

"I've got it!" Rechenko hollered. "I have a downlink from the mother ship. The laser link is working!"

"Great!" Angela said. "Let's see where everyone is."

"It will take a moment. I have to key in the badge signatures again." Rechenko typed on the keyboard.

"Find Judy," Angela said. "We have to make sure she didn't crash Ratty when we lost contact."

"There she is! She's about a half a mile from Angel Rock, moving at a good speed.

"What about Mac and Boyle? Are they still in the Valley?"

Rechenko input Matty's code. "I've got them! What the heck?" He stared at the screen, his jaw wide open.

"What is it?' Angela looked over his shoulder. "Is that right?"

"Yes, it is." Rechenko input Mac and Boyle's badge numbers.

"It's Mac, all right, and Boyle is with him."

"Victor, what if it's an ambush? We've got to let Judy know."

"I'll try, but she's going to have to reboot her onboard computer in order for her communications link to work."

"Would she know to do that?"

"I'm not sure, but as soon as the laser comes back online, I believe it sends a prompt to the onboard system to flash a reboot command."

As Judy came up a rise, her eyes focused on a beautiful sight that up until now, she had only heard of. A giant rock formation in the shape of an angel loomed in front of her. She had heard of Angel Rock described before, and even seen pictures, but nothing prepared her for the beauty and splendor of the extraordinary landmark. The formation made of bare rock gave the giant angel a white glow that set it apart from the surrounding formations.

As she rolled on toward Angel Rock, Judy noticed a prompt flashing on the computer: *Reboot*

"Great! The system is back on line! Maybe I can get some help," she said aloud. She hit the reset button and slowed Ratty to a crawl. Looking out in front, she felt a chill run through her body as if she was seeing a ghost. Only a few hundred feet in front of her stood Matty, parked next to the giant angel.

"She rebooted the system!" Rechenko shouted. "We should be able to get a picture from her cameras any second."

The camera mounted on Ratty's front grill came on, showing Matty parked directly in ahead.

"She's found them!" Rechenko said.

"Yes, but in what condition? Can we talk to her yet?"

"Not yet. She has to reset her communicator. It's on a separate system, so if the computer crashes, you still have local communications. But it still has to be reset. She should be getting a prompt from the console."

Judy stared at Matty, now just thirty yards in front of her, looking strangely abandoned. She slowed Ratty to a crawl and drove around to one side for a visual inspection.

"Oh, my God!" she gasped as she stopped Ratty. One entire side of Matty had a huge hole, with wires and insulation hanging out. She quickly sealed the helmet on her soft suit and depressurized the crew cab. She grabbed her emergency supplies and bounded out onto the surface.

"Mac!" she yelled, hoping he would pick her up on his helmet radio. "Mac! Can you hear me?" She approached the hole in the side of Matty, aware that Dr. Boyle could be about. The Doctor may well have gotten the better of Mac and then drove Matty to this point, waiting in ambush. She reached the opening and peered inside.

"At least she's being cautious." Angela observed, watching Judy's movements captured on Ratty's camera.

"We better keep an eye out for Dr. Boyle," Rechenko warned. "The screen shows that he and Mac are inside Matty, or at least close by."

From where she stood, Judy strained to see the airlock at the rear of the vehicle, hoping Mac might be inside. She could see it wasn't pressurized and was most likely empty. Judy pushed away some insulation, which blocked her view to the front of Matty, and saw a figure slumped over in the driver's seat. Her heart leaped as she pulled herself up through the gaping hole and into the vehicle. She could tell it was Mac by the Commander stripes on his arms and helmet. Debris lay everywhere in the dust-covered interior. Judy made her way over to Mac and saw that his suit was battered as if he had been in a brawl.

"Mac!" she yelled. "Mac! Can you hear me?" she yelled again, looking for any signs of life. She pulled him up and looked inside his visor at his ashen face. His eyes were closed and his breathing was shallow.

"Oh, Mac! What happened to you?" She pulled out an emergency oxygen bottle and clicked it into his suit. She grabbed his arm and checked his vitals on his wrist monitor. It showed a very weak pulse, but at least he was alive.

"I can't see anything now," Angela said. "She's moved inside Matty, I hope she's careful. Can you tell anything from the locator badges?"

"No, nothing specific," Rechenko answered. "I just show three people all on top of each other."

"Damn! I wish we could get closer." Angela suddenly sat up. "Hey! Did you see that?"

"See what?"

"I thought I saw a figure walk by the opening."

"Are you sure it wasn't Judy?"

"I don't know, but it moved toward the front."

Judy grabbed Mac by the shoulders and yanked him out of the chair and onto the floor. Any movement could possibly jump-start his breathing so she checked his face again. As she peered through his visor, she caught a glimpse of movement from behind her, reflected off Mac's helmet.

Before she could turn around, Judy felt a blow to the side of her head that knocked her to the floor next to Mac. She regained her bearings and looked up. Boyle, wearing a soft suit, stood over her. He reached out and tried to grab her by the neck, but she instinctively rolled onto her back and swung her legs into his. To her surprise, he immediately retreated, in obvious pain.

Several thoughts flashed through her head as she scrambled to her feet. Judging from the condition of Mac's hard suit, and the fact that Boyle no longer wore his, they must have had some sort of violent scuffle, or possibly were near the explosion that blew the hole in Matty, injuring Boyle in the process. He was vulnerable and she would take advantage. She recalled what Mac had said before, about knowing when to be compassionate, and when to be ruthless. With Mac dying at her feet, she knew what to do. She needed to get the cyanide syringe from Mac's leg pocket. If she could do it quickly, Boyle wouldn't be able to stop her before she had it in her hand. *Ruthless,* she reminded herself.

They faced each other, poised to attack. Boyle stood with his back to the hole in Matty's side, Judy with her back to the front passenger seat. Mac lay on the floor between them. Judy glanced quickly down at Mac's leg pocket, then at Boyle.

"You know I can't allow you to leave here alive," Boyle said, breaking the eerie silence between them. "It's just not in the cards, you surviving to tell the world what you know. You must die here."

Boyle's words struck fear in her very being. He had her cornered inside Matty, ready to pounce at any second. She tried to turn her fear into action as she felt herself beginning to shake. She couldn't let him win. *Be ruthless!*

Boyle inched forward. She glanced down at Mac again and noticed a spent oxygen bottle by his leg. As Boyle moved forward, she scooped up the bottle and in one motion, flung it at his head. He turned away and partially blocked the flying projectile with his arm, backing away as he did.

Falling to her knees she ripped open Mac's leg pocket; she reached inside and felt nothing! It was gone! Had Mac tried to use it already? She looked up at Boyle who stared back at her.

"Are you looking for this?" He held up the syringe in his left hand.

Judy's knees nearly buckled. She didn't have a chance with the syringe in Boyle's control. Like a caged animal, she decided to strike. She would charge at him with all her strength and try to force him out of the opening behind him.

Boyle raised the syringe high over his head, sensing her imminent charge.

"Come on, Doctor," he taunted. "Come and get some of this!"

Adrenaline pumped in her veins, fueling her rage. She steadied her feet, ready to launch herself across the ten feet that separated them. But then she saw the flash of Ratty's large silver claw burst through the opening and clamp around Boyle's chest.

"Aughh!" he screamed as the giant claw lifted him up and ripped him out of Matty like captured prey.

Stunned and elated, Judy stood at the opening and watched Boyle's arms flailing as Ratty, looking like a giant crab with a struggling victim in its claw, backed away. She picked up the cyanide syringe on the floor and jumped out on to the surface and walked toward her prisoner. She waved her arms at the ungainly beast like an animal trainer, directing Ratty to lower its claw toward her. She could hear Boyle's heavy breathing and groaning.

Judy held out the deadly syringe, ready to plunge it into Boyle's thigh, all the time thinking, *Ruthless, ruthless.* But another groan distracted her.

"Judy," Mac's voice cut to her heart.

He's alive!

She lowered her arm and recalled Mac's words: "Know when to be compassionate, and when to be ruthless."

Exhaustion gripped her as the adrenaline rush began to subside. She backed up and motioned Ratty to raise Boyle up high again. All she wanted to do at that moment was check on the most important person in her life. She turned and threw the syringe as far as she could, freeing herself from its burden. Then she made her way back to Mac's side.

"Yes! What a performance!" Rechenko helped Angela take off the virtual reality goggles she had used to remotely operate Ratty. "That was a one in a million shot! I'll bet Boyle never knew what hit him! Very impressive, young lady. You really have quite a touch with those claws! Any chance he could get away?"

"No, not out of those things." Angela slumped back in her chair. "He might end up with a couple of busted ribs, but I'd just keep him in the claws all the way back to base."

Judy looked at the long shadows that covered Mars Base in darkness and admired the bright peak of Sunset Ridge, still painted in the orange glow of the setting sun. With Boyle still in its mighty grip, she raised Ratty's claw skyward toward the ridge, in salute to the victims buried there. "We're home," she said to Mac who sat beside her, fading in and out of sleep.

He turned and gave her a tired smile. "No, we're going home tomorrow."

CHAPTER 29

JUDGMENT

Boyle's mind drifted in and out of consciousness before he realized he was back inside the radiation chamber in Mars 2. He began to feel a dull pain coursing through his body as he shook off the effects of a drug-induced coma. The catheter in his arm delivered a stimulant to revive him. *What a pitiful existence.*

His right arm throbbed, but he couldn't remember how it all happened. He recalled arguing with Mac and setting off the explosive, which he thought had destroyed Matty. He remembered waking up, bouncing around inside Matty's airlock with a busted right arm and bruises all over his body.

He had found a spare soft suit inside the airlock and struggled to climb out of his bulky hard suit, but the pain made it an hour-long task. By the time he put on the soft suit, Matty had come to a stop by Angel Rock. When he exited the airlock, he found Mac slumped over the driving console, either dead or dying. He remembered he had grabbed the syringe Mac carried and slipped it in his pocket. That's when Ratty appeared over the horizon and he retreated back to the airlock to wait. When he realized it was Judy, by herself, he decided to confront her; but he had underestimated her strength and resolve.

The last thing he remembered was pulling out the syringe and facing her. Now he found himself inside the radiation chamber, again sitting in the same chair, facing the same monitor. Only he wasn't strapped in as before. Boyle tried to sit up but felt a sharp pain across his ribs. He slumped back in the chair as the monitor in front of him switched on. He saw Mac on camera, staring down at him from the bridge.

Boyle looked away, refusing to make eye contact with his adversary. Regardless of how things had turned out, he refused to believe Mac had outsmarted him. He glanced back at the screen and noticed that Mac continued to stare, saying nothing, forcing him to speak first.

"Go away. Leave me alone." Boyle's voice was raspy, his mouth dry. He turned away from the screen.

Mac said nothing.

Boyle burned inside. *How obnoxious!* Mac taunted him with his silence! He turned back toward the screen. "I know what you're thinking. You think you've won, don't you? You think you've got the upper hand, but you're wrong! As I told you before, this is too big for you! You will be crushed like a bug when we return to Earth, and I will be the hero. There will be no trial, no tribunal, nothing. You are an international criminal, and that is how you will be treated. No one gets the upper hand on me!"

Finally, Mac began to speak, although it was with much more confidence than Boyle had heard before.

"Defiant to the end, Dr. Boyle? You disappoint me. I thought you might thank me for saving your life yesterday; but no, you're just a self-centered, egotistical fool. You're an ordinary man, and not a very smart one at that."

Boyle clenched his fist, trying to temper his rage. "I refuse to discuss this mission with you any further. You have already told me you are going to bring me up on charges, so I have the right to legal counsel. Besides, you have no credible evidence against me. It is you who will be prosecuted for your crimes."

"You don't have to speak to me, Boyle. This isn't an inquiry; this is more like a sentencing. You see, we have already convicted you of the murders of twelve human beings. But before we get to your sentence, I'd like to show you what the world thinks of our evidence against you. In less than twenty-four hours, the press has released their verdict based on the data we retrieved from your computer and sent back to Earth."

Headlines from familiar newspapers around the world began to flash on the screen. Boyle gasped. The New York Times headline read, **MARS CONSPIRACY!** in bold letters with a sub-headline reading, **Pyramids Discovered on Mars! Kept from Public.** The Washington Post headline said **MARS COVER-UP!** It also showed a picture of the Pyramid of the Sun with a smaller comparison picture of its twin pyramid in Mexico.

By far the most hurtful headline came from the London Times: **BRIT EXPOSED AS TRAITOR IN MARS CONSPIRACY!** The sub-headline read, **Dr. William Boyle Implicated in Twelve Deaths.**

Boyle leaned back in his chair, unable to speak. He was the international criminal, vilified by the world, his career and reputation in shambles. In one final taunting, Mac showed him a headline from the <u>Sacramento Bee</u>, accompanied by a picture of an elderly couple smiling outside a log cabin. The headline said, **MACTAVISH VINDICATED!** The sub headline read, **Local Family Celebrates Hero Son's Innocence.**

Boyle couldn't bear the insult. "Go to hell!" he yelled at the screen. "You've done more damage than you know!" As those words passed his lips, he knew Mac had gotten the best of him. He could only guess at the reaction of the Community, although he suspected they would turn invisible, leaving him exposed as a delusional mad scientist who acted alone.

His only hope would be to somehow prevent the launch of Mars 3. But what could he do from here? He knew Mac wouldn't move him to the launch vehicle until the last possible moment. Boyle realized his only salvation was to destroy the base, even at the cost of his own life. If he succeeded, the Community could easily discredit Mac's evidence, and his own reputation would remain intact.

Mac began to read the charges the crew had brought against him. "Dr. William Boyle, you are hereby charged in the death of Commander Russell F. Chandler, a human being. The murder of Lieutenant Alexander Holshevnikoff, a human being..."

Boyle scoffed. Mac's decision not to tie him up would be his last mistake. Once again, he would prove he had the superior intellect. His mind raced as he tried to formulate a plan to sabotage the base and the launch.

He glanced at Mac one more time, consumed by hate and contempt for his unworthy adversary who continued his judicial charade. "You bastard! You don't control me!" Boyle cursed. Then suddenly, something caught his eye that sent a shudder through his body. As Mac continued to read the charges against him, a pen floated freely in front of the Commander, weightless! *How could that be?*

Boyle ripped the catheter from his arm, stumbled to the ladder and climbed up to the hatch. It was unlocked! Ignoring the excruciating pain from his injuries, he pushed the hatch open and dragged himself out of the chamber and onto the floor of the flight deck. He limped to the bridge where Mac should have been. It was empty!

"Nooooooo!" Boyle wailed. He could hear Mac's voice echo through the base as he continued to read the charges. "...the murder of Katie Thompson, a human being. The death of Gina Gibson, a human being..."

Boyle slid down the ladder, making his way to the habitat airlock, "Is anyone here?" A horrendous fear sapped his strength. He was alone. He limped and stumbled down the airlock tunnel and collapsed to the floor of the gutted Habitat 2.

Making his way to the wall of the habitat, he peered outside. Mars 3 was gone!

"Nooooo!" he cried again as he limped to the center of the empty habitat and fell to his knees. "You can't do this to me!"

Mac continued his reading. "The murder of Lieutenant Michael Traveres, a human being. Dr. William Boyle, on all these counts we find you guilty. And in doing so, we hereby sentence you to life on Mars."

"Nooooo!"

"You are confined to the base for the remainder of your natural life. You will have no access to an environment suit of any kind. The computer operation has been altered to continue life support only. You will be responsible for maintaining the base recycling system and cultivating the Mars Garden, as your life will depend on it."

"You can't do this!" he wailed. "Come back! Come back for me! I can't stay here alone!" He collapsed to a fetal position, shaking.

Mac finished his reading with a final statement and question. "This transmission hereby ends all human contact with Mars Base until such time that another expeditionary mission returns. Dr. Boyle, do you have any last words or statement you wish to make?"

Boyle remained curled up in a ball, sobbing, allowing Mac the last word.

"Let the record show that Dr. William Boyle made no final statement. This transmission is terminated. May God have mercy on your soul."

The monitors throughout the base went dead, cutting off all communications to and from the base. Boyle curled up tighter. With Mac's transmission over, the base went silent. He was alone.

CHAPTER 30
HOMEWARD

Mac gazed out the window at the Martian surface below and soaked in his last close-up glimpse of the red planet. With their final pass around Mars, the computer would engage the hyperdrive, sending them into a trans-orbit trajectory to Earth.

"Two minutes to burn, Commander," Rechenko called out. "The ignition chamber is primed and ready to receive the matter stream."

"Copy that, Victor." Mac's eyes remained focus on Mars. Despite all that had happened, he felt a deep sadness for the planet he had called home for the past year and a half. He now understood Mars had witnessed much suffering and heartache long before an earthly footprint touched its barren soil, bringing more human drama and suffering. He hoped the red planet's future would be brighter than its immediate past.

"Ninety seconds, Commander. The matter-antimatter stream is flowing steadily into the fusion chamber; critical mass is imminent."

"Copy that." Mac glanced at the console. Ignition was moments away. Because of the alignment with Earth, there would be no live link to Houston at the time of the burn. He preferred it that way. The story of Mars Base and the Valley of the Sun had dominated the Worlds headlines for three days. Mission Control and the world media would be anxious to get confirmation on a successful jump to hyperspace. Mac dreaded the media frenzy they would endure upon their return.

"Sixty seconds."

"Okay, Victor. I'm powering up the fuel cells for manual override. The switch is armed." Mac looked over his shoulder at Judy and Angela strapped to their seats, holding hands in anticipation of the twelve-minute ride. He smiled. "Get ready, this should be quite a jolt. About six g's worth."

"We're ready!" Judy shouted. "Let's fire this popgun and go home!"

"San Francisco, here we come. Whoo!" Angela chimed in.

Mac laughed, the tension of the mission forgotten for a moment.

"Thirty seconds, injectors are primed. The fuel chamber is a go!" Rechenko barked. "Fifteen seconds! The chamber is open! Approaching critical mass."

With ignition imminent, and in this most crucial phase, Mac felt anxious about separating from a world he had grown to love and hate—a world where he had learned more about himself than he ever thought possible.

"...three...two...one...ignition!" Mars 3 accelerated, pinning all of them to their seats.

"We have a good burn, manual override off!" Rechenko shouted, struggling to speak as the g-forces quickly started to build.

With the added weight on his body, Mac felt as if he was being torn away from Mars' influence and all that had happened there. His mind wandered from one experience to another—the camaraderie, the great feeling of accomplishment. He promised himself he would never forget the simple pleasures such as bounding across the surface with so little effort, or taking in the magnificent view from Sunset Ridge as the long shadows reached across the Grand Arroyo Plains.

He thought about the crew he left buried on the ridge, always cherishing the time he had spent with them, particularly Traveres. He knew so little about this quiet hero who sacrificed so much for others.

With the g-forces pinning him against his seat, he closed his eyes and tried to picture what Sunset Ridge looked like from above, with the four graves overlooking the base. What a waste of humanity, a waste of good people led astray by a treacherous man.

He thought back to Boyle, lying on the floor of Habitat 2, curled up in a fetal position. What a life he had made for himself. Brilliant, but driven by ego, he had made a remarkable discovery; and now he paid the price for his short-sightedness, his reputation in shambles. Boyle was truly alone. Who would save him now? Certainly not the Community—that invisible giant always manipulating events behind the scenes, discrediting and vilifying anyone who attempted to reveal their true identities, and hiding the truth when that suited its purposes.

Indeed, the truth was the real casualty of this mission. Not only the truth about Mars, but about Earth and the link the two planets so obviously shared. He foresaw no cultural anarchy, as Boyle had warned. More than likely, some people would believe the evidence while others would remain skeptical. But at least the people of the world would be able to draw their own conclusions.

For all the power and influence the Community wielded, they were no match for the most powerful force in the universe: love—specifically, the love between Angela and Michael. Their bond proved impossible to break. In spite of all the intricate planning by the Community and Dr. Boyle, the strength of two star-crossed lovers prevailed.

Going against the Community had cost Traveres his life, but the results of his sacrifice would shake the world. His action had released undeniable proof of a lost civilization having visited Earth thousands of years ago to serve as our teachers. Mankind would be forced to look itself in the mirror and see who really was staring back.

"Commander, we have achieved maximum velocity. The burn is nominal, and we are prepared for shutdown in three minutes," Rechenko announced.

"Copy that, Victor, three minutes." Mac returned to his thoughts. He felt the final bonds of Mars slipping away and began to wonder about his relationship with this planet and the beings that once lived there. He considered the possibility that he had been selected not by the Community, but a higher power to go on this mission and fight for the preservation and protection of the ancient city in the Valley of the Sun. Destiny had led him to Magdalena, who in turn fueled the fires inside his heart—not only for her, but for the lost civilizations he had grown to admire and respect. He willingly accepted these mysterious beings as his teachers from another world, a world he was no longer a stranger to.

"We have main engine cutoff, Commander!"

"Congratulations, everyone, we're homeward bound." Mac unbuckled his belt and floated freely toward the window for a glimpse at Mars. Judy drifted up and joined him to look at the view.

"It looks so small already," she said. "I know this sounds crazy, but after all we've been through, I think I'm going to miss that little red planet."

Mac gave her a hug. "Remember, that little red planet has just revealed some extraordinary secrets. I think the world will be talking about our mission for a long time."

"You did one hell of a job, Mac. You know that, don't you?" She kissed him on the cheek and floated away.

He continued to stare out the window at Mars and wondered if he really could consider this a successful mission. He had lost four crew members and left one behind in permanent exile. But his mission had been to establish a permanent manned presence on Mars, and in an ironic twist of fate, with the involuntary help of Dr. Boyle, he had accomplished just that.

Mac chuckled at the absurdity of it all and glanced one more time at Mars, growing smaller by the minute. He felt pangs of separation from this glowing, rust-colored orb suspended in the cold vastness of eternity. He closed his eyes and thanked his teachers several millenniums removed for allowing him to revel in their greatness if only for a fleeting moment. Opening his eyes, he smiled and said goodbye, then drifted away from the window, never to look back again.

ACKNOWLEDGMENTS

There are countless people to thank for helping me get this project off the ground and running, but my key inspiration has to be my Dad who sadly passed away in 1980. I remember him waking me up in the early mornings to watch Alan Sheppard and John Glen launch into space on those early days of our burgeoning space program. As a kid growing up in Southern California I have fond memories of my Dad carefully pointing out the track of a new satellite as it glided overhead in the star filled evening sky. His work for the government on the early missile program and his lifelong career in aviation inspired me to dream beyond my feet planted firmly on the ground. To him and my Mom who stood firmly beside him, always encouraging my siblings and me to dream big, I am forever indebted and grateful.

New York Times best selling author James Rollins deserves special thanks for sharing his wisdom and insight to a complete novice. Jim's kindness not only to me but many aspiring writers in the Sacramento area is legendary. His recommendations and encouragement were pivotal in getting me on the right track early on.

Of course, this book could have never made it to its present form with out the diligent help and constructive input from the best readers group on the planet. Naida West, Pesia Wooley, Nan Mahon and Randy Haynes, all published authors, graciously endured my stodgy and awkward presentation and patiently dragged me, sometimes kicking and screaming, into the wonderful world of coherent writing. This thanks falls woefully short of my true appreciation.

A special acknowledgment to my cover artist Eric Warp, who along with my friend Brian Jacobson, actually read and enjoyed my original manuscript in all its many errors and flaws. Both were completely supportive and enthusiastic and kept me going in the early days of this project. Eric has been particularly helpful in developing an artful presentation for my future marketing needs.

My family has been of great support to me and I must thank my sister Chris, who halfway through reading said, "Wow, you actually wrote a book!" My brother John managed to pass on some great and sorely needed technical advice. Also thanks to my brothers Dan and Dave in Portland, Oregon. I believe Dave read a couple of different versions giving me much appreciated input and encouragement. Go Ducks! And of course my Mom, Olga, who has patiently waited all these years for me to get Red Storm published.

I'd like to thank the following people who either read my manuscript or helped and encouraged me with their constructive input. Ruth Younger, Jeff Knott, (thanks Rusty!), Sandy Bullock, Martin Khodabakhshian, Will Parrinello, Mary Mackey, Don Giroux, Kathy Anne Thompson, Jim Wilson, Ken Heiden, Dale Brown, Chris Beck, Alan Jacobson, Marcia Reimers, Suzy Rupp, Kevin Swartzendruber, Joyce Mitchell, Bill Pieper, Marty Hernandez, Charlotte Fadipe and Jennifer Whitney. Thank you all for your support.

And the best for last, I must thank my beautiful wife Lila and my son Matthew who both serve as my daily inspiration. I couldn't get out of bed and face the world without their love and support. Matthew is my cosmic conscience and I'm sure someday he'll rock the world with his own writing. Lila deserves special credit because before this book was a chapter long she was my first proofreader, editor and critic, whether she liked it or not. If she had doubts, she never showed it. Her support and belief in my personal dream sustained me through the dark ages of this project and continue to sustain me today. Thanks for giving me the strength to persevere.

BIOGRAPHY

Frank Luna is an Emmy award winning television director with 30 years working in broadcast news. He currently lives with his wife in Sacramento, California and they are proud to have their son Matthew serving in the United States Air Force. Frank is an avid golfer and also enjoys kayaking and cycling along with other outdoor activities in beautiful Northern California.

Made in the USA
Charleston, SC
21 July 2012